DARK
HORSE

Since the publication of her first book in 1988, Tami Hoag's novels have appeared regularly on the bestseller lists, including seven consecutive *New York Times* bestsellers. She lives on a horse farm in Virginia.

Also by Tami Hoag

DARK HORSE

Tami Hoag

ORION

First published in Great Britain in 2002 by
Orion Books, an imprint of The Orion Publishing Group,
Orion House, 5 Upper St Martin's Lane,
London, WC2H 9EA

A CIP catalogue record for this book is
available from the British Library

Printed and bound in Great Britain by
Clays Ltd, St Ives plc

This book was inspired by the adventures of Tess and Mati.
May there be many more, and may they live to tell the tales.

ACKNOWLEDGMENTS

As always, I have several people to thank for sharing with me their professional expertise as I wrote this story. Lieutenant Ed Serafin, Palm Beach County Sheriff's Office, Robbery/Homicide division. Robert Crais. Eileen Dreyer. Jessie Steiner. Mary Phelps. And most of all, Betsy Steiner, true friend and partner in international intrigue.

AUTHOR'S NOTE

Welcome to my other world.

In my life away from my desk, I am a competitive equestrian. In fact, I've been a rider longer than I've been a writer. Over the years horses have been my joy, refuge, therapy, salvation, and comfort. I've ridden in nearly every equestrian discipline, from barrel racing to jumping. When I was thirteen and my girlfriends were baby-sitting to earn spending money, my father was bringing home young horses for me to break to saddle.

Several years ago I settled on the equestrian sport of dressage as my out-of-office passion. Dressage is all about control and precision and the mastery of imperceptible cues between rider and horse. The ultimate result is something like equine ballet, which appears elegant and effortless but requires the same physical and mental fitness as power yoga.

I began competing in dressage in 1999. Being me, I didn't ease into the sport. I have one gear in everything I do: full-on. I bought a wonderful—if difficult—horse named D'Artagnon from Olympic rider Guenter Seidel, and within a year's time went from my first dressage competition to being a nationally ranked amateur rider in the U.S. Dressage Federation. At the end of my first season, my coach, trainer, mentor, and great friend, Betsy Steiner (a world-class rider herself), encouraged me to bring D'Artagnon along with several other horses from her stable to Florida for the winter season.

Every year top equestrians from the East Coast, Midwest, Canada, and Europe migrate to Welllington in Palm Beach County to spend three months in constant training and competition in some of the most prestigious dressage and jumper shows in the country. Thousands of horses and hundreds of riders converge to create a fascinating world, a world driven by the thrill of victory, the agony of defeat, and lots of money. A world populated by the ultrarich and the very poor; celebrities, royalty, and ordinary people who scrimp and save year-round in order to "do the season"; philanthropists, dilettantes, professionals, amateurs, con men, and criminals. People who love horses, and people who love to exploit people who love horses. A world with a glamorous surface and a tough underbelly. Yin and yang. Positive and negative.

By the end of that first season in Florida, my imagination was running wild with story ideas that would blend my two worlds. The result is *Dark Horse,* a classic private-eye novel set against the backdrop of international show jumping. I hope you enjoy this glimpse into the dark side of my other world.

If you come away from this book thinking the horse business is all bad, I'll tell you that's not so. Some of the finest, kindest, most generous people I have ever known have been in the horse business. But on the flip side of that coin, some of the most vile, vicious, loathsome people I have ever known have been in the horse business. The horse world can be a world of extremes and amazing adventures. I've had horses drugged, horses stolen. I've been stranded in a foreign country with a sociopathic horse dealer who canceled my transportation home. I've masqueraded as a groom and flown in the belly of a cargo plane with a horse bent on killing me. But these adventures don't happen every day. Every day I go to the stables and find friendship and partnership and calm within my soul.

My own horses appear in this book, in Sean Avadon's stable. But, in answer to the inevitable question, Elena is not me (if my life were so exciting, when would I write a book?). However, I do agree with her when she says, "On the back of a horse I felt whole, complete, connected to that vital place in the center of me ... and the chaos within me found balance."

DARK
HORSE

ACT ONE

SCENE ONE

FADE IN:

EXTERIOR: PALM BEACH EQUESTRIAN CENTER— SUNSET

Flat, open fields of scrub stretching to the west. A dirt road running north onto equestrian center property and south toward small horse farms some distance away. No one around. The fields are empty. No people, no horses. Sunday night: everyone has gone home.

Erin stands at the back gate. She's waiting for someone. She's nervous. She thinks she's here for a secret purpose. She thinks her life will change tonight.

It will.

She looks at her watch. Impatient. Afraid he won't show. She's not aware of the camera filming her. She thinks she's alone.

She's thinking: maybe he won't come, maybe she's wrong about him.

A rusted white van approaches from the south. She watches it come toward her. She looks annoyed. No one uses this back road this time of day. The gate to the show grounds has already been chained shut for the night.

The van stops. A masked assailant leaps out.

ERIN
No!

She starts to run toward the gate. He catches her arm from behind and spins her around. She kicks him. He backhands her across the face, knocking her sideways. She wrenches free of his grasp as she stumbles, and she tries to run again but can't get her feet under her. The assailant knocks her down from behind, coming down on top of her, his knee in her back. He pulls a hypodermic needle from the pocket of his jacket and rams the needle into her arm. She makes a sound of pain and starts to cry.

He pulls her to her feet and shoves her into the van. He slams the door shut, gets in the van, the van turns around and drives away.

Life changes in a heartbeat.

FADE OUT

1

Life can change in a heartbeat.

I've always known that. I've lived the truth of that statement literally from the day I was born. I sometimes see those moments coming, sense them, anticipate them, as if they have an aura that precedes their arrival. I see one coming now. Adrenaline runs through my bloodstream like rocket fuel. My heart pounds like a piston. I'm ready to launch.

I've been told to stay put, to wait, but I know that's not the right decision. If I go in first, if I go in now, I've got the Golam brothers dead-bang. They think they know me. Their guard will be down. I've worked this case three months. I know what I'm doing. I know that I'm right. I know the Golam brothers are already twitching. I know I want this bust and deserve it. I know Lieutenant Sikes is here for the show, to put a feather in his cap when the news vans arrive and to make the public think they should vote for him in the next election for sheriff.

He stuck me on the side of the trailer and told me to wait. He doesn't know his ass. He doesn't even know the side door is the door the brothers use most. While Sikes and Ramirez are watching the front, the brothers are dumping their money into duffel bags and getting ready to bolt out the side. Billy Golam's four-by-four is parked ten feet away, covered in mud. If they *run, they'll take the truck, not the Corvette parked in front. The truck can go off-road.*

Sikes is wasting precious time. The Golam brothers have two girls in the trailer with them. This could easily turn into a hostage situation. But if I go in now, while their guard is down . . .

Screw Sikes. I'm going in before these twitches freak.

It's my case. I know what I'm doing.

I key my radio. "This is stupid. They're going to break for the truck. I'm going in."

"Goddammit, Estes—" Sikes.

I click the radio off and drop it into the weeds growing beside the trailer. It's my case. It's my bust. I know what I'm doing.

I go to the side door and knock the way all the Golam brothers' customers knock: two knocks, one knock, two knocks. "Hey, Billy, it's Elle. I need some."

Billy Golam jerks open the door, wild-eyed, high on his own home cooking—crystal meth. He's breathing hard. He's got a gun in his hand.

Shit.

The front door explodes inward.

One of the girls screams.

Buddy Golam shouts: "Cops!"

Billy Golam swings the .357 up in my face. I suck in my last breath.

And then I opened my eyes and felt sick at the knowledge that I was still alive.

This was the way I had greeted every day for the past two years. I had relived that memory so many times, it was like replaying a movie over and over and over. No part of it changed, not a word, not an image. I wouldn't allow it.

I lay in the bed and thought about slitting my wrists. Not in an abstract way. Specifically. I looked at my wrists in the soft lamplight—delicate, as fine-boned as the wing of a bird, skin as thin as tissue, blue-lined with veins—and thought about how I would do it. I looked at those thin blue lines and thought of them as lines of demarcation. Guidelines. *Cut here.*

I pictured the needle-nose point of a boning knife. The lamplight would catch on the blade. Blood would rise to the surface in its wake as the blade skated along the vein. Red. My favorite color.

The image didn't frighten me. That truth frightened me most of all.

I looked at the clock: 4:38 A.M. I'd had my usual fitful four and a half hours of sleep. Trying for more was an exercise in futility.

Trembling, I forced my legs over the edge of the bed and got up, pulling a deep blue chenille throw around my shoulders. The fabric was soft, luxurious, warm. I made special note of the sensations. You're always more intensely alive the closer you come to looking death in the face.

I wondered if Hector Ramirez had realized that the split second before he died.

I wondered that every day.

I dropped the throw and went into the bathroom.

"Good morning, Elena. You look like shit."

Too thin. Hair a wild black tangle. Eyes too large, too dark, as if there was nothing within to shine outward. The crux of my problem: lack of substance. There was—is—a vague asymmetry to my face, like a porcelain vase that has been broken, then painstakingly restored. The same vase it was before, yet not the same. The same face I was born with, yet not the same. Slightly skewed and strangely expressionless.

I was beautiful once.

I reached for a comb on the counter, knocked it to the floor, grabbed a brush instead. Start at the bottom, work upward. Like combing a horse's tail. Work the knots out gently. But I had already tired of looking at myself. Anger and resentment bubbled up through me, and I tore the brush through my hair, shoving the snarls together and tangling the brush in the midst of the mess.

I tried maybe forty-five seconds to extricate the thing, yanking at the brush, tearing at the hair above the snarl, not caring that I was pulling hair out of my head by the roots. I swore aloud, swatted at my image in the mirror, swept the tumbler and soap dish off the counter in a tantrum, and they smashed on the tile floor. Then I jerked open a drawer in the vanity and pulled out a scissors.

Furious, shaking, breathing hard, I cut the brush free. It dropped to the floor with a mass of black hair wrapped around it. The pressure in my chest eased. Numbness trickled down through me like rain. Calm.

Without emotion, I proceeded to hack away at the rest of my mane, cutting it boy-short in ten minutes. The result was ragged with a finger-in-the–light-socket quality. Still, I'd seen worse in *Vogue*.

I swept up the mess—the discarded hair, the broken glass—tossed it in the trash, and walked out of the room.

I'd worn my hair long all my life.

The morning was cool, shrouded in a thick, ground-hugging fog, the air ripe with the damp scents of south Florida: green plants and the murky canal that ran behind the property; mud and manure and horses. I stood on the patio of the little guest house I lived in and breathed deeply.

I had come to this farm a refugee. Jobless, homeless, a pariah in my chosen profession. Unwanted, unloved, abandoned. All of it deserved. I had been off the job two years, most of that time spent in and out of hospitals as doctors repaired the damage done to my body that day at the Golam brothers' trailer. Piecing together shattered bone, patching torn flesh, putting the left side of my face together like a three-dimensional puzzle. They had been less successful with my psyche.

Needing something to do until I could make up my mind about reaching for that boning knife, I had answered an ad in *Sidelines,* a locally based, biweekly magazine for the horse industry: GROOM WANTED.

Life is strange. I don't want to believe anything is preordained. To believe that, one would have to accept the existence of a viciously cruel higher power in order to explain things like child abuse and rapists and AIDS and good men being shot dead in the line of duty. But the occasional twist of fate always makes me wonder.

The phone number in the ad belonged to Sean Avadon. I'd known Sean a hundred years ago in my riding days, when I was a spoiled, sulky, Palm Beach teenager and he was a spoiled, outrageous twenty-something spending his trust fund on horses and mad flings with pretty young men from Sweden and Germany. We had been friends, Sean always telling me I needed him to be my surrogate sense of humor and fashion.

Our families lived a couple of mansions down from one another on the Lake Worth side of the narrow island, Sean's father a real estate magnate, mine an attorney to the wealthiest crooks in south Florida. The slumlord and the shyster, each of them sire to ungrateful offspring. Sean and I had bonded in parental disdain and our love for horses. Wild child times two.

All that had seemed so long ago as to be a dream I could barely remember. So much had happened since. I had left Palm Beach, left that world. I had metaphorically lived and died in another life. Then I answered that ad: GROOM WANTED.

I didn't get the job. As bad a shape as I was in, even I could see the pity in his eyes when we met for drinks at The Players. I was a dark shadow of the girl Sean had known twenty years past, so pathetic I didn't have the pride to fake mental health. I guess that might have been rock bottom. I might have gone home that night to the apartment I was renting and tried to find that boning knife.

Instead, Sean took me in like a stray cat—a recurring theme in my life. He put me in his guest house and asked that I work a couple of his horses for the winter season. He claimed he needed the help. His ex-trainer/ex-lover had run off to Holland with his groom and left him in the lurch. He made it sound like he was giving me a job. What he was giving me was a stay of execution.

Three months had passed. I was still fantasizing about suicide, and every evening I took a bottle of Vicodin out of my nightstand, emptied out the pills, and looked at them and counted them and thought how one pill would ease the physical pain that had been with me every day since "the incident," as my attorney called it. (How sterile and neat that sounded. A small segment of unpleasantness that could be snipped from the fabric of life and isolated. How in contrast to my memories.) One pill could ease the pain. Thirty could end it. I had a stockpile of three hundred and sixty pills.

Every evening I looked at those pills, then put them back in the bottle and put the bottle away. I had never taken one. My evening ritual.

My daily ritual for the past three months was the routine of Sean's barn and time spent with his horses. I found both rituals comforting, but for very different reasons. The pills were a connection to death, and every night I didn't take them was a victory. The horses were a connection to life, and every hour spent with them was a reprieve.

Early on in my life I came to the conclusion that my spirituality was something uniquely and privately my own, something I could find only deep within a small quiet space in the very center of my being. Some people find that place through meditation or yoga or prayer. I find that place within me when I am on a horse. My Zen religion: the equestrian art of dressage.

Dressage is a discipline born on the battlefield in ancient times. Warhorses were trained in precision movements to aid their masters in battle, not only to evade enemies, but to attack them. Over the centuries the training went from the battlefield to the showring, and dressage evolved into something like equine ballet.

To the untrained eye it appears graceful and elegant and effortless. A skilled rider seems to be so quiet, so motionless as to virtually blend into the background. In reality, the sport is physically and mentally demanding on both horse and rider. Complex and complicated. The rider must be attuned to the horse's every footfall, to the balance of every inch of the horse's body. The slightest shift of the rider's weight, the smallest movement of a hand, the lightest tensing of a calf muscle will affect the quality of the performance. Focus must be absolute. Everything else becomes insignificant.

Riding was my refuge as a teenager, when I felt I had little control over any other aspect of my life. It was my stress release when I had a career. It had become my salvation when I had nothing else. On the back of a horse I felt whole, complete, connected to that vital place in the very center of me that had otherwise closed itself off, and the chaos within me found balance.

D'Artagnon and I moved across the sand arena through the last wisps of the morning ground fog, the horse's muscles bulging and rolling, his hooves striking the ground in perfect metronome rhythm. I massaged the left rein, sat into his back, tightened my calves around him. The energy moved from his hindquarters, over his back; his neck rounded and his knees came up into the stylized, slow-motion trot called *passage*. He seemed almost to float beneath me, to bounce like a huge, soft ball. I felt he might take wing if only I knew the one secret word to whisper to him.

We halted in the center of the ring at the place known as X. In that moment I felt joy and peace.

I dropped the reins on his neck and patted him. He lowered his head and started to walk forward, then stopped and came to attention.

A girl sat on the white board fence that ran along the road. She watched me with a sense of expectation about her. Even though I hadn't noticed her, I could tell she'd been there, waiting. I judged her to be about twelve. Her hair was long and brown, perfectly straight, and neatly held back from her face with a barrette on each side. She wore little round black-rimmed glasses that made her look very serious. I rode toward her with a vague feeling of apprehension that made no sense at the time.

"Can I help you?" I asked. D'Ar blew through his nostrils at her, ready to bolt and save us from the intruder. I should have let him.

"I'm here to see Ms. Estes," she said properly, as if she'd come on business.

"Elena Estes?"

"Yes."

"And you are . . . ?"

"Molly Seabright."

"Well, Molly Seabright, Ms. Estes isn't here at the moment."

"*You're* Ms. Estes," she declared. "I recognize your horse. His name is D'Artagnon, like in the *Three Musketeers.*" She narrowed her eyes. "You cut your hair." Disapproval.

"Do I know you?"

"No."

"Then how do you know me?" I asked, the apprehension rising up like bile through my chest to the base of my throat. Maybe she was a relative of Hector Ramirez, come to tell me she hated me. Maybe she'd been sent as a decoy by an older relative who would now pop out of nowhere to shoot me or scream at me or throw acid in my face.

"From *Sidelines,*" she said.

I felt like I'd walked into the middle of a play. Molly Seabright took pity on me and carefully climbed down from the fence. She was slightly built and dressed neatly in sensible dark slacks and a little blue T-shirt with a small daisy chain embroidered around the throat. She came up along D'Artagnon's shoulder and carefully held the magazine out to me, folded open to an interior page.

The photograph was in color. Me on D'Ar, riding through thin ribbons of early-morning fog. The sunlight made his coat shine as bright as a new penny. My hair was pulled back in a thick ponytail.

I had no memory of being photographed. I had certainly never been interviewed, though the writer seemed to know things about me I didn't know myself. The caption read: *Private investigator Elena*

Estes enjoys an early-morning ride on D'Artagnon at Sean Avadon's Avadonis Farm in Palm Beach Point Estates.

"I've come to hire you," Molly Seabright said.

I turned toward the barn and called for Irina, the stunning Russian girl who had beat me out for the groom's job. She came out, frowning and sulky. I stepped down off D'Artagnon and asked her to please take him back to the barn. She took his reins, and sighed and pouted and slouched away like a sullen runway model.

I ran a gloved hand back through my hair, startled to come to the end of it so quickly. A fist of tension began to quiver in my stomach.

"My sister is missing," Molly Seabright said. "I've come to hire you to find her."

"I'm sorry. I'm not a private investigator. This is some kind of mistake."

"Why does the magazine say that you are?" she asked, looking stern and disapproving again. She didn't trust me. I'd already lied to her once.

"I don't know."

"I have money," she said defensively. "Just because I'm twelve doesn't mean I can't hire you."

"You can't hire me because I'm not a private investigator."

"Then what are you?" she demanded.

A broken-down, busted-out, pathetic ex–sheriff's detective. I'd thumbed my nose at the life I'd been raised in, been ostracized from the life I'd chosen. What did that make me?

"Nothing," I said, handing the magazine back to her. She didn't take it.

I walked away to an ornate park bench that sat along the end of the arena and took a long drink from the bottle of water I'd left there.

"I have a hundred dollars with me," the girl said. "For a deposit. I expect you have a daily fee and that you probably charge expenses. I'm sure we can work something out."

Sean emerged from the end of the stable, squinting into the distance, showing his profile. He stood with one booted leg cocked and pulled a pair of deerskin gloves from the waist of his brown breeches. Handsome and fit. A perfect ad for Ralph Lauren.

I headed across the arena, anger boiling now in my stomach. Anger, and underlying it a building sense of panic.

"What the fuck is this?" I shouted, smacking him in the chest with the magazine.

He took a step back, looking offended. "It might be *Sidelines*, but I can't read with my nipples, so I can't say for certain. Jesus Christ, El. What did you do to your hair?"

I hit him again, harder, wanting to hurt him. He grabbed the magazine away from me, took another quick step out of range, and turned to the cover. "Betsy Steiner's stallion, Hilltop Giotto. Have you seen him? He's to die for."

"You told a reporter I'm a private investigator."

"They asked me who you were. I had to tell them something."

"No, you didn't have to. You didn't have to tell them anything."

"It's only *Sidelines*. For Christ's sake."

"It's my name in a goddam magazine read by thousands of people. Thousands of people now know where to find me. Why don't you just paint a big target on my chest?"

He frowned. "Only dressage people read the dressage section. And then only to see if their own names are in the show results."

"Thousands of people now think I'm a private investigator."

"What was I supposed to tell them? The truth?" Said as if that were the most distasteful option. Then I realized it probably was.

"How about 'no comment'?"

"That's not very interesting."

I pointed at Molly Seabright. "That little girl has come here to hire me. She thinks I can help her find her sister."

"Maybe you can."

I refused to state the obvious: that I couldn't even help myself.

Sean lifted a shoulder with lazy indifference and handed the magazine back to me. "What else have you got to do with your time?"

Irina emerged from the barn, leading Oliver—tall, elegant, and beautiful, the equine version of Sean. Sean dismissed me and went to his teak mounting block.

Molly Seabright was sitting on the park bench with her hands folded in her lap. I turned and walked to the barn, hoping she would just go away. D'Artagnon's bridle hung from the ceiling on a four-pronged hook near an antique mahogany cabinet full of leather-cleaning supplies. I chose a small damp sponge from the work table, rubbed it over a bar of glycerine soap, and began to clean the bridle, trying to narrow the focus of my mind on the small motor skills involved in the task.

"You're very rude."

I could see her from the corner of my eye: standing as tall as she could—five-feet-nothing—her mouth a tight little knot.

"Yes, I am. That's part of the joy of being me: I don't care."

"You're not going to help me."

"I can't. I'm not what you need. If your sister is missing, your parents should go to the cops."

"I went to the Sheriff's Office. They wouldn't help me either."

"*You* went? What about your parents? They don't care your sister is missing?"

For the first time Molly Seabright seemed to hesitate. "It's complicated."

"What's complicated about it? She's either missing or she's not."

"Erin doesn't live with us."

"How old is she?"

"Eighteen. She doesn't get along with our parents."

"There's something new."

"It's not like she's bad or anything," Molly said defensively. "She doesn't do drugs or anything like that. It's just that she has her own opinions, that's all. And her opinions aren't Bruce's opinions . . ."

"Who's Bruce?"

"Our stepfather. Mom always sides with him, no matter how asinine he is. It makes Erin angry, so she moved out."

"So Erin is technically an adult, living on her own, free to do whatever she wants," I said. "Does she have a boyfriend?"

Molly shook her head, but avoided my eyes. She wasn't so sure of that answer, or she thought a lie might better serve her cause.

"What makes you think she's missing?"

"She was supposed to pick me up Monday morning. That's her day off. She's a groom at the show grounds for Don Jade. He trains jumpers. I didn't have school. We were going to go to the beach, but she never came or called me. I called her and left a message on her cell phone, and she never called me back."

"She's probably busy," I said, stroking the sponge down a length of rein. "Grooms work hard."

Even as I said it I could see Irina sitting on the mounting block, face turned to the sun as she blew a lazy stream of cigarette smoke at the sky. Most grooms.

"She would have called me," Molly insisted. "I went to the show grounds myself the next day—yesterday. A man at Don Jade's barn told me Erin doesn't work there anymore."

Grooms quit. Grooms get fired. Grooms decide one day to become florists and decide the next day they'd rather be brain surgeons. On the flip side, there are trainers with reputations as slave masters, temperamental prima donnas who go through grooms like disposable razors. I've known trainers who demanded a groom sleep every night in a stall with a psychotic stallion, valuing the horse far more than the person. I've known trainers who fired five grooms in a week.

Erin Seabright was, by the sound of it, headstrong and argumentative, maybe with an eye for the guys. She was eighteen and tasting independence for the first time.... And why I was even thinking this through was beyond me. Habit, maybe. Once a cop...But I hadn't been a cop for two years, and I would never be a cop again.

"Sounds to me like Erin has a life of her own. Maybe she just doesn't have time for a kid sister right now."

Molly Seabright's expression darkened. "I told you Erin's not like that. She wouldn't just leave."

"She left home."

"But she didn't leave *me*. She wouldn't."

Finally she sounded like a child instead of a forty-nine-year-old CPA. An uncertain, frightened little girl. Looking to me for help.

"People change. People grow up," I said bluntly, taking the bridle down from the hook. "Maybe it's your turn."

The words hit their mark like bullets. Tears rose behind the Harry Potter glasses. I didn't allow myself to feel guilt or pity. I didn't want a job or a client. I didn't want people coming into my life with expectations.

"I thought you would be different," she said.

"Why would you think that?"

She glanced over at the magazine lying on the shelf with the cleaning supplies, D'Artagnon and I floating across the page like something from a dream. But she said nothing. If she had an explanation for her belief, she thought better of sharing it with me.

"I'm nobody's hero, Molly. I'm sorry you got that impression. I'm sure if your parents aren't worried about your sister, and the cops aren't worried about your sister, then there's nothing to be worried about. You don't need me, and believe me, you'd be sorry if you did."

She didn't look at me. She stood there for a moment, composing herself, then pulled a small red wallet from the carrying pouch strapped around her waist. She took out a ten-dollar bill and placed it on the magazine.

"Thank you for your time," she said politely, then turned and walked away.

I didn't chase after her. I didn't try to give her her ten dollars back. I watched her walk away and thought she was more of an adult than I was.

Irina appeared in my peripheral vision, propping herself against the archway as if she hadn't the strength to stand on her own. "You want I should saddle Feliki?"

Erin Seabright had probably quit her job. She was probably in the Keys right now enjoying her newfound independence with some cute good-for-nothing. Molly didn't want to believe that because it would mean a sea change in her relationship with the big sister she idolized. Life is full of disappointments. Molly would learn that the same way as everyone: by being let down by someone she loved and trusted.

Irina gave a dramatic sigh.

"Yes," I said. "Saddle Feliki."

She started toward the mare's stall, then I asked a question for which I would have been far better off not having an answer.

"Irina, do you know anything about a jumper trainer named Don Jade?"

"Yes," she said casually, not even looking back at me. "He is a murderer."

2
_____

The horse world is populated by two kinds of people: those who love horses, and those who exploit horses and the people who love them. Yin and yang. For every good thing in the world, there is something bad to counterbalance. Myself, I've always felt the bad far outweighs the good, that there is just enough good to buoy us and keep us from drowning in a sea of despair. But that's just me.

Some of the finest people I've known have been involved in the horse business. Caring people who would sacrifice themselves and their own comfort for the animals who relied on them. People who kept their word. People with integrity. And some of the most loathsome, hateful, twisted individuals I've ever known have been involved in the horse business. People who would lie, cheat, steal, and sell their own mother for a nickel if they thought it would get them ahead. People who would smile to your face, pat you on the back with one hand, and stab you in the back with the other.

From what Irina told me, Don Jade fit into that second category.

Sunday morning—the day before Erin Seabright didn't show to pick up her little sister to go to the beach—a jumper in training with Don Jade had been found dead in his stall, the victim of an allegedly accidental electrocution. Only, according to gossip, there was no such thing as an accident where Don Jade was involved.

I went online and tried to learn what I could about Jade from articles on horsesdaily.com and a couple of other equestrian sites. But I wanted the story in full, uncensored, and I knew exactly who to call.

If Don Jade defined my second category of horse people, Dr. Dean Soren defined the first. I had known Dr. Dean for a lifetime. Nothing went on in the horse world Dean Soren didn't know about. He had begun his veterinary career in the year aught on the racetrack, eventually moving on to show horses. Everyone in the business knew and respected Dr. Dean.

He had retired from his veterinary practice several years before, and spent his days holding court in the café that was social central of the large stable he owned off Pierson. The woman who ran the café answered the phone. I told her who I was and asked for Dr. Dean, then listened as she shouted across the room at him.

Dr. Dean shouted back: "What the hell does she want?"

"Tell him I need to ask him a couple of questions."

The woman shouted that.

"Then she can damn well come here and ask me in person," he shouted back. "Or is she too goddammed important to visit an old man?"

That was Dr. Dean. The words *charming* and *kindly* were not in his vocabulary, but he was one of the best people I had ever known. Whatever softer elements he lacked, he more than made up for in integrity and honesty.

I didn't want to go to him. Don Jade interested me only because of what Irina had said about him. I was curious, but that was all. Curiosity wasn't enough to make me want to interact with people. I had no desire to leave my sanctuary, especially in light of the photo in *Sidelines*.

I paced the house, chewing at what was left of my fingernails.

Dean Soren had known me off and on most of my life. The winter season I was twelve, he let me ride along with him on his rounds one day a week and act as his assistant. My mother and I had moved to a house in the Polo Club for the season, and I had a tutor so that I could ride every day with my trainer, and not have a school schedule interrupt my horse show schedule. Every Monday—rider's day off—I would bribe the tutor and slip off with Dr. Dean to hold his instrument tray and clean up used bandages. My own father had never spent that kind of time with me. I had never felt so important.

The memories of that winter touched me now in an especially vulnerable place. I couldn't remember the last time I had felt important. I could hardly remember the last time I had wanted to. But I could remember very clearly riding beside Dr. Dean in the enormous Lincoln Town Car he had tricked out as a rolling vet clinic.

Perhaps it was that memory that made me pick up my car keys and go.

The prime property Dr. Dean owned was populated by hunter/jumper people in one large barn and by dressage people in the other. The offices, Dr. Dean's personal stable, and the café were all located in a building between the two large barns.

The café was a simple open-air affair with a tiki bar. Dr. Dean sat at the centermost table in a carved wooden chair, an old king on his throne, drinking something with a paper umbrella in it.

I felt light-headed as I walked toward him, partly afraid to see him—or rather, for him to see me—and partly afraid people would come out of the woodwork to stare at me and ask me if I was really a private investigator. But the café was empty other than Dean Soren and the woman behind the counter. No one ran over from the barns to gawk.

Dr. Dean rose from his chair, his piercing eyes on me like a pair of lasers. He was a tall, straight man with a full head of white hair and a long face carved with lines. He had to be eighty, but he still looked fierce and strong.

"What the hell's wrong with you?" he said by way of a greeting. "Are you in chemotherapy? Is that what happened to your hair?"

"Good to see you, too, Dr. Dean," I said, shaking his hand.

He looked over at the woman behind the counter. "Marion! Make this girl a cheeseburger! She looks like hell!"

Marion, unfazed, went to work.

"What are you riding these days?" Dr. Dean asked.

I took a seat—a cheap folding chair that seemed too low and made me feel like a child. Or maybe that was just Dean Soren's effect on me. "I'm riding a couple of Sean's."

"You don't look strong enough to ride a pony."

"I'm fine."

"No, you're not," he pronounced. "Who is Sean using for a vet now?"

"Paul Geller."

"He's an idiot."

"He's not you, Dr. Dean," I said diplomatically.

"He told Margo Whitaker her mare needs 'sound therapy.' She's got headphones on the poor horse two hours a day, playing the sounds of nature."

"Gives Margo something to do."

"The horse needs not to have Margo hovering around. That's what the horse needs," he growled. He sipped his umbrella drink and stared at me.

"I haven't seen you in a long time, Elena," he said. "It's good you're back. You need to be with the horses. They ground you. A person always knows exactly where they stand with horses. Life makes more sense."

"Yes," I said, nervous under his scrutiny, afraid he would want to talk about my career and what had happened. But he let it go. Instead, he quizzed me about Sean's horses, and we reminisced about horses Sean and I had ridden in years past. Marion brought my cheeseburger and I dutifully ate.

When I had finished, he said, "You said on the phone you had a question."

"Do you know anything about Don Jade?" I asked bluntly.

His eyes narrowed. "Why would you want to know about him?"

"A friend of a friend has gotten mixed up with him. It sounded a little sketchy to me."

His thick white brows bobbed. He looked over toward the jumper barn. There were a couple of riders out on the jump field taking their mounts over colorful fences. From a distance they looked as graceful and light as deer bounding through a meadow. The athleticism of an animal is a pure and simple thing. Complicated by human emotions, needs, greed, there is little pure or simple about the sport we bring the horses into.

"Well," he said. "Don has always made a pretty picture with some ragged edges."

"What does that mean?"

"Let's take a walk," he suggested.

I suspected he didn't want anyone showing up to eavesdrop. I followed him out the back of the café to a row of small paddocks, three of them occupied by horses.

"My projects," Dr. Dean explained. "Two mystery lamenesses and one with a bad case of stomach ulcers."

He leaned against the fence and looked at them, horses he had probably saved from the knackers. He probably had half a dozen more stashed around the place.

"They give us all they can," he said. "They do their best to make sense out of what we ask them to do—*demand* they do. All they want in return is to be cared for properly and kindly. Imagine if people were like that."

"Imagine," I echoed, but I couldn't imagine. I had been a cop a dozen years. The nature of the job and the people and things it had exposed me to had burned away any idealism I might ever have had. The story Dean Soren told me about Don Jade only confirmed my low opinion of the human race.

Over the last two decades, Jade's name had twice been connected to schemes to defraud insurance companies. The scam was to kill an expensive show horse that hadn't lived up to potential, then have the owner file a claim saying the animal had died of natural causes and collect a six-figure payout.

It was an old hustle that had come into the spotlight of the national media in the eighties, when a number of prominent people in the show-jumping world had been caught at it. Several had ended up in prison for a number of years, among them an internationally well-known trainer, and an owner who was heir to an enormous cellular phone fortune. Being rich has never stopped anyone from being greedy.

Jade had lurked in the shadows of scandal back then, when he had been an assistant trainer at one of the barns that had lost horses to mysterious causes. He had never been charged with any crime or directly connected to a death. After the scandal broke, Jade had left that employer and spent a few years in France, training and competing on the European show circuit.

Eventually the furor over the horse killings died down, and Don

Jade came back to the States and found a couple of wealthy clients to serve as cornerstones for his own business.

It might seem inconceivable that a man with Jade's reputation could continue on in the profession, but there are always new owners who don't know about a trainer's history, and there are always people who won't believe what they don't want to believe. And there are always people who just plain don't care. There are always people willing to look the other way if they think they stand to gain money or fame. Consequently, Don Jade's stable attracted clients, many of whom paid him handsomely to campaign their horses in Florida at the Winter Equestrian Festival.

In the late nineties, one of those horses was a jumper called Titan.

Titan was a talented horse with an unfortunately mercurial temperament. A horse that cost his owner a lot of money and always seemed to sabotage his own efforts to earn his keep. He earned a reputation as a rogue and a head case. Despite his abilities, his market value plummeted. Meanwhile, Titan's owner, Warren Calvin, a Wall Street trader, had lost a fortune in the stock market. And suddenly one day Titan was dead, and Calvin filed a $250,000 claim with his insurance company.

The official story pieced together by Jade and his head groom was that sometime during the night Titan had become spooked, had gone wild in his stall, breaking a foreleg, and had died of shock and blood loss. However, a former Jade employee had told a different tale, claiming Titan's death had not been an accident, that Jade had had the animal suffocated, and that the horse had broken his leg in a panic as he was being asphyxiated.

It was an ugly story. The insurance company had immediately ordered a necropsy, and Warren Calvin had come under the scrutiny of a New York State prosecutor. Calvin withdrew the claim and the investigation was dropped. No fraud, no crime. The necropsy was never performed. Warren Calvin got out of the horse business.

Don Jade weathered the rumors and speculation and went on about his business. He'd had a convenient alibi for the night in question: a girl named Allison, who worked for him and claimed to have been in bed with him at the time of Titan's death. Jade admitted to the affair, lost his marriage, but kept on training horses. Old clients either believed him or left him, and new pigeons came to roost, unaware.

I had learned pieces of this story from my research on the Internet, and from Irina's gossip. I knew Irina's opinion of Jade had been based on the stories she'd heard from other grooms, information that was likely grounded in fact and heavily flavored with spite. The horse business is an incestuous business. Within the individual disciplines (jumping, dressage, et cetera) everyone knows everyone, and half of them have screwed the others, either literally or figuratively. Grudges and jealousies abound. The gossip can be vicious.

But I knew if the story came out of Dean Soren's mouth, it was true.

"It's sad a guy like that stays in business," I said.

Dr. Dean tipped his head and shrugged. "People believe what they want. Don is a charming fellow, and he can ride the hell out of a jump course. You can argue with success all you want, Elena, but you'll never win. Especially not in this business."

"Sean's groom told me Jade lost a horse last weekend," I said.

"Stellar," Dr. Dean said, nodding. His ulcer patient had come to our corner of the paddock and reached her nose out coyly toward her savior, begging for a scratch under the chin. "Story is he bit through the cord on a box fan hanging in his stall and fried himself."

The mare stepped closer and put her head over the fence. I scratched her neck absently, keeping my attention on Dean Soren. "What do you think?"

He touched the mare's head with a gnarled old hand, as gentle as if he were touching a child.

"I think old Stellar had more heart than talent."

"Do you think Jade killed him?"

"It doesn't matter what I think," he said. "It only matters what someone can prove." He looked at me with those eyes that had seen—and could see—so much about me. "What does your friend's friend have to say about it?"

"Nothing," I said, feeling sick in my stomach. "She seems to be missing."

On Monday morning Don Jade's groom, Erin Seabright, was to have picked up her little sister to take her to the beach. She never showed and hadn't been in contact with her family since.

I paced the rooms of the guest house and chewed on the ragged stub of a thumbnail. The Sheriff's Office hadn't been interested in the concerns of a twelve-year-old girl. It was doubtful they knew anything about or had any interest in Don Jade. Erin Seabright's parents presumably knew nothing about Jade either, or Molly wouldn't have been the only Seabright looking for help.

The ten-dollar bill the girl had given me was on the small writing desk beside my laptop. Inside the folded bill was Molly's own little homemade calling card: her name, address, and a striped cat on a mailing label; the label adhered to a little rectangle of blue poster board. She had printed her phone number neatly at the bottom of the card.

Don Jade had been sleeping with one of his hired girls when the horse Titan had died half a decade past. I wondered if that was a habit: fucking grooms. He wouldn't have been the first trainer with that hobby. I thought about the way Molly had avoided my eyes when she'd told me her sister didn't have a boyfriend.

I walked away from the desk feeling anxious and upset. I wished I'd never gone to Dr. Dean. I wished I had never learned what I'd learned about Don Jade. My life was enough of a mess without looking for trouble. My life was enough of a mess without the intrusion of Molly Seabright and her family problems. I was supposed to be sorting out the tangle of my own life, answering inner questions, finding myself—or facing the fact there was nothing worth finding.

If I couldn't find myself, how was I supposed to find someone else? I didn't want to fall down this rabbit hole. My involvement with horses was supposed to be my salvation. I didn't want it to have anything to do with people like Don Jade, people who would have a horse killed by electrocution, like Stellar, or by shoving Ping-Pong balls up its nostrils, cutting off its air supply, like Warren Calvin's Titan.

That was how suffocation was accomplished: Ping-Pong balls in the nostrils. My chest tightened at the dark mental image of the animal panicking, throwing itself into the walls of its stall as it desperately tried to escape its fate. I could see the eyes rolling in terror, hear the grunt as it flung itself backward and hit a wall. I could hear the animal scrambling, the terrible sound of a foreleg snapping. The nightmare seemed so real, the sounds blaring inside my mind. Nausea and weakness washed through me. My throat felt closed. I wanted to choke.

I went outside onto the little patio, sweating, trembling. I thought I might vomit. I wondered what it said about me that in all the time I'd been a detective, I'd never gotten sick at anything I'd seen one human being do to another, but the idea of cruelty to an animal undid me.

The evening air was fresh and cool, and slowly cleared the horrible images from my head.

Sean had company. I could see them in the dining room, talking, laughing. Chandelier light spilled through the tall casement windows to be reflected in the dark water of the pool. I had been invited to dinner, but turned him down flat, still furious with him for the *Sidelines* fiasco. He was probably, even as I stood there, telling his pals about the private investigator who lived in his backyard. Fucking dilettante, using me to amuse his Palm Beach pals. Never giving a thought to the fact that he was playing with my life.

Never mind he had saved it first.

I didn't want the reminder. I didn't want to think of Molly Seabright or her sister. This place was supposed to be my sanctuary, but I felt as if half a dozen unseen hands were grabbing at me, plucking at my clothes, pinching me. I tried to walk away from them, going across the damp lawn to the barn.

Sean's barn had been designed by the same architect who designed the main house and the guest house. Moorish arches created galleries down the sides. The roof was green tile, the ceiling teak. The light fixtures hanging down the center aisle had been taken out of an art deco–era hotel in Miami. Most humans don't have homes that cost what his stable cost.

It was a lovely space, a place I often came to at night to calm myself. There are few things as quieting and reassuring to me as horses browsing on their evening hay. Their lives are simple. They know they are safe. Their day is over and they trust the sun will rise the next morning.

They trust their keepers absolutely. They are utterly vulnerable.

Oliver abandoned his food and came to put his head out over his stall door to nuzzle my cheek. He caught the collar of my old denim shirt between his teeth and seemed to smile, pleased with his mischief. I hugged his big head and breathed in the scent of him. When I stepped back, extricating my collar, he looked at me with eyes as kind and innocent as a small child's.

I might have cried had I been physically able to do so. I am not.

I went back to the guest house, glancing in again at Sean's dinner party as I passed. Everyone looked to be having a grand time, smiling, laughing, bathed in golden light. I wondered what I would see if I were to walk past Molly Seabright's house. Her mother and stepfather talking around her, preoccupied with the details of their mundane lives; Molly isolated from them by her keen intelligence and her worry for her sister, wondering where to turn next.

When I went inside my house, the message light on my phone was blinking. I hit the button and braced myself to hear Molly's voice, then felt something like disappointment when my attorney asked me to please return his call sometime this century. Asshole. We'd been waging the battle for my disability pay since I had left the Sheriff's Office. (Money I didn't need, but was entitled to because I had been injured on the job. Never mind that it had been my own fault, or that my injuries were insignificant compared to what had happened to Hector Ramirez.) What the hell didn't he know about the situation after all this time? Why did he think he needed me?

Why would anyone think they needed me?

I went into my bedroom and sat on the bed, opened the drawer of the nightstand. I took out the brown plastic bottle of Vicodin and poured the pills out on the tabletop. I stared at them, counted them one by one, touching each pill. How pathetic that a ritual like this might soothe me, that the idea of a drug overdose—or the thought that I wouldn't take them that night—would calm me.

Jesus God, who in their right mind would think they needed me?

Disgusted with myself, I dumped the pills back in the bottle, put the bottle back in the drawer. I hated myself for not being what I had always believed myself to be: strong. But then I had long mistaken being spoiled for being strong, being defiant for being independent, being reckless for being brave.

Life's a bitch when you find out in your thirties that everything you ever believed to be true and admirable about yourself is nothing but a self-serving lie.

I had painted myself into a corner and I didn't know how to get out of it. I didn't know if I could reinvent myself. I didn't think I had the strength or the will to do it. Hiding in my own private purgatory required no strength.

I fully realized how pathetic that was. And I had spent a lot of nights in the past two years wondering if being dead wasn't preferable to being pathetic. So far I had decided the answer was no. Being alive at least presented the possibility for improvement.

Was Erin Seabright somewhere thinking the same thing? I wondered. Or was it already too late? Or had she found the one circumstance to which death was preferable but not an option?

I had been a cop a long time. I had started my career in a West Palm Beach radio car, patrolling neighborhoods where crime was a common career choice and drugs could be purchased on the street in broad daylight. I had done a stint in Vice, viewing the businesses of prostitution and pornography up close and personal. I had spent years working narcotics for the Sheriff's Office.

I had a head full of images of the dire consequences of being a young woman in the wrong place at the wrong time. South Florida offered a lot of places to get rid of bodies or hide ugly secrets. Wellington was an oasis of civilization, but the land beyond the gated communities was more like the land that time forgot. Swamp and woods. Open, hostile scrubland and sugarcane fields. Dirt roads and rednecks and biker meth labs in trailer houses that should have been left to the rats twenty years past. Canals and drainage ditches full of dirty black water and alligators happy to make a meal of any kind of meat.

Was Erin Seabright out there somewhere waiting for someone to save her? Waiting for me? God help her. I didn't want to go.

I went into the bathroom and washed my hands and splashed water on my face. Trying to wash away any feelings of obligation. I could feel the water only on the right side of my face. Nerves on the left side had been damaged, leaving me with limited feeling and movement. The plastic surgeons had given me a suitably neutral expression, a job so well done no one suspected anything wrong with me other than a lack of emotion.

The calm, blank expression stared back at me now in the mirror. Another reminder that no aspect of me was whole or normal. And I was supposed to be Erin Seabright's savior?

I hit the mirror with the heels of my fists, once, then again and again, wishing my image would shatter before my eyes as surely as it had shattered within me two years ago. Another part of me wanted the sharp cut of pain, the cleansing symbolized in shed blood. I wanted to bleed to know I existed. I wanted to vanish to escape the pain. The contradictory forces shoved against one another inside me, crowding my lungs, pushing up against my brain.

I went to the kitchen and stared at the knife block on the counter and my car keys lying beside it.

Life can change in a heartbeat of time, in a hairsbreadth of space. Without our consent. I had already known that to be the truth. In my deepest heart I suppose I knew it to be true in that moment, that night. I preferred to believe I picked up the keys and left the house to escape my own self-torment. That idea allowed me to continue to believe I was selfish.

In truth, the choice I made that night wasn't safe at all. In truth, I chose to move forward. I tricked myself into choosing life over purgatory.

Before it was all over, I feared I might live to regret it—or die trying.

3

Palm Beach Polo Equestrian Center is like a small sovereign nation, complete with royalty and guards at the gates. At the front gates. The back gates stood open during the day and could be reached from Sean's farm by car in five minutes. People from the neighborhood regularly hacked their horses over on show days and saved themselves the cost of stabling—ninety dollars a weekend for a pipe-and-canvas stall in a circus tent with ninety-nine other horses. A guard making night rounds would lock the gate at some point late in the evening. The guard hadn't made his rounds yet that night.

I drove through the gates, a yellow parking pass stolen from Sean's Mercedes hanging on my rearview mirror, just in case. I parked in a row of vehicles along a fence opposite the last of the forty big stabling tents on the property.

I drove a sea-green BMW 318i convertible I bought at a sheriff's auction. The roof sometimes leaked in a hard rain, but it had an interesting option that hadn't come from the factory in Bavaria: a small, foam-lined metal box hidden in the driver's door panel, just big enough to hold a good-sized bag of cocaine or a handgun. The Glock nine millimeter I kept there was tucked into the back of my jeans, hidden by my shirttail as I walked away.

On show days the show grounds are as busy and crazy as the streets of Calcutta. Golf carts and small motorcycles race back and forth between the barns and showrings, dodging dogs and trucks and trailers, heavy equipment, Jaguars and Porsches, people on horses and children on ponies, and grooms walking charges done up in immaculate braids and draped in two-hundred-dollar cool-out sheets in the custom colors of their stables. The tents look like refugee camps with portable johns out front, people filling buckets from pump hydrants by the side of the dirt road, and illegal aliens dumping muck buckets into the huge piles of manure that are carted away in dump trucks once a day. People school horses on every available open patch of ground, trainers shouting instructions, encouragement, and insults at their students. Announcements blare over the public address system every few minutes.

At night the place is a different world. Quiet. Almost deserted. The roads are empty. Security guards make the rounds of the barns periodically. A groom or trainer might drop by to perform the ritual night check or to tend an animal with a medical problem. Some stables leave a guard of their own posted in their elaborately decorated tack room. Baby-sitters for horseflesh worth millions.

Bad things can happen under cover of darkness. Rivals can become enemies. Jealousy can become revenge. I once knew a woman who sent a private cop everywhere with her horses after one of her top jumpers was slipped LSD the night before a competition offering fifty thousand dollars in prize money.

I'd made a couple of good busts at this show grounds when I'd worked narcotics. Any kind of drug—human or animal, remedial or recreational—could be had here if one knew whom and how to ask. Because I had once been a part of this world, I was able to blend in. I had been away from it long enough that no one knew me. Yet I could walk the walk and talk the talk. I had to hope Sean's little joke in *Sidelines* hadn't taken away my anonymity.

I made the dogleg turns from the back area known euphemistically as "The Meadows," the tent ghetto where show management always sticks the dressage horses that ship in for only several shows each season. From those back tents it takes twenty minutes to walk to the heart of the show grounds. Earth-moving equipment sat parked at one corner, backed into freshly cleared land amid the scrubby woods. The place was being expanded again.

Lights glowed in the tents. A woman's melodic laugh floated on the night air. A man's low chuckle underscored the sound. I could see the pair standing at the end of an aisle in tent nineteen. Elaborate landscaping at the corner of the tent set the stage around a lighted stable sign with one golden word on a field of hunter green: JADE.

I walked past. Now that I had found Jade's stalls, I didn't know what I was going to do. I hadn't thought that far ahead. I turned on the far side of tent eighteen and doubled back around, coming up through the aisles of nineteen until I could hear the voices again.

"Do you hear anything?" The man's voice. An accent. Maybe Dutch, maybe Flemish.

I stopped breathing.

"Gut sounds," the woman said. "She's fine, but we'll go through the drill with the vet anyway. Can't be seen looking careless after Stellar."

The man gave a humorless laugh. "People have made their minds up about that. They believe what they want."

"The worst," the woman said. "Jane Lennox called today. She's thinking of putting Park Lane with another trainer. I talked her out of it."

"I'm sure you did. You're very persuasive, Paris."

"This is America. You're supposed to be innocent until proven guilty."

"Innocent always if you're rich or beautiful or charming."

"Don is beautiful and charming, and everyone believes he's guilty."

"Like O.J. was guilty? He's playing golf and fucking white women."

"What a thing to say!"

"It's true. And Jade has a barn full of horses. Americans..." Disdain.

"I'm an American, V." An edge to the tone. "Do you want to call me stupid?"

"Paris..." Smarmy contrition.

"Stupid Americans buy your horses and line your pockets. You should show more respect. Or does that just prove how stupid we are?"

"Paris..." Smarmier contrition. "Don't be angry with me. I don't want you angry with me."

"No, you don't."

A Jack Russell terrier came sniffing around the corner then and stared at me while he raised his leg and peed on a bale of hay, considering whether or not to blow my cover. The leg went down and the dog went off like a car alarm. I stood where I was.

The woman called out: "Milo! Milo, come here!"

Milo stood his ground. He bounced up and down like a wind-up toy every time he barked.

The woman rounded the corner, looking surprised to see me. She was blond and pretty in dark breeches and a green polo shirt with a couple of gold necklaces showing at the throat. She flashed a thousand-watt toothpaste-ad smile that was nothing more than jaw muscles flexing.

"Sorry. He thinks he's a Rottweiler," she said, scooping up the Russell. "Can I help you?"

"I don't know. I'm looking for someone. I was told she works for Don Jade. Erin Seabright?"

"Erin? What do you want with her?"

"This is kind of awkward," I said. "I heard she was looking for another job. I have a friend in the market for a groom. You know how it is during the season."

"Do I ever!" She gave a dramatic, put-upon sigh, rolling the big brown eyes. An actress. "We're looking too. Erin quit, I'm sad to say."

"Really? When was that?"

"Sunday. Left us high and dry. Found something more interesting up in Ocala, I guess. Don tried to talk her out of it, but he said her mind was made up. I was sorry to hear it. I liked Erin, but you know how flighty these girls can be."

"Huh. I'm surprised. The way I understood it, she wanted to stay in the Wellington area. Did she leave an address—to have her paycheck sent?"

"Don paid her before she left. I'm Don's assistant trainer, by the way. Paris Montgomery." Keeping the dog tucked against her, she held a hand out and shook mine. She had a strong grip. "And you are...?"

"Elle Stevens." A name I had used undercover in my past life. It fell off my tongue without hesitation. "So, she left Sunday. Was that before or after Stellar went down?"

The smile died. "Why would you ask that?"

"Well . . . a disgruntled employee leaves and suddenly you lose a horse—"

"Stellar bit through an electrical cord. It was an accident."

I shrugged. "Hey, what do I know? People talk."

"People don't know shit."

"Is there a problem here?"

The man stepped into the picture. Mid-fifties, tall and elegant with silver temples highlighting a full head of dark hair. He wore a stern, aristocratic expression, pressed tan slacks, a pink Lacoste knit shirt, and a black silk ascot at his throat.

"Not at all," I said. "I was just looking for someone."

"Erin," Paris Montgomery said to him.

"Erin?"

"Erin. My groom. The one that left."

He made a sour face. "That girl? She's good for nothing. What would you want with her?"

"Doesn't matter," I said. "She's gone."

"What's your friend's name?" Paris asked. "In case I hear of someone."

"Sean Avadon. Avadonis Farm."

The man's cold blue eyes brightened. "He has some very nice horses."

"Yes, he does."

"You work for him?" he asked.

I supposed I did look like hired help with my hacked-off hair, old jeans, and work boots. "He's an old friend. I'm leasing a horse from him until I can find what I'm looking for."

He smiled then like a cat with a cornered mouse. His teeth were brilliantly white. "I can help you with that."

A horse dealer. The third-oldest profession. Forerunners of used-car salesmen the world over.

Paris Montgomery rolled her eyes. A truck pulled up at the end of the tent. "That's Dr. Ritter. I've got to go."

She turned the big smile back on and shook my hand again. "Nice meeting you, Elle," she said, as if we'd never had that moment of unpleasantness at the mention of Stellar's death. "Good luck with your search."

"Thanks."

She set the Russell down and followed the barking beast around the corner as the vet called for her.

The man held his hand out to me. "Tomas Van Zandt."

"Elle Stevens."

"My pleasure."

He held my hand a little too long.

"I'd better be going," I said, drifting back a step. "It's getting late for a wild-goose chase."

"I'll take you to your car," he offered. "Beautiful women shouldn't go around unescorted here in the dark. You don't know what kind of people might be around."

"I have a pretty good idea, but thanks for your concern. Women shouldn't get into cars with men they've only just met either," I said.

He laughed and placed a hand over his heart. "I am a gentleman, Elle. Harmless. Without designs. Wanting nothing of you but a smile."

"You'd sell me a horse. That would cost me plenty."

"But only the best horses," he promised. "I will find you exactly what you need and for a good price. Your friend Avadon likes good horses. Maybe you could introduce us."

Horse dealers. I rolled my eyes and gave him half a smile. "Maybe I just want a ride to my car."

Looking pleased, he led the way out of the tent to a black Mercedes sedan and opened the door for me.

"You must have a lot of satisfied customers if you can rent a car like this for the season," I said.

Van Zandt smiled like the cat that got the cream *and* the canary. "I have such happy clients, one gave me the loan of this car for the winter."

"My goodness. If only my ex had made me so happy, he might still be considered in the present tense."

Van Zandt laughed. "Where are you parked, Miss Elle?"

"The back gate."

As we started down the road toward The Meadows I said, "You

know this girl, Erin? She's not a good worker?"

He pursed his lips like he'd gotten a whiff of something rotten. "Bad attitude. Smart mouth. Flirting with the clients. American girls don't make good grooms. They're spoiled and lazy."

"I'm an American girl."

He ignored that. "Get a good Polish girl. They're strong and cheap."

"Can I get one at Wal-Mart? I've got a Russian now. She thinks she's a czarina."

"Russians are arrogant."

"And what are Dutchmen?"

He pulled the Mercedes in where I pointed, alongside my Beemer.

"I am from Belgium," he corrected. "Men from Belgium are charming and know how to treat ladies."

"Slick rascals, more like," I said. "Ladies should be on their guard, I think."

Van Zandt chuckled. "You are no pushover, Elle Stevens."

"It takes more than a smile and an accent to sweep me off my feet. I'll make you work for it."

"A challenge!" he said, delighted at the prospect.

I got out of the car without waiting for him to come around and open the door, and dug my keys out of my hip pocket. The back of my hand brushed over the butt of the gun tucked in my waistband.

"Thanks for the ride," I said.

"Thank you, Elle Stevens. You brightened an otherwise boring evening."

"Don't let Ms. Montgomery hear you say that."

"She's all gloom, talking about the dead gelding."

"Losing a horse worth that kind of money would bring me down too."

"It wasn't her money."

"Maybe she liked the horse."

He shrugged. "There's always another."

"Which I'm sure you'll be happy to supply to the grieving owner for a price."

"Of course. Why not? That's business—for me and for her."

"You sentimental fool, you."

In the harsh glow of the security light from above I saw the muscles of Van Zandt's jaw flex. "I am in this business thirty years, Elle Stevens," he said, a thread of impatience in his voice. "I am not a heartless man, but for professionals horses come and horses go. It's a shame the gelding died, but with professionals a sentimental fool is just that: a fool. People have to move on with their lives. Owners too. The insurance will pay for the dead horse, and his owner will buy another."

"Which you will be happy to find."

"Of course. I know already a horse in Belgium: clean X rays and twice as good as that one over the fences."

"And for a mere one-point-eight million he can belong to some lucky American and Don Jade can ride him."

"The good ones cost, the good ones win."

"And the rest can bite through electrical cords in the dead of night and fry themselves?" I asked. "Careful who you say that to, Van Zandt. Some insurance investigator might hear you and think the wrong thing."

He didn't shrug that off. I sensed him tense.

"I never said anyone killed the horse," he said, his voice tight and low. He was angry with me. I wasn't supposed to have a brain. I was supposed to be the next American with too much money and too little sense, waiting for him to charm me and sweep me off to Europe on a buying trip.

"No, but Jade has that reputation, doesn't he?"

Van Zandt stepped closer. My back pressed against the frame of my car's roof. I had to look up at him. There wasn't a soul around. There was nothing but a lot of open country beyond the back gates. I slipped one hand into the back of my waistband and touched my gun.

"Are you that insurance person, Elle Stevens?" he asked.

"Me?" I laughed. "God, no. I don't work." I said the word with the kind of disdain my mother would have used. "It's just a good story, that's all. Don Jade: Dangerous Man of Mystery. You know us Palm Beachers. Can't resist a juicy scandal. My biggest concern in life at the moment is where my next good horse is coming from. What goes on with this show-jumping crowd is nothing but good gossip to me."

He relaxed then, having decided I was sufficiently self-absorbed. He handed me his card and dredged up the charm again. Nothing like greed to rally a man. "Give me a call, Elle Stevens. I'll find you your horse."

I tried to smile, knowing only one side of my mouth moved upward at all. "I may take you up on that, Mr. Van Zandt."

"Call me V.," he suggested, his tone strangely intimate. "V. for Very Good Horses. V. for Victory in the showring."

V. for vomit.

"We are friends now," he announced. He leaned down and kissed my right cheek, then the left, then the right again. His lips were cold and dry.

"Three times," he said, Mr. Suave again. "Like the Dutch."

"I'll remember that. Thanks again for the ride."

I got into my car and backed out of the line. The back gate was locked. I turned and went back down the road past tent nineteen. Van Zandt followed me to the truck entrance. The lights blazed in the four big permanent barns to the right. A guard stood in the little booth between traffic lanes before the main gates, reggae music blasting from a radio on the counter. I waved at him. He waved me past without a question, his attention on the eighteen-wheel commercial horse van pulling in. I could have had a trunk full of stolen saddles. I could have had a body back there. I might have been anyone, may have done anything. An unsettling thought for the ride home.

I turned right on Pierson. Van Zandt turned right on Pierson. I watched him in the mirror, wondering if he hadn't believed me when I'd said I wasn't an insurance investigator. I wondered what his reaction would be if he saw the photo in *Sidelines* and put two and one together.

But people are funny that way, more easily fooled than the average person might like to believe. I didn't look like the woman in the photo. My hair was short. I hadn't given the name of the woman in the photo. The only real connection was Sean. Still, the words *private investigator* would set off alarms. I had to hope Sean was right: that only dressage people read the dressage section.

I turned right on South Shore. Van Zandt turned left.

I cut my lights, pulled a U-turn, and followed at a distance, past the polo stadium. He turned in at The Players club. Wining and dining. Part of a horse dealer's job. A new best friend at the bar in a place like that could turn out to have deep pockets and no self-restraint.

Van Zandt stood to make a tidy profit selling the Belgian jumper to Stellar's owner, who stood to collect a fat insurance payoff on a horse with no real future. And Don Jade—who had trained and shown Stellar, and would train and show the next one—stood in the middle of them, taking money at both ends of the deal. They might have all been in Players together right then, drinking to Stellar's timely demise.

Erin Seabright hadn't been heard from since the night Stellar died.

I dismissed the idea of going into the club. I wasn't prepared. I gunned my car's engine, turned it around, and headed home.

I was about to become a private investigator.

4

I wonder why I'm still alive.

Billy Golam had pointed that gun right in my face. In countless nightmares I have looked down the barrel of that .357 and sucked in what should have been my final breath. But Golam had turned and fired in another direction.

Was living my punishment, my purgatory? Or was I supposed to have chosen to end it myself to pay for my recklessness? Or was I just damn lucky and unwilling to believe it?

Four-thirty A.M.

I was lying in bed, staring at the blades of the ceiling fan go around. The guest house had been decorated by a Palm Beach interior designer who had gone amok with delusions of Caribbean plantations. It seemed a cliché to me, but no one had ever paid me to pick out paint chips and pillow shams.

At four I went out and fed the horses. By five I had showered. It had been so long since I'd had to introduce myself to people and care about what they thought of me that I couldn't remember how to go about it. I couldn't shake the idea that I would be rejected on sight, or if not on sight, on reputation.

What a strange conceit to believe everyone in the world knew all about me, all about what I'd done and what had happened to end my career. I had been a story on the evening news for a couple of days. A sound bite. Something to fill the airtime before the weather came on. The truth was probably that no one not directly involved with what had happened, no one not living in that world of cops, had given the story more than the most cursory attention. The truth is that people seldom really care about the catastrophic events of someone else's life beyond thinking, "Better her than me."

I stood in my underwear, staring at myself in the mirror. I put some gel in my hair and tried to make it look as if it had an intentional style. I wondered if I should attempt makeup. I hadn't worn any since the surgery to put my face back together. My plastic surgeon had given me the card of a woman who specialized in postsurgical makeup. The Post-Traumatic Avon Lady. I had thrown the card away.

I dressed, discarding a dozen different choices and finally settling on a sleeveless silk blouse the color of fresh-poured concrete and a pair of brown trousers that were so big around the waist, I had to pin them shut to keep them from sliding down my hips.

I used to care about fashion.

I killed some time on the Internet, chewed my nails, and made some notes.

I found nothing of interest on Tomas Van Zandt. His name did not appear even on his own Web site: worldhorsesales.com. The site listed on his business card showed photos of horses that had been brokered through Van Zandt's business. Phone numbers were listed for a business office in Brussels, a number for European sales, and for two U.S. subagents, one of whom was Don Jade.

I found several articles about Paris Montgomery in the *Chronicle of the Horse* and *Horses Daily* describing recent wins in the showring, talking about her humble beginnings riding ponies bareback in the Pine Barrens of New Jersey. According to the propaganda, she had worked her way up the ranks from groom to working student to assistant trainer; succeeding on hard work and raw talent. And charm. And the fact that she could have been a model.

She had been Don Jade's assistant trainer for three years and was so grateful for the opportunity, blah, blah, blah. So few people realized what a great guy he really was. He'd been unfortunate to do business with some people of questionable ethics, but shouldn't be condemned by association, et cetera, et cetera. Jade was quoted as saying Paris Montgomery had a bright future and the ambition and talent to attain whatever she set her sights on.

Photographs with the articles showed Montgomery going over a fence on a horse called Park Lane, and close-ups of her flashing the big smile.

The smile irritated me. It was too bright and came too easily. The charm seemed insincere. Then again, I'd only just met her for ten minutes. Maybe I didn't like her because I couldn't smile and wasn't charming.

I flipped the screen shut on my laptop and went outside. Dawn was a pale notion on the edge of the eastern sky as I let myself into Sean's house through the French doors into the dining room. He was alone in bed, snoring. I sat down beside him and patted his cheek. His eyelids pulled slowly upward, revealing a lot of red veins. He rubbed a hand over his face.

"I was hoping for Tom Cruise," he said in a voice full of gravel.

"Sorry to disappoint. If a horse dealer named Van Zandt comes around, my name is Elle Stevens and you're looking for a groom."

"What?" He pushed himself upright and shook his head to clear the cobwebs. "Van Zandt? Tomas Van Zandt?"

"You know him?"

"I know of him. He's the second-biggest crook in Europe. Why would he come here?"

"Because he thinks you might buy horses from him."

"Why would he think that?"

"Because I pretty much led him to believe it."

"Uh!!"

"Don't look offended," I said. "That expression emphasizes the lines around your mouth."

"Bitch."

He pouted for a moment, then caught himself and rubbed his hands over his face—outward and upward from his mouth. The ten-second face-lift. "You know I already have a European connection. You know I only work with Toine."

39

"Yes, I know. The last honest horse dealer."

"The only one in the history of the world, as far as I know."

"So let Van Zandt think he's wooing you away from Toine. He'll have an orgasm. If he comes around, pretend you're interested. You owe me."

"I don't owe you that much."

"Really?" I said. "Thanks to you, I now have a client and a career I didn't want."

"You'll thank me later."

"I'll exact my revenge later." I leaned over and patted his stubbled cheek again. "Happy horse dealing."

He groaned.

"And, by the way," I said, pausing at the door. "He thinks I'm a Palm Beach dilettante and that I'm leasing D'Artagnon from you."

"I'm supposed to keep this all straight?"

I shrugged. "What else have you got to do with your time?"

I was almost out the bedroom door when he spoke again.

"El..."

I turned back toward him, one hand on the door frame. He looked at me, uncharacteristically serious, a certain softness in his expression. He wanted to say something kind. I wanted him to pretend this day was like any other. We each seemed fully aware of the other's thoughts. I held my breath. One side of his mouth lifted in a smile of concession.

"Nice outfit," he said.

I waved at him and left the house.

Molly Seabright lived in a two-story stucco house on the edge of a development called Binks Forest. Upscale. Backyard on a fairway. A white Lexus in the drive. There were lights on in the house. The hardworking upper middle class preparing to face another day. I parked down the street and waited.

At seven-thirty kids in the neighborhood began drifting out of their homes and wandering past me toward the school bus stop at the end of the block. Molly emerged from the Seabright house pulling a wheeled book bag behind her, looking like a miniature corporate exec on her way to catch a plane. I got out of my car and leaned back against it with my arms crossed. She spotted me from twenty feet away.

"I've reconsidered," I said as she stopped in front of me. "I'll help you find your sister."

She didn't smile. She didn't jump for joy. She stared up at me and said, "Why?"

"Because I don't like the people your sister was mixed up with."

"Do you think something bad has happened to her?"

"We know something has happened to her," I said. "She was here and now she isn't. Whether or not it's something bad remains to be seen."

Molly nodded at that, apparently pleased I hadn't tried to falsely reassure her. Most adults speak to children as if they're stupid simply because they haven't lived as many years. Molly Seabright wasn't stupid. She was smart and she was brave. I wasn't going to talk down to her. I had even decided not to lie to her if I could help myself.

"But if you're not a private investigator, what good are you?" she asked.

I shrugged. "How hard can it be? Ask a few questions, make a few phone calls. It's not brain surgery."

She considered my answer. Or maybe she was considering whether or not to say what she said next. "You were a sheriff's detective once."

I might have been that stunned if she had reached up and hit me in the head with a hammer. I who wouldn't talk down to a child. It hadn't occurred to me Molly Seabright would run home and do her own detective work online. I felt suddenly naked, exposed in that way I had earlier convinced myself was unlikely to happen. Blindsided by a twelve-year-old.

I glanced away. "Is that your bus?"

A school bus had pulled up to the curb and the children gathered there were clambering aboard.

"I walk," she said primly. "I found a story about you in the computer archives of the *Post*."

"Only one? I'm offended."

"More than one."

"Okay, so my dirty secret is exposed. I was a detective for Palm Beach County. Now I'm not."

She understood to leave it at that. Wiser than most people I've known three times her age.

"We need to discuss your fee," she said. Ms. Business.

"I'll take the hundred you offered and we'll see what happens."

"I appreciate that you're not trying to patronize me."

"I just said I'd take a hundred dollars from a kid. Sounds pretty low to me."

"No," she said, those too-serious eyes staring at me through the magnifying lenses of the Harry Potter glasses. "I don't think so." She put her hand out. "Thank you for accepting my case."

"Jesus. You make me feel like we should sign a contract," I said, shaking her hand.

"Technically, we should. But I trust you."

"Why would you trust me?"

I had the feeling she had an answer, but that she thought it might be too much for me to comprehend and so thought better of sharing it with me. I began to wonder if she was really from this planet.

"Just because," she said. A child's pat answer to people who aren't really paying attention. I let it go.

"I'll need some information from you. A photograph of Erin, her address, make and model of her car, that sort of thing."

As I was asking, she bent down, unzipped a compartment of her book bag, and withdrew a manila envelope, which she handed to me. "You'll find everything in there."

"Of course." I shouldn't have been surprised. "And when you went to the sheriff's department, who did you speak with?"

"Detective Landry. Do you know him?"

"I know who he is."

"He was very rude and condescending."

"So was I."

"You weren't condescending."

A black Jag backed out of the Seabright garage, a suit at the wheel. Bruce Seabright, I assumed. He turned away from us and drove down the street.

"Is your mother home?" I asked. "I'll need to speak with her."

The prospect didn't thrill her. She looked a little nauseated. "She goes to work at nine. She's a real estate agent."

"I'll have to speak with her, Molly. And with your stepfather, too. I'll leave you out of it. I'll tell them I'm an insurance investigator."

She nodded, still looking grim.

"You should leave for school now. I don't want to be arrested for contributing to the delinquency of a minor."

"No," she said, heading back toward the house, head up, her little book case rattling along on the sidewalk behind her. We should all have so much character.

Krystal Seabright was on a cordless phone when Molly and I walked into the house. She was leaning over a hall table, peering into an ornate rococo mirror, trying to stick down a false eyelash with a long pink fingernail while she chattered to someone about an absolutely fabulous town house in Sag Harbor Court. No one would have picked her out of a lineup as Molly's mother. Having met Molly first, I might have pictured her mother as a buttoned-up attorney or a doctor or a nuclear physicist. I might have, except that I knew firsthand children and parents didn't always match.

Krystal was a bottle blonde who'd used one too many bottles in her thirty-some years. Her hair was nearly white and looked as fragile as cotton candy. She wore just a little too much makeup. Her pink suit was a little too tight and a little too bright, her sandals a little too tall in the spike heel. She glanced at us out of the corner of her eye.

". . . I can fax you all the details as soon as I get to my office, Joan. But you really need to see it to appreciate it. Places like this just aren't available now during the season. You're so lucky this just came up."

She turned away from the mirror and looked at me, then at Molly with a *what now?* expression, but continued her conversation with the invisible Joan, setting up an appointment at eleven, scribbling it into a messy daybook. Finally she set the phone aside.

"Molly? What's going on?" she asked, looking at me, not her daughter.

"This is Ms. Estes," Molly said. "She's an investigator."

Krystal looked at me like I might have beamed down from Mars. "A what?"

"She wants to talk to you about Erin."

Fury swept up Krystal's face like a flash fire burning into the roots of her hair. "Oh, for God's sake, Molly! I can't believe you did this! What is the matter with you?"

The hurt in Molly's eyes was sharp enough that I felt it myself.

"I told you something bad's happened," Molly insisted.

"I can't believe you do these things!" Krystal ranted, her frustration with her younger daughter clearly nothing new. "Thank God Bruce isn't here."

"Mrs. Seabright," I said, "I'm looking into a case at the equestrian center which might involve your daughter Erin. I'd like to speak with you in private, if possible."

She looked at me, wild-eyed, still angry. "There's nothing to discuss. We don't know anything about what goes on over there."

"But Mom—" Molly started, desperately wanting her mother to care.

Her mother turned a withering, bitter look on her. "If you've told this woman some ridiculous story, you're going to be in such hot water, young lady. I can't believe the trouble you're making. You don't have any consideration for anyone but yourself."

Two red dots colored Molly's otherwise paste-pale cheeks. I thought she might start to cry. "I'm worried about Erin," she said in a small voice.

"Erin is the last person anyone needs to worry about," Krystal said. "Go to school. Go. Get out of this house. I'm so angry with you right now . . . If you're late for school you can just sit in detention this afternoon. Don't bother calling me."

I wanted to grab a handful of Krystal Seabright's overprocessed hair and shake her until the hair broke off in my fist.

Molly turned and went outside, leaving the front door wide open. The sight of her wheeling away her little book bag made my heart ache.

"You can leave right behind her," Krystal Seabright said to me. "Or I can call the police."

I turned back to face her and said nothing for a moment while I tried to wrestle my temper into submission. I was reminded of the fact that I had been a terrible patrol officer when I'd first gone on the job because I lacked the requisite diplomatic skills for domestic situations. I have always been of the opinion that some people really do just need to be bitch-slapped. Molly's mother was one of those people.

Krystal was trembling like a Chihuahua, having some control issues of her own.

"Mrs. Seabright, for what it's worth, Molly has nothing to do with this," I lied.

"Oh? She hasn't tried to tell you her sister has vanished and that we should be calling the police and the FBI and *America's Most Wanted*?"

"I know that Erin hasn't been seen since Sunday afternoon. Doesn't that concern you?"

"Are you implying I don't care about my children?" Again with the bug-eyes and the practiced affront—always a sign of low self-esteem.

"I'm not implying anything."

"Erin is an adult. At least in her own mind. She wanted to live on her own, take care of herself."

"So you're not aware that she was working for a man who's been involved in schemes to defraud insurance agencies?"

She looked confused. "She works for a horse trainer. That's what Molly said."

"You haven't spoken with Erin?"

"When she left she made it very clear she wanted nothing more to do with me. Living a decent life in a lovely home was just all too boring for her. After everything I've done for her and her sister..."

She went to the hall table, glanced at herself in the mirror, and dug her hand into a big pink and orange Kate Spade purse. She came out of the bag with a cigarette and a slim lighter, and moved toward the open front door.

"I've worked so hard, made so many sacrifices..." she said, more or less to herself, as if it comforted her to portray herself as the heroine of the story. She lit the cigarette and blew the smoke outside. "She's done nothing but give me grief since the night she was conceived."

"Does Erin's father live in the vicinity? Might she have gone to spend time with him?"

Krystal burst out laughing, but not with humor. She didn't look at me. "No. She wouldn't have done that."

"Where is her father?"

"I wouldn't know. I haven't heard from him in fifteen years."

"Do you know who Erin's friends are?"

"What do you want with her?" she asked. "What's she done now?"

"Nothing I'm aware of. She may have some information. I'd just like to ask her some questions about the man she's been working for. Has Erin been in trouble in the past?"

She leaned way out the door, took another hard drag on the cigarette, and exhaled the smoke at a hibiscus shrub. "I don't see that my family is any business of yours."

"Has she ever been involved with drugs?"

She snapped a look at me. "Is that what this is about? Is she mixed up with drug people? God. That's all I need."

"I'm concerned about where she's gone," I said. "Erin's disappearance happened to coincide with the death of a very expensive horse."

"You think she killed a horse?"

I thought my head might split in two. Krystal's concern seemed to be about everyone except her daughter. "I just want to ask her some questions about her boss. Do you have any idea where she might have gone?"

She stepped outside, tapped her ash into a plant pot, and hopped back into the house. "Responsibility isn't Erin's thing. She thinks being an adult means doing whatever you damn well please. She's probably run off to South Beach with some boy."

"Does she have a boyfriend?"

She scowled and looked down at the tiled floor. Down and to the right: a lie. "How would I know? She doesn't check in with me."

"Molly said she hasn't been able to reach Erin on her cell phone."

"Molly." She puffed on the cigarette and tried to wave the smoke out toward the street. "Molly is twelve. Molly thinks Erin is cool. Molly reads too many mystery novels and watches too much A&E. What kind of child watches A&E? *Law and Order, Investigative Reports.* When I was twelve I was watching *Brady Bunch* reruns."

"I think Molly has reason to be concerned, Mrs. Seabright. I think you might want to speak with the Sheriff's Office about filing a missing person's report."

Krystal Seabright looked horrified. Not at the prospect that her daughter might have been the victim of foul play, but at the idea of someone from Binks Forest having to file a police report. What would the neighbors say? They might put two and two together and figure out her last house was a double-wide.

"Erin is not missing," she insisted. "She's just . . . gone somewhere, that's all."

A teenage boy emerged through a door into the upstairs hall and came thudding down the stairs. He looked maybe seventeen or eighteen and hungover. Gray-faced and glum, with platinum-tipped dark hair that stood up in dirty tufts. His T-shirt looked slept in and worse. He didn't resemble Krystal or her daughters. I made the assumption he belonged to Bruce Seabright, and wondered why Molly had made no mention of him to me.

Krystal swore under her breath and surreptitiously tossed her cigarette out the door. The boy's eyes followed it, then went back to her. Busted.

"Chad? What are you doing home?" she asked. A whole new tone of voice. Nervous. Obsequious. "Aren't you feeling well, honey? I thought you'd gone to school."

"I'm sick," he said.

"Oh. Oh. Uh . . . Would you like me to make you some toast?" she asked brightly. "I have to get to the office, but I could make you some toast."

"No, thank you."

"You were out awfully late last night," Krystal said sweetly. "You probably just need your sleep."

"Probably." Chad glanced at me, and slouched away.

Krystal scowled at me and spoke in a low voice. "Look: we don't need you. Just go away. Erin will turn up when Erin needs something."

"What about Erin?" Chad asked. He had come back into the hall, a two-liter bottle of Coke in one hand. Breakfast of champions.

Krystal Seabright closed her eyes and huffed. "Nothing. Just— Nothing. Go back to bed, honey."

"I need to ask her some questions about the guy she works for," I said to the boy. "Do you happen to know where I can find her?"

He shrugged and scratched his chest. "Sorry, I haven't seen her."

As he said it, the black Jag rolled back into the driveway. Krystal looked stricken. Chad disappeared down a hall. The man I assumed to be Bruce Seabright got out of the car and strode toward the open front door, a man on a mission. He was stocky with thinning hair slicked straight back and a humorless expression.

"Honey, did you forget something?" Krystal asked in the same tone she'd used with Chad. The overeager servant.

"The Fairfields file. I've got a major deal going down on a piece of that property this morning and I don't have the file. I know I set it on the dining room table. You must have moved it."

"No, I don't think so. I—"

"How many times do I have to tell you, Krystal? Do not touch my business files." There was a condescension in his tone that couldn't have been categorized as abusive, but was, in a subtle, insidious way.

"I'm—I'm sorry, honey," she stammered. "Let me go find it for you."

Bruce Seabright looked at me with a hint of wariness, like he suspected I might have a permit to solicit charitable donations. "I'm sorry if I interrupted," he said politely. "I have a very important meeting to get to."

"I gathered. Elena Estes," I said, holding my hand out.

"Elena is considering a condo in Sag Harbor," Krystal hurried to say. There was a hint of desperation in her eyes when she looked at me in search of a coconspirator.

"Why would you show her something there, darling?" he asked. "Property values in that neighborhood will only decline. You should show her something at Palm Groves. Send her to the office. Have Kathy show her a model."

"Yes, of course," Krystal murmured, swallowing down the criticism and the slight, allowing him to take away her sale. "I'll go find that file for you."

"I'll do it, honey. I don't want anything dropping out of it."

Something on the stoop caught Seabright's eye. He bent down and picked up the cigarette butt Krystal had thrown out. He held it pinched between his thumb and forefinger and looked at me.

"I'm sorry, but smoking is not allowed on my property."

"Sorry," I said, taking the thing away from him. "It's a filthy habit."

"Yes, it is."

He went into the house to find his errant file. Krystal rubbed at her forehead and stared down at her slightly too flashy sandals, blinking like she might have been fighting tears.

"Just go, please," she whispered.

I stuck the butt in the plant pot and went. What else could I say to a woman who was so under the thumb of her domineering husband, she would sooner abandon her own child than displease him?

Over and over in my life I've found that people are amazing, and seldom in a good way.

5

We never know the quality of someone else's life, though we seldom resist the temptation to assume and pass judgment. Plenty of women would have looked at Krystal Seabright's situation through the filter of distance and assumed she had it made. Big house, fancy car, career in real estate, land developer husband. Looked good on paper. There was even a Cinderella element to the story: single mother of two swept out of her lowly station in life, et cetera, et cetera.

So too with the apparently well-heeled folks who owned the four thousand expensive horses at the equestrian center. Champagne and caviar every day for a snack. A maid in every mansion, a Rolls in every five-car garage.

The truth was more checkered and less glamorous. There were personal stories full of nasty little plot twists: insecurities and infidelities. There were people who came to the Florida season on a dream and a shoestring, saving every dime all year so they could share a no-frills condo with two other riders, take a few precious lessons from a big-name trainer, and show their mediocre mount to anonymity in the amateur arena just for the love of the sport. There were second-tier professionals with second mortgages on farms in East Buttcrack, hanging on the fringes of the big stables, hoping to pick up a real client or two. There were dealers like Van Zandt: hyenas prowling the water hole, in search of vulnerable prey. The lush life has many shades of gray beneath the gold leaf. It was now officially my job to dig up some of those darker veins.

I thought it would be best to put in as much time as possible near the Jade stable before someone attached to Don Jade went into the bathroom with a copy of *Sidelines* and came out with a revelation. I'd spent enough time working undercover as a narc to know the chances of that were small, but there nonetheless. People see what they're programmed to see, they seldom look for anything else. Still, a cop's life undercover is never without the fear of being made. It can happen any second, and the deeper under, the worse the timing.

My strategy working undercover had always been to get as much information as possible, as fast as possible; to sketch my illusion boldly and quickly. Dazzle the mark, draw them in close, then hit with the sucker punch and get out. My superiors in the Sheriff's Office had frowned on my methods because I'd borrowed my style from con artists rather than cops. But they had seldom frowned on the outcome.

Sean's parking pass still hanging from my rearview mirror, I rolled past the guard at the gatehouse and into the maelstrom of the Wellington show grounds day shift. There were horses everywhere, people everywhere, cars everywhere, golf carts everywhere. A show was under way and would run through Sunday. Horses and ponies would be jumping over fences in half a dozen competition rings. The chaos would work in my favor, like running a game of three-card monte on a corner in Times Square. Difficult to keep your eye on the queen when you're in the middle of a circus.

I parked in the second lot, cut past the permanent barns and the vet clinic, bypassed the concession stands, and found myself on the show grounds' version of Fifth Avenue: a row of mobile tack shops and pricey boutiques in tricked-out fifth-wheel trailers. Custom jewelers, custom tailors, antiques dealers, monogramming shops, cappuccino stands. I hit a couple of the boutiques to pick up trappings for my role as dilettante. Image is everything.

I purchased and put on a wide-brimmed straw hat trimmed with black grosgrain ribbon. Men never take seriously a woman in a hat. I chose a couple of silk blouses and long wraparound skirts made from vintage saris. I made sure the clerks went overboard with the tissue paper, making the shopping bags look full to bursting. I bought some impractical sandals and trendy bracelets, and put them on. When I thought I looked frivolous enough, I went in search of Don Jade.

There was no sign of him or of Paris Montgomery at his stalls. An underfed Guatemalan man was mucking out a stall, head down, trying not to attract attention lest the next stranger be an INS agent. The front of another stall had been removed to create a grooming bay. In it an overfed girl in a too-revealing tank top was grudgingly brushing a dappled gray horse. The girl had the mean, narrow eyes of someone who blames everyone but herself for the shortfalls in her life. I caught her looking at me sideways, her expression sour.

I tipped my head back and regarded her from under the brim of the ridiculous hat. "I'm looking for Paris. Is she around?"

"She's riding Park Lane in the schooling ring."

"Is Don with her?" Don, my old pal.

"Yeah." And did I want to make something of it?

"And you are . . . ?"

She looked surprised I would bother to ask, then suspicious, then determined she would take advantage of the opportunity. "Jill Morone. I'm Mr. Jade's head groom."

She was Mr. Jade's only groom by the look of it, and by the anemic way she was wielding that brush, she defined the position loosely.

"Really? Then you must know Erin Seabright."

The girl's reactions were so slow, her brain might have been in another time zone. I could see her every thought move sluggishly through her mind as she tried to decide on an answer. She dragged the brush along the horse's shoulder. The horse pinned its ears and rolled an eye at her.

"She doesn't work here anymore."

"I know. Paris told me. Do you know where she went? A friend of mine wanted to hire her."

Jill shrugged, eyes sliding away. "I dunno. Paris said she went to Ocala."

"You guys weren't friends, I guess. I mean, you don't seem to know very much."

"I know she wasn't a very good groom." The pot calling the kettle.

"And I can assume you are?" I said. "Are you interested in moving?"

She looked pleased with herself, like she had a naughty little secret. "Oh, no. Mr. Jade treats me *very* well."

Mr. Jade probably barely knew her name—unless she was his latest alibi, which I doubted. Men like Don Jade went for girls who were pretty and useful. Jill Morone was neither.

"Good for you," I said. "I hope you still have a job to keep after that business with Stellar."

"That wasn't my fault."

"A horse dies like that. Suspicious circumstances. Owners get nervous, start making phone calls to other trainers . . . Business can go downhill fast."

"It was an accident."

I shrugged. "Did you see it happen?"

"No. I found him, though," she admitted with a strange spark of pride in her beady little eyes. The chance celebrity. She could be on the fringe of a dark spotlight for a week and a half. "He was just laying there with his legs straight out," she said. "And his eyes were open. I thought he was just being lazy, so I slapped him on the butt to make him get up. Turned out he was dead."

"God. Awful." I looked down the row of Jade's stalls—a dozen or more—each of them hung with a box fan outside the bars of the stall fronts. "I'm surprised you still have the fans up, considering."

She shrugged again and swiped the brush over the gray a couple more strokes. "It's hot. What else should we do?"

The horse waited for her to drift back a step, then whipped her with his tail. She hit him in the ribs with the brush.

"I wouldn't want to be the person who was careless enough to let that electrical cord hang into Stellar's stall," I said. "That groom would never work in this business again. I'd see to that if I had anything to do with it."

The little eyes went mean again in the doughy face. "I didn't take care of him. Erin did. See what kind of groom she was? If I was Mr. Jade, I would have killed her."

Maybe he had, I thought as I walked away from the tent.

I spotted Paris Montgomery some distance away in a schooling ring, golden ponytail bobbing, sunglasses shading her eyes as she guided her mount over a set of jumps. Poetry in motion. Don Jade stood on the sidelines, filming her with a camcorder, as a tall, skinny, red-haired, red-faced man spoke at him, gesturing angrily. He looked like a giant, irate Howdy Doody. I approached the ring a short way down the fence from the two men, my attention seemingly directed at the horses going around.

"If there's so much as a hint of something rotten in those test results, Jade, you'll face charges," the red-faced man said loudly, either not caring or else craving the attention of everyone in the vicinity. "This won't just be about whether or not General Fidelity pays out. You've gotten away with this crap for too long as it is. It's time someone put a stop to it."

Jade said absolutely nothing, nothing in anger, nothing in his own defense. He didn't even pause in his filmmaking. He was a compact man with the rope-muscled forearms of a professional rider. His profile looked like something that should have been embossed on a Roman coin. He might have been thirty-five or he might have been fifty, and people would probably still be saying that about him when he was seventy.

He watched his assistant go over a combination of fences with Park Lane, and frowned as the horse rapped his front ankles and took a rail down. As Paris cantered past, he looked up at her and called out a couple of corrections for her to make to get the horse to bring its hindquarters more fully under itself in preparation for takeoff.

The other man seemed incredulous that his threats had not elicited a response. "You're a real piece of work, Don. Aren't you even going to bother to deny it?"

Jade still didn't look at him. "Why should I bother, Michael? I don't want to be blamed for your heart attack on top of everything else."

"You smug bastard. You still think you can get people to kiss your ass and convince them it smells like a rose."

"Maybe it does, Michael," Jade said calmly, still watching his horse. "You'll never know the truth because you don't want to. You don't want me to be innocent. You enjoy hating me too much."

"I'm hardly the only one."

"I know. I'm a national pastime again. That doesn't change the fact that I'm innocent."

He rubbed the back of his sunburned neck, checked his watch, and sighed. "That's enough for her, Paris," he called, clicking the camera off.

"I'll be on the phone with Dr. Ames today," the other man said. "If I find out you've got connections at that lab—"

"If Ames tells you anything about Stellar, I'll have his license," Jade said calmly. "Not that there's anything to tell."

"Oh, I'm sure there's a story. There always is with you. Who were you in bed with this time?"

"If I have an answer to that, it's none of your business, Michael."

"I'm making it my business."

"You're obsessed," Jade said, turning toward the stables as Paris approached on Park Lane. "If you put as much energy into your work as you do into hating me, maybe you could actually make something of yourself. Now, if you'll excuse me, Michael, I have a business to run."

Michael's face was a twisted, freckled mask of bitter emotion. "Not for long if I can help it."

Jade walked off toward the barn, seemingly unaffected by the exchange. His adversary stood for a moment, breathing hard, looking disappointed. Then he turned and stalked off.

"Well, that was ugly," I said. Tomas Van Zandt stood less than ten feet from me. He'd watched the exchange between Jade and the other man surreptitiously, same as I had, pretending to watch the horses in the ring. He glanced at me in a dismissive way and started to walk off.

"I thought men from Belgium were supposed to be charming."

He pulled up short and looked at me again, recognition dawning slowly. "Elle! Look at you!"

"I clean up good, as they say down at the trailer park."

"You've never been to a trailer park," he scoffed, taking in the hat, the outfit.

"Of course I have. I once drove a maid home," I said, then nodded after the man Jade had argued with. "Who was that?"

"Michael Berne. A big crybaby."

"Is he an owner or something?"

"A rival."

"Ah...These jumper people are so dramatic," I said. "Nothing this exciting goes on in my neck of the equestrian woods."

"Maybe I should then sell you a jumper," Van Zandt suggested, eyeing my shopping bags, pondering my credit card limit.

"I don't know if I'm ready for that. Looks like a tough crowd. Besides, I don't know any of the trainers."

He took my arm. The courtly gentleman. "Come. I'll introduce you to Jade."

"Swell," I said, looking up at him out the corner of my eye. "I can buy a horse and collect the insurance. One-stop shopping."

Like flipping a switch, Van Zandt's face went from courtly to stormy; the gray eyes as cold as the North Sea, and frighteningly hard. "Don't say such stupid things," he snapped.

I stepped away from him. "It was a joke."

"Everything with you is a joke," he said in disgust.

"And if you can't take one, Van Zandt," I said, "fuck you."

I watched him struggle to put Mr. Hyde back in his box. The mood swing had come so quickly, I couldn't believe it hadn't given him whiplash.

He rubbed a hand across his mouth and made an impatient gesture.

"Fine. It's a joke. Ha ha," he said, still clearly angry. He started toward the tent. "Forget it. Come."

I didn't move. "No. Apologize."

"What?" He looked at me with disbelief. "Don't be silly."

"Keep digging that hole, Van Zandt. I'm stupid *and* silly, and what else?"

The muscles in his face quivered. He wanted to call me a bitch or worse. I could see it in his eyes.

"Apologize."

"You shouldn't have made the joke," he said. "Come."

"And you should apologize," I countered, fascinated. He seemed incapable of performing the act, and amazed that I was insisting.

"You are being stubborn."

I laughed out loud. "*I'm* being stubborn?"

"Yes. Come."

"Don't order me like I'm a horse to be moved from one place to another," I said. "You can apologize or you can kiss my ass."

I waited, expecting an explosion, not sure what would happen after it came. Van Zandt looked at me, then looked away, and when he turned back toward me he was smiling as if nothing had happened.

"You're a tigress, Elle! I like that. You have character." He nodded to himself, suddenly enormously pleased. "That's good."

"I'm so glad you approve."

He chuckled to himself and took my arm again. "Come along. I'll introduce you to Jade. He'll like you."

"Will I like him?"

He didn't answer. He didn't care what I liked or didn't like. He was fascinated that I had challenged him. I was sure he didn't get much of that. Most of his American clients would have been wealthy women whose husbands and boyfriends had no interest in horses. Women who gave him undue credit simply because he was European and paid attention to them. Insecure women who could be easily charmed and manipulated, impressed by a little knowledge, a little Continental elegance, and a big ego with an accent.

I had witnessed the phenomenon firsthand many times over the years. Women starved for attention and approval will do a lot of foolish things, including parting with large sums of money. That was the clientele that made unscrupulous dealers a hell of a lot of money. That was the clientele that made dealers like Van Zandt snicker and sneer "stupid Americans" behind the client's back.

Park Lane came out of the tent with Jill the groom in tow just as we were about to step into the aisle. Van Zandt snapped at the girl to watch where she was going, muttering "stupid cow" only half under his breath as the horse dragged her away.

"D.J., why can you not find any girls with brains in their heads?" he asked loudly.

Jade stood at the open door to a tack stall that was draped in green and hung with ribbons won in recent shows. He calmly took a drink of Diet Coke. "Is that some kind of riddle?"

Van Zandt took a beat to get it, then laughed. "Yes—a trick question."

"Excuse me," I said politely, "but do I look like I'm standing here with a penis?"

"No," Paris Montgomery said, coming out of the tack stall. "A couple of dicks."

Van Zandt made a growling sound in his throat, but pretended good nature. "Paris, you're the quick one with the tongue!"

She flashed the big grin. "That's what all the fellas say."

High humor. Jade paid no attention to any of it. He was looking at me. I stared back and stuck out my hand. "Elle Stevens."

"Don Jade. You're a friend of this character?" he asked, nodding at Van Zandt.

"Don't hold it against me. It was a chance meeting."

The corner of Jade's mouth flicked upward. "Well, if there's a chance, Tomas will be right there to take it."

Van Zandt pouted. "I don't wait for opportunity to come and knock on the door. I go and invite it politely.

"And this one came to steal your groom," he added, pointing at me.

Jade looked confused.

"The cute one. The blonde," Van Zandt said.

"Erin," Paris said.

"The one that left," Jade said, still looking at me.

"Yes," I said. "Apparently someone beat me to her."

He gave no kind of reaction at all. He didn't look away or try to express his sadness that the girl had left. Nothing.

"Yeah," Paris joked. "Elle and I are going to start a support group for people without grooms."

"What brought you looking for Erin in particular?" Jade asked. "She didn't have very much experience."

"She did a good job, Don," Paris said, defending the missing girl. "I'd take her back in a heartbeat."

"A friend of a friend heard your girl might be looking to make a change," I said to Jade. "Now that the season has started, we can't be too fussy, right?"

"True enough. You have horses here, Elle?"

"No, though Z. here is trying to remedy that."

"V.," Van Zandt corrected me.

"I like Z. better," I said. "I'm going to call you Z."

He laughed. "Watch this one, Jade. She's a tigress!"

Jade hadn't taken his eyes off me. He looked beneath the stupid hat and past the chic outfit. He wouldn't be easily fooled. I found I didn't want to look away from him either. Magnetism hummed from within him like electricity. I thought I could feel it touching my skin. I wondered if he had control of it; could turn it on and off, up and down. Probably. Don Jade hadn't survived at his game without skill.

I wondered if I was up to matching him.

Before I had to answer that question, a more imminent danger swaggered into the picture.

"God in heaven! What kind of sadist put my class at this uncivilized hour of the day?"

Stellar's owner: Monte Hughes III, known as Trey to friends and hangers-on. Palm Beach playboy. Dissolute, debauched drunk. My first big crush when I'd been young and rebellious, and had thought dissolute, debauched, drunken playboys were romantic and exciting.

Sunglasses hid undoubtedly bloodshot eyes. The Don Johnson *Miami Vice* haircut was silver and wind-tossed.

"What time is it, anyway?" he asked with a lopsided grin. "What day is it?"

He was drunk or on something or both. He always had been. His blood had to have a permanent alcohol level after all the years of indulgence. Trey Hughes: the happy drunk, the life of every party.

I held myself very still as he came toward us. There was little chance he would recognize me. I'd been a young thing when last he'd seen me—twenty years before—and the term "pickled brain" didn't mean preservation of any kind. I couldn't say he'd ever really known me, though he had flirted with me on several occasions. I remembered feeling very impressed with myself at the time, ignoring the fact that Trey Hughes flirted with every pretty young thing to cross his path.

"Paris, honey, why do they do this to me?" He leaned into her and kissed her cheek.

"It's a conspiracy, Trey."

He laughed. His voice was rough and warm from too much whiskey and too many cigarettes. "Yeah, I used to think I was paranoid, then it turned out everyone really was out to get me."

He was dressed to ride in buff breeches, a shirt and tie. His coat bag was slung over his shoulder. He looked exactly the same to me as he had twenty years ago: attractive, fifty, and self-abused. Of course, he'd been thirty at the time. Too many hours in the sun had lined and bronzed his face, and he'd gone gray at an early age—a family trait.

He had seemed dashing and sophisticated to me back when. Now he just seemed pathetic.

He leaned down and peered at me under the brim of my hat. "I knew there had to be a person under there. I'm Trey Hughes."

"Elle Stevens."

"Do I know you?"

"No. I don't think so."

"Thank God. I've always said I never forget a beautiful face. You had me thinking I might be getting Old Timer's."

"Trey, your brain is too drenched in alcohol for it to contract anything," Jade said dryly.

Hughes didn't so much as glance at him. "I've been telling people for years: I drink for medicinal purposes," he said. "Maybe it's finally paying off.

"Never mind me, darling," he said to me. "I never do." His brows drew together. "Are you sure . . . ?"

"I'm a new face," I said, almost amused at my own joke. "Have you ever been to Cleveland?"

"God, no! Why would I go there?"

"I was sorry to hear about Stellar."

"Oh, yeah, well . . ." he rambled, making a dismissive gesture with his hand. "Shit happens. Right, Donnie?" The question had a barb to it. He still didn't look at Jade.

Jade shrugged. "Bad luck. That's the horse business."

C'est la vie. C'est la mort.

Such is life. Such is death.

His grief was underwhelming.

"God bless General Fidelity," Hughes said, raising an imaginary glass. "Provided they cough up."

Again, there was a bite to his words, but Jade seemed unaffected.

"Buy the Belgian horse," Van Zandt said. "You'll then say: Stellar who?"

Hughes laughed. "It's not enough I've given you my Mercedes. Now you're spending my money before it even gets into my pocket, V.?"

"That seems wisest, knowing you, my friend."

"All my dough's going into the new barn," Hughes said. "Casa de Money Pit."

"What good is a fancy stable with no horses to put in it?" Van Zandt asked.

"Let someone like Mr. Jade here come in with a truckload of clients to pay the mortgage and buy me a new speedboat," Hughes answered. "Like half of Wellington."

True enough. A great many Wellingtonians paid a year's mortgage with the exorbitant rents they charged for the three or four months the winter people were in town.

"Trey, get on your horse," Jade ordered. "I want you sober enough to complete the course."

"Hell, D.J., booze is the only thing that gets me around. I couldn't do it sober." He looked around, searching. "Erin, my peach," he called. "Be a doll and bring my noble steed along."

"Erin doesn't work here anymore, Trey. Remember?" Paris said, taking his coat bag and handing him his hard hat.

"Oh, right. You got rid of her."

"She left."

"Huh." He looked off into the middle distance, smiling to himself. "Seems like I just saw her." He glanced around to see that the coast was clear and said to Paris in a stage whisper: "Honey, why couldn't you lose the little heifer instead?"

Paris rolled her eyes. "Get on your horse, Trey."

She called to the Guatemalan man in Spanish to bring the gray horse, and the entourage began to move out of the aisle. I turned to follow. Jade was still standing there, still watching me.

"It was nice meeting you, Elle. I hope we see you around— whether V. sells you a horse or not."

"I'm sure you will. I'm intrigued now."

"Like a moth to a flame?" he said.

"Something like that."

He shook my hand, and I felt that current pass through me again.

I watched the pack of them make their way toward the schooling ring. Van Zandt walked alongside the gray, bending Hughes' ear about the jumper in Belgium. Hughes listed to one side on the horse's back. Paris glanced backward, looking for Jade to catch up.

I started the hike back to my car, wishing I had time to go home and take a shower, to wash off the taint. There was a slick oiliness to Jade's crowd that should have had a smell to it, the same way I've always believed snakes should have a smell to them. I didn't want to have anything to do with them, but the wheels were turning now. The old familiar buzz of anxious excitement in my head. Familiar, not altogether welcome.

I'd been on the sidelines a long time. I lived one day to the next, never knowing whether I would decide I'd lived one day too many. I didn't know if I had my head together enough to do this. And if I didn't, Erin Seabright's life could hang in the balance.

If Erin Seabright still had a life.

You got rid of her, Trey Hughes had said. An innocent enough statement on the face of it. A figure of speech. And from a man who didn't even know what day it was. Still, it struck a nerve.

I didn't know if I should trust my instincts, they'd been so long out of use. And look what happened the last time I trusted them, I thought. My instincts, my choice, and the consequences. All bad.

But it wouldn't be my action that did the damage this time. It would be inaction. The inaction of Erin Seabright's mother, of the Sheriff's Office.

Someone had to do something. These people Erin Seabright had known and worked for were far too dismissive when it came to the subject of her, and far too cavalier when it came to the subject of death.

6

The address Molly had given me as Erin's was a three-car garage some entrepreneurial sort had converted into rental property. Geographically, it was only a few miles from the Seabright home in Binks Forest. In every other respect it was in another world.

Rural Loxahatchee, where the side roads are dirt and the ditches never drain; where no one had ever met a building code they wouldn't ignore. A strange mix of run-down places, new middle-class homes, and small horse properties. A place where people nailed signs to tree trunks along the road advertising everything from "Make $$$ in Your Own Home" to "Puppies for Sale" to "Dirt Cheap Stump Grinding."

The property where Erin had lived was overgrown with tall pines and scrubby, stunted palm trees. The main house was a pseudo-Spanish ranch style, circa mid-seventies. The white stucco had gone gray with mildew. The yard consisted of dirty sand fill and anemic, sun-starved grass. An older maroon Honda sat off to one side on the driveway, filthy and dotted with hardened gobs of pine sap. It looked like it hadn't gone anywhere in a long while.

I went to the front door and rang the bell, hoping no one would be at home in the middle of the day. I would have been much happier letting myself into the garage-cum-guest house. I'd had enough human interaction to last me the day. I swatted a mosquito on my forearm and waited, then rang the bell a second time.

A voice like a rusty hinge called out: "I'm around the back!"

Small brown geckos darted out of my path and into the overgrown landscaping as I walked around the side of the garage. Around the back of the house was the obligatory pool. The screened cage that had been erected to keep bugs out of the patio area was shredded in sections as if by a giant paw. The door was flung wide on broken hinges.

The woman who stood in the doorway was long past the age and shape anyone would care to see her in a two-piece swimming suit, but that was what she was wearing. Flab and sagging skin hung on her bent frame like a collection of half-deflated leather balloons.

"What can I do for you, honey?" she asked. A New York transplant in giant Jackie-O sunglasses. She must have been pushing seventy, and appeared to have spent sixty-eight of those years sunbathing. Her skin was as brown and mottled as the skin of the lizards that lived in her yard. She was smoking a cigarette and had two hugely fat ginger cats on leashes. I was momentarily stunned to silence by the sight of her.

"I'm looking for my niece," I said at last. "Erin Seabright. She lives here, right?"

She nodded, dropped her cigarette butt, and ground it out with the toe of her aqua neoprene scuba diver's boot. "Erin. The pretty one. Haven't seen her for a couple of days, darling."

"No? Neither has her family. We're getting kind of worried."

The woman pursed her lips and waved my concern away. "Bah! She's probably off with the boyfriend."

"Boyfriend? We didn't know she had a boyfriend."

"What a surprise," she said sarcastically. "A teenage girl who doesn't tell her family anything. I thought they were on the outs, though. I heard them fighting out in the yard one night."

"When was that?"

"Last week. I don't know. Thursday or Friday maybe." She shrugged. "I'm retired. What do I know from days? One's the same as the next. I know I came out to walk my babies the next morning and someone had run a key down the side of Erin's car and ruined the paint. I have a gate to keep the riffraff out, if my lazy son would come and fix it. He could care if I'm raped and killed. He thinks he inherits."

She chuckled and looked down at the ginger cats, sharing a joke telepathically. One of the cats lay on its back in the dirt with its hind legs stretched out. The other pounced at her foot, ears flat.

"Bah! Cecil! Don't bite Mommy's toe!" she scolded. "I got an infection the last time. I thought I would die of it!"

She swatted at the cat and the cat swatted back, then scuttled to the end of its leash and growled. It had to weigh twenty-five pounds.

"Could I possibly take a look in her apartment?" I asked politely. "Maybe I can get an idea where she's gone. Her mother's worried sick."

She shrugged. "Sure. Why not? You're a relative."

The kind of landlady we all want. Fourth Amendment? What Fourth Amendment?

She tied the cat leashes to the handle of the broken screen door and dug in the fanny pack slung around her waist, coming out with a set of keys, a cigarette, and a hot pink Bic lighter. She fired up as we went around to the front of the garage, where two doors flanked windows that had been set into the plywood wall where the original garage doors had once been.

"When I did the guest house I had them put in two apartments," the woman confided. "One bath. You can get more rent that way. Semiprivate. Seven-fifty a month per."

Seven hundred and fifty dollars a month to live in a garage and share a bathroom with a stranger.

"I'm Eva by the way," she said, sliding her sunglasses on top of her head. "Eva Rosen."

"Ellen Stuart."

"You don't look like family," Eva said, squinting at me as we went into the apartment.

"By marriage."

The apartment was a single room with dingy vinyl flooring and an assortment of hideous thrift store furniture. An efficiency kitchen setup was tucked into one corner: a small sink full of dirty dishes crawling with ants, two burners, a microwave, and a mini-fridge. The bed was at the back, unmade.

There was no other sign anyone lived there. There were no clothes, no shoes, no personal effects of any kind.

"It looks like she's moved out," I said. "You didn't see her packing stuff in her car?"

Eva turned around in the middle of the room, mouth agape, cigarette stuck to her lower lip and bobbing precariously. "No! No one said anything to me about moving out. And left me dirty dishes, no less! You give people a nice place and this is how they treat you!"

"Have you seen anyone else coming in and out in the past few days?"

"No. Just that other one. The chubby one."

"Jill Morone?"

"She's a mean one. Those beady little eyes. I'd never leave my babies with that one."

"She lives in the other half?"

"Someone is going to have to answer to me," Eva muttered. "They rented for the season. They have to pay."

"Who pays the rent?"

"The checks are from Jade Farms. That nice girl, Paris, always brings the check herself. She's so nice. I can't believe she would let this happen."

Puffing angrily on the cigarette, she went to the sink and turned the water on. The pipes kicked and spat. When the water finally ran, it looked brown. "People can't just move out in the middle of the night and think they don't have to pay. My no-good son is good for one thing: he's a bail bondsman. He knows people."

I followed as Eva opened a door and went through the shared bath to Jill Morone's side of the garage. The floor was piled with wet towels, the walls of the shower stall orange and black with rust and mildew.

"This one's still here," Eva muttered. "The little pig. Look at this mess."

The place looked like it had been tossed, but I suspected that was simply the girl's mode of housekeeping. Clothes and magazines were strewn everywhere. An ashtray heaped with butts sat on the coffee table. I spotted the issue of *Sidelines* with my photo in it lying on the floor, and surreptitiously toed it under the sofa.

"I wouldn't let dogs live like this," Eva Rosen muttered, freely pawing through Jill Morone's things. "Where does she get all this? Clothes from Bloomingdale's. The tags still on. I bet she steals. She's the type."

I didn't argue. I browsed through the tangled mess of jewelry on the girl's dresser, wondering if any of it might have walked over from next door. An even trade for a stack of dirty dishes.

"Were you around here Sunday, Mrs. Rosen?"

"It's *Miz*. I was here all day."

"What about Sunday night?"

"Sunday nights I go with my friend Sid to A-1 Thai. I had the chicken curry. So spicy! I had a heartburn for days."

"What time did you get home?"

"That would be none of your business."

"Please, Ms. Rosen, it could be very important. Erin is missing."

She pretended to be stubborn for a moment, then tipped her head on one side and shrugged. "Sid is a special friend, if you know what I mean. I didn't get home until Monday. Noon, maybe."

Ample time for Erin to have packed up her own stuff, or for someone to have done it for her.

"She's run off with a boy, that's what," Eva said, finishing off her smoke and adding it to the heap in the ashtray. "No offense to your family, but she had that look with the tight shirts and the bare belly button."

This from a seventy-year-old in a bikini.

"What can you tell me about her boyfriend?" I asked. "Do you know what kind of car he drives?"

"Sixty-seven years I lived in Queens. I should know from cars?"

I tried to breathe slowly. Another of my shortcomings as a cop: lack of diplomacy with the general public. "Color? Size? Anything I could give to the police?"

"Black, maybe. Or dark blue. I only saw it the one time, and it was night."

"What about the boy? What does he look like?"

"What's with the third degree?" she asked, pretending indignation. "I'm on *Law and Order* now? You're Miss District Attorney or something? Is Sam Waterston going to come out of the closet now?"

"I'm just concerned about my niece, Ms. Rosen. I'm afraid something might have happened to her. She didn't tell anyone she was moving. Her family doesn't know anything about this boyfriend. How can we be sure she went with him willingly?"

Eva thought about that, her eyes brightening for a second at the possibility of intrigue, then she waved a hand, pretending indifference. "I didn't get a good look. I heard arguing, I looked through the blinds, I saw the back of a head."

"Could you tell if he was tall or short? Younger or older?"

She shrugged. "He was average. His back was to me."

"Have you ever met the man Erin worked for?" I asked.

"What man? I thought she worked for Paris."

"Don Jade. Middle-aged, on the slight side, very good-looking."

"Don't know him. I only know Paris. She's such a nice person. Always takes the time to ask after my babies. I have to think she doesn't know Erin ran off, or she would have spoken to me about it."

"I'm sure that's true," I said. "Did you notice anything at all about the boyfriend, Ms. Rosen? Anything."

Eva Rosen shook her head. "I'm sorry, darling. I would help if I could. I'm a mother too, you know. Do you have children of your own?" she asked, looking suspiciously at my haircut.

"No, I don't."

"They drive you crazy with worry. And then there's the disappointment. It's a trial."

"Did you ever hear Erin call the boyfriend by name?" I asked.

She searched her memory. "Maybe. I might have heard her mention a name that night. Yes. It was something like it was from a soap opera. Brad? Tad?"

"Chad?"

"That's it."

Chad Seabright.

Forbidden love. I wondered if that Shakespearean story line had contributed to Erin's defection from the Seabright home. I couldn't imagine Bruce Seabright would have approved of his son and his stepdaughter dating, regardless of the fact they weren't blood relatives. And if Bruce didn't like it, Krystal wouldn't like it.

I wondered why Molly hadn't told me about Erin and Chad, why she hadn't told me about Chad at all. Maybe she believed I would disapprove too. If that was the case, she overestimated me. I didn't care enough to have an opinion on her sister's morality. My only interest in Erin's love life was as motive in her disappearance.

I drove back to the Seabright home. Chad the Invalid was in the driveway, washing his black Toyota pickup. The all-American boy in khakis and a white T-shirt. He glanced up at me through a pair of mirrored Oakley shades as he rinsed the soap off his wheel rims.

"Nice ride," I said as I walked up the driveway. "Eva Rosen told me about it."

"Who's Eva Rosen?"

"Erin's landlady. She doesn't miss a trick, old Eva."

Chad stood up, the hose and the wheels forgotten. "I'm sorry," he said politely. "I didn't get your name."

"Elena Estes. I'm looking for your stepsister."

"Like I told you this morning, Ms. Estes: I haven't seen her."

"That's funny, because Eva tells me you were in her yard just the other night. She seems to know some pretty interesting things about you," I said. "About you and Erin."

He shrugged and shook his head, then added a boyish grin to complete the whole Matt Damon look. "I'm sorry. I don't know what you're talking about."

"Come on, Chad," I cajoled. "I've been around the block a few times. It doesn't matter to me if you and Erin are involved. A boy fucking his stepsister isn't going to make me turn a hair."

He frowned at the accusation.

"That's why Erin left the house, isn't it?" I said. "Your father wouldn't put up with the two of you doing it under his nose."

"We're not involved," he insisted.

"Eva tells me the two of you had a fight the other night in her driveway. What happened, Chad? Did Erin dump you? Let me guess: you weren't nearly so interesting as a boyfriend once her Mommy and Stepdaddy weren't watching anymore."

He looked away from me, trying to decide how to play this. Respond with the truth, with outrage, stick with denial, stay calm? He had chosen the latter tack to start, but my bluntness was beginning to irritate him.

"I'm not sure who you are, ma'am," he said, still trying to hang on to the false good humor, "but you're crazy."

I found a dry patch along the front fender of the pickup, leaned back against it, and crossed my arms. "Who'd she dump you for, Chad? An older man? Her boss, maybe?"

"I don't know who Erin is seeing," he said curtly. "And I don't care."

He dumped the wash water on the driveway and carried the bucket into the garage. I followed.

"Okay. Maybe I'm way off base. Maybe the fight was about something else altogether," I offered. "If that hangover you had this morning is anything to go by, you're a guy who likes to party. From what I've heard, Erin might like a wild time. And there she is at the equestrian center, a whole new world of drug dealers and users. Maybe that's what you fought about in Eva Rosen's driveway: drugs."

Chad slammed the bucket onto a shelf where car care products were arranged like a display at Pep Boys. "You're way out of line, lady."

"She try to cut you out of a deal, Chad? Is that why you came back later and keyed her car?"

"What's with you?" he demanded. "Why are you here? Do you have a warrant or something?"

I was standing too close to him. He wanted to back away. "I don't need a warrant, Chad," I said quietly, my eyes steady on his. "I'm not that kind of a cop."

He didn't know quite what that meant, but it made him nervous. He put his hands on his hips, shuffled his feet, crossed his arms over his chest, looked out at the street.

"Where's Erin?" I asked.

"I told you, I don't know. I haven't seen her."

"Since when? Since Friday? The night you fought with her? The night you keyed her car?"

"I don't know anything about that. Talk to that fat cow she works with," he said. "Jill Moron. She's nuts. Ask her where Erin is. She probably killed her and ate her."

"How do you know Jill Morone?" I asked. "How would you know anything about the people Erin works with if you haven't been in touch with Erin?"

He went still and looked out the door.

Gotcha. It was nice to know I still had the touch.

"What did you fight about Friday night, Chad?" I asked again, then waited patiently while he struggled to decide on an answer.

"I dumped her," he said, turning toward the shelves again. He selected a white cotton towel from a stack of white cotton towels, all neatly folded. "I don't need the trouble."

"Uh-huh. Bullshit. You don't dump a girl, then come back and key her car. There's no point if you're not the dumpee."

"I didn't key her car!"

"I don't believe you."

"Well, that's your problem, not mine."

"I don't see you dumping her, Chad. Erin might have been off the hook with Krystal and Bruce because she moved out, but you could still pull your old man's chain by staying involved with her."

"You don't know anything about my family."

"Don't I?" I looked around the garage with its place for everything and everything in its place. "Your old man is a tight-ass control freak. His way is the only way. His opinion is the only opinion. Everyone else in the house is there to serve his needs and validate his superiority. How am I doing so far?"

Chad went to his truck in a huff and started trying to towel off the water spots that had already dried on the finish.

"He'll ride you if you don't get those spots out, won't he, Chad?" I said, following him around the truck. "Can't have spots on the cars. What would the neighbors think? And imagine if they found out about you and Erin. What a disgrace, doing it with your stepsister. It's practically incest. You really found Dad's hot button, didn't you?"

"Lady, you're pissing me off."

I didn't tell him that was the idea. I followed him around the hood to the other side of the truck. "Tell me what I want to know and I'll leave."

"There's nothing to tell. I don't know where Erin is, and I don't give a shit."

"I bet you'll give a shit when you've got a cop tailing you. Because maybe there's a drug angle to Erin's disappearance. I can tell you from experience, there are few things a narc likes better than getting his hooks into a kid with money and connections. And how about when your father gets questioned about your involvement? I guess you might enjoy that—"

He turned on me, hands up, as if I was holding him at gunpoint. "All right! All right. Jesus, you're something, lady," he said, shaking his head.

I waited.

"All right," he said again, letting out a sigh. "Erin and I used to be together. I thought it meant something, but it didn't mean anything to her. She dumped me. That's it. That's the whole story. There's nothing to do with drugs or deals or anything else. That's it. She dumped me."

He shrugged and his arms fell back to his sides, limp, the admission taking all the starch out of him. The male ego is a fragile thing at seventeen or seventy.

"Did she give you a reason?" I asked quietly. "I wouldn't ask," I added as his tension level came back up. "But something has happened where Erin was working, and now she's nowhere to be found."

"Is she in trouble?"

"I don't know."

He thought about that for a minute. "She said there was someone else. 'A man,' she said. Like I'm twelve or something." He shook his head in disgust.

"Did she say who?"

"I didn't ask. I mean, why should I care? I know she had a thing for her boss, but he's like fifty or something . . ."

"Did she tell you she was going anywhere? Did she say anything about changing jobs or moving?"

He shook his head.

"She never said anything about going to Ocala?"

"Ocala? Why would she go there?"

"Her boss says she quit her job and moved to Ocala to take another."

"That's news to me," he said. "No. She wouldn't do that. It doesn't make any sense."

"Thanks for the info." I pulled a card from my pocket, my phone number scribbled on it. "If you hear from her, would you call this number and leave a message?"

Chad took the card and stared at it.

I went back to my car and sat at the end of the Seabright driveway for a moment. I looked around the neighborhood. Quiet, lovely, expensive; golfers lining up a tee shot beyond the backyard. The American dream.

I thought about the Seabrights. Well-off, successful; neurotic, contentious, seething with secret resentments. The American dream in a fun house mirror.

I parked on the street in front of the school, the soccer moms and me. I would have felt less out of place in a chorus line. Kids began to pour out the doors and head for the buses or the car-pool line.

There was no sign of Krystal Seabright, not that I had expected to see her. It seemed quite clear to me that Molly was just a small person who happened to live in the same house as Krystal. Molly had turned out the way she had turned out by luck or self-preservation or watching A&E. She had probably watched all the drama and rebellion and parental conflict of Erin's life, and consciously turned in the other direction in order to win approval.

Funny, I thought, Molly Seabright was probably exactly who my little sister would have been, had I had a little sister. My parents had adopted me and called it quits. I was more than enough to handle. Too bad for them. The child learning from my mistakes might have been exactly the daughter they had wanted in the first place.

I got out of the car as I saw Molly come out of the school. She didn't spot me right away. She walked with her head down, pulling her little black case behind her. Though she was surrounded by other children, she seemed alone, deep in thought. I called out to her as she turned and started down the sidewalk. When she saw me, her face brightened with a carefully tempered expectation.

"Did you find her already?" she asked.

"No, not yet. I've spent the day asking a lot of questions. She may be in Ocala," I said.

Molly shook her head. "She wouldn't have moved without telling me, without calling me."

"Erin tells you everything?" I asked, opening the car door for her. I glanced around to see if anyone had me pegged as a child molester. No one was paying any attention at all.

"Yes."

I went around to the driver's side, got behind the wheel, and

73

started the engine. "Did she tell you she and Chad were involved with each other?"

Her gaze glanced off of mine and she seemed to shrink a little in the seat.

"Why didn't you tell me about Chad?"

"I don't know," she mumbled. "I would rather not acknowledge Chad's existence."

Or that Erin had shifted from sister to sexual being, I thought as I drove back toward the cul-de-sac where Molly lived. Erin had been her idol and protector. If Erin abandoned her, then Molly was all alone in the land of dysfunctional Seabrights.

"Chad was at Erin's apartment Friday night," I said. "They had an argument. Do you know anything about that?"

Molly shrugged. "Maybe they broke up."

"Why would you think that? Was Erin interested in someone else?"

"She had a crush on her boss, but he's too old for her."

That was a matter of opinion. From what I had learned about Erin so far, I wouldn't have been at all surprised to find out she had her sights set on a man old enough to be her father. And if past history was anything to go by, Jade wouldn't draw that line for her.

"Anyone else?"

"I don't know," Molly said irritably. "Erin liked flirting with guys. I didn't pay attention. I didn't want to hear about it."

"Molly, this is very important," I said as I pulled to the curb at the end of her street. "When I ask you questions about Erin, or about anything, anyone, you have to tell me the absolute truth as you know it. No glossing over details you don't like. Got it?"

She frowned, but nodded.

"You have to trust me," I said, and a bolt of white-cold fear ran through me.

Molly looked at me in that steady, too-wise way and said, "I already told you I do."

This time I didn't ask her why.

7

I stand at the side of the Golam brothers' trailer. I've been told to stay put, to wait, but I know that's not the right decision. If I go in first, if I go in now, I've got the brothers dead-bang. They think they know me. I've worked this case three months. I know what I'm doing. I know I'm right. I know the Golam brothers are already twitching. I know I want this bust and deserve it. I know Lieutenant Sikes is here for the show, to put a feather in his cap. He wants to look good when the news vans arrive. He wants to make the public think they should vote for him in the next election for sheriff.

He's stuck me on the side of the trailer and told me to wait. He doesn't know his ass. He didn't listen to me when I told him the side door is the door the brothers use most. While Sikes and Ramirez are watching the front, the brothers are dumping their money into duffel bags and getting ready to bolt out the side. Billy Golam's four-by-four is parked ten feet away, covered in mud. If they run, they'll take the truck, not the Corvette parked in front. The truck can go off-road.

Sikes is wasting precious time. The Golam brothers have two girls in the trailer with them. This could easily turn into a hostage situation. But if I go in now . . . They think they know me.

I key the button on my radio. "This is stupid. They're going to break for the truck. I'm going in."

"Goddammit, Estes—"

I drop the radio into the weeds growing beside the trailer. It's my case. It's my bust. I know what I'm doing.

I draw my weapon and hold it behind my back. I go to the side door and knock the way all the Golam brothers' customers knock: two knocks, one knock, two knocks. "Hey, Billy, it's Elle! I need some."

Billy Golam jerks open the door, wild-eyed, high on his own home cooking—crystal meth. He's breathing hard. He's got a gun in his hand.

Shit.

The front door explodes inward.

One of the girls screams.

Buddy Golam shouts: "Cops!"

Billy Golam swings the .357 up in my face. I suck in my last breath.

He turns abruptly and fires. The sound is deafening. The bullet hits Hector Ramirez in the face and blows out the back of his head, blood and brain matter spraying Sikes behind him.

The image faded slowly from my brain, and the building I had worked out of slowly came into focus before me.

The Palm Beach County Criminal Justice Complex is tucked away on a patch of landscaped acres off Gun Club Road near Lake Lytal Park. The complex houses the Sheriff's Office, the medical examiner's offices, the morgue, the county courts, and the jail. One-stop shopping for lawbreakers and their victims.

I sat in the parking lot looking at the building that held the Sheriff's Office, feeling sick in my stomach. I hadn't been through those doors in a long time. There was a part of me that believed everyone in the building would recognize me on sight and that all of them nursed a virulent hatred of me. Logically, I knew that wasn't true. Probably only half of them would know and hate me.

The clock was ticking toward change of shift. If I didn't catch James Landry now, it would have to wait until the next day. I wanted Erin Seabright's name in his mind, a mental thorn to rub at all night.

My legs felt weak as I walked toward the doors. Jail inmates in dark gray uniforms were working on the landscaping, overseen by a black guard in camo pants and a painted-on black T-shirt, a trooper's hat perched on his head. He exchanged bullshit with a couple of cops standing on the sidewalk smoking cigarettes. None of them looked at me.

I went inside to the desk. No one called out my name or rushed to assault me. Maybe it was the haircut.

The receptionist behind the bulletproof glass was a round-faced young woman with three-inch purple lacquered fingernails and a Medusa's head of intertwined black braids.

"I need to speak with Detective Landry," I said.

"What is this regarding, ma'am?"

"A missing persons case."

"Your name?"

"Elena Estes."

There was no flicker of recognition. No scream of outrage. I didn't know her, she didn't know me. She called Landry on the phone and told me to wait in the chairs. I stood with my arms crossed and stared at the door to the stairwell, barely breathing. It seemed an hour before the heavy gray door opened.

"Ms. Estes?"

Landry held the door back by way of invitation.

He was a compact, athletic-looking man, mid-forties, with a meticulous quality about him. There was still starch in his shirt at nearly four P.M. His hair was cropped almost military-short; black, heavily salted with gray. He had a stare like an eagle's: penetrating and slightly disdainful, I thought. Or perhaps that was my paranoia showing.

I had known several of the seventeen detectives in Robbery/ Homicide, the major case squad, but I hadn't known Landry. Because of the nature of their work, narcotics detectives usually keep—or are kept—to themselves, their paths crossing with the other detectives only over dead bodies.

We went up the stairs to the second floor without speaking. There was no one behind the glass in the small vestibule that led to the Robbery/Homicide squad room. Landry let us in with a card key.

Steel desks grouped together made islands across the expanse of the room. Most of the desks were empty. I recognized no one. The gazes that flicked my way were hooded, flat, and cold. Cop eyes. The look is always the same, regardless of agency, regardless of geography. The look of people who trust no one and suspect everyone of something. I couldn't tell what they were thinking. I knew only that some of the gazes lingered too long.

I took the seat Landry indicated beside his desk. He smoothed a hand over his tie as he settled into his chair, his eyes never leaving my face. He clicked his computer on and settled a pair of reading glasses on the bridge of his nose.

"I'm Detective Landry," he said, typing. "I'll be taking your statement. I understand you want to report someone missing."

"She's already been reported missing. Erin Seabright. Her sister spoke with you a couple of days ago. Molly Seabright. She told me you were rude and condescending and of no help to her."

Another chapter from *The Elena Estes Guide to Winning Friends and Influencing People.*

Landry pulled his glasses off and gave me the stare again. "The kid? She's twelve."

"Does that somehow change the fact that her sister is missing?"

"We don't take complaints from children. I spoke on the phone with the mother. She didn't want to file. She says the daughter isn't missing."

"Maybe she killed the girl," I said. "You're not going to look for her because her murderer doesn't want to file a complaint?"

His brows pulled together. "You have reason to think the mother killed her?"

"No. I don't think that at all. I'm saying you didn't know differently and you blew the girl off."

"So you came here to pick a fight with me?" he said, incredulous. "Are you mentally ill? What have you got to do with these people? Are they relatives of yours?"

"No. Molly is a friend."

"The twelve-year-old."

"She asked me to help her. I happen to believe she has good reason to think her sister is missing."

"Why is that?"

"Because her sister is missing. She hasn't been seen since Sunday."

I filled him in on the Don Jade saga and the death of Stellar. Landry was angry with me. Impatience hummed in the air around him. He didn't like that I'd done his job for him, even if he didn't believe he'd had a job to do. Cops can be territorial that way.

"You think something happened to this girl because of a dead horse." He said it as if it were the most ludicrous theory he'd ever heard.

"People are killed for their shoes," I said. "People are killed for turning down the wrong street. This dead horse by himself is worth a quarter of a million dollars in insurance money, and the sale of his replacement to his owner is probably worth nearly that much in sales commissions alone. I don't find it hard to believe someone would resort to violence for that kind of money, do you?"

"And the trainer says the girl quit her job and moved to Ocala."

"The trainer who probably had the horse killed and stands to profit handsomely by the next deal."

"Do you know that she didn't move to Ocala?" Landry asked.

"No. But it seems unlikely."

"Have you been to her apartment? Were there signs of a struggle?"

"I've been to her apartment. There's nothing there."

"Nothing. As if she moved out?" he suggested.

"Maybe. But we won't know if someone doesn't look for her. You could put a call in to Ocala."

"Or you could drive up there and look for her."

"Or you could call the local PD or SO or whatever they have in Ocala."

"And tell them what? That this girl might have moved up there and taken a job? She's eighteen. She can do whatever the hell she wants."

"Give them a heads-up on her car."

"Why? Has it been stolen?"

I stood up. I was angrier than he was and glad he couldn't see it on my face. "Okay, Landry. You don't give a shit this girl has vanished, couldn't care less that she might be dead, and you have no interest in a six-figure fraud case. What am I paying taxes for?"

"Insurance fraud isn't insurance fraud until the insurance company says so. And the girl isn't missing if she's eighteen and willingly moved elsewhere—unless her family reports her missing."

"Her family did report her missing. Her sister reported it. That fact aside, you're saying if she's estranged from her family and something happens to her, only she could report her own disappearance.

That's absurd. You're going to let God-knows-what happen to this girl because her mother is a self-absorbed airhead who's just happy to be rid of her.

"I guess I can see that," I said sarcastically. "After all, it might take an hour or two out of your busy day investigating purse snatchings to make a couple of phone calls, do some background checks, ask a few questions—"

Landry stood now too. His face was growing red beneath his tan. Everyone in the office was watching us. In my peripheral vision I could see one of the sergeants had come out of his office to watch. In the background a phone rang unanswered.

"Are you trying to tell me how to do my job, Estes?"

"I've done your job, Landry. It's not that hard."

"Yeah? Well, I don't see you working here now. Why is that?"

The phone stopped ringing. The silence in the room was the silence of outer space: absolute.

Half a dozen valid answers trailed through my head. I gave none of them. Only one answer counted—to the people in this room and to me. I didn't work here anymore because I'd gotten one of our own—one of *their* own—killed. Nothing trumped that.

Finally, I nodded. "All right. You win," I said quietly. "Cheap Shot of the Day Award goes to Landry. I figured you'd be a big asshole, and I was right. But Erin Seabright is missing, and someone has to care about that. If it has to be me, so be it. If that girl ends up dead because I couldn't find her quickly enough and you could have, that one will be on your head, Landry."

"Is there a problem here?" the sergeant asked, coming over. "Oh, yeah," he said, stopping in front of me. "I'm looking at it. You've got a hell of a nerve coming into this building, Estes."

"Sorry. I didn't realize crime fighting had become by invitation only. Mine must have gotten lost in the mail."

The path to the door seemed to elongate as I walked away. My legs felt like columns of water. My hands were shaking. I went out of the squad room, down the hall, and into the ladies' room, where I slumped over a toilet and vomited.

A handful of moments passed as I leaned against the wall of the stall, closed my eyes, and held my face in my hands. I was hot, sweating, breathing hard. Exhausted. But I was still alive, literally and metaphorically. I had bearded the lions in their den and survived. I probably should have been proud of myself.

I pushed myself to my feet, went and washed my face and rinsed my mouth with tap water. I tried to concentrate on my small victory. James Landry wouldn't be able to put Erin Seabright so easily out of his mind tonight, if for no other reason than that I had challenged him. If confronting him resulted in one phone call that turned up one lead, it would have been worth the effort and what it had cost me emotionally.

As I walked out to my car, I wondered dimly if I was developing a sense of purpose. It had been so long since I'd had one, I couldn't be sure.

I got into the BMW and waited. Just when I was ready to decide Landry had made his exit while I was hugging the porcelain life preserver, he came out of the building, sunglasses hiding his eyes, a sport coat folded over one arm. I watched him get into a silver Pontiac Grand Am and roll out of the parking lot. I pulled into traffic two cars behind him, wanting to know who I was dealing with. Did he go straight home to a wife and kids? Could I play that parental angle on him? He hadn't been wearing a ring.

He drove straight to a cop bar on Military Trail. Disappointingly predictable. I didn't follow him inside, knowing my reception would probably be openly hostile. This was where the rank and file blew off steam, complained about their superiors, complained about civilians, complained about their ex-spouses. Landry would complain about me. That was all right. I didn't care what James Landry thought of me . . . as long as thinking of me made him think of Erin Seabright too.

8

Unlike me, Sean still enjoyed embarrassing his proper Palm Beach family by occasionally showing up at the charity balls that are the life of Palm Beach society during the winter season. The balls are lavish, over-the-top affairs that cost nearly as much to put on as they raise for their various causes. The net for the charity can be shockingly low, considering the gross, but a good time will be had in the process. If one goes for that sort of thing—designer gowns, designer jewels, the latest in cosmetic surgery, the posturing and the catty mind games of the ridiculously rich. Despite having been raised in that world, I had never had the patience for it.

I found Sean in his closet—which is larger than the average person's bedroom—in an Armani tuxedo, tying his bow tie.

"What's the disease du jour?" I asked.

"It starts with a P."

"Pinkeye?"

"Parkinson's. That's a hot one with the celebs these days. This will be a younger crowd than some of the more traditional diseases." He slipped his tux jacket on and admired himself in the three-way mirror.

I leaned against the marble-topped center island and watched him primp. "One of these years they're going to run out of afflictions."

"I've threatened my mother I'm going to put on a ball for genital herpes," Sean said.

"God knows half the population of Palm Beach could benefit."

"And the other half would catch it at the after-party parties. Want to be my date?"

"To catch herpes?"

"To the ball, Cinderella. Your parents are sure to be there. Double your scandal, double your fun."

The idea of seeing my mother and father was less appealing than going into the Sheriff's Offices had been. At least facing Landry had the potential for something good to come of it.

My mother had come to see me in the hospital a couple of times. The maternal duty of a woman without a maternal bone in her body. She had pushed to adopt a child for reasons that had nothing to do with a love of children. I had been an accessory to her life, like a handbag or a lapdog.

A lapdog from the pound, my heritage was called into question by my father every time I stepped out of line—which was often. He had resented my intrusion on his life. I was a constant reminder of his inability to sire children of his own. My resentment of his feelings had only served to fuel the fires of my rebellion.

I hadn't spoken to my father in over a decade. He had disowned me when I'd left college to become a common cop. An affront to him. A slap in his face. True. And a flimsy excuse to end a relationship that should have been unbreakable. He and I had both seized on it.

"Gee, sorry," I said, spreading my arms wide. "I'm not dressed for it."

Sean took in the old jeans and black turtleneck with a critical eye. "What happened to our fashion plate of the morning?"

"She had a very long day of pissing people off."

"Is that a good thing?"

"We'll see. Squeeze enough pimples, one of them is bound to burst."

"How folksy."

"Did Van Zandt come by?"

He rolled his eyes. "Honey, people like Tomas Van Zandt are the reason I live behind gates. If he came by, I didn't hear about it."

"I guess he's too busy trying to sweet-talk Trey Hughes into spending a few million bucks on horses."

"He'll need them. Have you seen that barn he's building? The Taj Mahal of Wellington."

"I heard something about it."

"Fifty box stalls with crown molding, for God's sake. Four groom's apartments upstairs. Covered arena. Big jumping field."

"Where is it?"

"Ten acres of prime real estate in that new development next to Grand Prix Village: Fairfields."

The name gave me a shock. "Fairfields?"

"Yes," he said, adjusting his French cuffs and checking himself out in the mirror again. "It's going to be a great big gaudy monstrosity that will make his trainer the envy of every jumper jockey on the East Coast. I have to go, darling."

"Wait. A place like you're saying will cost the earth."

"And the moon and the stars."

"Can Trey really live that large off his trust fund?"

"He doesn't have to. His mother left nearly the entire Hughes estate to him."

"Sallie Hughes died?"

"Last year. Fell down the stairs in her home and fractured her skull. So the story goes. You really ought to keep up with the old neighborhood, El," he scolded. Then he kissed my cheek and left.

Fairfields. Bruce Seabright had just that morning been on his way to close a deal at Fairfields.

I don't like or trust coincidence. I don't believe coincidence is an accidental thing. In college I had once attended a lecture by a well-known New Age guru who believed all life at its most basic molecular structure is energy. Everything we do, every thought we have, every emotion we experience, can be broken down to pure energy. Our lives are energy, driving, seeking, running, colliding with the energy of the other people in our small worlds. Energy attracts energy, intent becomes a force of nature, and there is no such thing as coincidence.

When I feel like believing strongly in my theory, I then realize I have to accept that nothing in life can truly be random or accidental. And then I decide I would be better off believing in nothing.

Considering the people involved in Erin Seabright's life, whatever was going on was not positive. Her mother seemed not to have known who Erin was working for, and I could believe that was true. Krystal wouldn't have cared if Erin had been working for the devil himself, so long as her little world wasn't rocked because of it. She probably preferred not to think Erin was her daughter at all. But what about Bruce Seabright? Did he know Trey Hughes? If he knew Hughes, did he then also know Jade? And if he knew either or both of them, how did Erin fit into that picture?

Say Bruce wanted Erin out of his house because of her involvement with Chad. If he knew Hughes—and via Hughes had a connection to Don Jade—he might have gotten her set up with Jade as a means to that end. The more important question was whether or not Bruce Seabright cared about what happened to Erin once she was out of his house. And if he cared, would his caring be a positive or a negative thing? What if he wanted her gone permanently?

These were the thoughts and questions that filled my evening. I paced the guest house, chewing the stubs of my fingernails. Quiet, smooth jazz seeped out of the stereo speakers in the background, a moody sound track to the scenarios playing through my head. I picked up the phone once and dialed Erin's cell phone number, getting an automated voice telling me the customer's mailbox was full. If she had simply moved herself to Ocala, why wouldn't she have picked up her messages by now? Why wouldn't she have called Molly?

I didn't want to waste a day going to Ocala on what my gut told me would be a fool's errand. In the morning I would call a PI up there and give him the pertinent information, along with instructions. If Erin was working at the Ocala show grounds, I would know it in a day, two at the most. I would have the PI page her from the show office, say that she had an important phone call. If someone answered the page, he could verify whether or not it was, in fact, Erin Seabright. A simple plan. Landry could have done the same utilizing local law enforcement.

Asshole. I hoped he was lying awake.

It was after midnight. Sleep was nowhere in sight for me. I hadn't had a real night's sleep in years—partly because of my state of mind, partly because of the low-level chronic pain the accident had left me with. I didn't wonder what the lack of sleep was doing to my body or to my mind, for that matter. I didn't care. I'd gotten used to it. At least tonight I wasn't dwelling on thoughts of the mistakes I'd made or how I should pay for those mistakes.

I grabbed a jacket and left the house. The night was cool, a storm blowing across the Everglades toward Wellington. Lightning backlit the clouds to the far west.

I drove down Pierson, past the truck entrance to the Equestrian Club, past the extravagant stables of Grand Prix Village, made a turn and found the stone entrance gates of Fairfields. A sign showed the layout of the development in eight parcels ranging in size from five to ten acres. Three parcels were marked "Sold." Gracious beauty for exclusive equestrian facilities was promised, and a number was listed for Gryphon Development, Inc.

The stone columns were up, and a guardhouse had been constructed, but the iron gates had yet to be installed. I followed the winding drive, my headlights illuminating weeds and scrub. Security lights glowed white at two building sites. Even in the dead of night I had no trouble identifying which of the two properties belonged to Trey Hughes.

The stable was up. Its silhouette resembled a big Kmart. A huge, two-story rectangle that ran parallel to the road, flaunting its size. It stood back maybe thirty yards from the chain-link construction fence. The gate was chained and padlocked.

I pulled into the drive as far as the gate allowed and sat there trying to take in as much as I could. My headlights bathed a piece of earth-moving equipment, and revealed torn ground and mounded piles of dirt. Beyond the stable on the near end I could just make out what must have been the construction boss's office trailer. In front of the stables, a large sign advertised the construction company, proud to be building Lucky Dog Farm.

I could only ballpark the cost of the place. Ten acres this near the show grounds was worth a fortune with nothing on it. A facility the likes of what Trey Hughes was putting up had to go two, maybe three million just for the buildings. And that would be for horse facilities alone. Like Grand Prix Village, there would be no stately homes in Fairfields. The owners of these stables had posh homes at the Polo

Club or on the island or both. The Hughes family had a beachfront estate on Blossom Way, near the exclusive Palm Beach Bath and Tennis Club. Trey himself had had a mansion in the Polo Club when I'd last known of him. Now he had it all, thanks to Sallie Hughes taking a wrong step on the stair.

Lucky dog, indeed. Rid of the woman Trey used to call The Dominatriarch, and unfettered access to an obscene fortune in one simple fall. That idea writhed in the back of my mind like a snake in the shadows.

After speaking with Sean, I had gone online to find any stories on Sallie Hughes' death, and found nothing but her obituary. No story of any investigation.

Of course, there wouldn't be a story. How unseemly to allow such things in the papers, my mother would have said. The newspaper on the island was for social news and announcements. Not for such dirty business as death and police investigations. The newspaper my mother read was printed on glossy stock with ink that wouldn't rub off on the reader's hands. Clean in fact and in content.

The *Post*—printed in West Palm Beach (where the common folk live)—reported Sallie Hughes had died in her home at the age of eighty-two.

However it had happened, Trey Hughes was now a very fat golden goose. There were sure to be a few people willing to do him a little favor like getting rid of a jumper with more heart than talent. It didn't matter how much money Trey already had. Another quarter of a million was always welcome.

Don Jade had to be at the head of that list of helpful hopefuls. What a sweet deal for Jade, or any trainer: walking into a barn like this one, the kind of place that would give him legitimacy again and draw still more clients with bottomless pockets.

I wondered about the tension I'd sensed between the two men that morning. Trey Hughes could now afford to put nearly any big-name trainer he wanted in his stable. Why had he gone with Don Jade—a man whose reputation was based more on scandal than on success. A man with a reputation for doing bad deeds and getting away with them . . .

Whatever had put him there, Don Jade was in the catbird seat. That had to make him the envy of a lot of bitterly jealous people.

Michael Berne came to mind. I had recognized the name as soon as Van Zandt had blabbed it that morning. Berne had been mentioned in Stellar's obituary in the online magazine *Horses Daily*. He'd had the ride on Stellar before Jade, with only limited success in the showring. Then Jade got the horse. Got the horse, got the owner, got the Taj Mahal of Wellington. No wonder Berne was angry. He hadn't just lost a paycheck when Stellar had been led out of his barn. He'd lost a big-time meal ticket.

He wasn't just Jade's rival, as Van Zandt had said, he was an enemy.

An enemy could be a valuable source of information.

I drove back to the equestrian center, wanting time to prowl without having to worry about any of Jade's crowd seeing me. I wanted to find Berne's stable. If I could get a phone number off his stalls, I would be able to set up a meeting somewhere we weren't likely to be caught by any Jade confederates.

The guard came out of the gatehouse looking bored and unhappy.

"It is very late," he said in heavily accented English.

I heaved a sigh. "Tell me about it. We've got a horse with colic. I drew the short straw."

He frowned at me as if he suspected I might have just insulted him.

"A sick horse," I explained. "I have night watch, like you."

"Oh, yes." He nodded then. "I understand. I am very sorry to hear. Good luck with that, miss."

"Thank you."

He didn't bother to ask my name or what barn number this phantom horse was in. I had a parking pass and a believable story. That was enough.

I parked back in The Meadows, not wanting anyone's attention on my car. With my Maglite in hand and my gun in the back of my jeans, I walked the aisles of the tent barns, looking for Michael Berne's name, hoping not to run afoul of someone's groom or a roving security guard.

The storm was rolling closer. The wind was coming up, making tent tops billow and flap, making horses nervous. I kept my light low, looking at stall cards and emergency numbers, and still managed to spook some horses, sending them spinning around their small quarters, eyes rolling white. Others nickered at me, hoping for something to eat.

I cut the light as I walked the dogleg from The Meadows to the next set of tents. If I was lucky, Berne's horses were stabled relatively near Jade's. Their run-in had taken place at the schooling ring nearest Jade's barn. Maybe that was Berne's schooling area too. If I was unlucky, Berne had gone out of his way to pick a fight with Jade, and I would have to walk forty stables before I found what I wanted.

A gust swept in from the west, shaking the trees. Thunder rumbled overhead. I ducked into tent twenty-two and started checking names.

A quarter of the way down the first row I stopped and listened. The same sounds as in the other tents: horses moving, nickering, kicking against the pipes that framed the stalls. Only these sounds weren't coming from the horses around me. The disturbance was a couple of rows over. The creak and groan of a stall door opening. The shuffling sound of hooves moving through deep bedding. A horse whinnied loudly. The horse in the stall nearest me rushed its door and whinnied back.

I flicked the light up at it to see a bay, head high, ears pricked, white-rimmed eyes focused past me, past the horse across the aisle. The horse whinnied again and spun around. Another down the row followed suit.

I doused my light and crept down the aisle to the back end of the tent, the Maglite held like a club in my hand. The flashlight weighed three pounds. When I'd been in uniform I had once used this flashlight to defend my life against a 270-pound biker on PCP. He'd ended up in the hospital with a concussion.

I didn't draw my weapon. I wanted to see, not confront. The Glock was my last line of defense.

The wind howled and the tent top swelled upward like a balloon wanting to take flight. The thick ropes holding the tent stakes squeaked and groaned. I slipped around the end stalls, staying close to the wall. The land behind the tent dropped off sharply to ground that had been cleared and burned over the summer, being made ready for more tents, more schooling rings. It looked like a moonscape. The smell of ash flavored the air.

As I started to ease around the end stall to the next aisle, I heard a door swing back on its hinges, and there was a sharp, distinct sound that didn't register until the next thing had already happened.

Like a specter running from the otherworld, a huge, ghostly gray horse barreled down the aisle straight at me. He was nearly on top of me before I could react, knocking me backward. I scrambled to keep my feet moving, to throw myself out of his way. A tent spike caught my right ankle and jerked my leg out from under me, dumping me to the ground with a jarring thud. I tried to cover my head and pull myself into a ball, every inch of me braced for the horrible strike of steel-shod hooves and the driving weight of a half-ton animal coming down on soft tissue and fragile bones. But the gray leapt over me, then soared over the edge of the embankment. I scrambled to my knees and watched in horror as he stumbled hard down the bank, going down on his knees, hind legs still running. He squealed in fright, flailing to right himself, dragging himself up and running on into the night.

Pushing to my feet, I turned back toward the tent as another horse ran out. Dark with a blaze. Whinnying as it ran after the gray. I dove to the side as he bolted past.

A slap on the ass.

The sound I'd heard before: the flat of a hand slapping a horse's rump.

I ran back into the tent. The rest of the barn was in an uproar by now, horses screaming and banging in their stalls. The flimsy pipe-and-canvas stalls shaking and rattling. The tent walls shuddering as the wind kicked at them. I shouted, hoping to frighten the perpetrator with discovery and send him running.

Another horse pranced out of an open stall, saw me, snorted and bolted past, knocking me into the door of the stall behind me. Then that door shoved forward, pushing me with it, knocking me to my knees.

I scuttled ahead like a crab, reaching for the door across the way to pull myself up. The horse came out of the stall behind me like a rodeo bronc, a raw bellow coming from it as it bucked and kicked out at me. I felt the air whoosh past my ear as the hoof just missed its mark.

Before I could start to turn around, a smelly, suffocating blackness engulfed my head and upper body and I was shoved forward against a stall. I tried to claw at the blanket, but couldn't get my arms up. I wanted air. I wanted what little light there was. I wanted to be free to fight my assailant, who jerked me backward, then sideways, one way and then the other.

Dizziness swirled through my head and I staggered and stumbled and went down on one knee. Then something struck hard, hitting me across the back with enough force to make me see stars.

On the third blow I fell forward and lay still. My breath was a hot rasp in the shallowest part of my lungs. I couldn't hear anything but a roaring in my head, and I wondered if I would know what was happening before the next loose horse ran over me, crushing me beneath its hooves. I tried to push myself up and couldn't. The messages scattered somewhere between my brain and my nerve pathways. Pain kicked me in the back and I choked and coughed, needing air, unable to take a deep breath.

A moment passed. No horses trampled me. No pitchfork impaled me. I figured my attacker had run, which left me in a very bad place at a very bad time. Horses were running loose. If someone came rushing into this barn and found me . . .

I tried again to gather my strength and managed to shove the horse blanket off my head. Gulping air, fighting nausea, I grabbed hold of the stall door and dragged myself to my feet. Dizzy, the ground seeming to pitch beneath me, I stumbled out the back of the tent and fell down again.

The Maglite lay on the ground where it had landed when the first horse had hit me, its beam a yellow beacon in the dark. I scooped it up, grabbed hold of a tent rope, and pulled myself up.

Horses were running in the cleared ground down the slope. Some were running between this tent and the next. The wind was blowing harder, carrying the first pelting drops of rain. I heard someone shout in the distance. Time to go.

I stepped inside the tent just far enough to flick the beam across the front of an open stall.

In Case of Emergency Phone Michael Berne . . .

"Don't move. Drop the flashlight."

The voice came from behind me on a beam of light that spilled around my shoulders. I kept the Maglite in my hand, but held my arms away from my body.

"I heard a commotion," I said, turning slightly. "Someone was in here opening stall doors."

"Yeah, right," he said sarcastically. "Guess who. Drop the flashlight."

"It wasn't me," I said, turning a little more. "I tried to stop them. I've got the bruises to prove it."

"I'm not gonna tell you again, lady. Drop the flashlight."

"I want to see who you are. How do I know you're not the person who did this?"

"I'm with security."

I didn't find that reassuring. Security for the show grounds was contracted out to a private company that lowballed the bid for the job. The staff was probably as reliable and well trained as the people who let lunatics get on commercial airliners with guns and knives. For all I knew, half of them were convicted felons. With my back to him, I couldn't be sure he was even wearing the uniform.

"Let me see you."

He huffed an impatient sigh. Before he could say no, I turned around and hit him full in the face with the beam from the Maglite.

I noted his clothes second. I noted his gun first.

"Is that part of the uniform?" I asked.

"It's part of *my* uniform." He made a motion with it. "Enough with the questions. Cut the light and give it to me. Let's go."

I did as instructed, more than willing to get out in the open where I knew there were other people around. I considered and rejected the idea of making a break for it. I didn't want people looking for me, my description and sketch on the front page of the newspaper. Nor did I want to get shot in the back. Playing along for the moment could offer an opportunity to learn something.

Outside, people were calling, horses were whinnying. I could hear hoofbeats on the hard-packed road. The guard herded me to a golf cart parked on the side of tent nineteen—Jade's barn.

I wondered how long the cart had been parked there. I wondered how easy it would be to buy a guy like this to open some stall doors. Working nights for peanuts guarding horses worth more than the average man would make in a lifetime might alter a person's perspective of right and wrong.

I slid onto the passenger's side of the bench seat, the seat wet and slippery as the rain came harder. The guard kept his gun in his left hand as he started the cart and backed it around. I shifted positions, turning slightly toward him, and surreptitiously touched the Glock, still secure in the back of my jeans, beneath my jacket and turtleneck.

"Where are we going?"

He didn't answer. A walkie-talkie crackled on his belt. Other guards radioing about the loose horses. He didn't get on the air to tell anyone he'd apprehended me. I didn't like that. We started down the road toward the main part of the show grounds, a ghost town at two in the morning.

"I'll want to speak to your supervisor," I said with authority. "And someone will need to call Detective James Landry with the Sheriff's Office."

That turned his head.

"Why?"

I took my turn not answering. Let him wonder. We passed other guards, other people running through the rain to join in the fun of trying to catch half a dozen hot-blooded horses drunk on freedom.

We drove through the maze of tents and down a row of deserted retail shops. The rain came now in sheets. We drove farther and farther away from any source of help. My heart rate increased a beat. Adrenaline was like a narcotic in my bloodstream, the prospect of danger intoxicating and exciting. I stared at the security guard and wondered what he would think if he knew that. Most people would find it disturbing.

He pulled the golf cart alongside one of the big trailers that housed the various show grounds management offices and cut the engine. We clattered up the metal stairs and the guard ushered me inside. A heavyset man stood beside a metal desk, listening to the noise coming over a walkie-talkie the size of a brick. He had a throat like a bullfrog: a sack of flesh wider than his head, spilling over the collar of his shirt. He wore the blue security uniform too, with a couple of extra pins on the chest. Decorated for meritorious ass-sitting and delegating above and beyond the call, I guessed. He scowled at me as I stood dripping water all over the floor.

"She's the one," the guard said. "I caught her opening stall doors."

I looked him in the face and said with just enough point to make my meaning crystal clear: "Any more little surprises like that in your pocket?"

He had stuffed the gun. I could see him struggle with the notion that he'd blown it showing me the thing. I had something to use against him. He wasn't supposed to be carrying on the job. He probably didn't have a permit for it either. If that was true and I reported him to the police, there was a good chance he'd lose his job at the very least. I could see on his face all these things were just now occurring to him.

If he'd been overly bright he wouldn't have been working dog watch in a rent-a-cop uniform.

"You caught me standing in a barn with a flashlight," I said. "I was trying to help. Same as you."

"You got something against Michael Berne?" the bullfrog asked. He had the thick drawl of a panhandle Floridian, where the Sunshine State and the Deep South rub loins, as it were.

"I've never met Michael Berne, though I did see him having a loud, threatening argument with Don Jade this morning. You might want to find out where Mr. Jade is right now."

The supervisor stared at me. "Berne is on his way," he said. "And a couple of deputies. Have a seat, Miss . . . ?"

I didn't answer and I didn't sit, though my back was aching like a son of a bitch from the beating I'd taken.

"You'll need to tell the deputies to treat that stall area as a crime scene," I said. "In addition to letting the horses loose, your perp assaulted me when I tried to run him off. They'll find a pitchfork or a broom—something with a long handle—that may have his prints on it. I'll want to press charges. And I'll want to go to the emergency room for an examination, and to have them take photographs of my bruises. I may sue. What kind of management does this place have if they can't keep people or animals safe?"

Bullfrog looked at me as if he'd never seen one of my kind before. "Who are you?"

"I'm not telling you my name."

"I need your name, miss. I have to make a report."

"That's a problem then, because I'm not telling you," I said. "I don't have to tell you anything. You're not an officer of the court or of the government, and therefore you have no right to demand information of me."

"Deputies are on the way," he said by way of a threat.

"That's fine. I'll be happy to go with them, though they have no grounds to arrest me. Standing in a barn aisle is not a crime that I'm aware of."

"Bud says you let them horses loose."

"I think you should ask Bud again what he saw."

He looked at Bud. "Was she letting them loose or not?"

Bud looked constipated, unable to tell the lie he wanted to tell either to cover his own ass or to grab a little glory with his boss. "She was right there."

"So were you," I pointed out. "How do we know you didn't open those doors?"

"That's ridiculous," Bullfrog said. "Why would he do something like that?"

"I could only speculate. Money. Maliciousness. Mental illness."

"Maybe those motives all apply to you."

"Not in this particular instance."

"You have horses here on the grounds, Miss—?"

"I'm through speaking with you now," I announced. "May I use your phone to call my attorney?"

He squinted at me. "No!"

I sat then in a straight chair beside the desk. Bullfrog's radio crackled. The gate guard announcing the arrival of the sheriff's deputies. A stroke of luck. I didn't want to meet Michael Berne in these circumstances. Bullfrog instructed the gate guard to send the radio car to the security office.

"Letting them horses loose is a serious crime," he said to me. "You could do time for that."

"No, I couldn't, because I didn't let the horses loose. The perpetrator might be charged with malicious mischief, which is a misdemeanor. There would be a fine and maybe community service. It's nothing compared to, say, illegally carrying a concealed weapon," I said, looking at the scowling Bud.

"I thought you said you were through talking," he said.

I smoothed my wet hair back with my hands and stood up as a car door slammed outside the trailer. The deputy came in looking like he'd been awakened from a sound sleep to answer the call.

"What's up, Marsh? Somebody let some nags loose? This her?"

"She was in the vicinity," Bullfrog said. "She may have information about the crime."

The deputy looked at me, unimpressed. "Do you, ma'am?"

"I'll speak directly to Detective Landry," I said.

"What's your name, ma'am?"

I moved past him, going to the door, checking out his name tag as I passed. "We'll talk in the car, Deputy Saunders. Let's get going."

He looked at Bullfrog, who shook his head and said, "Good luck with that, son. She's a pistol."

9

You got me out of bed for this?" Landry looked from Deputy Saunders to me with the kind of disgust usually reserved for spoiled food.

"She won't talk to anyone else," Saunders said.

We walked down the hall toward the squad room, Landry muttering, "Aren't I the lucky one. I don't see what any of us are doing here. You could have handled this in the field in half an hour. Jesus."

"I was assaulted," I said. "I think that warrants a detective."

"Then you take whoever is up. You know that."

"But I've already established a relationship with you regarding this case."

"No, you haven't, because there isn't any case. What you talked to me about yesterday isn't a case."

We went into the division offices through reception. Landry handed his badge and his weapon to the security officer through the drawer beneath the bulletproof glass. Saunders followed suit. I pulled the Glock out of the back of my jeans, put it and my car keys in the tray. Landry stared at me.

I shrugged. "I've got a license."

He turned to Saunders. "You fucking idiot. She could have blown your empty head off in the car."

"Now, Detective," I cooed, slipping past him as the security officer buzzed the door open. "I'm not that kind of girl."

"Get out of here, Saunders," he snapped. "You're about as useful as a limp dick."

We left Saunders looking forlorn in the outer office. Landry stalked past me, the muscles in his jaw working. We went past his desk to an interview room. He pushed the door back.

"In here."

I went in and gingerly took a seat. The pain in my back wouldn't let me draw a full breath. I had begun to wonder if maybe I really should go to an ER.

Landry slammed the door. "What the hell were you thinking?"

"That's rather a broad question, so I'm just going to take my pick of moments," I said. "I went to the equestrian center to look for some hint of what might have happened to Erin Seabright."

"But you weren't in the barn where she worked, right? She worked for some guy named Jade. So how is it you were in this other barn?"

"Michael Berne is an enemy of Don Jade. This morning I witnessed Berne threaten Jade."

"Threaten him how?"

"In that if-I-find-out-you-killed-that-horse-I'll-ruin-you kind of way."

"So this Jade sneaks in and turns the guy's horses loose. Big deal."

"It's a big deal to the man whose livelihood depends on the soundness of those horses. It's a big deal to the trainer who has to explain to owners how a horse worth a quarter of a million or a half a million dollars came to break a leg running around loose in the dead of night."

Landry heaved a sigh and turned his head at an odd angle, as if to pop a vertebra in his neck. "And you'd drag me out of bed for this?"

"No. I did that just for fun."

"You're a pain in the ass, Estes. Not like you haven't been told that before."

"That and worse. It doesn't bother me. I don't have a very high opinion of myself either," I said. "I suppose you think I'm being flip, and that's all right. I don't care what you think of me. I want you to be aware there are bad things going on that all seem to center on Don Jade. Don Jade is the man Erin Seabright was working for. Erin Seabright is missing. Do you see the connection here?"

He shook his head. "So I'm told you're caught standing there in this other guy's barn. How do I know you didn't let these nags loose just to get attention? You want people looking at Jade, so you orchestrate this little opera—"

"Nice turn of phrase. And did I beat myself with a pitchfork handle too? I can assure you, I'm not that flexible."

"You're walking around. You don't look any worse for wear to me."

I slipped my jacket off and stood up. "All right. I don't usually do this on the first interrogation, but if you promise not to call me a slut..."

I turned my back to him and pulled my sweater up to my neck. "If those marks look anywhere near as bad as they feel—"

"Jesus."

He spoke the word softly, without anger, without energy, the wind knocked out of his sails. I knew it probably didn't have as much to do with the marks my assailant had left on me as it did with the patchwork of skin grafts I'd worn for the past two years.

That wasn't what I had wanted. Not at all. I had lived with those scars a long time now. They were a part of me. I had kept them to myself because I kept to myself. I didn't dwell on them. I didn't look at them. In a strange way, the damage that had been done to my body was unimportant to me, because I had become unimportant to myself.

Suddenly the damage was very important. I felt naked emotionally. Vulnerable.

I pulled the sweater down and picked up my jacket, my back still to Landry.

"Forget it," I said, embarrassed and angry with myself. "I'm going home."

"You want to press charges?"

"Against whom?" I asked, turning to face him. "The asshole

you're not going to bother to look for, let alone question, because nothing that goes on with that horse crowd is of any interest to you? Unless, of course, someone turns up murdered."

He couldn't think of anything to say to that.

The corner of my mouth moved in what passed for a bitter smile. "Imagine that: You at least have the humanity to feel sheepish. Good for you, Landry."

I stepped past him, going to the door. "How do you like my odds that Saunders is sitting in the parking lot catching twenty? Pretty good, I think. See you around, Landry. I'll call you when I find a body."

"Estes. Wait." He didn't want to meet my eyes when I turned again and looked at him. "You should go to an ER. I'll take you. You might have busted a rib or something."

"I've had worse."

"Jesus Christ, you're a hardhead."

"I don't want your pity," I said. "I don't want your sympathy. I don't want you to like me or care what happens to me. I don't want anything from you but for you to do your job. And apparently, that's too much to ask.

"I'll show myself out. I know the way."

He followed me back to reception. Neither of us spoke as we retrieved our weapons. I pretended he had ceased to exist as we walked down the hall and down the stairs.

"I'm good at what I do," he said as the front doors came into view.

"Really? What's that? You have a second career as a professional asshole?"

"You're a piece of work."

"I'm what I have to be."

"No, you're not," he said. "You're rude and you're a bitch, and that somehow makes you feel superior to the rest of us."

The rain was still coming down. It looked white as it passed through the beams of the security lights in the parking lot. Saunders and his radio car were gone.

"Great," I said. "I guess I have to take you up on that ride, after all."

Landry looked at me sideways as he flipped up the collar of his jacket. "Fuck you. Call a cab."

I watched him get into his car, and stood there in the rain until he'd backed up and driven away. Then I went back inside to use the phone.

I couldn't say I hadn't asked for it.

When the cabbie finally showed, he wanted to chat, curious about why I needed a ride from the Sheriff's Office at 3:45 in the morning. I told him my boyfriend was wanted for murder. He didn't ask any more questions after that.

I propped myself up in the back of the cab and spent the ride home wondering how Erin Seabright was spending the night.

ACT TWO

SCENE ONE

FADE IN:

INTERIOR: OLD TRAILER HOUSE

Night. A single lightbulb in a lamp with no shade. No curtains at the filthy window. A rusty old iron bed frame. Stained mattress with no sheets.

Erin sits on the bed, huddled against the headboard, frightened, naked. She is chained to the bed by one wrist. Her hair is a mess. Mascara rings her eyes. Her lower lip is split and bloody.

She is very aware of the camera and the director of the scene. She tries to cover as much of herself as she can. She is crying softly, trying to hide her face.

DIRECTOR

Look at the camera, bitch. Say your line.

She shakes her head, still hiding.

DIRECTOR
Say it! You want me to make you?

She shakes her head and looks at the camera.

ERIN
Help me.

FADE OUT

10

Landry didn't sleep for shit, and it was Estes' fault. Her fault he'd been dragged out of bed in the first place. Her fault he couldn't get back to sleep once he'd finally gotten back home. Every time he closed his eyes he saw her back, crisscrossed with lines where new flesh had been stitched into old. The bruises just coming to the surface from her run-in at the equestrian center were insignificant, pale shadows beneath the old damage.

Damage. He thought of Estes and what he knew about her. Their paths hadn't crossed when she was on the job. Narcs ran their own way. They spent too much time undercover, as far as he was concerned. It made them edgy and unpredictable. An opinion borne out in the incident that had ended her career, and ended the life of Hector Ramirez. What he knew about that incident was what everybody knew: Estes had jumped the gun, gone against orders to make the bust herself, and all hell had broken loose.

He had never given any thought to Estes, beyond thinking she'd gotten what she deserved, losing her job. He knew she'd been wounded, hospitalized, was suing the SO for her disability pay—which seemed pretty damned nervy, considering—but it had nothing to do with him, and he didn't give a shit about her. She was trouble. He had figured it, and now he knew it for a fact.

Pushy bitch. Telling him how to do his job.

He wondered about what had happened to her at the equestrian center, wondered if it really did have anything to do with this girl she said was missing...

If the girl was missing, why would a twelve-year-old child be the only one to report it? Why not her parents? Why not her employer?

Her parents who maybe wanted to be rid of her.

Her boss who maybe had a major scam going, and maybe beat Estes across the back with a broom handle.

He saw her back, a patchwork of mismatched flesh stretched taut over bone.

At five-thirty he got out of bed, pulled on a pair of running shorts, stretched, did a hundred sit-ups and a hundred push-ups, and started his day. Again.

I *stand at the side of the Golam brothers' trailer. I've been told to stay put, to wait, but I know that's not the right decision. If I go in first, if I go in now, I've got the brothers dead-bang. They think they know me. I've worked this case three months. I know what I'm doing. I know I'm right. I know the Golam brothers are already twitching. I know I want this bust and deserve it. I know Lieutenant Sikes is here for the show, to put a feather in his cap. He wants to look good when the news vans arrive. He wants to make the public think they should vote for him in the next election for sheriff.*

He's stuck me on the side of the trailer and told me to wait. He doesn't know his ass. He didn't listen to me when I told him the side door is the door the brothers use most. While Sikes and Ramirez are watching the front, the brothers are dumping their money into duffel bags and getting ready to bolt out the side. Billy Golam's four-by-four is parked ten feet away, covered in mud. If they run, they'll take the truck, not the Corvette parked in front. The truck can go off-road.

Sikes is wasting precious time. The Golam brothers have two girls in the trailer with them. This could easily turn into a hostage situation. But if I go in now... They think they know me.

I key the button on my radio. "This is stupid. They're going to break for the truck. I'm going in."

"Goddammit, Estes—"

I drop the radio into the weeds growing beside the trailer. It's my case. It's my bust. I know what I'm doing.

I draw my weapon and hold it behind my back. I go to the side door and knock the way all the Golam brothers' customers knock: two knocks, one knock, two knocks. "Hey, Billy, it's Elle! I need some."

Billy Golam jerks open the door, wild-eyed, high on his own home cooking—crystal meth. He's breathing hard. He's got a gun in his hand.

Shit.

The front door explodes inward.

One of the girls screams.

Buddy Golam shouts: "Cops!"

Billy Golam swings the .357 up in my face. I suck in my last breath.

He turns abruptly and fires. The sound is deafening. The bullet hits Hector Ramirez in the face and blows out the back of his head, blood and brain matter spraying Sikes behind him.

I go for my weapon as Billy bolts out the door and knocks me off the stoop.

He's running for the truck as I scramble to get my feet under me.

The engine roars to life.

"Billy!" I scream, running for the truck.

"Fuck! Fuck! Fuck!" The cords in his neck stand out as he screams. He throws the truck into reverse and hits the gas.

I throw myself at the driver's door, grab hold of the side mirror and the window frame, and get one foot on the running board. I don't think what I'm doing. I just act.

I'm screaming. He's screaming.

He brings the gun up and points it in my face.

I hit the gun, hit his face.

He cranks the wheel around as the truck runs backward. One of my feet slips off the running board. He throws the truck into drive and gravel spews out behind it.

I struggle to keep from falling. I try to grab the wheel.

The truck catches hold of pavement. Golam cranks the wheel hard left. His face is a contorted mask, mouth wide, eyes wild. I try to grab for him. He shoves the door open as the truck spins around in the road.

I'm hanging in space.

I'm falling.

The road slams against my back.

My left cheekbone shatters like an egg.

Then the black shadow of Billy Golam's four-by-four sweeps over me, and I die.

And I wake.

Five-thirty A.M. After two hours of fitful dozing, waiting for a rib fragment to deflate one or both of my lungs, I oozed over the side of my bed and forced myself to attempt stretching.

I went into the bathroom, stood naked in front of the mirror, and looked at my body. Too thin. Rectangular marks on both thighs where the skin grafts were taken. Gouges into the meat of the left leg.

I turned and tried to look over my shoulder at my back in the mirror. I looked at what I had shown Landry, and called myself stupid.

The one useful thing my father had ever taught me: never show a weakness, never appear vulnerable.

The bruises from my beating were dark maroon stripes. It hurt when I breathed.

At 6:15—after I'd fed the horses—I drove myself to the ER. The X rays showed no broken bones. A bleary-eyed resident, who'd had even less sleep than I, questioned me, clearly not believing my story of having fallen down a flight of stairs. All the staff looked at me askance with jaded eyes. Twice I was asked if I wanted to talk to a cop. I thanked them and declined. No one forced the issue, which led me to wonder how many battered women were allowed to simply walk out of the place and back into their own private hell.

The resident vomited up a big load of medical terms, trying to intimidate me with his expensive education.

I looked at him, unimpressed, and said, "I have bruised ribs."

"You have bruised ribs. I'll give you a prescription for painkillers. Go home and rest. No significant physical activity for forty-eight hours."

"Yeah, right."

He gave me a scrip for Vicodin. I laughed when I looked at it. I stuffed it in the pocket of my windbreaker as I left the building. My arms worked, my legs worked, no bones were protruding, I wasn't bleeding. I was ambulatory, I was fine. As long as I knew I wouldn't die of it, I had places to go, people to see.

My first call was to Michael Berne, or rather, to Michael Berne's assistant—the phone number on the stall doors. Michael was a busy man.

"Ask him if he's too busy to speak to a potential client," I said. "I can always take my business to Don Jade, if that's the case."

Miraculously, Michael's time suddenly freed up and the assistant handed off the phone.

"This is Michael. How can I help you?"

"By dishing some dirt on your friend, Mr. Jade," I said quietly. "I'm a private investigator."

11

I dressed in black from head to toe, slicked my hair back with a handful of gel, put on a pair of narrow black wraparound sunglasses, and stole Sean's black Mercedes SL. I looked like a character from *The Matrix*. Serious, mysterious, edgy. Not a disguise, but a uniform. Image is everything.

I had asked Berne to meet me in the parking lot at Denny's in Royal Palm Beach, a fifteen-minute drive from the show grounds. He had groused about the drive, but I couldn't take the risk of being seen with him near the equestrian center.

Berne arrived in a Honda Civic that had seen better days. He got out of the car looking nervous, glancing around. A private eye, a clandestine meeting. Heady stuff. He was dressed to ride in gray breeches with a couple of stains and a red polo shirt that clashed with his hair.

I buzzed down the Mercedes' side window. "Mr. Berne. You're here to meet me."

He squinted at me, doubtful, uncertain, unable to get any kind of a read on me. An agent for a shadow organization. Maybe he'd been expecting Nancy Drew.

"We'll talk out here," I said. "Please get in the car."

He hesitated like a child being offered a ride by a stranger. He looked around the parking lot again as if he expected something bad to happen. Masked operatives creeping out of the shrubbery to ambush him.

"If you have something to tell me, get in the car," I said impatiently.

He was so tall, he had to fold himself in to fit into the Mercedes, as if he were getting into a clown car. What a contrast he was to Jade's handsome, elegant image. Howdy Doody on growth hormones. Red hair and freckles, skinny as a rail. I'd read enough about Michael Berne to know he'd been a minor contender in the international show-jumping world in the early nineties, when he had ridden a horse called Iroquois. But the biggest thing he'd done was a tour of Europe with the second string of the U.S. Olympic team. Then Iroquois' owners had sold the stallion out from under him, and he hadn't had a big winner since.

When Trey Hughes had come into his barn, Berne had been quoted in an interview saying that Stellar was his ride back into the international spotlight. Then Stellar went to Don Jade's barn, and Michael Berne's star dimmed again.

"Who do you work for again, Ms. Estes?" he asked, taking in the pricey car.

"I didn't say."

"Are you with the insurance company? Are you with the police?"

"How many cops do you know drive a Mercedes, Mr. Berne?" I asked, allowing the barest hint of amusement to show. I lit one of Sean's French cigarettes and blew the smoke at the windshield. "I'm a private investigator—*private* being the operative word. There's nothing for you to be concerned about, Mr. Berne. Unless, of course, you've done something wrong."

"I haven't done anything wrong," he said defensively. "I run an honest business. There aren't any stories going around about me killing horses for the insurance money. That's Don Jade's territory."

"You think he had Stellar killed?"

"I know he did."

I watched him from the corner of my eye, and when I spoke I used a flat, monotone, business voice. "You have something to back that up? Like evidence?"

His mouth turned down in a sour pout. "Jade's too smart for that. He always covers his tracks. Last night, for example. No one will ever connect Don Jade to it, but he had my horses turned loose."

"Why would he do that?"

"Because I confronted him. I know what he is. It's people like Jade that give the horse business a bad name. Crooked deals, stealing clients, killing horses. People turn a blind eye as long as they aren't the victims. Someone has to do something."

"Did Trey Hughes ever approach you about doing something to Stellar?"

"No. I had Stellar on track. He was making progress. I thought we had a shot at the World Cup. I would never have anything to do with a scheme like that anyway."

"Why did Hughes take the horse away from you?"

"Jade poached him. He steals clients all the time."

"It didn't have anything to do with the fact that you weren't winning?"

Berne glared at me. "We were getting there. It was only a matter of time."

"But Hughes wasn't willing to wait."

"Jade probably told him he could do it faster."

"Yeah, well, now Stellar is going nowhere."

"What about the autopsy?"

"Necropsy."

"What?"

"It's called a necropsy when it's a horse."

He didn't like being corrected. "So what did it show?"

"I'm not at liberty to divulge those details, Mr. Berne. Were there any rumors going around before the horse died? I heard he wasn't sound."

"He was getting older. Older horses need maintenance—joint injections, supplements, things like that. But he was tough. He had a big heart and he always did his job."

"No one was hinting anything hinky was going on in Jade's barn?" I asked.

"There are always rumors about Jade. He's done this before, you know."

"I'm familiar with Mr. Jade's background. What kind of rumors lately?"

"The usual. What drugs his horses are on. Whose clients he's after. How he's got Trey Hughes by the balls—pardon my language."

"Why would anyone say that?"

"Come on," he said, defensive again. "He must have something. How else is he getting that barn Hughes is building?"

"Through merit? Good deeds? Friendship?"

None of my suggestions appealed.

"You worked for Trey Hughes," I said. "What could Jade have on him?"

"Take your pick: his drug du jour, whose wife he's been sleeping with—"

"How he came to inherit so suddenly?" I suggested.

Berne tried to sit back and study me for a moment, his expression not unlike Jill Morone's when she'd been trying to decide how to play me. "You think he killed his mother?"

"I don't think anything. I'm just asking questions."

He considered something and laughed. "Trey would never have the nerve. He stuttered whenever he talked about Sallie. She scared the crap out of him."

I didn't point out that Trey only needed nerve enough to hire someone else for the job. Delegating was something I was sure came quite easily to a man who had spent his entire life shirking any kind of responsibility.

"You haven't heard any rumors up that alley?" I asked.

"People make jokes behind his back. No one really thinks it. Trey has all he can do getting himself through the day. He couldn't organize his wallet, let alone plan a murder and get away with it. Anyway, he was with someone the night he got the call about his mother."

"Really? Who?"

He looked away. "What difference does that make?"

"It makes a difference if that person is in fact an accessory to murder."

"It's nothing like that."

"I'll get the answer one way or another, Mr. Berne. Do you want me asking all around the show grounds, opening up old wounds, stirring up old gossip?"

Berne stared out the window.

"Should I start guessing?" I asked. "Maybe it was you. That would put a fresh spin on an old story, wouldn't it?"

"I'm no fruit!"

"It's hardly a stigma in the equestrian community, is it?" I said on the verge of boredom. "From what I've seen, maybe every third guy is straight. Think of all the new friends you'll have if you come out of the closet. Or maybe you already have. I could look for an old boy-friend—"

"It was my wife."

Who he gave up in a heartbeat rather than have a perfect stranger think his switch clicked the other way.

"Your wife was with Trey Hughes the night his mother died? With him in the biblical sense?"

"Yes."

"With or without your consent?" I asked.

Berne turned purple. "What the hell kind of question is that?"

"If you thought you were on the verge of losing a client, maybe you and the missus cooked up a little incentive plan for him to stay."

"That's sick!"

"The world's a twisted place, Mr. Berne. No offense to you, but I don't know much about you as a person. For instance: I don't know if you're trustworthy. I need my name and my job description kept out of the public forum. I find people to be more closemouthed if they themselves have a secret they'd like kept. Are you getting my drift here, Mr. Berne? Or do I need to be more direct?"

He looked incredulous. "Are you threatening me?"

"I prefer to think we're reaching a mutual understanding on the importance of confidentiality. I'll keep your secret if you keep mine."

"You don't work for General Fidelity," he mused. "Phil would have said something."

"Phil?"

"Phil Wilshire. The claims adjuster. I know him. He would have said something about you."

"He's talked to you about this case?"

"I want Jade caught once and for all," he said, screwing up some self-righteous indignation. "He should be run out of the business. If there's anything I can do, I will."

"Anything?" I asked pointedly. "I'd be careful with my mouth if I were you, Mr. Berne," I cautioned. "A case could easily be made that you so hated Don Jade, you killed Stellar and you're trying to hang it on Jade in order to ruin him. There goes his career. There goes his position with Trey Hughes. You patch things up with Hughes, maybe you slip right back into the picture."

Berne exploded. "You asked me to come here so you could accuse me?! What are you? Crazy?"

"My, what a temper you have, Mr. Berne," I said calmly. "You should try anger management counseling. Rage is bad for your health."

He wanted to scream at me. I could see him almost choke on it.

"To answer your earlier question: No. I'm not crazy," I said. "I'm blunt. I have to cover all the bases, and I don't have time to screw around. I don't make friends doing it, but I get the answers I need.

"Maybe you're not guilty of a thing, Mr. Berne. Like I said, I don't know you. But in my experience, most crime is underpinned by three motives: money, sex, and/or jealousy. You score in all categories. So let's clear you right now, and I can concentrate on Jade. Where were you when Stellar died?"

"Home. In bed. With my wife."

I took a last long drag on the cigarette and exhaled through half a smile. "She's going to have to change her name to Alibi."

Berne held up his hands. "That's it. I'm through here. I came out of the goodness of my heart to help—"

"Put the violin away, Berne. We both know why you came here. You want Jade ruined. That's fine with me. I have my own agenda."

"Which is what?"

"My client's interest. Maybe we can both end up with what we want. How long after Sallie Hughes died did Trey take his horses to Jade?" I asked.

"Two weeks."

"And when did you hear Hughes had bought the property in Fairfields?"

"A month later."

My head felt like it had been put in a vise. I didn't want to know the sordid details of Trey Hughes' life or Michael Berne's life or Don Jade's life. I wanted to find Erin Seabright. My luck she lived in Pandora's box.

I pulled her photograph out of the inside pocket of my jacket and handed it to Berne. "Have you ever seen this girl?"

"No."

"She worked for Jade up until last Sunday. She was a groom."

Berne made a face. "Grooms come and go. I have all I can do to keep track of my own."

"This one vanished. Look again, please. You never saw her with Jade?"

"Jade always has women around him. I don't see the attraction, myself."

"Jade has a reputation in that area, doesn't he? Sleeps with the help?"

"The help, the clients, other people's clients. There's nothing he won't stoop to."

"That's what I'm afraid of, Mr. Berne," I said. I handed him a plain white card with a number printed on it. "If you have anything useful to tell, please call this number and leave a message. Someone will contact you. Thank you for your time."

Landry parked his car among the giant four-by-four trucks, BMWs, and Jaguars, and got out, already scanning the ground so he wouldn't step in anything. He'd grown up in a city. All he knew about horses was that they were huge and smelled bad.

The day was bright and warm. He squinted even through the lenses of his aviator shades as he surveyed the scene. It looked like a goddam refugee camp—tents and animals everywhere. People on bicycles and motor scooters. Dust billowed in clouds as trucks rumbled past.

He saw Jade's sign, went into the tent, and asked the first person he saw where Mr. Jade was. An Hispanic man with a pitchfork of shit in hand nodded to the side of the tent and said, "Outside."

Landry went in the direction of the nod. Halfway between Jade's tent and the next a man in riding clothes was sipping from a Starbucks cup, listening impassively as an attractive blonde talked at him. The blonde seemed upset.

"Mr. Jade?"

The pair turned and looked at him as he approached and showed them his badge.

"Detective Landry, Sheriff's Office. I'd like to ask you a few questions."

"Oh, my God!" the blonde laughed, flashing a big smile. "I knew you'd get caught! You never should have torn the tag off that mattress." She turned the smile on Landry. "Paris Montgomery. I'm Mr. Jade's assistant trainer."

Landry didn't smile back. Three hours' sleep didn't supply enough energy to waste on phony charm. He looked past the woman. "You're Mr. Jade?"

"What's this about?" Jade asked, striding into the tent and past Landry, trying to draw him back away from where passersby might see them.

"Are you aware of what happened here last night?" Landry asked. "Some horses were set loose a couple of tents down the row."

"Michael Berne's," Paris Montgomery supplied. "Of course we know. It's terrible. Something has to be done about security. Do you have any idea what these animals are worth?"

"Their weight in gold, apparently," Landry said, bored hearing about it. Why in hell should a horse be worth a million bucks if it wasn't on a racetrack?

"He's going to come after you, Don," she said to her boss. "You know Michael will be telling everyone who'll listen you did the deed—or had it done."

"Why would you say that, Ms. Montgomery?" Landry asked.

"Because that's how Michael is: bitter and vindictive. He blames everything but his lack of talent on Don."

Jade looked at her with hooded eyes. "That's enough, Paris. Everyone knows Michael is jealous."

"Of what?" Landry asked.

"Of Don," the woman said. "Don is everything Michael is not, and when Michael's clients see that and leave him, he blames Don. He probably turned those horses loose himself just so he could publicly blame Don."

Landry kept his eyes on Jade. "That must get old. You ever want to do something to shut him up?"

Jade's expression never changed. Calm, cool, controlled. "I learned a long time ago to ignore people like Michael."

"You should threaten to sue him for libel," Paris said. "Maybe that would shut him up."

"Slander," Jade corrected her. "Slander is spoken. Libel is written."

"Don't be such a prick," Paris snapped. "He's doing everything he can to ruin your reputation. And you walk around like you think you're in some kind of isolation bubble. You think he can't hurt you? You think he isn't in Trey's ear every chance he gets?"

"I can't stop Michael from spewing his venom, and I can't stop people from listening to him," Jade said. "I'm sure Detective Landry didn't come here to listen to us complain."

"I'm not here about the horses either," Landry said. "A woman was assaulted in the attempt to stop whoever set them loose."

Paris Montgomery's brown eyes widened in shock. "What woman? Stella? Michael's wife? Was she hurt?"

"I understand there was a scene yesterday between you and Mr. Berne, Mr. Jade," Landry said. "Would you care to tell me where you were around two A.M.?"

"No, I would not," Jade said curtly, going to stand beside the horse that was tied in an open stall. "Now, if you'll excuse me, Detective, I have a horse to ride."

"Maybe you'd rather discuss it at length at the Sheriff's Office," Landry suggested. He didn't like being dismissed like a servant.

Jade gave him a look. Haughty—even through the shades. "Maybe you'd rather take it up with my attorney."

"Save your money and my time, Mr. Jade. All you have to do is tell me where you were. It's only a trick question if you were here."

"I was with a friend. We were not here."

"Does this friend have a name?"

"Not as far as you're concerned."

He tightened a strap on the saddle. The horse pinned its ears.

Landry looked for a place to jump in case the beast went nuts or something. It looked mean, like it would bite.

Jade unsnapped the ties that held the animal in the stall.

"Our conversation is over," Jade announced. "Unless you have something that connects me to what happened, other than the hear-

say that Michael and I don't get along—and I know that you don't—
I don't intend to speak to you again."

He led the horse out of the stall and down the aisle. Landry
pressed back against a wall, holding his breath—a good idea regardless, in this place. The smell of manure and horses and Christ-knew-
what hung in the air like smog. When the horse was out of range to
kick him, he followed.

"What about you, Ms. Montgomery?"

The blonde caught a look from her boss, then turned to Landry.
"Ditto. What he said. With a friend."

They went out into the sunshine and Jade mounted the horse.
"Paris, bring my coat and hat."

"Will do."

Jade didn't wait for her, but turned the horse and started down the
road.

"With each other?" Landry asked, walking back into the tent with
Montgomery.

"No. God no!" she said. "I take orders from him all day. I'm not
interested in taking them all night too."

"He's got an attitude."

"He's earned it. People don't cut him a lot of breaks."

"Maybe that's because he doesn't deserve any."

He followed her into a stall draped in green with an oriental carpet on the floor and framed art on the walls. She opened an antique
wardrobe and pulled out an olive green jacket and a brown velvet-
covered helmet.

"You don't know him," she said.

"And you do. Who do you think he was with last night?"

She laughed and shook her head. "I'm not privy to Don's private
life. This is the first I heard he's seeing anyone."

Then it seemed unlikely he was, Landry thought. From what he'd
gathered, these horse people practically lived in each other's pockets.
And proximity aside, they were all rich, or pretended to be rich; and
the only thing rich people liked better than fucking each other over
was gossiping.

"He's very discreet," Montgomery said.

"I guess that's what's kept him out of prison: discretion. Your boss
has toed the wrong side of the line a couple of times."

"And has never been convicted of anything. Now, if you'll excuse me, I'd better get up to the schooling ring or he'll kill me." She flashed the bright smile. "Then you'll have a job to do."

Landry followed her out of the tent. She climbed behind the wheel of a green golf cart with the Jade logo on the nose, folded the coat, and put it on the seat beside her. The helmet went into a basket behind the seat.

"What about you, Ms. Montgomery? Does your mystery pal have a name?"

"Yes, he does," she said, batting her eyes coyly. "But I don't kiss and tell either, Detective. A girl could get a reputation that way."

She started the golf cart and drove away, calling and waving to people as she went past the tents. Ms. Popularity.

Landry stood with his hands on his hips for a moment, aware there was a girl watching him from inside the tent. He could see her from the corner of his eye: chubby, unkempt, tight T-shirt showing off curves and rolls better left to the imagination.

Landry wanted to get back in the car and leave. Estes was right: he didn't give a shit what these people did to each other. But he'd had to account for what had gone on in the office in the middle of the night with Estes demanding to see only him, and no paperwork being filed, and what a fucking nightmare. His lieutenant wouldn't take that Estes wasn't filing charges and leave it at that. He had to follow up.

He sighed and turned, drawing a bead on the girl.

"You work here?"

Her small eyes widened. She looked like she didn't know whether to shit her pants or have an orgasm. She nodded.

Landry went back inside, pulling his notebook out of his hip pocket. "Name?"

"Jill Morone. M-O-R-O-N-E. I'm Mr. Jade's head groom."

"Uh-huh. And where were you last night around two?"

"In bed," she said, smug with a secret she was dying to spill. "With Mr. Jade."

12

The offices of Gryphon Development were located in a stylish stucco wanna-be-Spanish building on Greenview Shores across the street from the Polo Club's west entrance. I parked in a visitor's slot next to Bruce Seabright's Jaguar.

A poster-sized ad for Fairfields filled the front window of the office, Bruce Seabright's photo in the lower right-hand corner. He had the kind of smile that said: I'm a big prick, let me sell you something overpriced. Apparently that worked for some people.

The offices were professionally done to look expensive and inviting. Leather couches, mahogany tables. There were photographs of four men and three women on the wall, each with professional accolades etched in brass on the picture frames. Krystal Seabright was not among them.

The receptionist looked a lot like Krystal Seabright. Too much gold jewelry and hair spray. I wondered if this was how Krystal and Bruce had met. The boss and the secretary. Trite but true too much of the time.

"Elena Estes to see Mr. Seabright," I said. "I have some questions about Fairfields."

"Wonderful location," she said, giving me a saleswoman-in-training smile. "There are some spectacular barns going up in the development."

"Yes, I know. I've been past."

"The Hughes property," she supplied with a look of near euphoria. "Is that to die for?"

"I'm afraid so."

She buzzed Seabright. A moment later, the door on the far side of the reception area opened and Bruce Seabright stepped out, hanging on to the doorknob. He wore a crisp tan linen suit with a regimental striped tie. Very formal for south Florida, land of loud aloha shirts and deck shoes.

"Ms. Estes?"

"Yes. Thank you for seeing me."

I walked past him into his office and took a position on the opposite side of the room, my back to a mahogany credenza.

"Have a seat," he offered, going behind his desk. "Can we get you anything? Coffee? Water?"

"No, thank you. Thank you for seeing me without an appointment. I'm sure you're a very busy man."

"I'm glad to say I am." He smiled the same smile from the photo on the Fairfields poster. "Business is booming. Our little jewel of Wellington is being discovered. Property here is as hot as any in south Florida. And the land you're asking about is a prime example."

"Actually, I'm not here to buy property, Mr. Seabright."

The smile faded to mild confusion. His features were small and sharp, like a ferret's. "I don't understand. You said you had questions about Fairfields."

"I do. I'm an investigator, Mr. Seabright. I'm looking into an incident at the equestrian center that involves a client of yours: Trey Hughes."

Seabright sat back in his chair, unhappy with this turn of events. "Of course I know Trey Hughes. It's no secret he bought in Fairfields. But I certainly don't go around talking about clients, Ms. Estes. I have my ethics."

"I'm not after personal information. I'm more curious about the development. When the land came up for sale. When Mr. Hughes bought his parcel."

"That's a matter of public record," Seabright said. "You could go to the county offices and look it up."

"I could, but I'm asking you."

Suspicion had overtaken confusion. "What's this about? What 'incident' are you investigating?"

"Mr. Hughes recently lost a very expensive horse. We have to cross all the *t*'s and dot all the *i*'s. You know."

"What does the property have to do with this horse?"

"Routine background information. Was the owner in financial straits, et cetera. The property Mr. Hughes is developing was expensive, and the development of the property itself—"

"Trey Hughes doesn't need money," Seabright said, offended by the suggestion. "Anyone will tell you he came into a large inheritance last year."

"Before or after he bought the Fairfields property?"

"What difference does that make?" he asked irritably. "He'd been interested in the property for some time. He purchased last spring."

"After the death of his mother?"

"I don't like what you're implying, Ms. Estes. And I'm not comfortable having this conversation." He rose from his chair, a heartbeat from throwing me out.

"Are you aware your stepdaughter has been working for Mr. Hughes' trainer?" I asked.

"Erin? What's Erin got to do with this?"

"I'd like an answer to that myself. But she seems to be missing."

Seabright's level of agitation went up a notch. "What are you— Who exactly do you work for?"

"That's confidential information, Mr. Seabright. I have my ethics too," I said. "Did you have anything to do with Erin getting that job?"

"I don't see how that's any of your business."

"Are you aware no one has had any contact with Erin in nearly a week?"

"Erin isn't close to the family."

"Really? I was told she was quite close to your son."

Bruce Seabright turned burgundy and jabbed a forefinger at me. "I want your license number."

I raised the one eyebrow I could and crossed my arms over my chest, sitting back against the credenza. "Why are you so upset with me, Mr. Seabright? I would think a father would be more concerned about his daughter than his client."

"I'm not—" He caught himself and closed his mouth.

"Her father?" I supplied. "You're not her father, therefore you don't have to be concerned about her?"

"I'm not concerned about Erin because Erin is responsible for herself. She's an adult."

"She's eighteen."

"And no longer lives under my roof. She does as she pleases."

"That's been a problem, hasn't it? What pleases Erin doesn't please you. Teenage girls..." I shook my head as if in commiseration. "Life is easier without her around, isn't it?"

I thought I could see his body vibrate with the anger he was trying to contain. He stared at me, burning my image into his brain so he could visualize and hate me when I'd gone.

"Get out of my office," he said, his voice tight and low. "And if I see you on this property again, I'm calling the police."

I moved away from the credenza, taking my time. "And tell them what, Mr. Seabright? That I should be arrested for caring more about what's become of your stepdaughter than you do? I'm sure they'll find that to be very curious."

Seabright yanked the door open and called out loudly to the receptionist: "Doris, call the Sheriff's Office."

Doris stared, bug-eyed.

"Ask for Detective Landry in Robbery/Homicide," I suggested. "Give him my name. He'll be happy to make an appearance."

Seabright narrowed his eyes, trying to decide if I was bluffing.

I left the Gryphon offices at my own pace, got in Sean's car, and drove away—just in case Bruce Seabright wasn't.

13

My God, El, you look like one of Robert Palmer's all-girl eighties' bands."

I had put the top down for the drive home, hoping the air would clear my head. Instead, the sun had baked my brain, and the wind had swept my hair up into a 'do from a fashion shoot for the tragically hip. I wanted a drink and a nap in the sun by the pool, but knew I would allow myself neither.

Sean leaned down and kissed my cheek, then scolded me peevishly. "You stole my car."

"It matched my outfit."

I got out of the Mercedes and handed him the keys. He was in breeches and boots, and a tight black T-shirt with the sleeves rolled up to show off biceps the size of grapefruits.

"Robert must be coming to teach you," I said.

"Why do you say that?" he asked, irritated.

"The muscle shirt. Darling, you're really so transparent."

"Well, meow, meow. Aren't we catty today?"

"A good beating will do that to me."

"I'm sure you deserved it. Invite me next time. I'd love to watch."

We walked together across the stable yard toward the guest house. Sean looked at me out of the corner of his eye and frowned.

"Are you all right?"

I gave the question undue weight and consideration, instead of tossing off the usual meaningless answer. What an odd moment to be struck by insight, I thought. But I stopped and acknowledged it within myself.

"Yes," I said. "I am."

As tangled and trying as this case was becoming, as unwilling a participant as I'd been, it felt good to use the old skills. It felt good to be necessary to something.

"Good," he said. "Now go powder your nose and transform yourself again, Cinderella. Your alter ego has company coming."

"Who?"

"Van Zandt." He spat the name out as if it were a bitter thing with a pit in it. "Don't say I never sacrificed for you."

"My own mother wouldn't do as much."

"You'd better believe that, honey. Your mother wouldn't let that slimebag in the service entrance. You've got twenty minutes to curtain."

I took a shower and dressed in one of the outfits I had purchased at the show grounds: a jewel-red wraparound skirt made from an Indian sari, and a yellow linen blouse. An armload of bracelets, a pair of thick-soled sandals, and tortoiseshell shades, and I was Elle Stevens, Dilettante.

Van Zandt had just arrived as I cut through the stables to the parking area. He was dressed to impress in the uniform of the Palm Beach patriarch: pink shirt, tan slacks, blue blazer, his signature ascot at his throat.

As he spotted me, he came toward me with his arms outstretched. My long-lost old friend.

"Elle!"

"Z."

I suffered through his cheek-kissing routine, bracing my hands against his chest so he couldn't embrace me.

"Three times," he reminded me, stepping back. "Like the Dutch."

"Sounds to me like an excuse to grope," I said with half a smile. "Clever lech. What other cultures do you steal from in order to cop a feel in the guise of good manners?"

He smiled the smarmy/suave smile. "That all depends on the lady."

"And I thought you'd come to see my horses," Sean said. "Am I just a beard?"

Van Zandt looked at him, puzzled. "Are you a beard? You don't even have a beard."

"It's a figure of speech, Z.," I explained. "You have to get used to Sean. His mother sent him to drama camp as a child. He can't help himself."

"Ah. An actor!"

"Aren't we all?" Sean said innocently. "I've asked my girl to saddle Tino—the gelding I was telling you about. I'd like to get eighty thousand for him. He's talented, but I've got too many that are. If you have any clients looking . . ."

"I may have," Van Zandt said. "I've brought my camera. I'll make a video to send to a client I have coming down from Virginia. And when you're ready to look for something new, I'll be happy to show you the best horses in Europe. Bring Elle along with you. We'll have a wonderful time."

He looked at me, taking in the skirt. "You are not riding today, Elle?"

"Too much fun last night," I said. "I'm recuperating. Sean and I went to the Pinkeye Ball."

"Elle can't resist a worthy cause," Sean said. "Or a glass of champagne."

"You missed all the excitement at the show grounds," Van Zandt said, pleased to have the gossip. "Horses being turned loose. Someone was attacked. Unbelievable."

"And you were there?" I asked. "In the dead of night? Might the police want to speak with you?"

"Of course I wasn't there," he said irritably. "How could you think I would do a thing like that?"

I shrugged. "Z., I have no idea what you might or might not do. I do know you can't take a joke. Really, these moods of yours are getting tedious, and I've only known you two days," I said, letting my irritation show. "You expect me to want to ride around Europe in a car with you and your multiple personalities? I think I'd rather stay home and hit my thumb with a hammer over and over."

He splayed a hand across his chest as if I'd wounded him. "I am a sensitive person. I want only good things for everyone. I don't go around accusing people for a joke."

"Don't take it personally, Tomas," Sean told him as we neared the barn. "Elle sharpens her tongue on a whetstone every night before bed."

"All the better to fillet you with, my dear."

Van Zandt looked at me, pouting. "It's not a sharp tongue that attracts a husband."

"Husband? Why would I want one of those?" I asked. "Had one once. Threw him back."

Sean grinned. "Why be a wife when you can have a life?"

"Ex is best," I agreed. "Half of the money, none of the headache."

Van Zandt wagged a finger at me, trying to rally a sense of humor. "You need taming, Miss Tigress. You would then sing a different song."

"Bring a whip and a chair for that job," Sean suggested.

Van Zandt looked like he'd already imagined that and then some. He smiled again. "I know how best to treat a lady."

From the corner of my eye I saw Irina coming. A flash of long bare legs and clunky hiking boots. I saw she had something in her hand. She looked angry, and I assumed—wrongly—angry with Sean for being late or upsetting her schedule, or one of the fifty other transgressions that regularly put Irina in a snit. She stopped five feet from us, shouted something nasty in Russian, and flung the thing in her hand.

Van Zandt cried out in surprise, just managing to bring an arm up and deflect the flight path of the steel horseshoe before it struck him in the head.

Sean jumped back in horror. "Irina!"

The groom launched herself at Van Zandt like a missile, screaming: "Pig! You filthy pig!"

I stood, flat-footed, watching in amazement as Irina pummeled him with her fists. She was slender as a reed, but strong as a teamster, the muscles in her arms clearly delineated. Van Zandt staggered backward and sideways, trying to shake her off, but she clung to him like a limpet.

"Crazy bitch!" he shouted. "Get her off! Get her off!"

Sean jumped to, grabbing hold of the girl's blond ponytail with one hand and catching a wildly swinging arm with the other. "Irina! Stop it!"

"Son of bitch! Stinking son of bitch!" she shouted as Sean peeled her off Van Zandt and pulled her backward down the aisle. She rattled off another slur in Russian and violently spat at the Belgian.

"She's crazy!" Van Zandt shouted, wiping blood from his lip. "She should be locked up!"

"I take it you two have met," I said dryly.

"I've never seen her before in my life! Crazy Russian cunt!"

Irina lunged against Sean's hold on her, the look on her face venomous with hate. "Next time I tear out your throat and shit in your lungs, cur! For Sasha!"

Van Zandt backed away looking stricken, his perfect hair standing up in all directions.

"Irina!" Sean shouted, appalled.

"Why don't we ladies retire for a moment?" I suggested, taking Irina by the arm and steering her toward the lounge.

Irina snarled and made a rude gesture in the direction of Van Zandt, but came with me.

We went into the lounge, a room paneled in mahogany and fitted with a bar and leather-upholstered chairs. Irina paced, muttering expletives. I went behind the bar, took a bottle of Stoli from the freezer, and poured three fingers in a heavy crystal tumbler.

"Here's to you, girlfriend." I raised the glass in a toast, then handed it to her. She drank it like water. "I'm sure he had it coming, but would you care to fill me in?"

She fumed and called Van Zandt more names, then heaved a sigh and calmed herself. Just like that: instant composure. "That is not a nice man," she said.

"The guy who delivers feed is not a nice man, but you've never gone to such an effort for him. Who is Sasha?"

She took a cigarette from a box on the bar, lit it, and took a long, deep drag. She exhaled slowly, her face tilted at an elegant angle. She might have been Greta Garbo in a past life.

"Sasha Kulak. A friend from Russia. She went to work for that pig in Belgium because he made all kinds of big promises. He would pay her and let her ride good horses and they would be like partners and he would make her a star in the horse shows. Stinking liar. All he wanted was to have her. He got her to Belgium and thought he owned her. He thought she should fuck him and be grateful. She said no. She was a beautiful girl. Why would she fuck an old man like him?"

"Why would anyone?"

"He was a monster to her. He kept her in a gypsy camper with no heat. She had to use the toilet in his stables and he spied on her through holes in the walls."

"Why didn't she leave?"

"She was eighteen and she was afraid. She was in a foreign country where she knew no one and could not speak their stupid language. She didn't know what to do."

"She couldn't go to the police?"

Irina looked at me like I was stupid.

"Finally, she went to bed with him," she said, shrugging in that way Americans can never mimic. "Still he was terrible to her. He gave her herpes. After a while she stole some money and ran away when they were looking for horses in Poland.

"He called her family and made threats because of the money. He told them lies about Sasha. When she came home, her father threw her out into the street."

"He believed Van Zandt over his daughter?"

She made a face. "They are two alike, those men."

"And what became of Sasha?"

"She killed herself."

"Oh, God, Irina. I'm sorry."

"Sasha was fragile, like a glass doll." She smoked a little more, contemplating. "If a man did this thing to me, I would not kill myself. I would cut off his penis and feed it to the pigs."

"Very effective."

"Then I would kill him."

"A little luckier in your aim with that horseshoe and you might have," I said.

Irina poured another three fingers of the Stoli and sipped at it. I thought about Van Zandt abusing his authority over a young girl that way. Most adults would have had a difficult time dealing with his mercurial temperament. An eighteen-year-old girl would have been in way over her head. He deserved exactly what Irina had imagined for him.

"I'd like to say I'll hold him down while you kick him," I said. "But Sean will expect you to apologize, Irina."

"He can kiss my Russian ass."

"You needn't be sincere."

She thought about that. If it had been me, I would still have told Sean to kiss my ass. But I couldn't afford to alienate Van Zandt, especially not in the light of what Irina had told me. Her friend Sasha was dead. Maybe Erin Seabright was still alive.

"Come on," I said before she could have a chance to set her mind against it. "Get it over with. You can kill him on your day off."

I led the way out. Sean and Van Zandt were standing on the grass near the mounting block. Van Zandt was still red in the face, rubbing his arm where the horseshoe had struck him.

Irina unhooked Tino from the grooming stall and led the gelding out.

"Sean, I apologize for my outburst," Irina said, handing him the reins. "I am sorry to have embarrassed you." She looked at Van Zandt with cold disdain. "I apologize for attacking you on Mr. Avadon's property."

Van Zandt said nothing, just stood there scowling at her. The girl looked at me as if to say, *See what a swine he is?* She walked away, climbed the stairs to the gazebo at the end of the arena, and draped herself on a chair.

"The czarina," I said.

Van Zandt sulked. "I should call the police."

"But I don't think you will."

"She should be locked up."

"Like you locked up her friend?" I asked innocently, wishing I could stick a knife between his ribs.

His mouth was trembling as if he might cry. "You would believe her lies about me? I have done nothing wrong. I gave that girl a job, a place to live—"

Herpes . . .

"She stole from me," he went on. "I treated her like a daughter, and she stole from me and fucked me in the ass, telling lies about me!"

The victim yet again. Everyone was against him. His motives were always pure. I didn't point out to him that in America if a man treated his daughter the way he had treated Sasha, he would go to prison and come out a registered sex offender.

"How ungrateful," I said.

"You believe her," he accused.

"I believe in minding my own business, and your sex life is not and never will be my business."

He crossed his arms and pouted, staring down at his tasseled loafers. Sean had mounted and was in the arena warming up.

"Forget about Irina," I said. "She's only hired help. Who cares what grooms have to say? They should be like good children: seen and not heard."

"These girls should know their place," he muttered darkly as he unzipped his camera case and took out a video camera. "Or be put in it."

A shiver ran down my spine like a cold, bony finger.

As we stood and watched Sean work the horse, I knew neither of us had our mind on the quality of the animal. Van Zandt's mood had gone to a very dark place. He had to be thinking about damage control to his reputation, probably believing Irina—and maybe I—would spread the Sasha story around Wellington and he would lose clients. Or maybe he was simply fantasizing about strangling Irina with his bare hands, the bones in her throat cracking like small dry twigs. Irina sat in the gazebo smoking, one long leg swinging over the arm of the big wicker chair, never taking her glare off Van Zandt.

My thoughts were running in another direction. I wondered if Tomas Van Zandt had thought Erin Seabright should be glad to accept his advances, or if he had "put her in her place." I thought about my feeling that Erin had dumped Chad, and wondered if Van Zandt or someone like him might have made her promises, then broken them in the most terrible way. And I wondered again if all these terrible possibilities had been made possible by Bruce Seabright.

Erin hadn't fit his idea of the perfect daughter, and now she was out of his way. If she turned up dead, would he feel a moment's guilt?

If she never turned up at all, would he feel a second's responsibility? Or would he be pleased for a job well done?

I thought about my own father and wondered if he would have been relieved to have his ungrateful daughter simply disappear. Probably. I had loudly opposed everything he was, everything he stood for. I'd thumbed my nose at him and taken up a profession putting away the people he defended in court, the people who provided for the lifestyle I'd grown up in. Then again, maybe I *had* disappeared for him. I hadn't seen or spoken to him in years. For all I knew, I had ceased to exist in his mind.

At least my father hadn't set me up for doom. That had been my own doing entirely.

If Bruce had set Erin up with Trey Hughes, and Hughes had set her up with Jade, and via Jade she had been exposed to Van Zandt, Erin had never really had any say in her destiny. The irony was that she had thought she was gaining independence, taking control of her life. But the longer she was missing, the longer the odds were she would come out of this with a life at all.

By the time Sean had finished showing Tino, Robert Dover had arrived to teach him, leaving me to see Van Zandt off the property.

"Do you think your client from Virginia will be interested?" I asked.

"Lorinda Carlton?" He gave the Continental shrug. "I will tell her to be, so she will be," he said. The word of Van Zandt, amen. "She's not a talented rider, but she has a hundred thousand dollars to spend. All I have to do is convince her this horse is her destiny and everyone will live happily ever after."

Except the woman who bought a horse she couldn't handle. Then Van Zandt would convince her to sell that one and buy another. He would make money on both deals, and the cycle would begin again.

"You shouldn't reveal your trade secrets," I said. "You'll disillusion me."

"You are a very smart woman, Elle. You know the ways of this horse world. It's a hard business. People are not always nice. But I take care of my clients. I am loyal to them and I expect them to be loyal to me. Lorinda trusts me. She gives me the use of her townhouse while I am here for the season. See how grateful my friends are to me?"

"That's one word for it," I said dryly.

And he would blithely betray the trust of his grateful friend so he could foster a more lucrative relationship with Sean Avadon. He told me without batting an eye, as if it were nothing to him, and in the next breath he spoke of loyalty as if he were the poster boy for personal virtue.

"Are you free for dinner, Elle?" he asked. "I'll take you to The Players. We can talk about what kind of horse I want for you."

I found the suggestion revolting. I was exhausted and in pain and fed up to my eyeballs with this nauseating character and his bipolar mood swings. I wanted to do what Irina had done, jump on him and pummel him and call him every vile name I could think of. Instead, I said, "Not tonight, Z. I have a headache."

He looked hurt and angry again. "I am not a monster. I have integrity. I have character. People in this business, they get angry, they spread rumors. You should know better than to believe them."

I held up a hand. "Stop. Just stop, will you? Jesus. I'm tired. My head hurts. I want to spend my evening in the Jacuzzi with no one talking at me. As impossible as this might be for you to grasp, it's not about you."

He didn't believe that, but he changed tack at least. He stood straighter and nodded to himself. "You will see, Elle Stevens. I will do for you. I will make you a champion," he said. "You will see what kind of man I am."

In the end, that was the one prophecy he made that actually came true.

14

Jill stood in front of the cheap full-length mirror wearing nothing but makeup, a black lace bra, and a thong. She turned this way and that, practicing her various looks. Shy, coy, sexy. She liked sexy best. It went with the bra.

The bra was too small by a couple of sizes and dug into her sides, but it made her boobs look all the bigger, which she thought was a good thing. Like the women in *Hustler,* her tits seemed to swell up out of the cups. She could easily imagine Jade burying his face in her cleavage. The idea gave her a tingle between her legs, which drew her attention to the thong.

It also was too small for her, the skinny little straps cutting into the fat on her hips. Pubic hair sprouted out on either side of the scrap of black lace at the front. She twisted around and looked at her butt, bare and white, wide and dimpled. She didn't like the way the thong felt going up her crack, but she thought she'd better get used to it. The thong was sexy. Men went for a thong. She just wished that bitch Erin hadn't been so fucking skinny. Maybe if the thong was for a normal-sized person it wouldn't be so uncomfortable.

Oh, well. It was free. And it kind of turned her on that it belonged to someone else. She was taking Erin's place—in the barn, in the world. With Erin gone, Jill could be the flirty one. Jill could be the clever one.

But she would still be in the shadow of Paris Montgomery.

That cunt.

Jill scowled at the reminder. It was not a pretty reflection that looked back at her.

She hated Paris. She hated her smile, hated her big eyes, hated her blond hair. She hated Paris more than she had hated Erin. And she had hated the two of them together more than anything. Together they had been like the popular girls in school: too cool to be friends with someone like Jill, full of private jokes and catty looks. At least she didn't have to put up with that shit anymore. But there was still Paris.

Men fell all over themselves for Paris. She could get anybody to do anything for her. Nobody seemed to see that she was just a big phony. Everyone thought she was so funny and sweet and nice. She wasn't nice at all. When people weren't looking she was bossy and bitchy and mean. She was always making snide remarks about Jill eating too much and Jill needing to exercise and Jill not knowing how to dress.

Jill looked at herself head to toe in the mirror and suddenly saw exactly what Paris Montgomery saw. Not a sexy woman in sexy lingerie, but a fat face with small, piggy eyes and a sour, downturned mouth; arms inflated with fat; fat legs with dimpled knees; a body she hated so much she often fantasized taking a knife and slicing off big slabs of it. Ugly and pathetic in her stolen, too-small underwear.

Tears squeezed out of her eyes and her face turned mottled red. It wasn't her fault she was fat. Her mother had let that happen when she was a kid. So she couldn't help it now that she ate the wrong things. And it wasn't her fault she didn't exercise. She was tired at the end of the day—never mind that bitch Paris was always accusing her of not working hard enough.

Why would she work any harder for Paris? Paris didn't give her any incentive to work hard, so if she wasn't getting as much done as Paris wanted, it was Paris's fault. And it wasn't her fault she didn't have nice clothes. She didn't get paid enough to buy nice things. She had to shoplift to get nice things. And she deserved them as much as anybody—more, really, considering people were so mean to her.

Well, she would show Paris Montgomery, she thought, digging through the pile of clothes tangled in the sheets of the unmade bed. She was going to take Paris Montgomery's place, just like she'd taken Erin's place.

Jill knew she could be just as good a rider as Paris if only someone would give her the chance. She had never had a good enough horse, that was all. Her father had bought her a crummy, cheap Appaloosa to ride. How was she supposed to get anywhere in the jumping world on that? She had once written a letter to her mother's brother to see if he wouldn't buy her a real horse. She couldn't see why he wouldn't. He was rich, after all. What was seventy or eighty thousand dollars to him? But she had never heard a thing from him. Cheap bastard.

She'd show him too. She'd show everybody. She was going to be rich, and she was going to ride the best horses and go to the Olympics. She had it all planned. All she needed was a break, and she knew right where she was going to get it.

She pulled a see-through white stretch lace blouse out of the pile of clothes Erin had left behind. Jill had claimed the stuff for herself. Why not? It wasn't even stealing if the other person just left it. She struggled into the top. Even with the stretch, the front gapped open between the buttons. She undid the top three, showing cleavage and black bra. That helped. And it was sexy. It was just the kind of thing Britney Spears wore all the time. That was why Erin had bought it. Erin always dressed that way: crop tops and hip huggers. And guys had always had their eyes on her—including Don.

Jill rummaged through another pile. She came up with a purple stretch miniskirt she'd stolen from Wal-Mart. It had been on clearance, anyway. The store wasn't out that much. She stepped into it and wriggled and pushed and pulled until she had it in place. She had a serious panty line from the too-small thong, but she figured that was a good thing. It was like advertising.

A pair of big hoop earrings and a necklace from the pile of jewelry that had belonged to Erin, and the bangle bracelets she'd lifted from Bloomingdale's, and she was set. She squeezed her feet into a pair of platform sandals, grabbed her purse, and left the apartment. She was going to show everybody, and she was going to start tonight.

Landry sat at his desk feeling like an asshole, scrolling through pages on the computer screen. Friday night, and this was what he had going on in his life.

It was Estes' fault, he thought, scowling. He had let that become his mantra for the day. Like a thorn, she'd gotten under his skin to irritate him. Because of her he was sitting at his desk reading old newspaper stories.

The squad room was mostly empty. A couple of the night-shift guys were doing paperwork. Landry's shift was long over, and the other four guys he worked with had gone home to girlfriends or wives and kids, or were sitting in the usual watering hole drinking and bitching, as cops are wont to do.

Landry sat at his desk trying to dig something up on the horse people. Neither Jade nor his assistant had a criminal record. The groom who was allegedly fucking Jade had been picked up a couple of times for shoplifting, and once on a DUI. She had struck him as trouble, and he'd been right about that. He didn't believe she'd been with Jade Thursday night, but she'd felt compelled to give the guy an alibi just the same. Landry had to wonder why.

Did the girl know Jade had been involved in letting Michael Berne's horses loose? Had she done the job herself, and by giving Jade an alibi, given herself one as well? Maybe Jade had put her up to it. He seemed too sharp to risk pulling a stunt like that himself. If the girl got caught, he could always deny knowledge of what she'd been up to. He could say it was a misguided attempt to gain his approval.

Michael Berne certainly believed Jade had been behind the incident. Landry had interviewed him in the afternoon, and he'd thought Berne was going to cry or choke as he blamed Don Jade for all the problems in his life. What had Paris Montgomery said? That Berne blamed Jade for everything except his own lack of talent. Berne seemed to think Jade was the Antichrist, responsible for all evil in the horse business.

Maybe he wasn't all wrong.

Estes had told Landry about Jade's past the first time she'd come in, the schemes to kill horses for the insurance money. No one had touched the guy for any of that. Jade had slipped out from under it all like a greased snake.

Insurance fraud, killing horses—what might Erin Seabright know about any of that, Landry wondered. And why wasn't she around to ask?

He had put a call in that afternoon to the Ocala authorities to see if they could locate the girl up there, and he had put out an alert for all law enforcement officers in Palm Beach County to be on the look-out for her car. She had probably split town for a new job or a new boyfriend, but in case she hadn't, it wouldn't hurt to cover the bases.

And if anyone asked him what the hell he was doing, he would say it was all Estes' fault, he thought irritably.

He sipped his coffee and glanced over his shoulder. The night guys were still into their paperwork. Landry tapped a couple of keys and brought up a newspaper account of the Golam brothers' bust, two years prior. He had read it earlier in the day, knew what was in it, knew exactly the paragraph his eyes would go to: the paragraph that described narcotics detective Elena Estes hanging on the door of Billy Golam's truck, then falling beneath it. She had been dragged fifty yards down Okeechobee Boulevard, and was hospitalized in critical condition at the time the story had been written.

He wondered what she must have gone through since that day, how many weeks, months she'd lain in a hospital bed. He wondered what had possessed her to jump on that truck and try to wrestle con-trol of it from Billy Golam.

Narcs. Cowboys, every last one of them.

Two years had passed. He wondered what she'd been doing all that time, and why she'd come out of the shadows for this case. He wondered why her life was crossing paths with his.

He sure as hell didn't want the trouble that came with her. But there it was. He'd taken the bait. He was on the case now.

It was all Estes' fault.

Jill ran out the front door of The Players, huffing and hiccuping, fat tears spilling down her cheeks with a dirty stream of black mascara. She swiped the back of her hand under her running nose, then scraped a stringy strand of hair back out of her eyes.

The valets stood off to the side, staring at her, saying nothing. They didn't ask if they could get her car, because they knew by looking at her, she wouldn't have a car worth letting them park. They parked cars for beautiful people, rich people, thin people.

"What are you looking at?" Jill snapped. They looked at each other, smirking. "Fuck you!" she shouted and ran, crying, across the parking lot, falling off one platform sandal and turning her ankle. Stumbling, she dropped the beaded handbag she'd stolen at Neiman Marcus, and the contents spewed out of it across the pavement.

"Goddammit!" Crawling on her hands and knees, she broke a fingernail as she scraped at a tube of lipstick and a pack of condoms. "Fuck! Fuck!"

Spittle and tears and snot ran from her face onto the concrete. Jill folded herself over into a ball and sobbed, a wrenching, ugly noise. She was ugly. Her clothes were ugly. Even her crying was ugly. Pain swelled inside her like a blister and burst with another wave of tears.

Why? She had asked the question a million times in her life. Why did she have to be the fat one, the ugly one; the one nobody liked, much less loved? It wasn't fair. Why was she supposed to have to work hard to change herself when bitches like Erin and Paris just had it all?

She wiped her face on the sleeve of the white lace blouse, gathered her stuff together, and struggled to her feet. An elegant older couple walking away from a Jaguar stared at her with something like horror. Jill gave them the finger. The woman gasped and the man put his arm around her protectively and hustled her toward the building.

Jill opened her car and flung her purse and the things that had come out of it in the direction of the passenger's seat. She flung herself behind the wheel, slammed the door, and burst into tears again. She pounded her fists on the wheel, then against the window, then hit the horn by accident and startled at the blast of sound.

Her big plan. Her big seduction. What a fucking joke she was.

She'd gone into Players, knowing Jade would be there, thinking he would invite her for a drink, and she could flirt with him and let him know how she'd helped him out with that cop. He was supposed to have been thankful and impressed with her quick thinking, and grateful for her loyalty. And they were supposed to have ended up at his place, where he would fuck her brains out. Phase one in her plan to get rid of Paris.

But everything had gone wrong, because she could never get a break. The whole stupid world was against her. Jade hadn't arrived yet when she got there, and the maître d' had wanted to throw her out. She could tell by the way he looked her up and down, like he thought she was some cheap hooker or something. He hadn't believed her when she told him she was meeting someone. And the waitress and the bartender had put their heads together and snickered at her as she sat at a table, waiting like an idiot drinking Diet Coke because they wouldn't go for her fake ID and serve her booze. Then that creep Van Zandt had showed up, half-drunk, and invited himself to sit with her.

What a jerk. All the mean, rotten things she'd heard him say about her, and he thought he could just suddenly pretend to be nice to her and charm his way into her pants. He'd never taken his eyes off her cleavage for the first fifteen minutes. And when she told him she was waiting for someone else, he had the nerve to be offended. Like she'd ever want to have sex with an old guy like him. So what he'd slipped her a couple of drinks? That didn't mean she owed him a blowjob, which was what he had wanted. If she was going to suck dick tonight, it wasn't going to be his.

And then Jade had finally walked in. And he'd looked at her with such disgust, she had wanted to shatter like a piece of glass. His angry words rang in her ears as if he'd screamed them at her, when in reality he'd asked her out into a quiet hall and had never raised his voice above a near whisper.

"What were you thinking, coming in here dressed like that?" he demanded. "You're my employee. The things you do in public reflect on me."

"But I was just—"

"I don't want the words *street whore* associated with my barn."

Jill had gasped as if he'd slapped her. That was when Michael Berne had come into the hall. She had seen him from the corner of her eye, pretending to make a phone call, watching them.

"I see clients here," Jade went on. "I conduct business here."

"I j-just w-wanted to see you," she'd said, her breath hitching in her throat as tears welled up. "I w-wanted to tell you about—"

"What's the matter with you? Thinking you can come here and interrupt my evening?"

"B–but I have t–to tell you— I know about Stellar—"

"If you need to speak with me about something, we'll do it at the barn during business hours."

"B–but—"

"Is everything all right here?" Michael Berne asked, butting in like it was any of his business, the skinny freckled dork.

"This doesn't concern you, Michael," Jade said.

"The young lady seems upset." But when he looked at her, Jill had known he didn't care whether or not she was upset. He had looked at her the same way every other man had looked at her tonight—like she was selling it and she ought to be cutting her prices.

She had glared up at him through a wavy sheen of tears and said, "Butt out! We don't need you around here or anywhere else!"

Berne had moved away. "You ought to take your personal business somewhere private, Jade," he said like a prissy fruit. "This is really unprofessional."

Jade had waited until Berne was out of sight, then turned on her again, angrier than before. "Get out of here. Get out of here before you embarrass me any more than you already have. We'll talk about this tomorrow, first thing in the morning. If I can stand the sight of you."

He might as well have cut her with a knife. The pain had gone as deep inside her as if he had.

Fuck him, Jill thought now. Don Jade was her boss, not her father. He couldn't tell her how to dress or where she could and couldn't go. He couldn't call her a whore and get away with it.

All the hard work she did for Don Jade, and this was the way he treated her. She would have been his partner—in bed and out. She would have been loyal to him. She would have done anything for him. But he didn't deserve her or her loyalty and devotion. He deserved to have people betray him and stab him in the back. He deserved whatever happened to him.

An idea slowly began to take shape in Jill's mind as she sat there in her car. She didn't have to put up with being treated like dirt. She didn't have to stand for being called names. She could get a job with any stable she wanted. Fuck Don Jade.

She drove out of the parking lot and took a left on South Shore, heading for the equestrian center, paying no attention to the car that pulled out behind her.

15

Molly could hear Bruce and her mother arguing. She couldn't make out all the words, but the tone was unmistakable. She lay on the floor of her bedroom, near the air-conditioning duct. Her room was right above Bruce's office, where he often summoned her mother or Chad or Erin to shout at them for their latest sin against him. Molly had learned long ago to make herself inconspicuous to the men her mother dated. She made no exception for Bruce, even if he was technically now her father. She didn't think of him that way. She thought of him as someone whose house she happened to live in.

The argument was about Erin. Her sister's name had stood out in the rise and fall of the conversation. Something was definitely up. Her mother had already been upset when Molly had gotten home from school, pacing, nervous, darting out the back door to smoke one cigarette after another. Dinner had been delivered from Domino's. Krystal hadn't eaten any of it. Chad had bolted down enough to choke a wolf, then beat it out of the house before Bruce got home.

And when Bruce walked in the door, Krystal had immediately asked to speak to him in his office.

Molly's stomach was churning with worry. She had made out

Erin's name and had heard the word "police." Her mother's tone had gone from urgent to angry to hysterical to tears. Bruce just sounded angry. And intermingled with the voices was a mechanical sound, like the VCR going on, going off, rewinding. Molly couldn't imagine what it meant. Maybe Krystal had found a porno tape in Chad's room. But then, why had she heard Erin's name, not Chad's?

Heart pounding, Molly left her room and crept down the back staircase. The house was dark except for the light coming from the office. She made her way down the hall on her tiptoes, holding her breath. If the office door opened, she was caught. The family room was adjacent to the office. If she could just slip in there . . . She ducked into the corner behind the ficus tree and crouched down against the wall.

"We are not calling the police, Krystal," Bruce said. "First of all, I don't believe it's real. It's some kind of hoax—"

"But what if it isn't?"

"They said don't call the police."

"My God, I can't believe this is happening," Krystal said, her voice trembling.

"I don't know why not," Bruce said. "She's your daughter. You know she's never been anything but trouble."

"How can you talk that way?"

"Easily. It's true."

"You can be so fucking cruel. I don't believe it. Ouch! You're hurting me! Bruce!"

Tears welled up in Molly's eyes. She hugged her knees to her chest and tried not to shake.

"I've asked you not to use foul language, Krystal. You can't be a lady with the mouth of a sailor."

Krystal rushed to apologize. "I'm sorry. I'm sorry. I'm upset. I didn't mean it."

"You're irrational. You have to get control of yourself, Krystal. Think this through logically. The tape says no police."

"What will we do?"

"I'll handle it."

"But I think—"

"Has anyone asked you to think?"

"No."

"Who makes the decisions in this house, Krystal?"

Krystal drew a shaky breath. "The person who is best equipped to make them."

"And who is that person?"

"You."

"Thank you. Now leave it to me. Go take a pill and go to bed. There's nothing we can do tonight."

"Yes," Krystal said softly. "I think I will do that."

Molly knew from past experience her mother would take more than one pill, and she would wash it down with vodka. She would retreat into her own little world and pretend everything in her life was lovely and fine. Molly, meanwhile, felt sick to her stomach. Everything she'd heard frightened her. What had Erin done now? Something terrible, if Krystal wanted to call the police.

"I'm going for a drive to clear my head," Bruce said. "I had a terrible day. Now this."

Molly held very still, praying neither of them would come into the family room for any reason. She heard her mother's heels on the tile in the hall. Krystal always went up the main staircase because it was beautiful and she had always dreamed of living in a beautiful house. Bruce walked past the family room on his way to the kitchen. Molly stayed still until she heard him go out the door to the garage. She waited to hear his car start and for the garage door to close, and then she waited a little longer. When she was sure he had gone, she crept out of her hiding place and went into his office.

No one was allowed in Bruce's office when Bruce wasn't there. He expected everyone to respect his privacy even though he regularly invaded everyone else's. This was his house, and he never let any of them forget it.

Molly turned on the desk lamp and looked around at the bookshelves and the walls covered with photographs of Bruce shaking hands with important people, with Bruce's awards for this and that having to do with his job and with his service to the community. Everything in the room was placed exactly as Bruce wanted it, and he would know if one little thing got moved a fraction of an inch.

Molly checked over her shoulder as she picked up the remote for the television and VCR. She hit the play button and waited, so nervous she was shaking all over.

The movie started without any credits or titles or anything. A girl standing by a gate on a back road. Erin. Molly watched in horror as a van pulled up and a man in a mask jumped out and grabbed her and threw her into the van.

A strange mechanical voice came out of the speakers: "We have your daughter. Don't call the police—"

Tears flooding her glasses, Molly hit the stop button, hit eject, scrambled onto a chair, and reached up to snag the video out of the machine. She wanted to cry out loud. She wanted to throw up. She did neither.

Clutching the tape, she ran through the house to the laundry room and grabbed her jacket off the hook. She wrapped the tape in the jacket and tied the jacket around her waist. She was shaking so badly, she didn't know if she would have the strength to do what she had to. All she knew was that she had to try.

She opened the garage door, climbed on her bike, and took off, pedaling as hard as she could down the street and into the night.

16

Despite the fact that every law enforcement agent in Palm Beach County hated me, I did still have contacts in the profession. I called an FBI agent I knew from the field office in West Palm. Armedgian and another agent had coordinated with PBSO narcotics on a case that involved heroine dealers in West Palm Beach and a connection in France. Armedgian had handled all the work between our respective offices, the FBI liaison in Paris, French authorities, and Interpol. The case had lasted six months, and in that time, Armedgian had become not only a contact, but a friend—the kind of friend I could call and ask for information.

I called him at the end of the day and reintroduced myself. *It's Estes. Remember me? We'll always have Paris . . .* Of course, he said, though there was a pause first, and a tension in his voice.

I asked him to get me what he could on Tomas Van Zandt and World Horse Sales from Interpol. Again the pause. Was I back on the job? He thought I'd left the profession, after . . . well, after . . .

I explained to him I was helping out a friend who had gotten mixed up with this character in a business deal, and I'd heard the guy was a crook. I wasn't asking for anything but to find out if he had a record. That didn't seem too much, did it?

Armedgian made the customary noises of complaint and fear of discovery and censure. Federal agents were the kids in school who really did worry that going to the lavatory without a hall pass would put a black mark in their permanent records that would ruin their lives. But in the end he agreed to do the deed.

Tomas Van Zandt hadn't become what he was overnight. It wasn't unreasonable to assume if he had terrorized one girl, he had terrorized others. Maybe one of them had dared to go to the authorities. Then again, part of his control over Sasha Kulak had been the fact that she was a stranger in a strange land, and probably there illegally.

It made me furious to think about it. He was a predator preying on vulnerable women, whether they were his employees or his clients. And the truly infuriating thing about that was the fact that vulnerable women often either refuse to see the danger in a man like Van Zandt, or convince themselves they have no recourse but to suffer through. And a sociopath like Van Zandt could smell that a mile away.

I picked up his business card and looked at it. It was late, but I could still call him on his cell phone, apologize again for Irina's behavior, ask to meet him for a drink. . . . Maybe I'd get lucky and have to kill him in self-defense at the end of the evening.

I was reaching for the phone when something hit my front door with force. My hand went for the Glock I'd laid on the table to clean. My mind raced through scenarios in the blink of an eye. Then the pounding started and a small voice penetrated the wood.

"Elena! Elena!"

Molly.

I pulled the door open and the girl fell inside as if she'd been blown to the house by a hurricane. Her hair was matted with sweat. She was as pale as parchment.

"Molly, what's wrong? What's happened?"

I guided her to a chair and she melted into it like a limp noodle, so out of breath she was panting.

"How did you get here?"

"My bike."

"God. It's the dead of night. Why didn't you call me if you needed to see me?"

"I couldn't. I didn't dare."

"Have you heard something from Erin?"

She pulled off the jacket she'd worn tied around her waist and fumbled through the folds of cloth. Her hands were shaking violently as she fished out a videotape and thrust it at me.

I took the thing to the VCR, rewound it, and hit the play button. I watched the drama unfold as I knew Molly had, but with a quality to my sense of dread I knew she didn't have because she hadn't lived as long as I had or seen the things that I had seen. I watched her sister knocked to the ground and shoved into the white van. Then came the voice, mechanically altered to disguise or to frighten or both: "We have your daughter. Call the police, she dies. Three hundred thousand dollars. Directions later."

The picture went to static. I stopped the VCR and turned to look at Molly. Molly the Mini-Exec was gone. Molly the adult in disguise was nowhere in sight. Sitting at my table, looking small and fragile, was Molly the child, twelve years old and terrified for her big sister. Tears trapped behind the lenses of her Harry Potter glasses magnified the fear in her eyes.

She was trying very hard to be brave as she waited for something from me. That almost frightened me more than the video had.

I crouched in front of her, my hands braced on the arms of the chair. "Where did you get this, Molly?"

"I heard Mom and Bruce fighting about Erin," she said quickly. "When they went out of his office, I went in, and I found it."

"They've seen it."

She nodded.

"What did they do?"

The tears rolled out the sides of the glasses and down her cheeks. She spoke in a very, very small voice. "Nothing."

"They didn't call the police?"

"Bruce said he would handle it. Then he sent Mom to bed." She shook her head in disbelief. I could see the anger rise up inside her, bringing color to her face. "And he went for a drive to clear his head, because he had a *bad day*! I hate him!" she cried, slamming a small fist on the table. "I hate him! He won't do anything because he doesn't want her back! Erin's going to die because of him!"

The tears came in earnest now, and Molly fell against me, throwing her arms around my neck.

I've never known how to comfort people. Perhaps because I wasn't taught by example. Or perhaps I had always taken my own personal pain so deeply within me, I wouldn't allow anyone to touch it. But Molly's pain was overflowing, and she gave me no choice but to share it with her. I closed my arms around her and stroked her hair with one hand.

"It won't be up to him, Molly," I said. "You've got me, remember?"

In that moment I knew real fear. This was no longer a case I didn't want with a probable outcome of no big consequence. It wasn't a simple matter of working a job. I had a connection to this child in my arms. I had made a commitment. I who had wanted nothing more than to hide with my misery until I could find the nerve to check out.

I held her tighter, not for her, but for me.

I made a copy of the videotape, then we put Molly's bike in my trunk and headed for Binks Forest. It was nearly midnight.

17

Jill let herself into Jade's tack room and turned on the small lamp that sat on an antique chest. She grabbed a jug of leather oil from the supply shelves, twisted off the top, pulled open the drawer with Jade's show breeches in it, and doused the pants with oil. She knew from looking in the catalogs those breeches cost at least two hundred dollars each. She threw open the armoire, pulled out his two custom-made jackets, and soaked them both, then did the same with his freshly pressed, custom-made shirts.

It didn't seem enough. She wanted more satisfaction.

She was supposed to have cleaned the stalls at the end of the day because Javier, the Guatemalan guy, had to leave early. But Jill didn't like pitching shit, and so she had simply stirred the bedding around to cover it. She snickered now as she went to the first stall and took out Trey Hughes' gray horse. She put the horse in the empty stall where Stellar had lived, then took a pitchfork into the gray's stall and uncovered the piles of manure and the spots wet with urine. The smell of ammonia burned her nose and she smiled a malicious smile.

Setting the fork aside, she went back to the tack stall and grabbed up the pile of clothes.

Jade would have a fit when he found this mess. He would know she had done it, but he wouldn't be able to prove it. And he was supposed to be in the showring in the morning. He wouldn't have any clothes. His horses wouldn't be ready. And Jill would be busy lying on the beach, getting a tan and looking for a hot guy.

She spread the clothing out in the stall, over the piles of shit and spots of pee, then went around and around the stall, stomping on Don Jade's expensive clothing, grinding it into the mess. This would teach him not to treat people like servants. He couldn't humiliate her and get away with it. Big asshole. He was going to regret what he'd done to her. She could have been his ally, his spy. Instead, he could rot.

"Fuck you, Don Jade. Fuck you, Don Jade." She chanted the words as she marched around the stall.

She had no fear of being caught by Jade. He was back at that snotty club, trying to impress some client or some woman. Paris was supposed to have night check, but Jill knew for a fact she hardly ever did it when it was her turn.

It didn't occur to Jill that someone from another stable might come through the barn, or that a security guard might be making rounds. She almost never got caught doing stuff. Like keying stupid Erin's car. Everyone assumed Chad did it because Chad had been there that night and he and Erin had argued. And Jill had once had a job at a Wal-Mart where she had stolen all kinds of stuff, right under her manager's nose. It served the store right, getting ripped off, if they were stupid enough to hire a guy as dumb as that guy had been.

"Fuck you, Don Jade. Fuck you, Don Jade," she chanted, happily grinding his clothes into the muck.

And then the stable lights went out.

Jill stopped marching and stood very still. She could feel her heart beating. The sound of it in her ears made it impossible to hear if someone was coming. As her eyes adjusted she could make out shapes, but the stall she was in was too far to the back of the tent to get much light from the big light pole out by the road.

Some of the horses turned around in their stalls. Some nickered— nervously, Jill thought. She felt around the wall blindly, trying to find the pitchfork. She'd left it on the far side of the stall. She turned her back to the door as she groped for it.

It happened so fast, she couldn't react. Someone rushed in behind her. She heard the rustle of the stall bedding, felt the presence of another person. Before she could scream, a hand was over her mouth. Her own hands closed desperately on the handle of the pitchfork, and she twisted around, trying to wriggle from her captor's grasp, breaking the hold, stumbling backward, swinging the pitchfork in a wide arch, hitting something. Her grip on the handle was too near the end of it, giving her little control or strength in her swing, and it flew out of her hands and thumped against the canvas wall.

She tried to scream then, and couldn't. As in a nightmare, the sound died in her throat. In that split second she knew she was going to die.

Still, she tried to run for the door. Her legs felt as heavy as lead. Her feet tangled in the clothes on the floor of the stall. Like a lasso around her ankles, the clothes pulled her feet out from under her. She fell forward, heavily, knocking the wind from her lungs. Her attacker came down on top of her from behind.

There was a sound—a voice—but she couldn't hear it above the pounding in her ears and the wrenching sound from her own throat as she tried to breathe and sob and beg. She felt the miniskirt being pulled up over her butt, a hand digging between her legs, tearing at the too-small thong.

She tried to pull herself forward. There was a terrible pressure in the middle of her back, then against the back of her head, forcing her head down, pushing her face into the manure she was supposed to have cleaned out of the stall that day. She couldn't breathe. She tried to turn her head and couldn't; tried to suck in air and her mouth filled with shit; tried to vomit and felt a terrible burning in her chest.

And then she didn't feel anything at all.

18

The Seabrights' neighborhood was silent, all the big lovely homes dark, their inhabitants blissfully ignorant of the dysfunction next door. There were still lights on downstairs on one end of the Seabright home. The second story was dark. I wondered if Krystal really was sleeping.

Bruce had "sent her to bed," Molly had said. As if she were a child. Her daughter had been abducted and her husband told her to go to bed. He would handle it. If Krystal hadn't seen the tape, I wondered if Bruce would have simply thrown it in the trash like a piece of junk mail.

Molly let us in the front door and led the way to Bruce Seabright's home office, the source of the lights. The office door stood open. Bruce was inside, muttering under his breath as he searched the bookcases near the television.

"Looking for this?" I asked, holding up the video.

He spun around. "What are you doing here? How did you get into my house?"

His glare hit on Molly half hiding behind me. "Molly? Did you let this person in?"

"Elena can help—"

"Help with what?" he said, choosing denial even while I stood there with the tape of his stepdaughter's kidnapping in hand. "We don't need her help for anything."

"You think you can handle this on your own?" I asked, tossing the tape on his desk.

"I think you can leave my home or I can call the police."

"That threat doesn't work with me. I thought you learned that lesson this morning."

His mouth pulled into a tight knot as he stared at me with narrowed eyes.

"Elena used to be a detective with the Sheriff's Office," Molly said, moving out of my shadow. "She knows all about those people Erin worked with, and—"

"Molly, go to bed," Seabright ordered curtly. "I'll deal with you tomorrow, young lady. Eavesdropping on conversations, coming into my office without permission, bringing this person into my home. You've got a lot to answer for."

Molly kept her chin up and gave her stepfather a long look. "So do you," she said. Then she turned and left the room with the dignity of a queen.

Seabright went to the door and closed it. "How did she know to call you?"

"Believe it or not, the people living in *your* house do have lives and minds of their own, and allow themselves to think without asking your permission. I'm sure you'll put a stop to that, now that you know."

"How dare you criticize the way I run my house? You don't know anything about my family."

"Oh, I know all about your family. Believe me," I said, hearing an old bitterness in my tone. "You're the demigod and the mortals revolve around you like planets around the sun."

"Where do you get off speaking to me this way?" he asked, advancing toward me, trying to get me to back away literally and figuratively. I didn't move.

"I'm not the one who has explaining to do, Mr. Seabright. Your stepdaughter has been kidnapped and Molly is the only person who seems to care whether she's ever seen alive again. What do you have to say about that?"

"I don't have anything to say to you. None of this is any of your business."

"I've made it my business. When, where, and how did this tape arrive?"

"I don't have to answer your questions." He walked past me as if to dismiss me, going back to the bookcases to close the doors on his television.

"Would you rather answer the questions of a sheriff's detective?" I asked.

"They said no police," he reminded me as he moved a bookend two inches to the left. "Do you want to be responsible for the girl's death?"

"No. Do you?"

"Of course not." He straightened a stack of books, his eyes already moving in search of the next piece of his kingdom out of place. Nervous, I thought.

"But if she simply never came back, you wouldn't exactly mourn her loss, would you?" I said.

"That's an obnoxious thing to say."

"Yes, well . . ."

He stopped rearranging and put on a face of high affront. "What kind of a man do you think I am?"

"I don't think you'd really like me to answer that right now. When did this tape arrive, Mr. Seabright? Erin hasn't been seen or heard from in nearly a week. Kidnappers usually want their money ASAP. It's rather the point of the thing, you see. The longer they hang on to a victim, the shorter the odds of something going wrong."

"The tape just came," he said, but he didn't look at me when he said it. I was willing to bet he'd had it for a couple of days.

"And the kidnappers haven't called."

"No."

"How did the tape arrive?"

"In the mail."

"To the house or to your office?"

"The house."

"Addressed to you or to your wife?"

"I—I don't recall."

To Krystal. And he'd kept it from her. He probably screened all her mail, the controlling prick. And when she'd finally seen it, he'd sent her to bed and gone out for a drive.

"I'd like to see the envelope," I said.

"I threw it out."

"Then it's in your trash. Let's go get it. There could be fingerprints on it, and the postmark could provide valuable information."

"It's gone."

"Gone where? Your trash was at the curb yesterday. If the tape arrived today..."

He had no answer for that, the son of a bitch. I heaved a sigh of disgust and tried again.

"Have they called?"

"No."

"God help you if you're lying, Seabright."

His face flushed purple. "How dare you call me a liar."

"You are."

We both turned toward the door to find Krystal standing there looking like an aging crack whore. Her face was drawn and pale. Mascara ringed her eyes. Her bleached hair stood up like a fright wig. She wore a short pink robe trimmed with feathery flounces around the neck and cuffs, and matching high-heeled mules.

"You are a liar," she said, glassy eyes fixed on her husband.

"You're drunk," Bruce accused.

"I must be. I know better than to speak to you out of turn."

I watched Seabright. He was furious, trembling with anger. If I had not been there, I don't know what he might have done. But then, if I hadn't been there, Krystal would never have had the nerve to say anything. I turned to her, taking in the dilated pupils and the smudged lipstick.

"Mrs. Seabright, when did you first see the tape of your daughter's kidnapping?"

"I had seen the box. It had my name on it. I didn't know why Bruce hadn't given it to me. I thought it was something I had ordered through the mail."

"Krystal..." Bruce growled.

"What day was that?"

Her mouth trembled. "Wednesday."

Two days.

"I didn't see any point in upsetting you with it," Seabright said. "Look at you. Look what it's done to you."

"I found it today," she said to me. "My daughter's been kidnapped. Bruce didn't think I should know about that."

"I told you, I will handle it, Krystal," he said through his teeth.

Krystal looked at me, tragic, pathetic, terrified. "In our family, we leave the decisions to the person best equipped to make them."

I looked hard at Bruce Seabright. He was perspiring. He knew he could intimidate a woman like Krystal, but he could not intimidate me.

"I'm going to ask you one last time, Mr. Seabright. And before you answer, know that the Sheriff's Office can pull your local usage details from the phone company and verify the information. Have the kidnappers called?"

He put his hands on his hips and looked up at the ceiling, weighing the pros and cons of denial. He wasn't the type to openly defy the cops. If he took my word on the phone records, and thought about what would happen if the Sheriff's Office became involved...his public image could be damaged...I held my breath.

"Last night."

A strange sound of anguish wrenched out of Krystal Seabright and she doubled over the back of a fat leather chair as if she'd been shot.

Seabright puffed himself up like a furious pigeon as he tried to justify his behavior. "First of all, I think the whole thing is a hoax. This is just Erin trying to humiliate me—"

"I'm up to my back teeth with men and their persecution theories today," I said. "I don't want to hear yours. I saw the tape. I know the kind of people Erin has been mixed up with. I wouldn't be willing to bet her life against your fear of embarrassment. Who called? A man? A woman?"

"It sounded like the voice on the tape," he said impatiently. "Distorted."

"What did it say?"

He didn't want to answer. His mouth pulled into that pissy little knot I wanted to slap off his face.

"Why should I tell you any of this?" he said. "I don't know anything about you. I don't know who you're working for. I don't know that you're not one of them."

"For God's sake, tell her!" Krystal cried. She slipped around the side of the leather chair and crawled into it, curling herself into a fetal position.

"And how do I know you're not?" I returned. "How does your wife know you're not?"

"Don't be ridiculous," Seabright snapped.

"*Ridiculous* isn't the word I'd use to describe it, Mr. Seabright. Erin has been a source of considerable irritation to you. Maybe you saw a way to eliminate the problem."

"Oh my God!" Krystal cried, putting her hands over her mouth.

"That's absurd!" Seabright shouted.

"I don't think the Sheriff's Office will think so," I said. "So you'd better start coming up with the details."

He heaved another sigh, the put-upon patriarch. "The voice said to put the money in a cardboard box and leave it in a specific spot at the Equestrian Estates horse-show grounds out in Loxahatchee somewhere."

I knew the area. Twenty minutes from Wellington, Equestrian Estates was an as-yet-undeveloped development. More or less wide-open spaces with a show grounds used only several times a year.

"When?"

"Today. Five o'clock."

"And did you leave the money?"

"No."

Krystal was sobbing. "You killed her! You killed her!"

"Oh, for God's sake, Krystal, stop it!" he snapped. "If she's really kidnapped, they aren't going to kill her. What would be the point?"

"The only point is to get the money," I said coldly. "They'll try to get it whether she's alive or not. Did they promise you would see Erin at the drop site? Did they say you'd be able to pick her up somewhere else if you came through with the cash?"

"They didn't say."

There was no guarantee Erin wasn't already dead. If the kidnapper was ruthless enough, she might have been killed in short order after the abduction to eliminate her as a possible witness later, and simply to make the kidnapper's life easier. Or that might have been the point all along—to eliminate her—with a dummied-up kidnapping plot thrown over it for camouflage.

"Have they called since?"

"No."

"I find that hard to believe. If I was expecting three hundred thousand at five in the afternoon and it didn't show, I'd want to know why."

He lifted his hands and walked away to a window where half-opened plantation shutters let in the darkness. I watched him and wondered just how cold a man he was. Cold enough to knowingly throw his stepdaughter to a sexual predator? Cold enough to have her killed? Maybe.

The one thing I had difficulty accepting was the idea of Seabright relinquishing control in any kind of collaborative scheme that would leave him vulnerable. But his only other choice would have been to dirty his hands himself, and that I didn't see at all. Conspiracy was the lesser of evils. Conspiracy could always be denied.

My gaze fell on Seabright's desk, immaculate in its organization. Perhaps I would see a file lying there labeled: KIDNAP ERIN. Instead, I stopped at the telephone, a Panasonic cordless with a caller ID window on the handset. The same phone I had in Sean's guest house. I went behind the desk, sat down in the leather executive's chair, and picked up the phone. The caller ID light on the base was blinking red.

"What are you doing?" Bruce demanded, hurrying back across the room.

I pressed the search button on the handset, and a number appeared in the display window. "I'm taking advantage of the miracle of modern technology. If the kidnapper called you on this line from a phone that wasn't blocked, the number will be stored in the memory of this unit and can be checked against a reverse directory. Isn't that terribly clever?"

I jotted the number on his spotless blotter, scrolled to the next stored number, and noted it. He wanted to snatch the phone out of my hand. I could see the muscles working in his jaw.

"My clients and business associates call me here," he said. "I won't have you harassing them."

"How do you know one of them isn't the kidnapper?" I asked.

"That's insane! These are wealthy and respectable people."

"Maybe all but one."

"I don't want people dragged into this mess."

"Do you have any enemies, Mr. Seabright?" I asked.

"Of course not."

"You've never pissed anybody off? A man in land development in south Florida? That would be astonishing."

"I'm a reputable businessman, Ms. Estes."

"And you're about as likable as dysentery," I said. "I can't believe you don't have a list of people who would be pleased to see you suffer. And I'm only thinking of your immediate family."

He hated me. I could see it in his small, mean eyes. I found the notion satisfying, the feeling mutual.

"I will have your license number," he said tightly. "I have every intention of reporting you to the proper authorities."

"Then I would be stupid to give it to you, wouldn't I?" I said, making note of another call. The phone reported having stored thirteen numbers since last having been cleared. "Besides, I don't see that you're in any position to complain about me, Mr. Seabright. I know too much you'd rather not read about in the newspapers."

"Are you threatening me?"

"I'm always amazed when people have to ask that question," I said. "Do you owe money to anyone?"

"No."

"Do you gamble?"

"No!"

"Do you know a man named Tomas Van Zandt?"

"No. Who is he?"

"Did you arrange for Erin to get the job working for Don Jade?"

I noted the last of the stored phone numbers and looked up at him.

"What difference does that make?" he asked.

"Did you?"

He seemed nervous again. He straightened a humidor on the desktop a sixteenth of an inch.

"It would be quite a coincidence if Erin had simply stumbled into a job with the trainer of the client you sold a hugely expensive property to."

"What does this have to do with anything?" he demanded. "So I might have mentioned she was looking for a job with horses. So what?"

I shook my head, tore the page of numbers off the blotter, and stood. I looked at Krystal, still huddled in the leather chair, eyes glassy, locked in her own private hell. I wanted to ask her if she thought it was worth it—the house, the clothes, the car, the money—but she was probably suffering enough without me accusing her of selling out her own child. I gave her one of the cards with my phone number on it, and laid one on the desk.

"I'll run these numbers and see what I come up with," I said. "Call me immediately if you hear from the kidnappers. I'll do what I can. In my professional opinion, you should call the Sheriff's Office, the detective division, and ask to speak directly to Detective James Landry."

"But they said no police," Seabright said, a little too happy to comply with that demand.

"Plain clothes, plain car. No one will know he isn't a Jehovah's Witness."

Seabright pouted. "I don't want other people making decisions for my family."

"No? Well, contrary to your egomania, you are not best equipped to make these decisions," I said. "You need professional help with this. And if you don't want to accept it, I'll cram it down your throat."

19

Two-forty A.M. Bruce Seabright couldn't sleep. He didn't try. He had no desire to share a bed with Krystal tonight, even though he knew she was unconscious. He was too agitated to sleep, or even to sit. He had spent an hour cleaning his office: polishing the fingerprints from the furniture, wiping down every item on the desk, spraying the telephone with Lysol. His inner sanctum had been breeched, contaminated.

Krystal had come in here without his knowledge and pawed through the mail on his desk, even though he had told her very specifically never to do that. He always handled the mail. And Molly had come in and taken the videotape. He had expected better of both of them. The disappointment was bitter in his mouth. The order of his world had been upset, and now that bitch private investigator was trying to take over. He wouldn't stand for it. He would find out who she was working for, and he would make sure she never worked again.

He paced the room, breathing deeply the scents of lemon oil and disinfectant, trying to calm himself.

He never should have married Krystal. That had been a mistake.

He had known her eldest daughter would be a problem he would end up having to deal with, and here he was.

He opened the television cabinet, pulled a video from the shelf, and popped it in the VCR and hit play.

Erin, naked, chained to a bed, trying to cover herself.

"Look at the camera, bitch. Say your line."

She shakes her head, tries to hide her face.

"Say it! You want me to make you?"

She looks at the camera.

"Help me."

Bruce ejected the tape and put it in its cardboard sleeve. He went to the small secret wall safe hidden behind a row of books on real estate law, opened the safe, put the tape inside, and locked it away. No one else would see the tape. That was his decision. He was best equipped to make it.

20

I have never been hindered by the belief that people are basically good. In my experience, people are basically selfish, and often cruel.

I slept for three hours because my body didn't give me a choice. I woke because my brain wouldn't let me rest. I rose and fed the horses, then showered and went to my computer in a T-shirt and underpants and started tracing the phone numbers from Bruce Seabright's phone using a reverse directory on the Internet.

Of the thirteen numbers, six were unlisted with a Wellington prefix, four came back with names, one came back to Domino's Pizza, and two calls had come from the same Royal Palm Beach number, also with no listing. Seabright claimed the kidnapper had called only once, but I didn't believe him. He'd been a no-show for the drop. I couldn't believe he wouldn't have gotten a call after that.

I dialed the Royal Palm number and listened to it ring unanswered. No cheerful greeting: Kidnappers R Us.

I dialed the unlisted numbers, one by one, getting answering machines and maids, and waking up a couple of very cranky people who would no doubt be calling Bruce Seabright's office to complain about his new assistant.

I dialed the Sheriff's Office, wending my way through the various receptionists to get to Landry's voice mail, at the same time checking my e-mail for word from my FBI contact on the inquiry to Interpol. Nothing yet. As I listened to Landry's message and jotted down his pager number, I considered calling Armedgian to hasten a response, but decided not to press my luck. Any info from abroad would just be corroboration. I already knew Van Zandt was a world-class sleaze.

Was he bold enough to try kidnapping? Why not? He'd been just a step away from it with Irina's friend, Sasha Kulak. If Bruce Seabright had set up Erin's job through Trey Hughes, it stood to reason Van Zandt could have found out Erin was connected to the Fairfields developer. Developers take in a lot of money, he might have reasoned. Why shouldn't he be entitled to some? Motive: greed. He knew the girl, knew the show grounds, knew when people would be around and when they wouldn't. Opportunity.

Means? I knew Van Zandt had a video camera, so he could have made the tape. The distortion device would have disguised his accent. What about the white van? Where had it come from, and if Van Zandt had been running the video camera, then who was the guy in the mask?

Scum finds its own level. There were plenty of people skulking in the shadows of the show grounds who could have been persuaded to do just about anything for money. Decent people might not have been able to find them, but Tomas Van Zandt was not a decent person.

The truly disturbing possibility of Van Zandt as the kidnapper was his possible connection to Bruce Seabright and Seabright's lack of action on the ransom demand. But if Seabright was connected, then why would the videotape have been addressed to Krystal? And why would he have tried to hide it from her? If the projected outcome was in fact to get rid of Erin but make it look like a kidnapping gone wrong, Seabright needed corroboration on his end. It didn't make sense for him to keep it to himself.

His lack of action couldn't be denied, whatever his motive. I was willing to bet he had yet to act, despite my threat.

I dialed Landry's pager and left my number. Avadonis Farms would come up in his caller ID. That gave me a better shot for a return call. He would have taken one look at my name and hit the erase button.

While I waited for the phone to ring, I poured a cup of coffee, paced, and considered other angles. The fact that Erin had cared for Stellar and Stellar was dead; the possible connections to Jade, with his shadowy past. The fact that Erin had been involved with Chad Seabright; the fact they had been seen arguing two days before her disappearance. She'd dumped him—for an older man, Chad said. She'd had a thing for her boss, Molly said.

The phone rang. I scooped it up and answered.

"This is Detective James Landry. I received a page from this number."

"Landry. Estes. Erin Seabright has been kidnapped. Her parents received a videotape and a ransom demand."

Silence on the other end as he digested that.

"Do you still think it's not a case?" I asked.

"When did they get the demand?"

"Thursday. The stepfather was supposed to make the drop yesterday. He took a pass."

"Excuse me?"

"It's a long story. Let's meet somewhere. I'll fill you in, then take you to them."

"That won't be necessary," he said. "I'll get the details from the parents. Thanks for the tip, but I don't want you there."

"I don't care whether you want me there or not," I said flatly. "I'll be there."

"Hindering an official investigation."

"So far, hindering has been your area of expertise," I said. "There wouldn't be an investigation but for me. The stepfather doesn't want to do anything. He'd be happy to say 'oh well' and hope the perps dump the girl in a canal with an anchor around her waist. I've got a three-day jump on you and an in with the people the girl worked for."

"You're not a cop anymore."

"And I needed you to remind me of that. Fuck you, Landry."

"I'm just saying. You don't call the shots, Estes. You want to lord it over somebody, hire a minion. I don't work for you or with you."

"Fine. Then I'll keep what I know to myself. See you there, asshole."

I hung up and went to dress.

There are few creatures on earth more pigheaded than cops. I can say this with surety, because I am one. I may no longer have carried a badge, but that isn't what being a cop means. Being a cop is in the nature, in the bones. A cop is a cop, regardless of status, regardless of uniform, regardless of agency, regardless of age.

I understood Landry because we were related by calling. I didn't like him, but I understood him. I suspected he understood me on one level as well as anyone could. He wouldn't admit to it, and he didn't like me, but he knew where I stood.

I pulled on a pair of tan slacks and a black sleeveless T-shirt. The phone rang again as I was strapping on my watch.

"Where do you live?" he asked.

"I don't want you coming to my house."

"Why not? Are you selling crack? Fencing stolen goods? What are you afraid of?"

I didn't want my sanctuary breached, but I wouldn't tell him that. Never willingly reveal a vulnerability to an adversary. My reluctance was telling enough. I gave him the address and cursed myself for giving him that tiny victory.

"I'll be there in thirty," he said, and hung up.

I buzzed him through the gate in twenty-three.

"Nice digs," Landry said, looking at Sean's house.

"I'm a guest." I led the way from the parking area near the barn toward the guest house.

"It pays to know people who don't live in cardboard boxes and eat out of Dumpsters."

"Is that your social circle?" I asked. "You could aim a little higher. You live at the marina, after all."

He gave me the look—suspicious, offended I would have knowledge of him without his permission. "How do you know that?"

"I checked you out. Idle hands and the World Wide Web . . ."

He didn't like that at all. Good. I wanted him to know I was smarter than he was.

"Your blood type is AB negative, and you voted Republican in the last election," I said, opening my front door. "Coffee?"

"Do you know how I take it?" he asked sarcastically.

"Black. Two sugars."

He stared at me.

I shrugged. "Lucky guess."

He stood on the other side of the kitchen peninsula with his arms crossed over his chest. He should have been on a recruiting poster. Starched white shirt with thin burgundy stripes, blood-red tie, the aviator shades, the military posture.

"You look like a fed," I commented. "What's up with that? Agency envy?"

"Why are you so curious about me?" he asked, irritated.

"Knowledge is power."

"So this is some kind of game to you?"

"Not at all. I just like to know who I'm dealing with."

"You know me as well as you're going to," he said. "Fill me in on the Seabrights."

I played the videotape for him and told him what had happened the night before at the Seabright house. He didn't bat an eye at any of it.

"You think the stepfather has some kind of angle on this?" he asked.

"There's no question how he feels about Erin, and it's certainly strange the way he's handled things so far. I don't like his connections. But if this kidnapping is staged and he's a party to it, why be secretive with the tape? I don't get that."

"Control, maybe," Landry said, running the tape back and playing it again. "Maybe he waits until it's over and the girl is dead, then he shows the tape to the wife and tells her how he was protecting her from the awful truth and he handled the situation as he thought best."

"Ah, yes. The decisions in the family are left to the person best equipped to make them," I muttered.

"What?"

"The family motto. Bruce Seabright is a serious control freak. Pathological. Egotistical, a bully, psychologically abusive. The family is something out of Tennessee Williams."

"Then it fits."

"Yes," I agreed. "The thing is, this girl existed in a veritable snake pit. I can name three other legitimate suspects."

"Then do."

I told him about Chad Seabright, and told him again about Don Jade.

"And I'm waiting to hear from a connection to Interpol about priors on Tomas Van Zandt. He has a history of bad behavior toward young women, and by all accounts he's as crooked as a dog's hind leg."

"Charming crowd these horse people," Landry said.

"The horse world is a microcosm. The good, the bad; the beautiful, the ugly."

"The haves and have-nots. That's what keeps the prisons full," Landry said. "Jealousy, greed, and sexual perversion."

"Make the world go round."

Landry sighed and backed the tape up again. "And what's your stake in this mess, Estes?"

"I told you. I'm helping out the little sister."

"Why? Why did she come to you?"

"It's a long story that doesn't really matter. I'm in it now, and I'm staying in it to the end. Do you have a problem with that?"

"Yeah, I do," he said, his attention on the television. "But I'm sure that won't stop you."

"No, it won't."

He hit the pause button and squinted at the screen. "Can you make out that tag number?"

"No. I tried. I couldn't make it out on Seabright's tape either. You'll need a technical wizard.

"Look, Landry, I'm already on the inside with Jade's people," I said. "I'm more than willing to work with you. You'd be stupid to take a pass on that. You're a lot of things, I'm sure, but I don't think stupid is one of them."

He gave me a long look, trying to see something beyond what I would allow him to see.

"I've done my homework too," he said. "You're a loose cannon, Estes. You always were, the way I hear it. I don't like that. You think this Seabright guy is a control freak. I consider that a virtue. When I'm on a case, I own it. Period. I don't want to be in this thing and wondering what the hell you're going to pull next. And I can guarantee no one else in the SO is going to stand for that either. My lieutenant finds out you've got your fingers in this, he'll have my ass."

"I can't do anything about that. I am in it, and I'm staying in it. I said I'll work with you, but I don't work for you. You don't control me, Landry. If that's your focus, we have a problem. There's only one goal here: getting Erin Seabright out alive. If you think it's some kind of contest, you can keep your dick in your pants. I'm sure yours is bigger than anybody's, but I don't want to see it. Thanks anyway.

"Now can we get on this?" I asked. "We're burning daylight."

Landry took a beat, then motioned toward the door. "Lead the way. I hope I don't regret this."

I returned his look and his sentiment. "That makes two of us."

Bruce Seabright was not happy to see me. He came to the door himself—no doubt having forbidden everyone else to—dressed for golf in khakis and a tangerine polo shirt. He had the same tasseled loafers as Van Zandt. It was now 8:15 A.M.

"Mr. Seabright, this is Detective Landry with the Sheriff's Office," I said. Landry held up his shield. "He tells me he hasn't heard from you."

"It's Saturday," Seabright said. "I didn't know how early I could call."

"So you thought you'd get eighteen in before you tried?" I asked.

"Ms. Estes tells me your stepdaughter has been abducted," Landry said.

Seabright glared at me. "The kidnappers said no police, so I didn't call the police. I certainly hope Ms. Estes hasn't put Erin in greater danger by bringing you here."

"I don't think this trumps blowing off the ransom drop," I said. "May we come in?"

He stepped back reluctantly, and closed the door behind us lest the neighbors see.

"Have you received any further communication from the kidnappers?" Landry asked as we followed Seabright to the inner sanctum. There was no sign of Krystal. The house was as silent as a mausoleum. I spied Molly crouched in the upstairs hall, peering down at us through the balusters.

"No."

"You last heard from them when?"

"Thursday night."

"Why didn't you pay the ransom, Mr. Seabright?"

Seabright closed the doors of his office and turned around to go behind his desk. Landry had already taken a position there, standing behind the desk chair with his hands resting on the chair back.

"I'm sure Ms. Estes has told you, I'm not convinced this whole thing isn't a hoax."

"You're convinced enough not to call the Sheriff's Office for fear of what might happen to Erin, but not enough to pay the ransom?" Landry said. "I'm not sure I understand that, Mr. Seabright."

Seabright paced the end of the room with his hands on his hips. "I'm sorry I don't know the protocol for kidnapping victims. This is my first time."

"Do you have the money?"

"I can get it."

"On a Saturday?"

"If I have to. The president of my bank is a personal friend. I do an enormous amount of business with him."

"Good," Landry said. "Call him. Tell him you may need to ask him a favor later today. You need three hundred thousand dollars in marked bills. He'll need some lead time to get that together. Tell him someone from the Sheriff's Office will meet him at the bank to assist him."

Seabright looked shocked. "B–but we're not actually going to give them the money, are we?"

"You are if you ever want to see your stepdaughter alive again," Landry said. "You do want that, don't you, Mr. Seabright?"

Seabright closed his eyes and huffed a sigh. "Yes. Of course."

"Good. I'll have people out here within the hour to put a tap on your phone. When the next call comes in we'll be able to trace its origin. You'll set up the drop. You'll tell them you'll show with the money, but Erin has to be there where you can see her or it's a no-go. They already know you're not a pushover. If they haven't already killed her, they'll bring her. They want the money, not the girl."

"I can't believe any of this is happening," Seabright muttered. "You'll be there? At the drop?"

"Yes. I've already spoken with my lieutenant about your situation. He'll be calling shortly to speak with you himself."

"What about the FBI?" Seabright asked. "Don't they always get involved with kidnappings?"

"It's not automatic. They can be called in if you like."

"I don't. This is way out of hand already. They said not to call the police, now my home is going to be crawling with them."

"We'll be very discreet, Mr. Seabright," Landry said. "I'll want to speak to everyone living in the house."

"My wife is sedated. Other than Krystal, it's just myself, my son Chad, and Krystal's younger daughter, Molly."

"Detective Landry is aware of the sexual relationship between Erin and Chad," I told him. Color spread up Seabright's neck like the red in a thermometer. "He'll definitely want to speak with Chad."

"My son has absolutely nothing to do with this."

"Because you say so?" I challenged. "Your son had plenty to do with Erin. He was seen at her apartment two nights before she disappeared, arguing with her."

"That was all her doing," Seabright said bitterly. "Erin goaded him into a relationship just to spite me."

"You don't think Chad would want to spite you for his own sake?"

Seabright came over and stuck a finger in front of my face. "I've had it with you and your accusations. I don't care who you're working for, I don't want you here. The Sheriff's Office is involved now. I'm sure they don't have any use for a private investigator either. Do you, Detective?"

Seabright looked to Landry. Landry looked at me, his face as unreadable as mine.

"Actually," Landry said. "Ms. Estes' cooperation in this is very important, Mr. Seabright. I wouldn't be here if not for her."

Good cop, bad cop. I almost smiled.

"Perhaps you'd like to explain *that* to Detective Landry's lieutenant," I said to Seabright.

He wanted to put his hands around my throat and choke me. I could see it in his eyes.

"I'm sure he'll be very interested to hear all about how you didn't want to be bothered with your stepdaughter's kidnapping," I went on, walking away from him. "You know, Detective Landry, maybe you *should* call in the FBI. I've got a friend in the regional office I could reach out to. After all, this could have international implications if one of the foreign nationals at the equestrian center is involved. Or it could involve some out-of-state client of Mr. Seabright's. If Erin has been taken across a state line, it automatically becomes a federal case."

All I had to do was mention his business dealings and Seabright's sphincter curled into a French knot.

"I don't like being threatened," he pouted.

I walked past him again, leaning toward his ear as I murmured, "That would be the point."

"Your focus needs to be on your stepdaughter, Mr. Seabright," Landry said. "Complaining about the people who seem to care more about this girl than you do isn't going to stand you in very good stead. Do you understand what I'm saying?"

"You're making me feel like I should call my attorney," Seabright said.

"Feel free to do that if you have concerns about talking to me."

That shut him up. He rubbed his hands over his face and looked up at the ceiling.

"Do you consider *me* a suspect?" he asked.

"Investigations of this type of crime are always of a two-pronged nature, Mr. Seabright. We have to consider possibilities both outside the family and within it," Landry said. "I'd like to speak with your son now. Is he home?"

Seabright went to an intercom panel on the wall and pressed a button. "Chad, would you come to my office, please?"

I imagined being elsewhere in the Seabright home, Bruce Seabright's voice ringing out of the walls. All he needed was a remote-control burning bush and his image would be complete.

"Has Chad been in any kind of trouble with the law, Mr. Seabright?" Landry asked.

Seabright looked offended. "My son is an honor student."

A polite knock sounded against the door and Chad Seabright stuck his head in the room, then slipped inside with the expression of a shy, hopeful puppy. He was dressed neatly in khakis and a navy Tommy Hilfiger polo. He looked ready to hit the links with the Young Republicans.

"Chad, this is Detective Landry and Ms. Estes," Bruce Seabright said. "They want to ask you some questions about Erin."

Chad put on big eyes. "Wow. Sure. I've already spoken with Ms. Estes. She knows I haven't seen Erin. I wish I could be more helpful."

"You and Erin had a relationship," Landry said.

Chad looked embarrassed. "That was over. I admit that was wrong. It just sort of happened. Erin is very persuasive."

"You had an argument with her last week. What was that about?"

"We broke up."

"Chad!" Bruce Seabright snapped. "You told me it was over months ago! When Erin moved out."

Chad looked at the floor. "It was . . . mostly. I'm sorry, Dad."

"Chad, where were you last Sunday between four and six P.M.?" Landry asked.

Chad looked around as if the answer might be pasted on the walls. "Sunday? Um . . . I was probably—"

"We were at the movies," Bruce Seabright said. "Remember, Chad? Wasn't it Sunday we went to that new Bruce Willis movie?"

"Was that Sunday? Oh, yeah." Chad nodded and looked at Landry. "At the movies."

"Which movie?"

"*Hostage.* It was great. Have you seen it?"

"I don't go to movies," Landry said.

"You don't happen to have a ticket stub, do you?" I asked.

Chad flashed a goofy smile with a little laugh. "Who keeps those things? Anal-retentives?"

"Then I'll ask you, Mr. Seabright. You strike me as a man who would keep his stub and have it laminated."

"No, I'm not."

"You're just the kind of man who would encourage his child to lie to a sheriff's detective," I said.

"Did you go with friends?" Landry asked. "Anybody who could say they saw you there?"

"No," Bruce said. "It was a father-son outing."

"Which theater?"

"The big one on State Road Seven."

"What time did the movie start?" I asked.

Seabright was on the verge of losing his temper again. "The late matinee." He glared at Landry. "Why are you standing here grilling us? If someone has taken Erin, they probably knew her from the equestrian center. Aren't there all kinds of lowlifes involved in the horse business? Shouldn't you be speaking with them?"

"Have you?" I asked. He looked at me blankly. "You set her up for that job through Trey Hughes. Have you spoken with him? Asked him if he's seen Erin, if he knows anything, if he's heard anything?"

Seabright's mouth moved, but nothing came out.

"After you saw the tape and knew Erin had been taken from the show grounds, you didn't call the one person you knew who had a connection to her?"

"I—well—Trey wouldn't know anything about it," he stammered. "Erin was just a groom."

"To Hughes. She's your stepdaughter."

Landry's cell phone rang and he excused himself from the office, leaving me and the Seabright males looking at each other. I thought they both should have been strung up by their scrotums and beaten with canes, but that isn't proper procedure even in south Florida.

"I've dealt with a lot of cold, rotten people in my time," I said to Bruce. "But you, Mr. Seabright, really must be crowned king turd on the shit pile. I'm going to step out for a moment now. I'm having anger management issues."

Landry was standing near the front door, brows drawn together as he spoke quietly into the phone. I looked upstairs and saw Molly, still sitting against the railing. She looked small and forlorn. She had to feel absolutely alone in this house. Krystal was of no help to her, and Bruce and his spawn were the enemy.

I wanted to go up the stairs and sit with her, and put my arm around her shoulders, and tell her I knew how she felt. But Landry had finished his call.

The look on his face made my stomach clutch.

"What is it?" I asked quietly, braced for the worst. And that was just what I heard.

"A girl's body has been found at the equestrian center."

21

There is nothing so humbling to a self-proclaimed cynic than to be so deeply affected by something as to be knocked breathless by it.

I literally felt the blood drain from my head when Landry told me about the body. He left me standing in the hall and went to tell Bruce Seabright.

Was it Erin? How had she died? Had she died because I'd failed her? What a selfish thought. If Erin was dead, the blame went first to the perpetrator, second to Bruce Seabright. In terms of culpability, I ranked way down the list. I thought perhaps it wasn't Erin, and in the next microsecond thought it couldn't be anyone else.

"What's happened?"

Molly suddenly appeared at my side. My tongue, which was usually quicker than my brain, was stuck in my mouth.

"Is it about Erin?" she asked, frightened. "Did somebody find her?"

"We don't know." It was the truth, but it tasted like a lie, and it must have sounded like one too. Molly took a step back from me.

"Tell me. I deserve to know. I'm not some—some stupid child everyone has to talk around and hide things from," she said angrily.

"No, you're not, Molly," I said. "But I don't want to scare you without knowing all the facts."

"You already have."

"I'm sorry." I took a breath to buy a moment so I could think through my delivery of the news. "Detective Landry just had a call from his captain. A body has been found at the equestrian center."

Her eyes went huge. "Is it Erin? Is she dead? It's because of the police. On the tape they said no police!"

"We don't know who it is, Molly," I said, taking hold of her by the shoulders. "But I can tell you, no one has killed Erin because Landry is here. The kidnappers have no way of knowing who he is or that he's from the Sheriff's Office."

"How do you know?" she demanded. "Maybe they're watching the house. Maybe the house is bugged!"

"That's not what's happened. The house is not bugged. That only happens in the movies. In real life, criminals are lazy and stupid. And whoever this dead body is, she's been dead longer than Landry has been in this house," I said. "I'm going to the show grounds now. I'll let you know as soon as I find out what's what."

"I'm coming with you," she said stubbornly.

"Absolutely not."

"But she's my sister!"

"And I'm doing my job. I can't have you there, Molly, for a whole list of reasons. And I don't want you there for a whole list of reasons."

"But I hate just sitting here," she argued. "Erin's in trouble. I want to help."

"If you want to help, keep your eyes open for any kind of a delivery. If the kidnappers send another video, we need to know about it the second it lands. That's your assignment. All right?"

I understood her frustration. She was the one person who had taken action to find Erin, and now she was being made to feel helpless.

"All right," she said on a sigh. I started to turn away. "Elena?"

"What?"

She looked up at me with wide eyes. "I'm really scared."

I touched her head as if I were giving some kind of benediction, wishing I had that kind of power, and knowing too well that I didn't. "I know. Hang in there. We're doing everything we can."

Landry came out of the office. Bruce Seabright did not emerge. I wondered if he was giving Krystal the news over the intercom.

"I'll call as soon as I know anything," I said to Molly, and went out the door, Landry right behind me.

"Do you know where barn forty is?" he asked.

"Yes. It's at the rear of the property. Follow me. I'll take you in the back way. It'll be much faster. Do you have any details?"

He shook his head. "Not that made any sense to me. The lieutenant said somebody dug her up. I don't know what that means—if it's a fresh body or a skeleton or what."

"We'll find out soon enough," I said, going around the front of my car. That sounded like a lie too. Every minute I didn't know felt like an hour. Because of Molly. I didn't want to have to tell her her sister was dead.

I took a route from Binks Forest through Aero Club—a housing development for people with their own planes—on to Palm Beach Point, to the dirt road that led to the back gate of the equestrian center. The gate where Erin Seabright had been snatched nearly a week before. Barn forty was in The Meadows, just beyond that gate.

As it was every weekend during the season, the area was bustling with riders and grooms and dogs and kids; cars and trucks and golf carts and motor bikes. The biggest crowd, however, was gathered around a rusty yellow front-end loader and a dump truck parked near one of the three-sided muck pits out in front of the tents. I could see a number of blue shirts. Security. A white and green county cruiser had parked in the mud at the edge of the road.

I pulled into a parking spot opposite the excitement, grabbed a hat out of my backseat, and got out of the car. Landry stopped in the road and opened his window. I leaned down and said, "You don't know me."

He rolled his eyes. "My fondest wish."

He drove ahead and pulled up alongside the radio car.

My heart was thumping as I neared the scene. I asked a girl with a ponytail sticking out the back of a baseball cap if she knew what had happened.

She looked excited. "They found a dead body."

"God. Does anybody know who it is?"

"Someone said a groom. I don't know."

I moved past her and threaded my way around the crowd. The security guards were telling people to go back to what they had been doing. The driver of the dump truck was sitting on his running board, blank-faced, hands hanging down between his knees. The driver of the front-end loader was standing beside his machine, gesturing as he spoke with a security guard, the deputy, and Landry.

I had reached the front of the mob. Beyond the loader, the muck pit was half dug out. Sticking out of the pile was a human arm. Female, purple fingernails, a cuff of bracelets sparkling in the blazing sun. A horse blanket had been thrown over whatever other body parts had been exposed.

"Miss?" Landry said, coming over to me. "The guard said you might be able to help us. If you could..."

"Oh— I don't know. I'm sure I couldn't," I said for the benefit of the spectators who were looking at me and wondering who the hell I was.

Landry took me by the arm and led me, protesting, toward the muck pit. When we were out of earshot of the crowd, he said, "The guy was cleaning out this pit and dug her up. Buried in shit. There's respect for the dead. He says this pit hasn't been cleaned out since Thursday, but it was emptied to the ground then."

"If it's Erin, I want ten minutes alone with Bruce Seabright and a large serrated knife."

"I'll hold him down, you cut his heart out."

"Deal."

Making a face at the smell of manure and urine, he leaned over the body and lifted the edge of the horse blanket.

I steeled myself for the worst. The body was white and stiff. Smudged mascara, blue eye shadow, and berry-red lipstick gave the face the impression of a macabre work of art. There was a thumb-sized bruise on the cheek. Her mouth was partially open, crumbled chunks of old manure spilling out.

I let go of my held breath, relieved and sickened at once. "It's Jill Morone."

"You know her?"

"Yes. And guess who she worked for."

Landry frowned. "Don Jade. She told me yesterday she was sleeping with him."

"Yesterday? What were you doing out here?" I asked, forgetting the audience, forgetting the role I was supposed to be playing.

He looked perturbed and wouldn't meet my eyes. "Following up on your assault."

"Gee. And I thought you didn't care."

"I care that you caused me paperwork," he complained. "Get out of here, Estes. Go play dilettante. Make yourself useful."

I put on a tragic face for the onlookers and hurried away to my car, where I called Molly Seabright to tell her her sister wasn't dead . . . as far as I knew. Then I set off to Don Jade's barn in search of a killer.

22

When I arrived at the Jade stalls there was a major cleanup under way. Paris was supervising as the Guatemalan man carried articles of clothing out of a stall and dumped them into a muck cart. She alternated snapping at the man with snapping at someone on the other end of her cell phone.

"What do you mean clothing isn't covered? Do you know what this stuff is worth?"

I looked at the pile in the muck cart. White and buff show breeches; an olive green three-season wool jacket, probably custom-made; custom tailored shirts. All of it worth a lot of money. All of it stained with manure.

"What happened?" I asked.

Paris clicked her phone shut, furious, dark eyes burning with anger. "That rotten, ugly, stupid, fat girl."

"Your groom?"

"Not only has she not shown up, not gotten the horses groomed, did not clean the stalls yesterday when Javier was gone; she did *this*." She thrust a finger at the pile of ruined clothing. "Spiteful, hateful, little—"

"She's dead," I said.

Paris pulled up mid-tirade and looked at me like I'd sprung a second head. "What? What are you talking about?"

"Haven't you heard? They found a body in the manure pile at barn forty. It's Jill."

She looked at me, then looked around as if there might be a hidden camera somewhere. "You're kidding, right?"

"No. I drove in the back way. The cops are there now. I'm sure they'll be here soon enough. They know she worked for Don."

"Oh, great," she said, thinking about the inconvenience, not the girl. I saw her catch herself mentally and put on an appropriate expression of concern. "Dead. That's terrible. I can't believe it. What happened to her? Did she have an accident?"

"I don't suppose she accidentally buried herself in horseshit," I said. "She must have been murdered. I wouldn't move anything around here if I were you. God knows what the detectives will think."

"Well, they can't think any of us would kill her," she said huffily. "She's the only groom we had left."

As if that was the only reason not to kill her.

"Why do you think she made this mess?" I asked, pointing at the clothes.

"Spite, I'm sure. Don said he saw her at The Players last night and he reprimanded her for something. Oh, my God," she said, eyes widening. "You don't think she was killed here, do you?"

I shrugged. "Where else would she have been?"

"I don't know. She might have been meeting a guy in one of the other barns or something."

"She had a boyfriend?"

Paris made a face. "She talked about guys like she was the village slut. I never believed she had one."

"Looks like she had one last night," I said. "You jumper people have all the excitement. Murder, mayhem, intrigue . . ."

Javier asked her in Spanish if he should keep cleaning the stall. Paris looked in through the bars. I looked too. The stall was a mess of churned-up muck and pine shavings and leather oil.

"Is that blood?" I asked, pointing. There were some drops that might have been blood splashed on curls of white pine bedding. It might have belonged to the dead girl. It might have belonged to her killer. It might have belonged to the horse that normally occupied the stall. Only a lab would tell us for sure. Who knew what else had already been dug out of the stall and hauled away.

Paris stared. "I don't know. Maybe. Oh, this is just too creepy for words."

"Where's Don?"

"Off buying clothes. He has to show today."

"I wouldn't count on that. He saw Jill last night. She came here and did this, and now she's dead. I think the cops are going to want to talk to him."

Paris found her way to a director's chair with JADE embroidered on the seat back. "Elle, this is just horrible," she said, sitting down, as if she suddenly didn't have the strength to stand. "You don't think Don could have...?"

"It doesn't matter what I think. I barely know the man. What do you think? Is he capable of something like that?"

She stared off into the middle distance. "I want to say no. I've never seen him violent. He's always so in control..."

"I heard he'd been in trouble for killing horses for the insurance money."

"Nothing was ever proven."

"What about Stellar?"

"That was an accident."

"Are you sure? What did the claims adjuster say?"

She put her head in her hands for a moment, then smoothed them back over her golden hair. On her right hand she wore an antique emerald and diamond ring that looked to be worth a fortune.

"The company will look for any reason not to pay," she said with disgust. "Because Don's involved. It's fine for owners to pay thousands in premiums, but God forbid they actually file a claim."

"But if it was an accident..."

"The adjuster called this morning and claimed the postmortem on Stellar turned up a sedative in the horse's bloodstream. It's ridiculous, but if they can deny the claim, I know they will. Trey is going to be furious when he hears."

And there goes the million-dollar stable, I thought. Even if

Hughes had wanted the horse dead, he didn't want to be caught involved with insurance fraud. He would blame Jade and fire him.

"Was there any reason the horse would have had anything in his system?" I asked.

Paris shook her head. "No. We have the stuff around, of course. Rompun, acepromazine, Banamine—every stable has that stuff on hand. A horse colics, we give him Banamine. A horse is difficult having his feet worked on by the farrier, we give him a little ace. It's no big deal. But there wasn't any reason for Stellar to have anything in his system."

"Do you think Jill might have known something about it?" I asked.

"I can't imagine what. She barely did her job. She certainly wouldn't have been here in the middle of the night when Stellar died."

"She was last night," I pointed out.

Paris looked to the end of the aisle as Jade came into the tent. "Well. I guess we never really know the people we work with, do we?"

Jade held shopping bags in both fists. Paris jumped out of the chair and went into the tack room with him to break the news about Jill. I strained to hear, but couldn't make out more than the urgent tone and the odd word, and Jade telling her to calm down.

I looked at Javier, who was still standing at the door of the stall waiting for instructions, and asked him in Spanish if this was a crazy business or what. More than you know, señora, he told me, then he took his pitchfork to a stall farther down the row.

Landry's car pulled up at the end of the tent. He had had to wait for the crime scene unit and the medical examiner's people to arrive at the dump site, and he had probably called in extra deputies to canvass the grounds, looking for anyone who might have seen Jill Morone the night before. He came in with another plainclothes cop at the same time Michael Berne stormed into the tent from the side, red-faced.

Berne stopped at the tack room door, sweeping the curtain back with one hand. "You're through, Jade," he said loudly, his voice full of excitement. "I'm telling the cops what I saw last night. You can get away with a lot of things, but you're not getting away with murder."

He seemed almost gleeful at the idea that someone had died.

"What do you think you saw, Michael?" Jade asked, annoyed. "You saw me speaking with an employee."

"I saw you arguing with that girl, and now she's dead."

Landry and the other detective arrived to hear the last of Berne's declarations. Landry flashed his badge in Berne's face.

"Good," Berne said. "I definitely want to talk with you."

"You can speak with Detective Weiss," Landry said, moving past him into the tack room. "Mr. Jade, I need you to come with me."

"Am I under arrest?" Jade asked calmly.

"No. Should you be?"

"He should have been a long time before now," Berne said.

Landry ignored him. "We believe an employee of yours has been found dead. I'd like you to come with me to identify the body and answer some routine questions."

"Ask him what he was doing with her at The Players last night," Berne said.

"Ms. Montgomery, we'll need to speak with you as well," Landry said. "I think we'll all be more comfortable at the Sheriff's Office."

"I have a business to run," Jade said.

"Don, for God's sake, the girl is dead," Paris snapped. "She may have been killed right here in our barn for all we know. You know she was here last night, busy ruining your wardrobe, and now—"

"What was she doing here last night?" Landry asked.

Jade said nothing. Paris got an oh shit look on her face and clamped her pretty mouth shut.

Landry stared at her. "Ms. Montgomery?"

"Uh . . . well . . . someone came in late last night and vandalized some things. We assumed it was Jill because she knows the combination to the lock on the tack room door."

Landry looked at Weiss, communicating something telepathically. Weiss went out to the car. Calling the CSU to come to Jade's stalls when they finished at the dumping site. Calling deputies to come secure the area until the CSU could get here.

Berne pointed at Jade. "I saw him fighting with the dead girl last night at The Players."

Landry held up a hand. "You'll get your turn, sir."

Perturbed by Landry's lack of interest in him, Berne stepped back out of the stall and turned to me. "They were in the bar together," he said loudly. "She was dressed like a hooker."

He looked back into the tack stall.

"You're not getting out of this noose, Jade. I heard that girl say she knew about Stellar. You killed her to shut her up."

"That's completely ridiculous. I did nothing of the sort."

"Let's go, Mr. Jade," Landry said. "The medical examiner's people are going to want to move the body."

"You don't want me to look at her here, do you?" Jade said. "I won't be the centerpiece of a sideshow."

Bad for business. Don Jade seen peering at his dead groom.

"We can meet them at the morgue."

"Can't we do this later? After I've finished my day?"

"Mr. Jade, a girl is dead. Murdered. I think that's a little more serious than your average day's work," Landry said. "You'll come with us now, voluntarily or not. How do you think it would be for your reputation to be seen in handcuffs?"

Jade heaved a big put-upon sigh. "Paris, call the clients and let them know what's going on. I don't want them hearing the news from unreliable sources," he said, glaring at Michael Berne. "Then stop at the show office and scratch our rides for the day."

"Scratch them for the rest of his life," Berne said with a sneer. "And I couldn't be happier."

I watched them walk out of the tent: Landry, Jade, and Paris Montgomery; Michael Berne bringing up the rear, mouth flapping. I thought about what Berne had said. I had punched his buttons the day before, suggesting he might have killed Stellar himself in order to ruin Jade. But maybe there was something to it. To Berne's way of thinking, Jade had robbed him of a dream life when he'd taken Trey Hughes away from him. What would it have been worth to get that dream back, to get revenge? The life of an animal? The life of a human? Jealousy can be a powerful motivator.

Stellar had had a sedative in his system when he died. Like Paris had said: those kinds of drugs were in every tack room on the grounds—Berne's included, no doubt.

The horse had died of electrocution—the method of choice

among equine assassins, because it left no obvious signs and mimicked death by colic, a common and sometimes fatal illness in horses. The murder was easily accomplished by one person with a couple of wires and a power source. Done correctly, it was difficult to prove the death was anything other than natural.

If the rumors about his past were true, Jade certainly knew that. But having a sedative show up in the postmortem was a big red flag, and Jade knew that as well. If he had killed the horse, he never would have put anything in the animal's system that would show up in the tox screen.

For that matter, if Jade had killed Stellar, why wouldn't he have claimed the horse died of colic? Why wouldn't he have simply said he didn't know what happened? Why the story about the accidental electrocution? There must have been some kind of evidence. Too bad the person who had found the horse dead was no longer around to tell us what that evidence might have been.

"I heard her say she knew about Stellar."

Berne had said it to further implicate Jade, but if Berne had killed the horse and Jill Morone knew and had been about to tell Jade . . . Motive.

Berne had seen the girl at The Players. He could have seen her leave. He could have followed her here . . . Opportunity.

I sank back into the chair Paris had occupied and wondered how Erin Seabright's kidnapping figured into any of this.

"This is some glamorous business you're involved with," Landry muttered as he came back. "A girl gets murdered, and all these people can think about is the inconvenience of it all."

"Take a good look at Berne," I said quietly as he stopped beside me. "If the girl's death is connected to the horse's death, he could be as much a suspect as Jade. He lost a big opportunity when the owner moved his horses to Jade's care."

"All right. You can explain that to me later. I don't even know these people ten minutes and I can believe they might be capable of anything. What about the Belgian guy?"

"Haven't seen him, but he's sure to turn up. There might be some blood in this stall," I said, tipping my head in that direction. "You'll want to give the CSU a heads-up."

He nodded. "Okay. I'm running Jade in for questioning. Weiss has Berne. The techno-geeks and my lieutenant are at the Seabrights' hooking up the phones."

"I hope to God it isn't too late."

An uneasy feeling crept down my right side, then Van Zandt came into focus in my peripheral vision. I didn't know how long he'd been standing there.

"Really, I don't know anything, Detective," I said. "I knew the girl by sight, that was all." I turned toward Van Zandt. "Z., did you see Jill last night?"

He looked like he had a sour stomach and a bad disposition. "Jill who?"

"Jill. The groom. Don's groom."

"Why would I see her?" he snapped irritably. "He should fire her. She's good for nothing."

"She's dead," Landry said.

Van Zandt looked perturbed. "Dead? How is she dead?"

"That's for the medical examiner to find out. My job is to find out why she's dead and who killed her. Did you see her last night?"

"I don't pay attention to grooms," Van Zandt said with disdain, and went into the tack room.

"Sir, I have to ask you not to touch anything," Landry said.

Van Zandt had the mini-fridge open. He closed the door and gave Landry an imperious look. "And who are you to ask anything of me?"

"Detective Landry. Sheriff's Office. Who are you?"

"Tomas Van Zandt."

"And what's your connection to Don Jade?"

"We are business associates."

"And you don't know anything about this girl Jill? Except that she was good for nothing."

"No."

The deputies came in then to secure the scene, and herded us out of the tent into the blinding sun. Landry got in his car with Jade and drove away.

"They are arresting Jade?" Van Zandt said. He looked pasty and ill in the daylight. He was wearing a blue and red ascot at the throat of his blue dress shirt. Perhaps it was cutting off the blood supply to his brain.

"No. Routine questioning," I said. "His employee was murdered.

Don't you find that shocking?" I asked. "I've never known anyone who was murdered."

Van Zandt shrugged. He didn't seem disturbed in the least. "The girl was a slut, always talking about this boy and that boy, dressing like a whore. It's no surprise she would come to a bad end."

"Are you saying she was asking for it?"

"I am saying if you lie down with the dogs, sometimes they bite."

"Well, there you go. A lesson to us all."

"This fucking sun," he complained, putting on his shades, changing the subject as if a girl's violent death was of no more consequence than a bad round in the showring. Less.

"What's your story, Z.?" I asked. "You look like death, yourself. Were you out partying last night without me?"

"Bad food. I don't get a hangover," he said stubbornly. "I never become drunk."

"Is that from lack of trying or are you superior to the rest of us?"

He mustered a thin smile. "The second, Elle Stevens."

"Really? And I thought the Germans were supposed to be the master race."

"It is only Germans who think that."

"You've got it all figured out, Z. Come on," I said, taking him by the arm. "I'll buy you a Bromo-Seltzer and you can tell me all about the New World Order."

23

You saw her at The Players last night. You had an argument."

"It wasn't an argument," Jade said calmly. "She was dressed inappropriately—"

"What's it to you? Was she there with you?"

"No, but she's my employee. The way she conducts herself in public reflects on me."

"You weren't there to meet her?"

"No. She worked for me. I didn't socialize with the girl."

Landry raised his brows. "Really? That's funny, because she told me yesterday you were sleeping with her."

"What? That's a lie!"

Finally, a human reaction. Landry had begun to suspect Jade didn't have a nerve in his body. They sat on opposite sides of a table in an interview room, Jade—until that moment—perfectly composed, every hair in place, a crisp white shirt accentuating his tan, his monogram on the cuff of the sleeve.

Michael Berne was next door with Weiss. The blonde was cooling her heels in the reception area. Jill Morone was on a slab in the morgue with an assortment of contusions but no obvious fatal injuries.

Landry figured strangulation or suffocation. She appeared to have been sexually assaulted.

Landry nodded as he took a bite out of his tuna salad sandwich. "She told me she was with you Thursday night when Michael Berne's horses were being turned loose."

Jade rubbed his hands over his face and muttered, "Oh, that stupid girl. She thought she was helping me."

"Helping you, as in giving you an alibi? Why would she think you needed one? She was right there when you told me you were with someone that night. Did she know otherwise?"

"Of course not. Jill didn't know anything about anything. She was a dim, pathetic girl with a vivid fantasy life."

"She had a thing for you."

He let go a long sigh. "Yes, I suppose she did. That was why she was at the club last night. She was waiting for me, apparently with ideas to seduce me."

"But you didn't want to see her."

"I asked her to leave. She was embarrassing herself."

"And you."

"Yes," Jade admitted. "My clients are wealthy, sophisticated people, Detective. They want to be represented in a certain way."

"And Jill didn't fit the bill."

"I wouldn't take Javier to The Players either, but I didn't kill him."

"He hasn't claimed you were fucking him," Landry said, reaching again for his sandwich. "That I know of."

Jade looked annoyed. "Do you need to be so crude?"

"No."

Landry sat back and chewed on his lunch, more to be irritating than out of hunger.

"So," he said, making a show of running the facts through his head as he formed a thought, "she got all dolled up and went to The Players to meet you . . . just on the off chance maybe you'd be interested?"

Jade made a gesture with his hand and shifted positions on his chair. He was bored.

"Come on, Don. She was around, she was hot for it, it was free. You're telling me you never took advantage?"

"That suggestion is repugnant."

"Why? You've fucked your help before."

The zinger hit its mark. Jade twitched as if at a small electrical shock. "I once had an affair with a groom. She was not Jill Morone. Nevertheless, I learned my lesson, and have made it a policy ever since, not to become involved with the help."

"Not even Erin Seabright? She's no Jill Morone either, if you get my drift."

"Erin? What's she got to do with this?"

"Why isn't she with you anymore, Don?"

He didn't like the familiarity. His eyes narrowed ever so slightly every time Landry used his name.

"She quit. She told me she took another job elsewhere."

"So far as I've been able to find out, you're the only person she actually told about this big change in her life," Landry said. "Taking a new job, moving to a new town. She never even told her family. I find that strange. She only told you. And no one has seen or heard from her since."

Jade stared at him for a moment, speechless, or knowing the wisdom of holding his tongue. Finally, he stood up. "I don't like the direction this conversation is taking. Are you charging me with something, Detective Landry?"

Landry stayed in his seat. He leaned back in the chair and rested his elbows on the arms. "No."

"Then I'd like to leave now."

"Oh. Well . . . I just have a few more questions."

"Then I'd prefer to have my attorney present. It's becoming clear to me you have an agenda that isn't in my best interest."

"I'm just trying to get a clear picture of the things going on in your business, Don. That's part of my job: to map out the victim's world, put all the pieces in place. You don't want me to get to the truth behind Jill Morone's death?"

"Of course I do."

"Do you feel you need an attorney present to do that? You're not under arrest. You've told me you don't have anything to hide."

"I don't."

Landry spread his hands. "So . . . what's the problem?"

Jade looked away, thinking, considering his options. Landry figured he was maybe good for another five minutes, tops. A sergeant supervisor sat in a room down the hall watching the interview via closed-circuit TV, watching the readout of a computer voice-stress analysis machine, looking for lies.

"Feel free to call your attorney if you like," Landry said generously. "We can wait for him..."

"I don't have time for this," Jade muttered, coming back to the table. "What else?"

"Mr. Berne said he heard Jill tell you she knew something about Stellar—this horse that died. What did she know?"

"I have no idea what she was talking about. The horse died accidentally in the middle of the night. There was nothing for her to know."

"There was plenty to know if it wasn't an accident."

"But it *was* an accident."

"Were you there when it happened?"

"No."

"Then you don't really know what happened. If it was an accident, why did the horse have a sedative in its system?"

Jade stared at him. "How do you know that?"

Landry looked back at him like he was an idiot. "I'm a detective."

"There was nothing criminal in Stellar's death."

"But the owner stands to pick up a big check from the insurance, right?"

"If the insurance company decides to pay, which is unlikely now."

"Would you have gotten a cut of that money?"

Jade stood again. "I'm leaving now."

"What time did you leave Players last night?"

"Around eleven."

"Where did you go?"

"Home. To bed."

"You didn't swing by the show grounds, check on your horses?"

"No."

"Not even after what went on the night before? You weren't worried?"

"Paris had night check last night."

"And she didn't notice anything wrong? She didn't see the vandalism?"

"Obviously, she was there before it happened."

"So, you went home to bed. Alone?"

"No."

"Same friend as Thursday night?"

Jade sighed again and looked at the wall.

"Look, Don," Landry confided, rising from his chair. "You need to tell me. This is serious business. This isn't just some nags running around in the middle of the night. A girl is dead. I realize in your world, she might not have counted for much, but in my world, murder is a big deal. Everyone who knew her and had a problem with her is going to have to account for their whereabouts. If you have a corroborating witness, you'd better say so or I'm going to end up wasting a lot more of your valuable time."

He thought Jade might let his arrogance get the best of him and just walk out. But he wasn't a stupid man. Landry imagined the guy's mind sorting information like a computer. Finally he said, "Susannah Atwood. She's a client. I would appreciate if you didn't mention this to any of my other clients."

"Everybody wants to be the trainer's pet?" Landry said. "That's quite a gig you've got going, Don. Ride the horses, ride the owners too."

Jade went for the door.

"I'll need her address and phone number, and the name and number for Jill Morone's next of kin," Landry said.

"Ask Paris. She takes care of my details."

His details, Landry thought, watching him go. That was what a young girl's life came down to for Don Jade: details.

"Thank you for your time, Mr. Jade."

Jade needs to run his business differently," Van Zandt pronounced.

We stood alone along the rail of one of the competition rings, watching a pint-sized rider take her pony over a course of small, elaborately decorated fences. Both girl and pony wore expressions of absolute concentration, eyes bright with determination and the fire of competitive spirit. They were a team: girl and pony against the world.

I remembered that feeling well. Me and a bright copper pony called Party Manners. My very best friend and confidant. Even after I had outgrown him, I had taken all my troubles to Party and he had listened without prejudice. When he died at the ripe old age of twenty-five I mourned his loss more deeply than the loss of any person I had known.

"Are you listening to me?" Van Zandt asked peevishly.

"Yes. I thought you were making a rhetorical statement." I had offered to buy him lunch, he had declined. I had offered to buy milk shakes and he had told me they would make me fat. Asshole. I bought one anyway.

"Yes," I agreed. "Murder puts off potential clients."

Van Zandt scowled. "I am in no mood for your sense of humor."

"You think I was joking? One groom disappears. One turns up dead—"

"Disappears?" he said. "That one left."

"I don't think so, Z. The detective was asking about her."

He turned sharply and looked down his nose at me. "What did you tell him?"

"Nothing. I've never even met the girl. I'm just letting you know. He'll probably ask you too."

"I have nothing to say about her."

"You had a lot to say the other night. That she flirted with clients, that she had a smart mouth— Come to think of it, pretty much the same things you said about Jill. You know, you shouldn't speak ill of the dead, Z. Especially not when there's a detective in earshot."

"They have no right to question me."

"Of course they do. You knew both girls. And frankly, you didn't have a very good attitude toward either of them."

He puffed up in offense. "Are you accusing me?"

"Oh, for God's sake," I said, rolling my eyes. "Behave this way with the cops and they'll pin the murder on you out of spite. And I'll volunteer to push the plunger when they stick the needle in your arm."

"What are you talking about? What needle?"

"This is a death penalty state. Murder is a capital offense."

"That's barbaric," he said, highly offended.

"So is burying a girl in a pile of horseshit."

"And you think I could do such a terrible thing?" Now he put on his expression of hurt, as if he were being betrayed by a lifelong friend.

"I didn't say that."

"This is all because of that Russian whore—"

"Watch it, Van Zandt," I said, giving him a little temper back. "I happen to be fond of Irina."

He huffed and looked away. "Are you lovers?"

"No. Is that your attempt to offend me? Accuse me of being a lesbian?"

He made a kind of shrugging motion with his mouth.

"That's pathetic," I said. "I'll bet you say every woman who won't fuck you is a lesbian."

A hint of red came into his face, but he said nothing. The conversation was not going his way. Again.

"Not that it's any of your business," I informed him as the girl and the pony concluded their round and the spectators applauded, "but as it happens, I am happily heterosexual."

"I don't think happily."

"Why? Because I haven't had the pleasure of your company in my bed?"

"Because you never smile, Elle Stevens," he said. "I think you are not happy in your life."

"I'm not happy with you trying to get inside my head—or my pants."

"You have no sense of purpose," he announced. He was thinking he was back in control of the situation, that I would listen to him the way too many weak, lonely women listened to him. "You need to have a goal. Something to strive for. You are a person who likes a challenge and you don't have one."

"I wouldn't say that," I muttered. "Just having a conversation with you is a challenge."

He forced a laugh.

"You have a nerve, making presumptions about me," I said calmly. "You don't know a thing about me, really."

"I am a very good judge of people," he said. "I am a long time in the business of assessing people, knowing what they need."

"Maybe I should set solving Jill's murder as my goal," I said, turning the tables around on him again. "Or solving the disappearance of the other girl. I can start by interviewing you. When was the last time you saw Erin Seabright alive?"

"I was more thinking you need a horse to ride," he said, unamused.

"Come on, Z., play along," I needled. "You might start me on the path to a career. Did you hear her say she was going to quit, or is that just D.J.'s story? Inquiring minds want to know."

"You are giving me a headache."

"Maybe she was kidnapped," I said, pretending excitement, watching him carefully. "Maybe she's being held as a sex slave. What do you think of that?"

Van Zandt stared at me, his expression blank. I would have paid a fortune to know where his mind was at that moment. What was he imagining? Was he thinking about Erin, hidden away somewhere for his own perverse pleasure before he cashed in? Was he remembering Sasha Kulak? Was he considering me as his next victim?

His cell phone rang. He answered it and started conversing in fluent French. I sucked on my milk shake and eavesdropped.

Europeans generally make the correct assumption that Americans can barely speak their own language, let alone anyone else's. It never occurred to Van Zandt that I had an expensive education and a talent for languages. From listening to his side of the conversation, I gleaned that Van Zandt was cheating someone in a deal and was pissed off that they weren't being entirely cooperative pigeons. He told the person on the other end of the call to cancel the horse's transportation to the States. That would teach them they couldn't fuck with V.

The conversation segued then into arrangements for several horses being flown to Florida from Brussels via New York, and two others being sent on the return flight to Brussels.

The horse business is big business in Europe. As a teenager I had once flown back home from Germany with a new horse, traveling in a cargo plane with twenty-one horses being shipped to new owners in the States. Flights like that one land every week.

Van Zandt ended the conversation and put the phone back in his pocket. "My shipping agent, Phillipe," he said. "He is a stinking crook."

"Why do you say that?"

"Because it's true. He is always wanting me to send things to him from the States. Pack it in with horse equipment and ship it with the horses. I do it all the time," he confessed blithely. "No one ever checks the trunks."

"And you're angry because he's cheating customs?"

"Don't be stupid. Who pays customs? Fools. I am angry because he never wants to pay me. Five hundred dollars' worth of Ralph Lauren towels, for which he still owes me. How can you trust a person like that?"

I didn't know what to say to that. I might have been standing with a serial sex offender, a kidnapper, a killer, and his biggest concern was getting stiffed for five hundred bucks of smuggled towels.

I disentangled myself from him when another dealer came by and they started talking business. I slipped away with a little wave and a promise that I was off in search of the meaning of my life.

A sociopath's stock-in-trade is his ability to read normal humans in order to see their vulnerabilities and take advantage of them. Many a corporate CEO hit the Fortune Five Hundred on those skills, many a con man lined his pockets. Many a serial killer found his victims...

Van Zandt wasn't smart, but he was cunning. It was with that cunning he had lured Irina's friend to Belgium to work for him. I wondered how he might have used that instinct on Erin, on Jill. I didn't like the way he had turned it on me when he'd said he didn't believe I was happy. I was supposed to be the carefree dilettante to him. I didn't like to think he could see anything else. I didn't like to think anyone could see inside me, because I was embarrassed by what little there was to see.

He was wrong about one thing, though. I had a goal. And if I found him in my crosshairs on my way to that goal, I was going to be all too happy to take him down.

I made my way back to Jade's barn on foot. Yellow tape blocked off the stalls from either end of the aisle. Despite the warning printed on the tape, Trey Hughes had crossed the line and was sitting in a chair with his feet up on a tack trunk, a beer in one hand and a cigarette in the other.

He squinted and grinned. "I know you!"

"Not really," I reminded him. "Are you part of the crime scene?"

"Honey, I'm a one-man walking crime scene. What's going on around here? It's like a goddam morgue."

"Yes, well, that would be because of the murder."

"But that was days ago," he said.

"What was days ago?"

His thoughts were tripping over each other in his beer-soaked brain. "I think I missed something."

"I think *I* missed something if there was a murder here days ago. Who are you talking about? Erin?"

"Erin's dead?"

I ducked under the tape and took a seat across from him. "Who's on first?"

"What?"

"What's on second."

"I dunno."

"Third base."

Hughes threw his head back and laughed. "God, I must be drunk."

"How could you tell?" I asked dryly.

"You're a quick study. Ellie, right?"

"Close enough."

He took a drag on his cigarette and flicked a chunk of ash onto the ground. I'm sure it never entered his head that he might start a fire in a tent full of horses. "So, who died?" he asked.

"Jill."

He sat up at that, sobering as much as he probably could. "You're joking, right?"

"No. She's dead."

"What'd she die of? Meanness or ugliness?"

"You're a kind soul."

"Shit. You never had to be around her. Is she really dead?"

"Someone murdered her. Her body was found this morning over by barn forty."

"Jesus H.," he muttered, running the hand with the cigarette in it back through his hair. Despite his comments, he looked upset.

"So far, no one misses her," I said. "Poor thing. I heard she was hot for Don. Maybe he'll miss her."

"I don't think so." Hughes leaned his head back and closed his eyes. "He'd have gotten rid of her a long time ago if he'd known it was that easy."

"She was a problem?"

"She had a big mouth and a little brain."

"Not a good combination in this business," I said. "I heard she was at The Players last night saying she knew something about Stellar."

One bleary blue eye tried to focus on me. "What could she know?"

I shrugged. "What is there to know?"

"I don't know. I'm always the last to know."

"Just as well, or you might end up like Jill."

"Somebody killed her," he said to himself. Leaning forward, he put out his cigarette on the toe of his boot and sat there with his head down and his hands dangling between his knees, as if he was waiting for a wave of nausea to pass.

"The cops are questioning Don," I said. "Do you think he could kill a person?"

I expected a quick denial. Instead, he was silent so long, I thought he might have gone into a catatonic state. Finally he said, "People can do the goddamnedest things, Ellie. You just never know. You just never know."

Paris Montgomery sat staring at him with her big brown eyes wide and bright. Not a deer in the headlights, Landry thought. The expression was more focus than fear. She had brushed her hair and put on lipstick while he'd been interviewing Jade.

"When did you last see Jill yesterday?" he asked.

"Around six. She was complaining about having to stay so late. She'd been dropping hints all day that she had big plans for the evening."

"Did you ask her what those plans were?"

"No. I hate to speak ill of the dead, but I have to admit I didn't like the girl. She had a bad attitude and she lied all the time."

"Lied about what?"

"Whatever. That she'd done a job she hadn't, that she knew people she didn't, that she'd trained with big-name people, that she had all these boyfriends—"

"Did she name names of these boyfriends?"

"I didn't want to hear about it. I knew it wasn't true," she said. "It was just creepy and pathetic. I was looking for someone to replace her, but it's hard to find good help once the season has started."

"So, she left around six. Were you aware of anything going on be-tween her and your boss?"

"Don? God, no. I mean, I know she had a crush on him, but that's as far as it went. Don had been after me to get rid of her. He didn't trust her. She was always flapping her mouth to anyone who would listen."

"About what?"

She blinked the big eyes and tried to decide how much she should tell him. "About everything that went on in our barn. For instance, if a horse was a little lame or—"

"Dead?" Landry suggested.

"This is a very gossipy business, Detective," she said primly. "Rep-utations can be made or lost on rumors. Discretion is an important quality in employees."

"So if she was running around shooting her mouth off about the horse that died, that would probably piss you off."

"Yes. Absolutely."

"And Don?"

"He would have been furious. Stellar's death has been a nightmare for him. He didn't need his own employee adding fuel to the fire." She stopped herself and frowned. "I'm not saying he would have hurt her. I won't believe that. I just won't."

"He doesn't have a temper?"

"Not like that. Don is very controlled, very professional. I respect him enormously."

Landry leaned over his notes and rubbed at the tightness in his forehead. "You didn't see Jill later last night?"

"No."

"You had night check last night. What time—"

"No, I didn't," she said. "Don did. I offered, but he insisted. After what happened in Michael Berne's barn the other night, he said it wasn't safe for a woman to wander around out there at night."

"He told me you had the job last night," Landry said.

Paris Montgomery's pretty brow furrowed. "That's not right. He must have forgotten. God, if one of us had been there last night, maybe we could have prevented what happened."

Or one of them *had* been there and caused what had happened.

"What time would he have done the check—if he had remembered?" Landry asked.

"Normally, one of us will check the horses around eleven."

Jade had said he'd been at The Players. If he'd gone to the barn later, he would surely have seen the vandalism, might even have caught the girl in the act. It wasn't a stretch to think they might have argued, things might have gotten out of hand . . .

"Where were you last night?" he asked.

"Home. Doing my nails, doing my bills, watching TV. I don't like to go out when we've got horses showing in the morning."

"You were alone?"

"Just me and Milo, my dog. We fight over the remote control," she said with a flirtatious smile. "I hope we didn't keep the neighbors up."

Landry didn't smile back. He'd been at this job too long to be swayed by charm. It was a form of dishonesty, as far as he was concerned.

That should have meant Estes was the girl for him. He'd never known anyone as blunt as Elena.

"Have you noticed anyone strange hanging around your stalls?" he asked.

Paris made a face. "There are plenty of strange people around the equestrian center. I can't say that I've noticed anyone in particular."

"So, you're fresh out of grooms now," he said. "I hear you lost one a week ago."

"Yes. Erin. Boom. Just like that. Quit and went somewhere else."

"Did she give you any explanation as to why?"

"She didn't talk to me about it. Never even said she was thinking about it. End of the day Sunday she told Don she was leaving, and off she went."

"No forwarding address?"

She shook her head. "I have to say, that really hurt, her just dumping us that way. I liked Erin. I thought she would be with us a long time. She talked about how cool it was going to be when we moved into the new barn. She was looking forward to going with us to show in Europe in the spring. I just never expected her to leave."

"You last saw her when?"

"Sunday afternoon. I left the equestrian center around three. I had a migraine."

"And Erin seemed fine when you spoke with her?"

She started to give an automatic answer, then stopped herself and thought about it. "You know, I guess she'd been distracted the last week or so. Boyfriend blues. She had broken up with some guy her own age and had her eye on someone else. I don't know who. Someone who wasn't a child, she said. Then some jerk keyed her car a couple of nights before. She was upset about that. My money's on Jill for that. She was horribly jealous of Erin."

She stopped herself again, looking confused. "Why are you asking about Erin?"

"She seems to be missing."

"Well, I think she went to Ocala—"

"No. She didn't."

The big brown eyes blinked as she took that in. "Oh, my God," she said quietly. "You don't think— Oh, my God."

Landry slid a business card across the table to her and rose to his feet. "Thank you for your time, Ms. Montgomery. Please call if you think of anything that might be helpful."

"We're finished?"

"For now," Landry said, going to the door. "I'll need you to call with a number for Ms. Morone's next of kin."

"Yes, of course."

"Oh—and a number for a Susannah Atwood and the rest of your clients, but first and foremost for Ms. Atwood."

"Susannah? Why Susannah?"

"Seems Mr. Jade was performing a night check of his own last night," he said, curious to see her reaction. He expected jealousy. He was disappointed.

Paris raised her eyebrows. "Don and Susannah?" she said, amusement turning one corner of her mouth. "I learn something new every day."

"I would think it'd be hard to keep a secret in such a small world."

"Oh, you'd be surprised, Detective Landry," she said, standing too close to him, her hand just below his on the edge of the open door. "There are two things the horse world is full of: secrets and lies. The trick is telling which is which."

24

People can do the goddamnedest things.

Words of insight from Monte Hughes III. Perhaps there was a scrap of substance beneath the self-absorbed, alcohol-soaked narcissist after all. Certainly there was something lurking beneath his well-worn surface, something that had penetrated the fog enough to trouble him.

". . . that would be because of the murder."

"But that was days ago."

I had to think he'd been referring to Stellar, and in that, admitting the horse had been killed. But at the same time, I couldn't get the image of Jill Morone's corpse out of my mind. The connection between Jill and Erin made me anxious. If one could be murdered, why not the other?

I hated that all of this was happening in the world that had been my refuge. But people are people. The setting doesn't change basic human emotions—jealousy, greed, lust, rage, envy. The players in this drama could have been plucked from this particular stage and placed on any other. The story would have been the same.

I left Trey Hughes and went in search of the one person no one had questioned who I thought might have something relevant to contribute. The one person in Jade's barn who was ever-present, but practically invisible. Javier.

His inability to speak English did not render him blind or deaf or stupid, but it did give him a cloak of anonymity. Who knew what he might have witnessed among the staff and clients of Jade's operation. No one paid any attention to him except to order him around.

But Javier had vanished that morning when Landry had come down the barn aisle, and I had no luck finding him. The Hispanic workers in the neighboring barns had nothing to say to a well-dressed woman asking questions, even if I did speak their language.

I felt at loose ends. For the first time that day I admitted to myself that I wished I still had a badge and could have been sitting in an interview room, pushing the buttons and pulling the strings of the people who had known and disliked Jill Morone, the people who had known Erin Seabright and may have held the key to her whereabouts. I knew those people and understood them in a way the detectives interviewing them never would.

At the very least I wanted to be there putting questions in Landry's ear. But I knew I would never openly be allowed that near an active investigation. And, despite my threats to Bruce Seabright, I would now be held completely outside the kidnapping investigation. I couldn't bully my way into that house with half the Palm Beach County detective division involved. I couldn't even call Molly on the phone because the calls would be traced and recorded.

I had been relegated to the role of informant, and I didn't like it— even though I had been the one dragging Landry into it in the first place.

I who had wanted no part of this case.

Grinding my teeth on my frustration, I left the show grounds and drove to a strip mall, to a cell phone store, where I purchased a prepaid, disposable phone. I would get it to Molly somehow so we could stay in contact without the Sheriff's Office listening in.

I thought about the caller who had rung Bruce Seabright twice in that long list of numbers from his home office phone, and wondered if the kidnappers had been smart enough to do what I was doing. Did they have a phone they could ditch? Had they bought it with cash, given a phony ID?

I had given the list of phone numbers to Landry, who would be able to get a line on all of them through the phone company. I doubted we would be lucky enough to have one of the numbers come back listed to Tomas Van Zandt or Don Jade or Michael Berne. Landry would know by the end of the day. I wondered if he would tell me. Now that he was in this mess up to his neck, I wondered if he would include me at all. A small hollow ball of fear had taken up residence in my stomach at the thought that he might not.

Sean waved me to the barn as I drove into the yard. The afternoon was slipping away in the west. The sky was orange with a drift of black smoke billowing along the horizon. Farmers burning off the stubble of their sugarcane fields. Irina was feeding the horses their dinner. I breathed in the scent of animals and molasses and grass hay. Better than a Valium to me. D'Artagnon stuck his head out over the door of his stall and nickered to me. I went to him and stroked his face and rested my cheek against his and told him that I missed him.

"Just in time for cocktails, darling. Come along," Sean said, leading the way to the lounge. He was still in breeches and boots.

"Sorry I haven't been any help the last few days," I said. "Are you going to fire me and throw me out into the street?"

"Don't be silly. You've embroiled me in international intrigue. I'll dine out on this for years to come." He went to the bar and poured himself a glass of merlot. "Want some? Blood red. That should appeal to you."

"No, thanks. I'll be giddy."

"That will be the day."

"Tonic and lime sounds nice."

He fixed the drink and I crawled onto a bar stool, tired and body sore.

"I spoke today with friends in Holland," he said. "They had already heard Van Zandt had been in my barn."

"That's some grapevine."

"Apparently, Van Zandt didn't waste any time putting the word out that I might be buying and selling horses with him."

"I'm sure he didn't. You're a plum catch, my peach. Great taste and lots of money. I'm sure he wanted that news to get to your long-time agent as soon as possible."

"Yes. Thank Christ I had called Toine ahead of time and warned him I was sacrificing myself for a noble cause. He would have been on the first plane over from Amsterdam to rescue me from Van Zandt's evil clutches."

"And what did your other friends have to say about the evil Z.?"

"That he's a pariah. He's been banished from the best farms in Holland. They simply won't do business with him."

"But plenty of other people will."

He shrugged. "Dealers always manage to find clients, and people with horses to sell need clients to sell them to. If no one did business with shady characters like Van Zandt, not much business would get done."

"I'll tell him you said so over dinner tonight."

He made a face. "You're having dinner with him? You'll want to buy a case of liquid Lysol."

"To drink?"

"To bathe in afterward. Seriously, Elle," he said, frowning at me, "be careful with that creep. Irina told me what he did to her friend. And now there's been a murder at the show grounds. Is he involved in that? That's where you were all day, isn't it?"

"I don't know if he was involved. Other people may have had reason to want the girl dead."

"Jesus, Elle."

"I know what I'm doing. And the cops are involved now."

"Is that who was here this morning?" he asked, a sly look coming into his eyes. "Mr. Very Good Looking in the silver car?"

"Detective," I corrected. "Is he good-looking? I hadn't noticed."

"Honey, you need an optometrist if you haven't noticed that."

"His personality leaves something to be desired."

"So does yours," he said, trying not to grin. "Could be a perfect fit."

"Could be you need your head examined," I complained. "This mess I'm involved in—thanks to you, by the way—involves a lot of ugly stuff. Romance is not on the agenda even if I was interested—which I'm not."

He hummed a note to himself, thinking something I was certain I didn't want to know. I was uncomfortable with the idea of anyone thinking of me as a sexual being, because I had ceased to think of myself in that way two years before.

Deeper than the scars on my body, my sense of self had been stripped down to nothing that day in rural Loxahatchee when Hector Ramirez had been killed and I had gone under the wheels of Billy Golam's truck.

Despite the fact that surgeons had spent the last two years repairing the physical damage to my body—mending broken bones, patching skin burned away by the road, rebuilding the shattered side of my face—I didn't know that I would ever feel whole again. Essential parts of me were missing—parts of my soul, of my psychological self. Maybe the layers would fill in eventually. Maybe that process had begun. But I had a very long way to go, and most days I doubted I had the strength or the will for the journey. I did know I didn't want anyone close enough to watch the process. Certainly not James Landry.

"Never say never, darling." Sean finished his wine and went off to ready himself for a night on the town in Palm Beach. I went to the guest house and checked my e-mail.

Special Agent Armedgian, my contact with the FBI field office in West Palm, had come through with the Interpol info.

According to Armedgian, Van Zandt had no arrest record, but Interpol had a file on him, which said something. He had dabbled in a lot of business pies, always skirting the line of what was legal and what was not, but never quite crossing over it—or not getting caught, at any rate.

There was no mention of him coming under scrutiny for anything of a sexual nature. I was disappointed, but not surprised. If there were other victims of his dubious charms, they were probably like Irina's friend: young, inexperienced, alone in a foreign country, afraid to tell anyone.

Needing to clear my head before the evening's mind games, I changed into a swimsuit and went to the pool to let the warm, silky water soothe my body and clean the layers of grit from my brain.

The sun was gone, but the pool shimmered midnight blue, lit from within its walls. I thought of nothing at all as I swam lazy laps with slow-motion underwater turns at the end of each. The tension washed away, and for a short time I was simply a sleek, aquatic animal, bone and muscle and instinct. It felt good to be something that fundamental and uncontrived.

When I'd had enough, I rolled over onto my back and floated, looking up at the pinpoint stars in the black velvet sky. Then Landry came into view, standing at the water's edge.

I dove under and came back up, shaking the water from my head.

"Detective. You got the drop on me," I said, treading water.

"I'm sure that doesn't happen very often."

He was still in his work clothes, though he had jerked the tie loose and rolled up the sleeves of his shirt.

"My fault for giving you the gate code," I said. "Hard day turning the thumbscrews?"

"Long."

"Sorry I missed it. No one makes a better bad cop than me."

"I have no doubt about that," he said with half a smile. "Aren't you going to invite me in? Say the water's fine?"

"That would be a cliché. I abhor predictability."

I swam to the ladder and climbed out, forcing myself not to rush to cover my body with my towel. I didn't want him to know how vulnerable I felt. Somehow I thought that even in the dim light around the pool he would see every scar, every imperfection. It made me angry that I cared.

I toweled myself off, rubbed my hair dry, then wrapped the towel around my waist like a sarong to hide the pitted, scarred flesh of my legs. Landry watched, his expression unreadable.

"Nothing about you is predictable, Estes."

"I'll take that as a compliment, though I don't think you consider unpredictability a virtue. Do you have any good news?" I asked, leading the way to the guest house.

"The deputies found Erin Seabright's car," he said. "Parked under about six inches of dust in a corner of that first lot at the truck entrance of the equestrian center."

I stood with my hand on the doorknob, holding my breath, waiting for him to tell me Erin had been found dead in the trunk.

"The CSU is going over it for prints, et cetera."

I let go a sigh at the initial sense of relief. "Where was it?"

"In the first parking lot as you come in the truck entrance, over by the laundry place."

"Why would it be there?" I asked, not expecting an answer. "She would have parked near Jade's barn, not half a mile away. Why would it be there?"

Landry shrugged. "Maybe she had dropped stuff off at the laundry."

"Then walked all the way to Jade's barn? And then walked to the back gate to meet whoever she thought she was meeting? That doesn't make sense."

"It doesn't make sense for the kidnappers to move it there either," Landry said. "They kidnapped her. Why would they care where her car was parked?"

I thought about that as we went into the house. "To buy time? Monday would have been Erin's day off. If not for Molly, no one would have missed her until Tuesday morning."

"And no one would have missed her then, because Jade claimed she'd quit and moved to Ocala," Landry finished the theory.

"How did he take the questioning?"

"It was an inconvenience to him. The interview and the murder."

"Any nerves?"

"Not worth mentioning."

"Well...the guy makes a living riding horses over fences taller than I am. It's not a game for the faint of heart."

"Neither is murder."

A game. It would be difficult for the average person to consider murder and kidnapping a game, but in a macabre way it was a game. A game with very serious stakes.

"Any word from the kidnappers?"

Landry sat against the back of a chair, hands in his pockets. He shook his head. "No. The phones are rigged at the Seabright house. I've had a couple of guys checking out the neighbors. That's a dead end."

"There's a bar in that armoire under the TV," I said, pointing into the living room. "You look like you need it. Help yourself while I change."

I made him wait while I took a quick shower, then stood in front of the mirror for five minutes, staring at myself, trying to read my own inscrutable expression.

I didn't like the anxious feeling lingering in my belly. The bubble of fear had been replaced by something I almost didn't recognize:

hope. I didn't want it to mean so much that Landry had come back, that he was filling me in, including me.

"You told Seabright you're a private investigator," he said. His voice was strong and clear. He must have been standing just on the other side of the bedroom door. "Are you?"

"Not exactly."

"That's fraud."

"No. It's a lie," I corrected. "It would only be fraud if I were misrepresenting myself and accepting money from the Seabrights based on that misrepresentation. I'm not."

"You'd make a hell of a lawyer."

So my father had always said, which was the reason I had become a cop. I hadn't wanted to be like him, bending the law like it was made of wire, bending it to suit the needs of corrupted people, corrupted wealth. I hadn't realized at the time that as a cop I would end up bending it as many ways myself and excusing my actions because I believed my cause was just. I still wasn't like him. That was the important thing.

"I checked the Seabright kid's record," Landry said. "He's never been in any trouble. Good student, lots of extracurricular activities."

"Like screwing his stepsister?"

"And the math club."

"I don't like that he's lying about where he was Sunday," I said.

"Like father, like son."

I pulled on black underwear, checking over my shoulder, half-expecting to see Landry standing in the doorway. He wasn't.

"Seabright's going to stick by his own flesh and blood," I said. I put on a white tuxedo shirt and a pair of black cigarette pants. "He isn't going to allow for the possibility Chad might be involved somehow."

"That's assuming the father is the one providing the alibi. It works the other way too."

I tied the shirt at the waist and escaped the bedroom. Landry stood leaning back against the kitchen counter, a scotch in hand. He took in the outfit with hooded eyes.

"You didn't have to dress up for me," he said.

"I didn't. I can't see Bruce Seabright actively participating in the kidnapping. Even if he wanted Erin gone, he wouldn't get his hands dirty. Too risky. So why would he need an alibi?" I asked. "Chad was the one involved with Erin."

"And Erin is the one with the juvie record," Landry said. "Shoplifting. Possession."

"Of what?"

"Ecstasy. Busted at a party. She got a slap on the wrist. I've got someone in the Juvenile Division checking out the pals she was arrested with," Landry said. "And I reached out to a guy I know in Narcotics to get a line on the dealer."

"Who in Narcotics?"

"Brodie. You know him?"

I looked at my feet and nodded. I stood across from Landry, leaning back against the other counter, my arms crossed over my chest. The room was so small, my bare feet were nearly toe-to-toe with his shoes. Good quality, brown leather oxfords. No tassels for Landry.

Matt Brodie had been a friend once. Or so I had thought. I wished I hadn't asked the question. Now Landry was waiting for me to elaborate. "He's good enough," I said.

"I'm sure he'd be happy to have your approval," Landry said with a dry edge of sarcasm.

I wondered what Brodie might have said about me, not that it mattered. Landry would think what he wanted.

"Jade is the one who claims the girl just up and left," he said. "He's the last one who saw her. I think it goes this way: Erin knew something about the dead horse. Jade wanted her out of the way. He set up the kidnapping to make some extra money for his trouble. The girl is probably as dead as the one in the shit pile."

"I'll hope you're wrong about the last part," I said, knowing he could well be right. I'd had the thought myself.

"Look, Estes, I owe you an apology," he said. "That's why I'm here. Maybe if I'd listened to you the first time you came in, Jill Morone wouldn't be dead. Maybe we'd have Erin Seabright back by now."

I shrugged. "I don't know what to say to that."

He was right and we both knew it. I wasn't going to offer platitudes like some good wife excusing a husband's minor transgressions.

Nor was I going to grind the truth in his face. He had made a judgment call, a bad one. I was the last person with a right to criticize on that count.

"It's not all about you," I said. "I was there ahead of you. I didn't stop that girl getting killed. I didn't find Erin. Sometimes things just play out the way they play out."

"You believe that?"

"I have to. If I didn't, then I'd be to blame for every rotten thing that ever happened, and I know for a fact I'm only to blame for two-thirds of them."

He looked at me for a moment that stretched on. I wanted to turn away or move, but I didn't.

"So, did Jade have an alibi for last night?" I asked.

"A woman. A client. Susannah Atwood."

"She confirmed?"

He nodded.

"And did she have anyone to corroborate *her* story?"

He rolled his eyes. "Sure. Jade. Why? Do you know her?"

"I know of her. Sean knows her. She has a reputation as a social dragonfly."

"Don't you mean butterfly?"

"No."

He raised his brows.

"I know her type," I said. "Susannah might just think providing an alibi to a murderer is the oral sex of the new millennium. I wouldn't trust her. Then again, I don't trust anyone."

I checked my watch and moved away from the counter. "I'm going to throw you out now, Landry. I've got a dinner date with the devil."

"Which one?"

"Van Zandt."

As I went in search of a pair of shoes, I told him what I'd learned through Sean and through Interpol via Armedgian. I had told Van Zandt I would meet him at The Players at eight. I had wisely declined his offer to pick me up.

Landry stood staring into the closet, hands on his hips. "You're telling me you think this guy could be a sexual predator, but you're going out to dinner with him?"

"Yes."

"What if he killed Jill Morone? What if he's got Erin stashed somewhere?"

"Hopefully, I'll learn something to help nail him."

"Are you on crack?" he asked, incredulous. "Are you stupid?"

"He won't try to pull anything with me," I said, coming out of the closet one heel on, one in hand. "First: He knows he doesn't scare me and can't control me. Second: He thinks I'm worth money to him as a client, not as a victim."

"And if he's just a fucking pervert who wants to rape you and slit your throat?"

"Then I will have made a gross misjudgment of his character—which I haven't."

"Estes, he may have killed that girl last night, for all you know. He lied about seeing her. He was there at The Players. The bartender and the waitress said he was there, drooling all over the girl. We'd have hauled him in by now, but we don't know where he is."

"What time did he leave the bar?"

"No one could say for certain."

"So pull him in and rake him over the coals if you want," I said. I stepped into the bathroom and looked at my hair. There was nothing to be done about it. "I'll gladly spend the evening in the tub reading a book. But if he's got Erin stashed somewhere, he's sure as hell not going to tell you about it."

"And you think he'll just up and tell you?" Landry asked, blocking the doorway. "Like that's some kind of smooth line: wanna come back to my place and see the girl I kidnapped? Jesus Christ!"

"So tail us! What are you getting so upset about?"

He shook his head and turned around in a circle, moving back into the bedroom. "This is why I don't want you involved in this," he said, pointing at me as I came out of the bathroom. "You've got your own agenda, you run off half-cocked—"

"So look the other way," I said, pushing his finger out of my face, my temper rising. "I'm a private citizen, Landry. I don't need your permission and I don't need your approval. If I turn up dead, you'll know who to arrest. I'll make your fucking case for you. You'll be a hero in the Sheriff's Office—getting rid of me and catching a killer all in one fell swoop."

"It's not my job to let you get yourself killed!" he shouted.

"Believe me, if I haven't done the job myself by now, I'm not about to let some hump like Van Zandt do it for me."

We were nearly nose to nose, the air in the scant inches between us charged with electricity. Landry held whatever it was he wanted to say tight in his chest. Maybe he was counting to ten. Maybe it was all he could do to keep from strangling me with his bare hands. I didn't know what he was thinking. I was thinking I was standing too damn close to him.

"I was good too, Landry," I said quietly. "On the job. I know that's not what anyone wants to remember about me, but I was good. You'd be a fool not to take advantage of that."

Another eternity came and went. We stood there staring at each other like a couple of angry porcupines—all defenses up. Landry blinked first and took a step back. I thought I should have been proud of that, but what I felt was more like disappointment.

"Van Zandt wants to impress me," I said. I went back into the closet and found a small clutch purse to stash my microcassette recorder in. "He wants to come across like a hotshot, but his mouth is bigger than his brain. I can get him to say things he shouldn't. I'll tape the conversation. I'll call you after."

"After what?" he asked pointedly.

"After coffee," I said. "I draw the line at prostituting myself. Glad you have such a high opinion of me, though."

"I'm glad you have a line," he muttered.

He pulled his cell phone out of his pocket, dialed a number, and stood staring at me while he waited for someone to pick up on the other end. I knew what he was doing. A part of me wanted to ask him not to, despite what I'd said earlier. But I wouldn't allow it. I had come as close to begging as I was going to.

"Weiss. Landry. Van Zandt is at The Players. Pick him up."

Never taking his eyes off me, he put the phone back in his pocket. "Thanks for the tip."

I wanted to tell him to go to hell, but I didn't trust my voice. It felt like I had a hard, hot rock stuck in my throat. I much preferred feeling nothing, caring about nothing but getting from one day to the next—and not caring very much about that. If you have no expectations, no purpose, no goal, you can't be disappointed, you can't feel hurt.

Landry turned and walked out, taking the information I'd given him, taking my plans for the evening with him, taking my hope to make a break in the case. I felt like a fool. I thought he had come to me to include me, but all he had wanted was to absolve his conscience. The case was his case. He owned it.

"Thanks for the tip."

I paced the house, trying to shove back the emotions crowding in on me. I needed to do something. I needed a new plan. I wasn't going to sit home with all these feelings to contemplate, and I didn't have a good book to take to the bathtub.

An idea began to take shape in my mind. Before it was more than an embryo, I had changed clothes and was out the door.

My life would have been easier if I had gone to Barnes & Noble.

25

Lorinda Carlton's Wellington address was a town house on Sag Harbor Court. Unless Van Zandt made a revelation during his interview with Landry, there was not probable cause for a warrant to search the premises. But if Van Zandt had been involved in Erin's kidnapping or Jill's murder, and had kept a souvenir, there was a good chance he would get rid of it as soon as he came back to the town house.

I parked in a visitor's slot at the end of the block of buildings where Carlton's unit was located. Half the places on the block had lights on, but there was no activity going on outdoors. No friendly neighbors sitting on their front stoop, watching Saturday night go by.

Because of the nature of Wellington and the winter show season, rentals experience a big turnover of tenants every year. While some of the horse people own homes, many find themselves in a different apartment every winter. The nature of horse people being what it is, the accommodations for their horses are arranged first, accommodations for themselves often wait until the last minute. The town house and apartment complexes consequently do not have a strong feeling of community.

Carlton's unit was on the far end of the dead-end street and completely dark. I peered in the sidelight at the front door, looking for a security system panel. If there was one, it was located out of my limited range of sight. If there was an alarm and I tripped it, I was in a bad position to get back to my car. I would have to find a way to make my escape through or over the tall hedge that ran along the end of the complex, hoping that no one would see me, then double back around later to get my car.

With that much of a plan in mind, I slipped a couple of picks out of my coat pocket and went to work on the front door lock. Any casual passerby would be far less suspicious of someone unlocking a front door than trying to sneak in the back. I could always shrug and say I'd lost my key, make up a story about how I was in for the weekend to see my friend Van Zandt, who had rudely forgotten about me.

I held my breath as I worked the picks in the lock. Lock picking is not a skill taught at the police academy. I learned it from a groom when I was eleven years old. Bobby Bennet had spent many years working the south Florida racetracks until an unfortunate misunderstanding about a burglary had landed him in prison for three to five. He claimed to have mended his wicked ways after he got out, but he had retained his old skills and passed them on to me because I was a pest and he got a kick out of me.

I thanked God for Bobby Bennet as the lock's tumblers fell into place. My heart was still thumping as I opened the door and went inside. Many security systems allow entry with a key, but then require the proper code to be entered on the keypad within a minute or two or the alarm sounds both within the house and with whatever agency the system is connected to, whether it be a private security company or the Sheriff's Office.

I found the system control panel on the wall adjacent to the hinged side of the door. A small green light declared the system unarmed.

Relieved, I moved on about my business. I flipped on a table lamp in the living room. Any neighbors bothering to notice the lights on would simply assume the person in the town house was the person who was supposed to be in the town house, because what thief would turn the lights on?

The place was vaguely shabby and smelled of stale dog. The carpet had been white once. So had the fake leather sofas that were now cracked and dingy. Van Zandt needed to get a wealthier client to put him up free of charge. He probably had Sean in mind for that. He was probably already scheming to get the guest house next season.

I passed through the galley kitchen, doing a cursory check of drawers and cupboards. Nothing but the usual assortment of mismatched utensils, cereal boxes, and laundry soap. He liked Heineken beer and orange juice with extra pulp. There were no amputated body parts in the refrigerator or freezer. A small load of laundry lay clean, dry, and wrinkled in the dryer. Slacks, socks, and underwear. As if he had undressed and thrown everything into the washing machine together. Except that there was no shirt. I wondered why.

The living room offered nothing of interest. A collection of videos in the TV cabinet. Science fiction and romances. Lorinda Carlton's, I assumed. I couldn't picture Van Zandt sitting through *Titanic,* weeping as Leonardo DiCaprio went under for the third time. There was no sign of the video camera he had brought to Sean's.

I climbed the stairs to the second floor, where the bedrooms were located—one small and decorated with dog toys, one master with cheesy laminated furnishings. This room smelled of Van Zandt's cologne. The bed was made, his clothes were put away neatly in the closet and in the drawers. He might have made some woman a good husband if not for those unfortunate sociopathic and misogynistic tendencies.

The video camera was in the closet, sitting on the floor beside a row of shoes. I opened the leather case and looked through the tapes, all of them labeled with the names of sale horses. Van Zandt would tape the horses, then copy the tapes (judiciously edited to show only the best traits of each horse) for prospective buyers to preview. I popped one of the VHSC cassette tapes into the camera, rewound it, and hit the play button. A gray horse appeared on the viewing screen, going over a series of jumps. Good form. The tape fuzzed out, then refocused, and a chestnut came into view. I hit the stop button and swapped tapes. More of the same. Van Zandt managed to get not only film of the horse in question, but also a smiling shot of some sweet young thing attached to the horse in some way or another. Rider or groom or owner. Cause for an eye roll, not alarm.

On the third tape I found Paris Montgomery astride a black gelding with a white star on his forehead. Stellar.

It broke my heart to watch him perform. He was a handsome animal with a mischievous sparkle in his eye and a habit of flipping his tail up like a flag as he jumped. He went to the fences with enthusiasm, but there wasn't a lot of spring in his jump and he didn't always get his hind legs out of the way in time to miss brushing the top rail of the fence. But I could see the will in him, the heart Dr. Dean had spoken of. When Stellar knocked a rail he pinned his ears and shook his head as he landed, as if angry with himself for not doing better. He had a lot of "try," as horse people say, but it took more than try to win at the elite level or be sold at an elite price.

Behind the camera, Van Zandt clearly became bored with the horse. There were far too many close-ups of Paris and her model's smile. I wondered just how close they were, whether or not Paris Montgomery drew the same line I did when it came to getting what she wanted from a man.

Then came one long shot of a girl holding Stellar by the reins, posing the riderless animal for a side view. Erin Seabright in a skin-fitting T-shirt and a pair of shorts that showed off slender, tan legs. Just as she got the horse positioned to best show him off, he butted her with his head and sent her staggering backwards, laughing. Pretty girl, pretty smile. She took hold of the horse's head and planted a kiss on his nose.

The tough, mouthy, bad girl. Not in this scene. I could see Erin's connection to the horse. I could see it in the way she spoke to him, the way she touched him, the way her hand lingered on his neck as she moved him. Knowing her family situation, it wasn't hard to imagine Erin felt closer to the horses she cared for than she did to most of the Seabright household. The horses didn't judge her, didn't criticize her, didn't let her down. The horses didn't know or care if she had broken rules. They only knew whether or not she was kind and patient, whether or not she brought them treats and knew where they liked to be scratched.

I knew these things about Erin Seabright because I had been Erin Seabright a lifetime ago. The girl who didn't fit the family mold, didn't want to live up to family expectations; the girl who chose acquaintances based on their objectionable qualities. Her only true friends lived in the stables.

The tape revealed more to me about Erin than it did about Van Zandt. I rewound it and watched Erin's part again, hoping I would have the opportunity to see her smile like that in person, though I knew even if I could get her out of this mess, it could be a very long time before she felt like smiling.

I swapped the tape for another and zoomed fast-forward through three more horses, then Sean and Tino popped up, and I let the tape play. The pair made a lovely picture as they moved around the arena. Sean was an excellent rider, strong, elegant, quiet and centered in his body. The brown gelding was lean and leggy and had a stylish way of going. The camera followed as they moved laterally across the ring toward the gazebo, diagonal pairs of legs crossing with the grace of a ballet dancer, the horse's body curving like a bow around Sean's leg. And then they went out of the frame.

The camera lingered on the gazebo, zooming in on Irina. She stared out of the picture with an expression of cold hatred, brought her cigarette to her lips, and blew the smoke right at the glass eye. It didn't seem to unnerve her that Van Zandt was watching her. It made my skin crawl. I wanted to go to Irina's apartment and lecture her on locking her door at night.

Elena Estes, Mother Hen.

I put the camera back where I had found it and went back into the bedroom, to the TV stand that housed another television and VCR. And a collection of porn. Multiple girls with one guy. Multiple guys with one girl. Lesbian sex. Lots of lesbian sex. Gay men. Some of the movies looked like they might have been violent, most didn't.

An equal opportunity perv, our Mr. Van Zandt.

I searched the drawers of the dresser and nightstands. I looked under the bed and found dust bunnies and some petrified dog turds. Van Zandt's patron needed a new cleaning person.

I found no tapes related to Erin's kidnapping. I knew the kidnapper had to have them. The tape that had been sent to the Seabrights was a full-sized VHS tape. Most modern camcorders were either digital or recorded on eight millimeter or a small VHSC cassette like the ones in the closet. The tape would then have been copied via VCR onto the larger tape. The kidnapper had also had access to more sophisticated audio equipment than any I had seen in the town house. The voice on the tape had been mechanically altered. If Van Zandt was involved in the kidnapping, he had the tapes and recording equipment stashed elsewhere.

Disappointed, I turned out the lights and went back downstairs. My internal clock was telling me it was time to go. I had lingered too long over the videotapes of the horses. I knew Landry would try to keep Van Zandt in the interview room as long as he could, but there was always the possibility Van Zandt would just get up and leave. He wasn't under arrest—that I knew of. He didn't even think the laws of the United States should apply to him.

I looked at the front door, but didn't move toward it. The idea of striking out had never appealed to me. I wanted to find something more incriminating than a porn habit, something—anything—that, even if it didn't tie him directly to the murder or the kidnapping, could at least be used as leverage against him in a future interview.

I went through the kitchen and let myself into a garage just large enough for one car and some storage lockers along one wall. The locker doors had padlocks on them. I didn't have the time to pop them. On top of the lockers were precarious piles of junk: a Styrofoam cooler, pool toys, cases of Diet Rite soda, a twelve-roll package of cheap toilet paper. In other words: nothing.

Plastic trash cans and recycling bins sat along the wall at the far end of the garage. I wrinkled my nose and went to them.

A criminal's garbage can be a treasure trove of evidence. Egg-coated, stinking evidence in most cases, but evidence nonetheless.

I pulled the lid off the first can and peered down into it. The only lightbulb in the garage was on the wall beside the kitchen door. The wattage wasn't enough to be of any real help to me. I wished I had brought my flashlight from the car, but there wasn't time to go get it.

I dug through the trash, having to get much too close to see what I was looking at. Junk mail, boxes and microwave trays from frozen dinners, egg cartons, egg shells, egg goo, Chinese take-out cartons, pizza boxes. The same garbage anyone might have. No credit card receipts, no to-do list that included murder and kidnapping.

I found a note that listed names of horses, a date, a departure time from Palm Beach, an arrival time in New York, flight number and times for a flight to Brussels. The horses he was shipping to Europe. I slipped the note into my jeans pocket. If Van Zandt was shipping horses out of the country, he could ship himself out of the country with them. He could fly with the horses and be gone from Landry's jurisdiction like a thief in the night.

Then I pulled the lid off the second trash container, and adrenaline rushed through my system like a drug.

The only item in the can was a shirt. The shirt that hadn't been run through the wash with the pants and socks and underwear—clothes taken off in haste and thrown in the machine together.

I had to lean down into the container to pick the shirt off the bottom. The smell of the can assaulted me, made my eyes water, turned my stomach. But I came back up with the shirt in hand and took it over by the light for a closer inspection.

Fine Egyptian cotton in a warm French blue. I held the shirt up to the light, looking for a monogram, wanting some positive ID the shirt belonged to Van Zandt. I found none, but there was something on the left side of the collar that might just as positively identify the owner: dark stains that looked like blood. The left front panel of the shirt had a large tear in it about halfway down with more blood.

My heart was racing.

Van Zandt might have cut himself shaving, a defense attorney would argue. And did he stab himself shaving too, a prosecutor would ask. The evidence suggested he might have been injured in a struggle, the prosecution would say.

I could easily picture Jill Morone fighting her attacker, arms flailing, fingers curled into claws, raking at him. She might have caught him on the neck, scratched him, he bled on the shirt. If the autopsy revealed skin beneath her fingernails . . . If Van Zandt had corresponding wounds on his neck . . . I hadn't noticed any, but he could have hidden them with his ever-present ascot. I thought of the stall in Jade's barn, of what I had thought might be blood on the pine bedding. Maybe from the second injury. She might have struck him with something, cut him with something. Maybe it wasn't liquor that accounted for Van Zandt's pallor that morning after all.

My heart was pounding so hard, my hands were shaking. I'd hit the jackpot. In the old days, I would have bought a round for the house after a find like this. Now I couldn't even claim the victory, and I wouldn't be welcome in the cop bars even if I could have. I stood there in the dim light of the garage, trying to temper my excitement, forcing myself to think through the next crucial steps I had to take.

Landry needed to find the shirt. As much as I would have enjoyed throwing it in his face, I knew that if I took it to him, it would never make it into a trial. As a private citizen, I didn't need a warrant to search someone's house. The Fourth Amendment protects us from agents of the government, not from each other. But neither could I be in that house illegally. If Van Zandt had invited me over, and during the course of my visit I had found the shirt, that would have been a different story. And still there might have been complications. Because I had once been a law enforcement agent, and because I had had contact with the Sheriff's Office about this case, a good defense attorney would argue that I should be considered a de facto agent of the Sheriff's Office, thereby blowing my status as an innocent citizen and rendering the evidence I had found inadmissable.

No. This had to be done by the book. Chain of custody had to be established. The SO needed to come into the garage with a warrant. An anonymous tip, along with Van Zandt's history and his connection to Jill Morone, might be enough to get it.

Still, I didn't want to put the shirt back into the trash container. I couldn't trust that something wouldn't go wrong; that Van Zandt wouldn't spook after his chat with Landry, come back here and get rid of the evidence. I needed to hide it somewhere Van Zandt wouldn't find it.

No sooner had that thought crossed my mind than came the sound of a car pulling into the drive, and the garage door opener started to growl.

The door was already a third of the way up as I turned and ran for the kitchen door, the car's headlights illuminating the wall like spotlights on a prisoner escape.

The car horn blasted.

I bolted into the kitchen, slammed the door, and locked the dead bolt, buying a few precious seconds. Frantically, I looked around the room for place to hide the shirt.

No time. No time. Ditch it and run.

I stuffed the shirt into the back of a lower kitchen cupboard, shut the door, and ran on as the key turned in the dead bolt.

Jesus Christ. If Van Zandt recognized me . . .

Running through the dining area, I caught a chair with my hip, tripped, stumbled, struggled to stay on my feet, my eyes on the sliding door to the screened patio.

Behind me I heard a dog barking.

I hit the patio door, yanked the handle. The door was locked.

A voice—a woman? "Get him, Cricket!"

The dog: growling. I could see him coming out of the corner of my eye: a small, dark missile with teeth.

My thumb fumbled at the lock, flipped it up. I yanked the door back on its track and went through the opening as the dog hit my calf with its teeth.

I jerked my leg forward and the dog yelped as I tried to slam the door on his head.

I dove across the small patio for the screen door, fell against it, then through it as it swung open. I was in the backyard.

Lorinda Carlton's town house was the last on its row. A tall hedge bordered the development. I needed to be on the other side of that hedge. On the other side of the hedge was an open, undeveloped space owned by the village of Wellington, and at the far end of that property, the Town Square shopping center.

I ran for the hedge. The dog was still coming behind me, barking and snarling. I took a hard right and sprinted along the hedge, looking for an opening to the other side. The dog was snapping at my heels. I pulled my jacket off as I ran, wrapped one sleeve of the windbreaker tight around my right hand, and let the rest of it trail the ground.

The dog lunged for and caught the jacket between his jaws. I grabbed hold of the one sleeve with both hands, planted one foot, and pivoted around, swinging the dog around on the end of the jacket. Around once, twice, like a hammer thrower in the Olympics. I let go.

I didn't know how far the dog's weight and momentum would carry him, but it was far enough to buy me a few seconds. I heard a crash and a yelp just as I caught sight of a way over the hedge.

A pickup sat parked beside another of the end unit town houses. I scrambled up onto the hood, onto the roof, and over the hedge.

I landed like a skydiver—bent knees, drop and roll. The pain that went through my body was sharp and shattering, starting in my feet and rocketing through all of me to the top of my head. For a moment I didn't try to move, I simply lay in a heap in the dirt. But I didn't know if anyone had seen me go over the hedge. I didn't know that horrid little mongrel wasn't going to come tearing, teeth bared, through the foliage like the shrunken head of Cujo.

Cringing, I pulled my feet under me, pushed myself up, and moved on, staying as close to the hedge as I could. Twin lightning bolts of pain shot from my lower back down my sciatic nerves to the backs of my knees, making me gasp. My bruised ribs punished me with every ragged breath. I would have been cursing, but that would have hurt too.

Another fifty yards and I would be at the shopping center.

I broke into a jog, fell back to a quick walk, and tried to will myself along. I was sweating like a horse, and I thought I smelled of garbage. I could hear a siren in the distance behind me. By the time the deputies arrived at Lorinda Carlton's/Van Zandt's town house and got the lowdown on the break-in, I would be safe. For the moment, anyway.

Of all the rotten luck. If I had left the house two minutes sooner... If I hadn't spent too much time looking at the horse tapes or marveling at Van Zandt's porn collection...If I hadn't stayed those extra few minutes and gone into the garage to dig through Van Zandt's garbage...I would never have found the shirt.

I had to call Landry.

I walked into the lights of Town Square. It was Saturday night. People were on the sidewalk in front of the Italian place, waiting for a table. I walked by, head down, trying to look casual, trying to regulate my breathing. Music spilled out the door of Cobblestones, the next restaurant on the row. I passed China-Tokyo, breathing in the deep-fried MSG, reminding me I hadn't eaten.

Normal human beings were having a lovely evening eating kung pao chicken and sushi. There probably wasn't a woman in the place who had ever broken into a house to search for evidence in a murder.

I've always been different.

I wanted to laugh and then cry at that thought.

In Eckerd's drugstore, I bought a bottle of water, a Power Bar, a cheap denim shirt, and a baseball cap, and got change for the pay phone. Outside, I tore the tags off the shirt and put it on over my sweat-soaked black T-shirt, broke in the bill of the ball cap and pulled it on.

I pulled a couple of scraps of paper out of my jeans pocket—one: the note from Van Zandt's garbage, the other: Landry's numbers. I rang Landry's pager, left the pay phone number, and hung up. While I waited, I tormented myself wondering how clearly the woman at Van Zandt's had seen me, wondered who she was, wondered if Z. had been with her.

I didn't think she'd gotten a very good look. She had told the dog to get "him." She'd seen the short hair and assumed, as most people would, that burglars are men. The cops would be looking for a man—if they looked at all. A simple B&E, nothing taken, no one hurt. I didn't think a lot of effort would go into it. I hoped to hell not.

Even if they bothered to dust the place for prints, mine weren't in any criminal database, and no other database was checked as a matter of routine. Because I had been in law enforcement, my prints were on file with Palm Beach County, but not with the prints of the common bad folk.

Still, I should have worn gloves. If nothing else, they would have been nice to have while I was digging through the trash.

I kept the wrapper around the Power Bar as I ate it.

They would have my jacket—or what was left of it when the dog finished with it—but nothing about the jacket connected it to me. It was a plain black windbreaker.

I tried to think if there had been anything in the pockets. A Tropicana lip sunblock, the end of a roll of Breathsavers, a cash receipt from the Shell station. Thank Christ I hadn't paid with a credit card. What else? When had I last worn that jacket? The morning I went to the emergency room.

The bottom dropped out of my stomach.

The prescription. The prescription for painkillers, which I'd had no intention of filling. I had stuffed it in my pocket.

Oh, shit.

Had I taken it out? Had I thrown it away and forgotten? I knew I hadn't.

I felt sick.

I leaned back against the wall and tried to remember to breathe, to think. My name was on the scrip—Elena Estes, not Elle Stevens. The name wouldn't mean anything to Van Zandt. Unless he had seen the photograph in *Sidelines*. The photograph with the caption that identified me riding at Sean's farm. And if that happened, how long before all the puzzle pieces fell into place?

Stupid, careless mistake.

If the deputies came knocking on my door, I would deny having been on Sag Harbor Court. I would say I'd lost that jacket at the show grounds. I wouldn't have a witness to corroborate the lie that would be my alibi, but why would I need an alibi, for heaven's sake? I would say with indignation. I was no criminal. I was a well-brought-up citizen with plenty of money. I wasn't some crack addict forced to steal to buy my next fix.

And they would show my photograph to Van Zandt and ask him if he recognized me, and I would be fucked.

Dammit, why wasn't Landry calling back? I called his pager again, left the pay phone number with 911 after it, hung up, and started to pace.

The worst of this mess wasn't going to be explaining my way out of charges. The worst of this was going to be if Van Zandt found that shirt before Landry could get there with a warrant.

Damn, damn, damn. I wanted to bang my head against the concrete wall.

I didn't dare go back to Van Zandt's. Even if I could have cleaned up and changed clothes, showed up as Z.'s abandoned dinner date in the hopes of finding him there, I couldn't risk that woman recognizing me—or Van Zandt himself identifying me as the person in his garage, if Van Zandt had been in that car too. At this point I didn't even dare go back to the complex to get my car.

What a fuckup. I'd had the best of intentions, but there was a real chance my actions were going to result in the loss of a potentially crucial piece of evidence, and a chance I'd blown my cover with Van Zandt—and thereby with all of Jade's crowd.

This was why I shouldn't have gotten involved in the first place, a nasty little voice inside told me. If a killer got away because of this, it was on my conscience. Another weight pressing down on me. And if Erin Seabright ended up dead as a result—

Why didn't Landry fucking call?

"Screw him," I muttered. I picked up the phone and called 911.

26

The phone on the other end of the line rang unanswered. Landry swore and hung up. He didn't recognize the number. The 911 on the end of it made him think it was Estes. Up to her pretty ass in God knew what. It was a sure bet she hadn't stayed home and gotten into the tub with a book.

She was something. Going off to dinner with a possible sex killer like it was no big deal. Landry supposed he had overreacted to the plan. She was a cop, after all—had been. And she was the last woman any man should have felt compelled to protect, but he had just the same. There was something about her lack of a sense of self-preservation that got to him, that made her seem, of all things, vulnerable. He kept thinking of her jumping on the running board of Billy Golam's truck, trying to wrench the wheel out of his hands... going under the goddam thing... being dragged down the pavement like a rag doll.

She didn't know enough—or care enough—to take care of herself. And it was a safe bet she didn't appreciate him doing the job for her. He could still see the look in her eyes when he'd called Weiss and told him to pick up Van Zandt. Anger, hurt, disappointment—all just beneath a scrim of tough indifference.

He stood in the hall outside an autopsy suite in the medical examiner's building. He had run straight from interviewing Van Zandt to catch the ME at the tail end of Jill Morone's slice-and-dice.

Van Zandt had provided nothing but frustration, mouthing off for fifteen minutes about the inferiority of the United States justice system, then exercising his right to an attorney. End of interview. They hadn't had anything solid to back up an arrest warrant. As had been pointed out to him recently, being an asshole was not against the law.

He had really screwed the pooch with this move. If he had waited until after the autopsy to bring in Van Zandt, he would have had some facts to play off, to twist around, to use against the man, maybe get him scared, get him to say something he would never say now.

Landry told himself again he had needed to maintain control of the situation, not have a wild card—Elena—adding to the mayhem.

He wondered what she was tangled up in right that moment. Nothing good, he was sure.

She would want to hear all about the autopsy. She would want to know Jill Morone had been pushed facedown into the floor of a horse stall. There had been pieces of wood shavings and horse manure lodged in her throat and in her mouth and nose. She had died from suffocation. A hand had gripped her neck from behind, exerting enough pressure to leave finger marks on the skin. At some point she had struggled with her assailant, breaking off several fingernails in the process. But there had been no skin or blood or anything else under her remaining nails.

That didn't make sense to Landry. If she'd fought hard enough to break fingernails, there should have been something to find. She had been held facedown in filth. There should at least have been traces of the stall bedding and the manure under her remaining nails, wedged there as she tried to struggle to push herself up. But there was nothing.

And while her clothes had been torn in a way that suggested a sexual assault, there had been no semen present in or on the body. In fact, evidence of rape was minimal. Some scratches on the thighs and labia, but no vaginal bruising or tearing. Could have been Jill's attacker had worn a condom, or he'd lost his erection and hadn't been able to close the deal. Or the attempted rape was an afterthought, staged to make a straight murder look like something else.

Landry could have used all this information against Van Zandt before the man had demanded an attorney, particularly the apparently failed attempt at rape. He could have gone straight at Van Zandt's ego with that, taunted him, mocked him. Van Zandt would have blown up. The man was too arrogant to stand for having his masculinity questioned, too arrogant to control his temper. He was smart enough to ask for a lawyer, though, and now there would be no questioning, no taunting, no mocking, without that lawyer present.

Who was too arrogant?

Landry cursed himself as Weiss came out of the autopsy suite. Weiss, a transplant from New York, was a small man who spent too much time in the gym and consequently had an upper body that looked like it had been inflated to the point of discomfort. Little man syndrome. His arms could not lie entirely flat at his sides.

"What do you think?"

"I think it's pretty goddam strange her fingernails were clean," Landry said. "What kind of perp kills a girl in what is essentially a public place, then takes the time to clean under her fingernails?"

"A smart one."

"One who's been caught before—or learned by doing," Landry mused.

"One who watches the Discovery Channel."

"One who knows there would have been evidence."

"Meaning she scratched him," Weiss said. "Did Van Zandt have any marks on him?"

"Not that I could see. He was wearing a turtleneck. I couldn't see anything on Jade either. We're not going to get a good look at either of them unless we have some pretty strong evidence to hold them on. Any word back on whether or not that was blood in the stall?"

Weiss shook his head and rolled his eyes. "It's Saturday night. If Dr. Felnick didn't have his in-laws staying at his house, we wouldn't have gotten the autopsy tonight."

"I think we would have," Landry said. "The management at the equestrian center have friends in high places. They want this thing solved and swept away ASAP. Murder is bad for morale among the patrons."

"People don't get murdered in Wellington."

"No. You have to come to West Palm for that."

"What about that assault the other night?" Weiss asked. "When the horses got turned loose. Think they're connected?"

Landry frowned, remembering the bruises on Estes' back that night, though at the time the bruises had hardly registered in his mind. He'd been too stunned by the old scars and lines of demarcation where skin had been grafted over tissue.

She had taken a beating Thursday night, but she hadn't said anything about a sex angle. She had surprised someone in the act of letting the horses loose. Wrong place, wrong time. Now he wondered if she'd come off lucky. Jill Morone had been in the wrong place at the wrong time too. Just two tents over.

"I don't know," he said. "What did the security people have to say?"

"Nothing. According to them, the place is virtually crime-free. The odd theft here and there. Nothing serious."

"Nothing serious. They've got serious now. Estes said she didn't like the guard she ran into that night. I spoke with him the next day. I didn't like him either. I meant to run a check on him, then—"

"Estes?" Weiss looked at him as if he was certain he had heard wrong.

"The vic," Landry qualified.

"What's her first name?"

"What's it matter?" Landry said defensively.

"Not *Elena* Estes?"

"What if it is?"

Weiss turned his head, and his thick neck made a sound like heavy boots on crushed shell. "She's a problem, that's what. Plenty of people would be happy if she was the one on that table in there," he said, looking at the door to the autopsy suite.

"Are you one of them?" Landry asked.

"Hector Ramirez was a hell of a guy. That bitch got his head blown off. I have a problem with that," Weiss said, puffing up, his arms raising another inch from his sides. "What's she doing in this? I heard she'd gone off and crawled into a bottle."

"I don't know anything about that," Landry snapped. "She's in the middle of this mess because she's helping somebody out."

"Yeah? Her kind of help I don't need," Weiss said. "Does the lieutenant know she's in it?"

"Oh, for Christ's sake. What is this, Weiss? Kindergarten? Are you gonna tell on her?" Landry said sarcastically. "She got the crap beat out of her Thursday. Be happy about that and get your head where it belongs. We've got a dead girl here and one kidnapped."

"Why are you defending her?" Weiss demanded. "Are you fucking her or something?"

"I'm not defending her. I barely know her, and what I do know, I don't like," Landry said. "I'm doing my job. Are we picking and choosing vics now? Did I miss that briefing? Can I just go sit on my boat every goddam day until we get a vic I feel is worthy of my services? I've gotta say that's going to cut my hours by a lot. No more crack whores, no more white trash—"

"I don't like that she's involved in this," Weiss declared.

"So? I don't like that I just watched a dead girl get carved up like a side of beef. If you don't like the job, go drive a cab," Landry said, turning away and starting down the hall. "If you don't think you can work this case, tell the boss and get the hell out of the way for someone who can."

His pager went off again. He swore, checked the display, then went back to the phone and dialed.

"Landry."

He listened as he was told about an anonymous tip stating the exact location of evidence in the murder of Jill Morone. A kitchen cupboard in a town house occupied by Tomas Van Zandt.

"Make up your mind, Weiss," he said as he hung up the phone. "I've got to go see about a search warrant."

I had no real way of knowing what happened to my 911 call. The operator had given me a hard time, clearly thinking I was trying to pull a hoax, and keeping me on the line so she could send a radio car to my location. I was as adamant as I could be that I knew Van Zandt had murdered "my friend" Jill Morone at the equestrian center, that Detective Landry could find Van Zandt's bloody shirt in the kitchen cupboard of the town house owned by Lorinda Carlton at the specific address on Sag Harbor Court. I described the shirt in as much detail as I could, then I hung up, wiped my prints off the phone, and went to sit on a bench outside the Chinese place. A deputy cruised by shortly after.

I hoped the message had gotten to Landry. But even if it had and he had decided to do something about it, a lot of time was going to pass before he made it to Van Zandt's.

A search warrant isn't something a detective can just run off his computer. He can't simply go to his boss and get one. He has to write an affidavit, substantiating the reasons for his request, specifying probable cause for the search, and specifying in detail what he intends to search for. If he wants to execute the search at night, he needs to make a convincing argument that there is imminent danger of evidence being destroyed or of another crime being committed, otherwise executing a search at night can be considered grounds for harassment charges. The affidavit has to go to a judge, who decides whether or not to issue the warrant.

It all takes time. And during that time the suspect might do anything—ditch evidence, bolt and run.

Had Van Zandt been in the car with the woman? I couldn't say. I knew the car was a dark color, but I hadn't taken the time to register make and model. It might have been the Mercedes Trey Hughes had given Van Zandt to use for the season, or not. I assumed the woman was Lorinda Carlton.

Whoever had seen me, if they had seen the shirt in my hands, I had to hope it would be assumed I had taken it with me.

I checked my watch and wondered if there were uniforms knocking on doors in the neighborhood around my car. If I nonchalantly showed up with the key to a BMW in my hand, would I be questioned? I walked to the Chevron station, used the bathroom and washed up, checked my watch again. More than an hour had passed since my escape.

I took the long way back to Sag Harbor Court. There were no cops, no searchlights. Van Zandt's black Mercedes was sitting in the drive at Lorinda Carlton's unit.

He did not come running down the street to accost me. Things seemed as quiet on Sag Harbor Court as they had when I had arrived.

I wondered if Carlton had called in the break-in after all, or if the siren I had heard had gone elsewhere. I wondered where in that time frame Van Zandt had shown up, and if he might have dissuaded her from calling because he didn't want a bunch of deputies in the house.

Unable to get answers to those questions, still twitching with the idea of being found out, I drove out of Sag Harbor Court and headed toward home with a detour through Binks Forest.

There were a couple of cars parked on the street on the Seabrights' block. Probably surveillance from the SO. The house was lit up.

I wanted to be inside, assessing the level of strain among the natives. I wanted to see Molly, to let her know she wasn't all alone. She had me on her side.

And I had just made the fuckup of the century, compromised my cover, and compromised evidence that might have linked Van Zandt to a murder.

Yeah. That would be a comfort to her. Me on her side.

Depressed and upset, I went home to regroup and wait for the worst to happen.

This is an outrage!" Van Zandt ranted. "Is this now a police state?"

"I don't think so," Landry said, opening a cupboard door and peering in. "If the police ran the state, I'm pretty sure I'd be making more money."

"I can't believe anyone would think Tommy could do such a horrible thing!"

Lorinda Carlton had that look of someone who wished she had been a hippy once, but had probably gone to boarding school. She was forty-something with long dark hair in braids, and she wore a T-shirt with some kind of New Age bullshit saying on it. She would probably claim to be descended from Indian shamans or reincarnated from the ancient Egyptians.

She stood beside Van Zandt, trying to cling to him. He shrugged her off. *Tommy*.

"This is not even my home," Van Zandt said. "How can you come into Lorinda's house this way?"

Weiss showed him the warrant again, tipping his head back so he could manage to look down his nose at a man half a foot taller than he was. "Can you read English? It has her name and address right on it."

"He lives here, right?" Landry said to the woman.

"He's my friend," she said dramatically.

"Yeah. You might want to rethink that."

"He's the kindest, most honest man I know."

Landry rolled his eyes. This one needed "Victim" tattooed on her forehead. Her rotten little shit-ass dog circled her feet, growling and barking. He was built like a little torpedo with hair and teeth. No question he'd bite if he got the chance.

"I don't know what you think you are going to find," Van Zandt said.

Weiss looked under the sink. "Bloody shirt. Torn, bloody shirt."

"Why would I have such a thing? And why would I keep it in a kitchen cupboard? It's ridiculous. Do you think I am stupid?"

Neither detective answered.

Landry reached up to move a stack of phone books off the refrigerator, and dust rained down in a thick cloud. The tip had specified the shirt was in a cupboard, but he had expanded the scope of the warrant to include the entire property, on the chance that Van Zandt had moved it. It was looking like he had. They had been through all the kitchen cupboards. A deputy was upstairs going through the cabinets and dresser drawers.

"On what grounds did you get this warrant?" Van Zandt asked. "Or are you allowed to persecute just anyone who is not a citizen?"

"A judge determined we have probable cause to believe this item is in your possession, Mr. Van Zandt," Landry said. "We have a witness. How's that for grounds?"

"Lies. You have no witness."

Landry arched a brow. "And how would you know that if you weren't there and didn't kill that girl?"

"I haven't killed anyone. And who could know what I have in this house? I have had no one here but a burglar. I'm sure you don't care about that."

"When did you have a burglar?" Landry asked casually as he looked in the closet that housed the washer and dryer.

"Tonight," Lorinda said. "Just as I got here from the airport. There was someone in the garage. Cricket chased him through the house, but he got away."

The dog started barking again at the mention of his name.

"Was anything taken?"

"Not that we've been able to see. But that doesn't change the fact that someone broke in."

"Was there a sign of forced entry?"

Carlton frowned.

"Did you call nine-one-one?"

Van Zandt pulled a face. "What would you have done? Nothing. Nothing was taken. You would say to be more careful locking the doors. A waste of time. I told Lorinda not to bother."

"You'd had your fill of law enforcement for one evening?" Landry said. "That's great. For all you know, this person killed someone last week, and now they're still running around loose thanks to you."

"Then you should have caught that person when they killed someone," Van Zandt pronounced.

"Yeah. We're working on that," Weiss said, bumping Van Zandt as he passed him to go into the living room.

"Did you get a good look at this person, Ms. Carlton?" Landry asked, thinking he was going to have to lock Estes in a cell for the duration of this mess. And if Lorinda Carlton had called 911, that job might already have been taken care of.

"Not really," she said, squatting down to catch hold of her dog. "It was dark."

"Man? Woman? White? Hispanic? Black?"

She shook her head. "I couldn't say. White, I think. Maybe Hispanic. I'm not sure. Slight build. Dark clothes."

"Nnn," Landry said, chewing his lip. Jesus Christ. What had Estes been thinking?

That she might find a bloody shirt. But she'd gotten caught in the act, and Van Zandt had ditched the evidence in the time it had taken to get the warrant.

"Do you want to file a report?" Weiss asked.

Carlton kind of shrugged, kind of shook her head, her attention on her dog. "Well . . . nothing was taken . . ."

And Van Zandt didn't want the cops going over the place with a fine-tooth comb. That was why they hadn't called it in. And what the hell was this woman thinking? How could she listen to him tell her not to call the cops after a break-in and not think he had something to hide?

The rationale of the serial victim never ceased to amaze him. He was willing to bet Lorinda had a rotten ex-husband or two in her background, and this asshole had somehow managed to convince her he was a good guy—while he lived off her largesse.

"That person might have been here *planting* evidence," she said. And now Landry knew how Van Zandt had explained away a bloody shirt.

"The evidence we're not finding?" Weiss asked.

"We can dust the place for prints, see if we get a hit on a known criminal," Landry said, looking at Van Zandt. "Of course, we'd have to fingerprint both of you for elimination purposes. You know, the guy might have been a serial killer or something. Wanted all over the world."

Van Zandt's eyes were narrow and hard as flint. "Fucking assholes," he muttered. "I'm calling my attorney."

"You do that, Mr. Van Zandt," Landry said, moving past him to go into the garage. "Waste your money—or the money of whatever sucker you've got supplying you with a lawyer like Bert Shapiro. There's nothing he can do about us searching this house. And you know, even if you've gotten rid of that shirt, we have blood evidence from the stall where Jill Morone died. Not her blood. Yours. We'll nail you on it eventually."

"Not mine," Van Zandt declared. "I wasn't there."

Landry stopped with his hand on the doorknob. "Then you would be willing to submit to a physical exam to prove your innocence?"

"This is harassment. I'm calling Shapiro."

"Like I said"—Landry smiled a nasty smile—"it's a free country. You know what's funny about this murder, though? It looked like a rape, but there wasn't any semen. The ME didn't find any semen. What happened, Van Zandt? You didn't want to do her after she suffocated? You like 'em kicking and screaming? Or could you just not get it up?"

Van Zandt looked like his head would explode. He grabbed at the

239

phone on the wall and knocked the receiver on the floor. He was shaking with anger.

Landry went out the door. At least he'd gotten in a shot.

They searched the premises for another forty minutes—and ten of those were just to annoy Van Zandt. If there had been a bloody shirt, it was gone. All they found was a video porn collection and that no one in the house ever bothered to clean. Landry was certain he could feel fleas biting his ankles through his socks.

Weiss sent the deputy on his way, then looked at Landry like *what now?*

"So this burglar," Landry said as they stood in the foyer. "Did you see which way he went?"

"Through the patio and that way through the yards, along the hedge," Lorinda said. "Cricket went after him. My brave little hero. Then I heard a terrible yelp. That awful person must have kicked him."

The dog looked up at Landry and snarled. Landry wanted to kick him too. Filthy, flea-ridden, vicious mutt.

"We'll take a look," he said. "Maybe the guy dropped his wallet on the way out. Sometimes we get lucky."

"You won't find anything," Van Zandt said. "I already have looked."

"Yeah, well, you're not exactly playing on our team," Weiss said. "We'll see for ourselves. Thanks anyway."

Van Zandt went off in a huff.

Weiss and Landry went to the car and got a flashlight. Together, they walked around to the back of the town house, shining the light on the shrubbery, on the grass. They walked in the direction Lorinda Carlton had pointed until they ran out of real estate, and found not so much as a gum wrapper.

"Pretty strange coincidence Van Zandt's place gets broken into while he's being interviewed," Weiss said as they walked.

"Crime of opportunity."

"Nothing was taken."

"Thievery Interruptus."

"And then we happen to get that tip."

Landry shrugged as they reached their car and he opened the driver's door. "Don't look a gift horse in the mouth, Weiss. They bite."

27

The call came at 3:12 A.M.

Molly had taken the handset from the portable phone in the living room, snuck it upstairs, and hidden it under a magazine on her nightstand. She wasn't allowed to have her own telephone, even though practically every girl in her class did. Bruce believed a girl and her own phone were a recipe for trouble.

He didn't let Chad have a phone either, though Molly knew Chad had a cell phone *and* a beeper so he and his stupid loser friends could send text messages back and forth, and page each other like they were important or something. Bruce didn't know about that. Molly kept the secret because she disliked Bruce more than she disliked Chad. According to Bruce, everyone in the house—except him—was supposed to make calls from the kitchen, where anybody could hear the conversation.

The phone rang three times. Molly stared at the handset she clutched in one hand, holding her breath, holding her microcassette recorder tight in her other small, sweating hand. She was afraid Bruce was going to sleep through the call. He didn't care what happened to Erin. But just as she decided she would answer, the ringing stopped.

She bit her lip and punched the on button on the phone and the record button on the tape recorder.

The voice was that terrible, creepy, distorted voice from the video, like something from a horror movie. Every word drawn-out and deliberate, metallic and ominous. Molly's eyes filled with tears.

"You broke the rules. The girl will pay the price."

"What are you talking about?" Bruce asked.

"You broke the rules. The girl will pay the price."

"It wasn't my choice."

"You broke the rules. The girl will pay the price."

"It wasn't my fault. I didn't call the cops. What do you want me to do?"

"Bring the money to the place. Sunday. Six P.M. No police. No detective. Only you."

"How much?"

"Bring the money to the place. Sunday. Six P.M. No police. No detective. Only you. You broke the rules. The girl will pay the price. You broke the rules. The girl will pay the price."

The line went dead.

Molly clicked the phone off, clicked the recorder off. She was shaking so hard, she thought she might get sick. *You broke the rules. The girl will pay the price.* The words played over and over, so loud, she wanted to slam her hands over her ears to drown them out, but the sound was inside her head.

It was all her fault. She had thought she was doing the right thing, the smart thing. She had thought she was the only one who would do anything to save Erin. She had taken action. She had gone for help. Now Erin could die. And it was her fault.

Her fault and Elena's.

You broke the rules. The girl will pay the price.

28

In the uncertain hour before the morning
Near the ending of the interminable night

Strange the things we remember and the reasons we remember them. I remember those lines from a T. S. Eliot poem because at eighteen, as a headstrong freshman at Duke, I had an obsessive crush on my literature professor, Antony Terrell. I remember a passionate discussion of Eliot's works over cappuccino at a local coffeehouse, and Terrell's contention that *Four Quartets* was Eliot's exploration of issues of time and spiritual renewal, and my argument that Eliot was the root cause of the Broadway musical *Cats* and therefore full of shit.

I would have argued the sun was blue just to spend time with Antony Terrell. Debate: my brand of flirtation.

I didn't think of Antony as I sat curled in the corner of the sofa, chewing on my thumbnail, staring out the window at the darkness before dawn. I thought about uncertainty and what would come at the end of the unending night. I didn't allow myself to contemplate issues of spiritual renewal. Probably because I thought I may have blown my chance to hell.

A tremor went through me and I shivered violently. I didn't know how I would live with myself if my getting caught at Van Zandt's caused the loss of evidence that could prove him to be a murderer. If he was somehow tied to Erin Seabright's disappearance, and I had blown the chance for him to be charged with something, and in charging him pressure him to give up Erin...

Funny. Before I had ever heard of Erin Seabright, I hadn't known how I would live with myself because Hector Ramirez had died as a consequence of my actions. The difference was that now it mattered to me.

Somewhere in all this, hope had snuck in the back door. If it had come knocking, I would have turned it away as quickly as I would turn away a door-to-door missionary. *No, thanks. I don't want what you're selling.*

> *"Hope" is the thing with feathers*
> *That perches in the soul*
> *And sings without the words*
> *And never stops—at all*

Emily Dickinson

I didn't want to have hope for myself. I wanted to simply exist.

Existence is uncomplicated. One foot in front of the other. Eat, sleep, function. Living, truly living, with all the emotion and risk that entails, is hard work. Every risk presents the possibility of both success and failure. Every emotion has a counterbalance. Fear cannot exist without hope, nor hope without fear. I wanted neither. I had both.

The horizon turned pink as I stared out the window, and a white egret flew along that pink strip between the darkness and the earth. Before I could take it for a sign of something, I went to my bedroom and changed into riding clothes.

No deputies had come knocking on my door in the dead of night to question me about my jacket and the break-in at Lorinda Carlton's/Tomas Van Zandt's town house. My question was: if the deputies didn't have my jacket, who did? Had the dog dragged it back to Lorinda Carlton? His trophy for his efforts. Had Carlton or Van

Zandt followed my trail and found it? If ultimately Van Zandt had possession of the prescription with my name on it, what would happen?

Uncertainty is always the hell of undercover work. I had built a house of cards, presenting myself as one thing to one group of people and something else to another group. I didn't regret the decision to do that. I knew the risks. The trick was getting the payoff before I was found out and the cards came tumbling down. But I felt no nearer to getting Erin Seabright back, and if I lost my cover with the horse people, then I was well and truly out of it, and I would have failed Molly.

I fed the horses and wondered if I should call Landry or wait to see if he would come to me. I wanted to know how Van Zandt's interview had gone, and whether or not the autopsy had been performed on Jill Morone. What made me think he would tell me any of that after what he had done the night before, I didn't know.

I stood in front of Feliki's stall as she finished her breakfast. The mare was small in stature and had a rather large, unfeminine head, but she had a heart and an ego as big as an elephant's, and attitude to spare. She regularly trounced fancier horses in the showring, and if she had been able to, I had no doubt she would have given her rivals the finger as she came out of the ring.

She pinned her ears and glared at me and shook her head as if to say, what are *you* looking at?

A chuckle bubbled out of me, a pleasant surprise in the midst of too much unpleasantness. I dug a peppermint out of my pocket. Her ears went up at the crackling of the wrapper and she put her head over the door, wearing her prettiest expression.

"Some tough cookie, you are," I said. She picked the treat delicately from my palm and crunched on it. I scratched her under her jaw and she melted.

"Yeah," I murmured, as she nuzzled, looking for another treat. "You remind me of me. Only I don't have anybody giving me anything but grief."

The sound of tires on the driveway drew my attention out the door. A silver Grand Am pulled in at the end of the barn.

"Case in point," I said to the mare. She looked at Landry's car, ears pricked. Like all alpha mares, Feliki was ever on the alert for intruders and danger. She spun around in her stall, squealed and kicked the wall.

I didn't go out to meet Landry. He could damn well come to me. Instead, I went to D'Artagnon, took him out of his stall, and led him to a grooming bay. Out of the corner of my eye, I watched Landry approach. He was dressed for work. The morning breeze flipped his red tie over his shoulder.

"You're up bright and early for someone who was out prowling last night," he said.

"I don't know what you're talking about." I chose a brush from the cabinet and started a cursory grooming job that would have made Irina scowl at me and mutter in Russian if it had not been her day off.

Landry leaned sideways against a pillar, his hands in his pockets. "You don't know anything about a B&E at the town house of Lorinda Carlton—the town house where Tomas Van Zandt is living?"

"Nope. What about it?"

"We got a nine-one-one call last night claiming there was a piece of evidence there that would lock Van Zandt into the murder of Jill Morone."

"Terrific. Did you find it?"

"No."

My heart sank. There was only one piece of news that would have been worse, and that would have been that they had found Erin's body. I hoped to God that wasn't the next thing coming.

"You weren't there," Landry said.

"I told you I was going to bed with a book."

"You told me you were getting in the tub with a book," he corrected me. "That's not an answer."

"You didn't ask a question. You made a statement."

"Were you at that town house last night?"

"Do you have reason to believe I was? Do you have my fingerprints? Something that fell out of my pocket? Video surveillance tapes? A witness?" I held my breath, not sure which answer I feared most.

"Breaking and entering is against the law."

"You know, I kind of remember that from when I was on the job. And there was evidence of forcible entry at this town house?"

He didn't look amused by the clever repartee. "Van Zandt made it back to his place before I could get the warrant. If that shirt was there, he got rid of it."

"What shirt is that?"

"Goddammit, Estes."

He grabbed my shoulder and pulled me around, startling D'Artagnon. The big gelding scrambled and pulled back against the cross-ties, jumped ahead, then sat back and reared.

I hit Landry hard in the chest with the heel of my hand. It was like punching a cinder block. "Watch what you're doing, for Christ's sake!" I hissed at him.

He let me go and backed away, more leery of the horse than of me. I went to the horse to calm him. D'Artagnon looked at Landry, uncertain that calming down was the wisest choice. He would have sooner run away.

"I've had zero sleep," Landry said in lieu of an apology. "I'm not in the mood for word games. You haven't been properly Mirandized. Nothing you say can be used against you. Neither Van Zandt or that goofy woman wants to pursue the matter anyway, because, as I'm sure you know, nothing was stolen. I want to know what you saw."

"If he got rid of it, it doesn't matter. Anyway, I have to think you had an accurate description of whatever it was or you wouldn't have gotten the warrant. Or did he give you grounds during your interview? In which case you should have been smart enough to hold him while you got the warrant and executed the search."

"There was no interview. He called a lawyer."

"Who?"

"Bert Shapiro."

Amazing. Bert Shapiro was on a par with my father in terms of high-profile clients. I wondered which of Van Zandt's grateful pigeons was footing that bill.

"That's unfortunate," I said. And doubly so for me. Shapiro had known me all my life. If Van Zandt showed him that prescription slip, I was cooked. "Too bad you didn't wait until the autopsy was done to pull him in. You might have had something to rattle his cage with before he used the L word."

I struck a nerve with that. I could see it in the way his jaw muscles flexed.

"Was there anything in the autopsy?" I asked.

"If there was, I wouldn't be standing here. I'd be in the box busting that asshole's chops, lawyer or no lawyer."

"It's hard to imagine he's clever enough to get away with murder."

"Unless he's had practice."

"He hasn't been caught at it," I said.

I chose a white saddle pad with the Avadonis logo embroidered on the corner and tossed it on D'Artagnon's back, lifted his saddle off the rack, and settled it in place. I thought I could feel Landry's inner tension as he watched me. Or maybe the tension was my own.

I moved around the horse, adjusting the girth—a job that had to be done gradually and in ridiculously small increments with D'Ar because he was, as Irina called him, a delicate flower. I tightened the girth one hole, then knelt to strap on his protective leg boots. I watched Landry shuffle his feet as he shifted positions restlessly.

"The Seabrights had another call," he said at last. "The kidnapper said the girl would be punished because Seabright broke the rules."

"Oh, God." I sat back on my heels, feeling weak at the news. "When did the call come?"

"Middle of the night."

After my screw-up at Van Zandt's. After Landry had executed the search warrant.

"Do you have someone sitting surveillance on Van Zandt?"

Landry shook his head. "The LT wouldn't approve it. Shapiro was already screaming harassment because of the search. We don't have a goddam thing on him. How do we justify surveillance?"

I rubbed at the tension in my forehead. "Great. That's great."

Van Zandt was free to do as he pleased. But even if he wasn't, we knew he wasn't in the kidnapping alone. One person had run the camera, one had grabbed the girl. There was nothing stopping the partner from hurting Erin even if Van Zandt was under twenty-four-hour guard.

"They're going to hurt her because I brought you into it," I said.

"First of all, you know as well as I do, the girl could already be dead. Second, you know you did the right thing. Bruce Seabright wouldn't have done anything at all."

"That's not a lot of comfort at the moment."

I pushed myself to my feet and leaned back against the cabinet, crossing my arms tightly against my body. Another tremor rattled through me, from my core outward, as I thought of the consequences Erin Seabright was going to suffer for my actions. If she wasn't dead already.

"They set up another drop," Landry said. "With luck, we'll have the accomplice by the end of the day."

With luck.

"Where and when?" I asked.

He just looked at me, his eyes hidden by his sunglasses, his face like stone.

"Where and when?" I asked again, moving toward him.

"You can't be there, Elena."

I closed my eyes for a moment, knowing where this conversation was going to end. "You can't shut me out of this."

"It's not up to me. The lieutenant will run the show. You think he's going to let you ride along? Even if it was my call, you think I'd let you in after that stunt you pulled last night?"

"That *stunt* netted a torn, bloody shirt from a murder suspect."

"Which we don't have."

"That's not my fault."

"You got caught."

"None of that would have happened if you hadn't had to flex your muscles last night and take Van Zandt in when you did," I argued. "I might have gotten something out of him over dinner. You could have had him afterward, after the autopsy. You could have held him, gotten the warrant, found the shirt yourself. But no. You couldn't play it that way, and now this guy is running around loose—"

"Oh, it's *my* fault you broke into that house," Landry said, incredulous. "And I suppose it was Ramirez's fault he walked in front of that bullet."

I heard myself gasp as if he had slapped me. My instinct was to step back. Somehow, I managed not to.

We stood there staring at each other for a long, horrible moment, the weight of his words hanging in the air. Then I turned, very deliberately, and went back to D'Artagnon to put on his other boot.

"Jesus," Landry murmured. "I'm sorry. I shouldn't have said that."

I didn't say anything. My focus was on tightening the boot straps just so, aligning them perfectly.

"I'm sorry," he said again as I stood. "You just make me so god-dam mad—"

"Don't put this on me," I said, turning to face him. "I'm carrying enough guilt without taking on yours too."

He looked away, ashamed of himself. I could have done without the small victory. The price for it had been too high.

"You're a son of a bitch, Landry," I said, but not with any strong emotion. I could have as easily said, you have short hair. It was a simple statement of fact.

He nodded. "Yeah. I am. I can be."

"Don't you have a ransom drop to arrange? I've got a horse to ride."

I took D'Ar's bridle down from the hook and went to put it on him. Landry didn't move.

"I have to ask you a question," he said. "Do you think Don Jade could be Van Zandt's partner in this? In the kidnapping?"

I thought about that. "Van Zandt and Jade were both connected to Stellar—the horse that was killed. They both stand to make a lot of money if Trey Hughes buys this jumper from Belgium."

"So, they're partners of a sort."

"Of a sort. Jade wanted rid of Jill Morone—maybe because she was lazy and stupid, or maybe because she knew something about Stellar. Erin Seabright was Stellar's personal groom. She might have known something too. Why? Do you have something on Jade?"

He debated whether or not to tell me. Finally, he drew a deep breath and let it out, and lied to me. I could feel it. I could see it in the way his eyes went flat and blank. Cop eyes. "I'm just trying to connect the dots," he said. "There are too many coincidences for this not all to be tied together."

I shook my head and smiled my bitter, ironic half smile, and thought of Sean's matchmaking talk. Oh, yeah. Me and Landry. A match made in hell.

"So what came out in the autopsy?" I asked again. "Or is that a state secret too?"

"She suffocated."

"Was she raped?"

"My personal feeling: he tried to rape her and couldn't get the job done. He had her facedown in that stall, and she suffocated while he was trying. She aspirated vomit and horse manure."

"God. Poor girl." To die like that, and not one person she'd known here mourned her.

"Or the rape attempt was staged," Landry said. "No semen anywhere."

"Anything under her nails?"

"Not so much as a flake of skin."

I finished doing up the buckles on the bridle, turned and looked at him. "He *cleaned* her fingernails?"

Landry shrugged. "Maybe he's not as dumb as he seems."

"That's a learned behavior," I said. "That's not: oops, I've accidentally suffocated this girl and now I have to panic. That's an MO. He's done this before."

"I'm already running it as an MO through the VICAP database, and I've got a call in to Interpol and to the Belgian authorities for similar cases."

My thoughts were already on what it could mean for Erin if she was in the hands not of a kidnapper whose only motive was money, but of a serial killer whose dark motive was his own.

"That's why they have a file on him," I said more to myself than to Landry. "That bullshit about his business practices—I knew that didn't add up to Interpol involvement. Armedgian, you son of a bitch," I muttered.

"Who's Armedgian?"

The Interpol information had been filtered through him. If I was right, and Van Zandt had a documented history as a predator, my good friend at the FBI had kept that information to himself. And I knew why. Because I wasn't part of the club anymore.

"Have the feds been in contact with your office?" I asked.

"Not that I'm aware of."

"I hope that means I'm wrong, not just that they're assholes."

"Oh, they're assholes," Landry pronounced. "And if they try to horn in on my case, they'll each have a new one."

He looked at his watch. "I've got to go. We're executing a search warrant at Morone's and Seabright's apartments. See if there's anything that might point us in a direction."

"You'll find a lot of Erin's personal effects in Jill's apartment," I said, taking my horse by the reins.

"How do you know that?"

"Because in the photograph I have of Erin, she's wearing the blouse Jill Morone died in. That's why it looked like Erin had moved out—Jill stole everything."

I led D'Artagnon out of the barn to the mounting block, leaving Landry to see himself out. From the corner of my eye, I could see him just standing there with his hands on his hips, looking at me. Behind him, the door to the lounge opened and Irina emerged in ice blue silk pajamas, coffee mug in hand. She gave Landry a scathing look as she glided past on her way to the stairs to her apartment. He didn't notice.

I got on my horse and we walked away to the arena. I don't know how long Landry stayed. As I took up the reins, I cleared the detritus of our encounter from my mind. I breathed in the scent of the horse, felt the sun warm my skin, listened to the jazz guitar of Marc Antoine coming over the arena speakers. I was there to cleanse myself, to center my being, to feel the comfort of familiar muscles working and the trickle of sweat between my shoulder blades. If I hadn't earned a moment of peace, I was going to take one anyway.

By the time I had finished, Landry was gone. Someone else had come to call.

Tomas Van Zandt.

29

So she was the dead person they found at the show grounds?"

Landry looked sideways at the old lady. She was wearing pink tights, an off-the-shoulder sweater, and furry bedroom slippers. She held a hugely fat orange cat in her arms. The cat looked like it would bite.

"I really can't say, ma'am," Landry said, looking around the tiny apartment. The place was a dump. And filthy. And it looked like it had been tossed. "Has anyone been in here since Friday evening?"

"No. No one. I've been here the whole time. And my friend Sid has been staying," she confided with a coy blush. "Since I found out the other one disappeared, I figure a girl can't be too careful."

Landry motioned to the room at large. "Why does it look this way?"

"Because she's a little pig, that's why! Not that I would speak ill of the dead, but..." Eva Rosen looked at the nicotine-stained ceiling to see if God was watching her. "She was mean too. I know she tried to kick my Cecil."

"Your what?"

"Cecil!" She hefted the cat. It growled.

Landry moved to pick through a pile of clothes left on the

unmade bed. Many items that looked too small for Jill Morone. Many items with price tags still attached.

"I think she stole," Eva said. "So how did she die?"

"I'm not at liberty to comment on that."

"But someone murdered her, right? They said on the news."

"Did they?"

"Was it a sex crime?" Clearly, she was hoping it was. People were amazing.

"Do you know if she had a boyfriend?" Landry asked.

"This one?" She made a face. "No. The other one."

"Erin Seabright."

"Like I told your little friend in the other room. Thad Something."

"Chad?" Landry said, moving on to a coffee table littered with candy wrappers and an overflowing ashtray. "Chad Seabright?"

Eva was horror-stricken. "They had the same last name? They were married?"

"No, ma'am." He picked through a stack of magazines. *People, Playgirl, Hustler.* Jesus.

"*Oy vey.* Under my own roof!"

"Did you ever see anyone coming in and out?" Landry asked. "Friends? Their boss?"

"The boss."

"Don Jade?"

"I don't know him. Paris," she said. "Blond, pretty, a very nice girl. She always takes time to chat. Always asks after my babies."

"Babies?"

"Cecil and Beanie. She was the one who paid the rent—Paris. Such a nice girl."

"When was she last here?"

"Not lately. She's very busy, you know. She rides those horses. Zoom! Over the fences." She swung the fat cat in her arms as if she meant to toss him. The cat flattened its ears and made a sound in its throat like a siren.

Landry went to the nightstand beside the bed and opened the drawer.

Bingo.

He took a pen from his pocket and gingerly moved aside a hot-pink vibrator, then lifted out his prize. Photographs. Photographs of Don Jade sitting astride a black horse with a winner's ribbon around its neck. Pictures of him jumping another horse over a huge fence. A photo of him standing beside a girl whose face had been scratched out of the picture.

Landry turned the photograph over and looked at the back. The first half of the inscription had been scratched over with a pen that had been pressed so hard it had carved a groove into the paper, but so carelessly it could still be read.

To Erin.
Love, Don.

30

He must be rounder, softer in the downward transitions."

Van Zandt had parked along the road—a dark blue Chevy, not the Mercedes—and stood leaning on the fence, watching me. My stomach flipped at the sight of him. I had hoped to next see him—if not on the news, being taken into custody by the authorities—at the equestrian center in a throng of humanity.

He climbed carefully over the board fence and came toward the ring, his eyes hidden by mirrored sunglasses, his expression flat and calm. I thought he still looked ill, and wondered if it was killing that upset his system, or the danger of being caught. Or perhaps it was the idea of having a loose end dangling. Me.

I glanced at the parking area adjacent to the barn. Irina's car was gone. She had left while I'd been engrossed in my ride.

I hadn't seen any sign of Sean. If he had returned home from his night out, he was sleeping late.

"You must be looser in your back so that the horse may be looser in his back," Van Zandt said.

I wondered if he knew, and knew in a fatalistic corner of my soul that he did. The possibilities ticked through my mind as they had every hour since my blunder at the town house: He had found the prescription and recognized my name from *Sidelines,* or Lorinda Carlton had recognized the name. The magazine might have been in the town house somewhere. They might have looked at the photograph together. Van Zandt might have recognized the horse, or my profile, or put the puzzle pieces together from the mention of Sean's farm. He might have found the jacket and the prescription, assumed Elena Estes was a cop conducting a search while he'd been in the interview room with Landry; called his attorney and asked to have the name checked out. Shapiro would have recognized my name.

It didn't matter how he might have found me out. What mattered was what he was going to do about it. If he knew I had been in his home Saturday night, then he knew I had seen the bloody shirt. I wished now I had kept the thing and damned the admissibility consequences. At least he would be in jail for the moment, and I would not be alone with a man I believed to be a murderer.

"Try again," he said. "Pick up the canter."

"We were just finishing for the day."

"Americans," he said with disdain, standing at the edge of the ring with his hands on his hips. "He is hardly warm. The work is only just beginning. Pick up the canter."

My natural inclination was to defy him, but staying aboard the horse seemed preferable to a level playing field where he had six inches and sixty pounds on me. At least until I could get a better read on him and what he may or may not know, it seemed best to humor him.

"On the twenty-meter circle," Van Zandt instructed.

I put the horse on a circle twenty meters in diameter, tried to breathe and focus, though my hands were so tight on the reins, I thought I could feel my pulse in them. I closed my eyes for two strides, exhaling and sinking into the saddle.

"Relax your hands. Why are you so tense, Elle?" he asked in a silky voice that made a chill go down my back. "The horse can sense this. It makes him also tense. More seat, less hand."

I made an attempt to react accordingly.

"What brings you out so early?"

"Aren't you happy to see me?" he asked.

"I would have been happy to see you at dinner last night. You stood me up. That doesn't win you any points with me."

"I was unavoidably detained."

"Taken to a desert island? A place with no phones? Even the police let you make a phone call."

"Is that where you think I was? With the police?"

"I'm sure I don't know or care."

"I left word with the maître d'. I couldn't call you. You have not given me your number," he said, then changed tones in the next breath. "Collect, collect, collect!" he demanded. "More energy, less speed. Come! Sit into him!"

I gathered the horse beneath me until I held him nearly on the spot, his feet pounding the sand in three-beat time. "Are you trying to make up to me with a free riding lesson?"

"Nothing is free, Elle," he said. "*Carry* him into the walk. Like setting down a feather."

I did as instructed—or tried to, rather—and failed because of my tension.

"Don't let him fall out of the gait that way!" Van Zandt shouted. "Is your horse to be on its forehand?"

"No."

"Then why did you let this happen?"

The implied answer was that I was stupid.

"Again! Canter! And more energy in the transition, not less!"

We went through the exercise again and again. Each time, something was not quite worthy, and that something was glaringly my fault. Sweat became lather on D'Artagnon's massive neck. My T-shirt was soaked through. My back muscles began to cramp. My arms were so tired, they trembled.

I began to question my wisdom. I couldn't stay on the horse all day, and by the time I got off, I was going to flop on the ground, limp, boneless, like a jellyfish washed ashore. For his part, Van Zandt was punishing me, and I knew he was enjoying it.

"... and make him float into the walk like a snowflake landing."

Again I brought the horse to the walk, holding my breath in anticipation of another outburst.

"Better," he said grudgingly.

"Enough," I said, letting the reins out to the buckle. "Are you trying to kill me?"

"Why would I do such a thing to you, Elle? We are friends, are we not?"

"I thought so."

"I thought so too."

Past tense. Intentional, I thought, not a misuse of the language that was probably third or fourth on his list.

"I called the restaurant later in the evening," he said. "The maître d' told me you never came."

"I was there. You weren't. I left," I lied. "I didn't see the maître d'. He must have been in the men's room."

Van Zandt considered the story.

"You are very good," he said.

"At what?" I watched him as I walked D'Artagnon on the circle, waiting for the gelding's breathing to slow.

"At the dressage, of course."

"You just spent half an hour screaming at me to get one decent transition."

"You need a strong coach. You are too willful."

"I don't need to be abused."

"You think I am abusive? An asshole?" he asked with a lack of emotion that was more disturbing than his usual attitude. "I believe in discipline."

"Putting me in my place?"

He didn't answer.

"What brings you out so early?" I asked again. "It couldn't be to apologize for last night."

"I have nothing to apologize for."

"You wouldn't recognize the occasion if it slapped you in the face. Did you come to see Sean about Tino? Is your client down from Virginia yet?"

"She arrived last night. Imagine her shock when she arrived at the house to interrupt an intruder."

"Someone broke into your house? That's terrible. Was anything stolen?"

"Oddly, no."

"Lucky. She wasn't hurt, was she? I saw a story on the news just the other night about an elderly couple being robbed in their home by two Haitians with machetes."

"No, she was not injured. The person ran away. Lorinda's dog gave chase through the lawns, but came back with only a jacket."

My stomach rolled again. My arms pebbled with goose bumps despite the heat.

"Where is your groom?" Van Zandt asked, looking toward the barn. "Why is she not here to take your horse?"

"Taking a coffee break," I said, wishing that were true. I watched Van Zandt's gaze go to the parking area where my BMW sat alone.

"A good idea, coffee," he said. "Put the horse in the cross-ties. We can have a cup of coffee together and make new plans."

"He needs to be hosed off."

"The Russian can do it. That's her job, not yours."

I considered picking up the reins and running him down. Easier said than done. He would be a moving target, and D'Ar would try to avoid hitting him. Even if I could knock him down, then what? I would have to go over a fence to get off the property. I didn't know if D'Artagnon would jump. He might as easily refuse at the fence and throw me.

"Come," Van Zandt ordered. He turned and started for the barn.

I didn't know if he had a weapon. I knew I did not. If I went into the building with him, he would have a big advantage.

I gathered the reins. My legs tightened around D'Artagnon's sides. He danced beneath me and blew through his nostrils.

A flash of color near the fence caught my eye and my attention. Molly. She had propped her bike and climbed through the fence, and was now running toward me.

I raised a finger to my lips in the hopes of keeping her from calling out my name. As if it mattered. My training as the child of a defense attorney: never admit anything. Even in the face of overwhelming evidence: deny, deny, deny.

Molly pulled up, looked at me, looked at Van Zandt, who had just noticed her. I climbed off D'Artagnon and held my hand out toward the girl.

"It's Miss Molly the Magnificent!" I exclaimed. "Come to call on her Auntie Elle."

Uncertainty filled her eyes, but her expression was a blank. Too much practice with volatile situations between Krystal and the men in her life. She came to me, breathing hard, her forehead shiny with sweat. I put my arm around her narrow shoulders and gave her a squeeze, wishing I could make her invisible. She was here because of me, and now because of me, she was in danger.

Van Zandt looked at her with something like disapproval. "Auntie Elle? You have family nearby?"

"Honorary Auntie," I said. My fingers tight on her arm, I said to Molly, "Molly Avadon, this my friend Mr. Van Zandt."

I didn't want Van Zandt to associate her with Erin. And I also thought it might be one thing for Van Zandt to make me disappear, but he might think twice about killing a relative of Sean's. He had to believe with the conceit of a sociopath that he had a good chance of getting away with what he'd done so far. Otherwise I thought he would already have been on a plane to Brussels or places unknown. If he still believed he could come away unscathed, he could still have a business here, could still hobnob with the rich and famous.

Molly looked again from me to Van Zandt, and said hello with cool reserve.

Van Zandt smiled a brittle smile. "Hello, Molly."

"I promised Molly we'd go to the horse show today," I said. "I'd better take a rain check on that coffee, Z. I don't see Irina, and I have to get this horse put away."

He frowned at that, considering his options.

"Let me help you, then," he said, taking D'Artagnon's reins.

Molly looked up at me with worried eyes. I thought I should tell her to slip away, to run for help. Van Zandt turned back toward us before I could do it.

"Come, Miss Molly," he said. "You are interested in horses? Like your Uncle Sean?"

"Kind of," Molly said.

"Come, then, and help with taking off this horse's boots."

"No," I said. "If she gets stepped on, it's my fault." I looked at Molly, trying to will her to read my mind. "Molly, honey, why don't you run to Uncle Sean's house and see if he's up?"

"He is not home," Van Zandt said. "I called as I was driving here. I got his machine."

"That only means he didn't answer," Molly said. Van Zandt frowned and continued on toward the barn with the horse.

I bent as if to brush a kiss against Molly's cheek and whispered in her ear, "Call nine-one-one."

She turned and ran for the main house. Van Zandt glanced over his shoulder and watched her go.

"Isn't she a doll?" I said.

He didn't comment.

We went into the barn and he put D'Artagnon into the grooming stall, removing his bridle and putting on his halter. I went to the opposite side of the horse and crouched to pull one of his boots off, keeping my feet under me and one eye on Van Zandt.

"You owe me dinner," I said.

"You owe me for a lesson."

"Are we even then?"

"I don't think so," he said. "I don't believe I'm through teaching you, Elle Stevens."

He came around the front of the horse. I moved behind the horse to the other side and bent to pull off another boot.

"You are if I say so."

"There are many kinds of lessons," he said enigmatically.

"I don't need a mentor. Thanks anyway."

I moved to the cabinet with the grooming supplies and surreptitiously pulled out a scissors. I wouldn't hesitate to stab him with it if he made a wrong move.

Maybe, I thought, I should stab him anyway—the best defense being a good offense. He was a murderer. Why run the risk of him hurting me, hurting Molly? I could step in close, shove the scissors to their hilt in his stomach at his navel. He would bleed out before he could do more than realize I'd killed him.

I would plead self-defense. The 911 call would establish I had felt in danger. Van Zandt was already known to the Sheriff's Office as a murder suspect.

I could call on my father to defend me. The press would eat it up. Father and prodigal child reunited as he fights to save her from the death chamber.

I had never purposefully taken a life. I wondered if I would feel remorse, knowing what I knew about Van Zandt.

"We could have made a good team, you and I," he said.

He moved back around the front of the horse.

I palmed the scissors and watched him come toward me.

My arms were trembling with fatigue and nerves. I wondered if I would have the strength to drive the blade into his body.

"You make it sound as if I'm never going to see you again," I said. "Are you going somewhere? Am I?"

He still had the sunglasses on. I couldn't see his eyes. His face was without expression. I didn't think he would kill me here, now. Even if he was willing to kill Molly too, he couldn't know for certain Sean wasn't in the house.

"I am not going anywhere," he said, stepping closer.

"Tomas!" Sean's voice rang down the aisle. Relief washed through me like a tidal wave, taking my strength with it. "I thought you might never come back! No one has tried to injure you this time, have they?"

"Only his pride," I said, leaning against the cabinet, setting the scissors aside. "I've denied him the joy of becoming my coach."

"Oh, my God!" Sean laughed. "Why would you want that job? She eviscerated the last one and served his remains in a spaghetti sauce with fava beans and a fine Chianti."

"She needs taming," Van Zandt said, finding a thin smile.

"And I need to be twenty again, but that's never going to happen either," Sean said, coming to me. He kissed my cheek and gave my arm a reassuring squeeze. "Darling, Molly is waiting impatiently. Why don't you run? I'll see to D'Artagnon."

"But I know you need to get going too," I said. "You have that luncheon today, don't you?"

"Yes." He gave Van Zandt a look of apology. "Riders Against Rheumatoid Rumps, or some equally worthy cause. Sorry to give you the bum's rush, Tomas. Call me tomorrow. We'll do dinner or something. Maybe when your client from Virginia arrives we could all go out."

"Of course, yes," Van Zandt said.

He came to me, put his hands on my shoulders, and kissed my cheeks. The right one, the left one, the right one. Like the Dutch. He looked at me and I thought I could feel the hate in his gaze, even through the mirrored lenses. "Until later, Elle Stevens."

31

I started to shake as I watched Van Zandt drive away. He might have killed me. I might have killed him.

Until later . . .

"What the hell was that about?" Sean demanded. "Your little friend came running, telling me to call nine-one-one."

"I told her to. I didn't think you were home. Did you make the call?"

"No. I beat it out here to save you! For God's sake, I'm not waiting in the house for the fucking deputies to get here while some maniac is dismembering you."

I put my arms around him and hugged him. "My hero."

"Explanation, please," he said firmly.

Moving away from him, I glanced out to make sure the devil hadn't changed his mind and come back.

"I have pretty good reason to believe Van Zandt murdered that girl at the show grounds."

"Jesus, Elle! Why isn't he in jail? What was he doing here?"

"He's not in jail because he ditched the evidence. I know that because I saw it and called the cops. But when Landry got there it was gone. I think Van Zandt knows I know."

Sean stared at me, shocked, trying to process it all. Poor boy. He really hadn't known what he was in for when he'd taken me in.

"I'm going to take advantage of this moment of silence to remind you: you got me into this," I said.

He looked at the ceiling, looked down the aisle, looked at D'Artagnon, who stood waiting patiently in the cross-ties.

"This is supposed to be a genteel sport," Sean said. "Lovely animals, lovely people, polite competition..."

"Every business has an underside. You've seen it."

He shook his head, sober, sad. "Yes, I've seen people cheated, I know people who've gotten conned in a horse deal, I know people who've gotten away with some questionable practices. But my God, Elle. Murder? Kidnapping? You're talking about a world I don't know anything about."

"And I'm up to my chin in it." I reached up and gently patted his handsome cheek. "You wanted me to be something interesting."

"If I'd had any idea...I'm sorry, honey."

"No. I'm sorry," I said, not knowing quite how one apologized for visiting a murderer upon one's friends. "I could have said no. Or I could have bailed when the Sheriff's Office took the case. I didn't. My choice. But I shouldn't have dragged you into it."

We stood there, both of us shell-shocked, feeling drained. Sean put his arms around me and hugged me, and kissed the top of my head.

"Please be careful, El," he murmured. "I didn't save you so you could get yourself killed."

I could hardly remember the last time anyone had held me. I'd forgotten how good it felt to be enveloped by another person's warmth. I'd forgotten how precious and fragile was the genuine concern of a real friend. I felt very lucky—another first time in too long a time.

The corner of my mouth turned up as I looked up at him. "No good deed goes unpunished," I said.

From the corner of my eye I saw Molly peek around the corner of the barn, eyes wide.

"He's gone, Molly," I said. "It's okay."

She composed herself as she came down the aisle, shaking off the traces of the frightened child who had run for help.

"Who was that?" she asked. "Is he one of the kidnappers?"

"I can't say yet. He might be. He's a bad guy. I know that for certain. I was lucky you showed up when you did, Molly. Thank you."

She glanced at Sean, said, "Excuse me," then looked up at me with her Junior Businesswoman expression. "I need to speak with you in private, Elena."

Sean raised his brows. "I'll see to D'Ar," he offered. "I need to do something to calm my nerves. It's too early in the day to drink."

I thanked him and took Molly into the lounge. The scent of the coffee Irina had made filled the room. I wondered absently why she had come down from her apartment to make it. She had a small kitchen of her own. It didn't matter. Grateful for what was left in the pot, I poured myself a cup, took it to the bar, and dropped a healthy shot of whiskey into it.

Too early my ass.

"Would you like something?" I asked Molly. "Water? Soda? Double-malt scotch?"

"No, thank you," she said politely. "You're fired."

"Excuse me?"

"I'm sorry, but I have to terminate our arrangement," she said.

I gave her a long, hard look, trying to see where this was coming from. Landry's news came back to me, cutting through the smog of Van Zandt's veiled threats.

"I know about the latest call, Molly. Landry told me."

Her earnest little face was white with fear. Tears rose up in her eyes behind the lenses of her glasses. "They're going to hurt Erin, because of me. Because I hired you and you brought in the sheriff's detectives."

I had never seen anyone look so forlorn. Molly Seabright stood in the middle of the room in red pants and a navy blue T-shirt, her small hands clasped in front of her as she tried valiantly not to cry. I wondered if I had looked half that despondent when I had said basically those same words to Landry earlier.

Coming around from behind the bar, I motioned her to one of the leather chairs and took another for myself.

"Molly, don't blame yourself for what was said in that call. You did the right thing getting help. Where would Erin be if you hadn't come to me? What would Bruce have done to get her back?"

The tears were falling now. "B-but they s-said no police. Maybe if—if it was only you—"

I took hold of her hands and squeezed them. They were as cold as ice. "This isn't a job for one person poking around, Molly. We need every resource available to us to try to get Erin back and to catch the people who took her. The Sheriff's Office has access to phone records, criminal records; they can tap phones, analyze evidence. It would have been a mistake not to call them in. You didn't do anything wrong, Molly. Neither did I. The only ones doing wrong here are the people who have your sister."

"B-but the voice kept saying over and over sh-she's going to pay the price because we b-broke the rules."

She pulled her hands away from me to dig in the fanny pack she had strapped around her waist, coming out with a microcassette recorder.

She held it out to me. "You have to listen."

"You recorded the call?"

She nodded and dug around in the fanny pack for a scrap of paper, which she handed to me. "And I wrote down the number from the caller ID."

I took the recorder and the slip of paper from her and punched the play button on the machine. The metallic, machine-altered voice came out of the tiny speaker: *You broke the rules. The girl will pay the price.* Over and over, separated by Bruce Seabright's terse comments. Then: *Bring the money to the place. Sunday. Six P.M. No police. No detective. Only you. You broke the rules. The girl will pay the price. You broke the rules. The girl will pay the price. You broke the rules. The girl will pay the price.*

Molly pressed a hand over her mouth. Tears rolled down her face.

I wanted to rewind the tape and play it again, but I wouldn't do it in front of her. She was going to be hearing that voice in her nightmares as it was.

I thought about the things that had been said, the way they had been said.

No police. No detective.

Did they mean Landry? Did they mean me? How had they known

either way? No marked cars, no uniforms had been sent to the Seabright home. There had been no direct contact with the kidnappers. If they were watching the house from a distance, they would have seen a few different men in and out of the house Saturday.

No police. No detective.

Landry and Weiss had spoken with most of Jade's crowd, asking about Jill Morone and about Erin. All of those people would know the Sheriff's Office was involved in investigating the murder. But I was willing to bet no mention had been made of the kidnapping, only that Erin was missing and had anyone seen or heard from her.

No police. No detective.

Why differentiate if the detective—singular—was Landry? Who knew we were both involved?

"What time did this call come?" I asked.

"Three-twelve A.M."

After my fiasco at Van Zandt's town house.

Aside from Van Zandt, who knew about my involvement? The Seabrights themselves, Michael Berne, and Landry. Eliminate Molly. Eliminate Krystal. Bruce had taken the call, therefore couldn't have made it. That didn't absolve him of involvement, since we knew there was more than one kidnapper, and knew that Bruce had lied about his whereabouts at the time of the kidnapping.

It seemed doubtful Van Zandt would have made the call from the town house, knowing the cops were already looking at him for the murder and asking questions about Erin. He might have gone out of the house to make the call. Or I supposed he could have made the call from the comfort of his bedroom, using a cell phone while watching one of his porn videos. Lorinda Carlton in the next room with her horrible little dog.

"I wanted to call the number back, but I was afraid," Molly said. "I knew the sheriff's detectives would be listening. I thought I would get in trouble."

I got up and went to the phone on the bar, dialed the number, and listened to it ring unanswered on the other end. I looked at Molly's note, her careful, girlish printing. What a kid—taping the call, getting the number. Twelve years old and she was more responsible than anyone else in her family.

I wondered what Krystal was doing as Molly was here saving my life and trying to save her sister's.

"Come with me," I said.

We went to the guest house and I pulled the list of numbers from Bruce Seabright's phone out of my notes for comparison. The number matched the two calls that came in to Bruce's phone. The Royal Palm Beach prefix.

I had given Landry the list of numbers. He had names to go with all of them by now—if there were names to be had for all of them.

Do you think Don Jade could be Van Zandt's partner in this? In the kidnapping?

Had Landry traced this number to Jade? Was that the thing he had decided to keep to himself?

It didn't make sense to me that Jade would be so careless as to use a traceable phone number to make ransom demands. Any fool would know enough to make that kind of call from a pay phone or from a disposable cell phone.

If the call had come from a disposable phone, like the one I had purchased the day before, and the SO had been able to trace the number to a phone sold at a particular store, they might have been able to get an ID on Jade from a salesperson.

"What happens now?" Molly asked.

"First, I'm giving you this," I said, handing her the phone I'd bought for her, along with a slip of paper with my numbers on it. "This is for you to contact me. It's prepaid for one hour of time, then it quits working. These are my numbers. You see or hear anything regarding Erin, call me right away."

She looked at the cheap phone like I'd handed her a gold brick.

"Do your folks know you're out of the house?"

"I told Mom I was going for a ride on my bike."

"Was she conscious at the time?"

"Mostly."

"I'll drive you home," I said. "We don't need the deputies out looking for you too."

We both started for the door, then Molly turned and looked up at me.

"Will you go to the place for the ransom?" she asked.

"I won't be allowed, but I have other leads to follow. Do I still work for you?"

She looked unsure. "Do you want to?"

"Yes," I said. "I do. And even if you fired me, I would stay in this to the end. When I start something, I finish it. I want to see Erin back safe."

Phone still clutched in her hand, Molly came and put her arms around my waist and hugged me tight.

"Thank you, Elena," she said, more serious than any twelve-year-old should ever be.

"Thank you, Molly," I returned, more serious than she knew. I hoped I would prove worthy of her trust and her gratitude.

"You're a very special person," I said as she stepped back. "It's a privilege to know you."

She didn't know what to say to that, this special child I knew went unnoticed by the people who should have treasured her most. In a way, I supposed it was just as well. Molly had done a far better job raising herself than her mother could have done.

"I wish I didn't have to be special," she confessed softly. "I wish I could just be normal and have a normal family and live a normal life."

Her words hit home with me. I had been twelve once, wishing I had a normal family, wishing I wasn't the sore thumb, the outsider. Unwanted by the man who was supposed to be my father. A burden to the woman who was supposed to be my mother. At twelve I had long since lost my value as an accessory to her life.

I said the only thing I could: "You're not alone, Molly. Us special chicks stick together."

32

"Do we pull him in?" Weiss asked.

They had crammed into the lieutenant's office—Landry, Weiss, and two other detectives: Michaels and Dwyer; and an unwelcome newcomer to the party—Special Agent Wayne Armedgian, FBI. Robbery/Homicide lieutenant William Dugan stood behind his desk, hands on his hips, a tall, tanned, gray-haired man who aspired to retire and go on the Senior PGA tour.

Dugan looked to Landry. "What do you think, James?"

"I think what we've got is too thin and circumstantial, unless Jade's blood type happens to match what we got out of the stall where Jill Morone was killed. Even that would be a stretch to hold him on. *If* we had a clue what his blood type is. He sure as hell isn't going to tell us. We'd need a court order to get a sample. Besides, we know that blood is likely Van Zandt's, anyway."

"You think," Weiss challenged. "Jade was seen arguing with the girl at Players. And he lied about not going back to the equestrian center."

"He lied about not *having* to go back," Landry corrected. "No one at the guard gate saw him come through. No one in the barn area saw him."

"No one saw Van Zandt either," Weiss said.

Landry shrugged. "They both know the back way in. Van Zandt was all over Jill Morone at Players before Jade got there. And we had the tip about the bloody shirt."

"The shirt we don't have," Weiss reminded him. "We don't even know that it really exists. We do know Jill Morone vandalized a couple of grand's worth of Jade's stuff. If he walked in and caught her... He could have killed her in the heat of the moment, then made it look like a rape attempt to try to put it on Van Zandt. Maybe he planted the shirt and made the nine-one-one call."

"Let's say they both did it," Landry offered. "I could be happy with that. They can have side-by-side executions."

"What do we know about the nine-one-one?" Dugan asked.

"It came from a pay phone outside Publix in the Town Square shopping center, half a block from the town house Van Zandt is staying in," Weiss said, watching Landry.

"Van Zandt's lawyer is screaming harassment and conspiracy," Dugan said.

Landry shrugged. "Judge Bonwitt said we had sufficient grounds for the search. Bert Shapiro can kiss his ass *and* mine."

"Conspiracy with whom?" Armedgian asked.

"Someone broke into Van Zandt's place last night while we had him here," Weiss explained. "And then we got the tip about the bloody shirt."

"Just as well you didn't find it," Armedgian said. "It probably would have gotten tossed out of court. Shapiro would have argued the shirt could have been planted."

"Van Zandt could move to Miami. Him and O.J. could become golf partners," Weiss suggested. Everyone but Landry chuckled politely at the bad joke.

"Or we could have that cocksucker dead to rights on a murder, locked up in jail while we nail the case down," Landry said, "instead of running around loose, free to get on a plane and leave the country anytime he wants."

"You think Van Zandt and Jade are in the kidnapping together?" Armedgian asked.

"Could be. Van Zandt's the pervert, Jade's the mastermind. Or it's Jade and someone else."

"Motive?"

"Money and sex."

"And what have you got on him?"

"Jade was last to see Erin Seabright. He claims she quit her job and left town, but she never told anyone else she was quitting," Landry explained.

Dwyer picked up. "Phone calls made from the kidnappers to the Seabright house came from a prepaid cell phone. With the phone number, we were able to get the name of the company that produced the phone, and from them we were able to get a serial number on the phone the calls came from. The phone was purchased at the Radio Shack on Okeechobee in Royal Palm Beach.

"The store has records of sales, but not of the serial numbers of the individual phones sold. They sold seventeen cell phones in the week prior to Erin Seabright's abduction. We've tracked three buyers through credit cards. The rest were cash transactions."

"We showed Jade's picture to the staff," Michaels said. "No one could ID him, but one of the clerks thought the name rang a bell."

"Why would Jade use his own name?" Armedgian asked.

"We could bring him in and ask him," Landry said. "But he's already threatened to call a lawyer, and if he pulls in the same breed of lawyer Van Zandt did, he's out of here in three minutes, and we've blown the ransom drop with nothing to show for it. This close to the appointed hour, they could panic and kill the girl—or kill her just because we pissed them off."

"Or you could hold Jade and try to get him to turn on his partner," Armedgian suggested.

Landry gave him the did-anybody-ask-you? look. "Do you know these people? Have you talked with Don Jade?"

"Well, no—"

"Ice wouldn't melt in his asshole. He's not copping to anything. We go near him, he's calling the dogs. It's a waste of time. Our best bet is to tail Van Zandt and Jade from a good distance, see if one of them goes to the girl, or if we can nail one or both of them at the drop. Then we've got real leverage and the lawyers will want to talk deal."

Armedgian fussed with the knot in his tie. "Do you really believe they're going to carry through with the drop?"

"Do we have a choice?" Landry said. "What do you want to do, Armageddon? Blow it off and go eat clams at Chuck and Harold's?"

"Landry," Dugan growled.

"What? What did I say?"

"The attitude . . . Special Agent *Armedgian* is here to assist us."

"I know what he's here for."

Armedgian raised his eyebrow. He appeared to have only one. A thick black caterpillar that crawled from one side of his bowling ball head to the other. "And what's that?"

Landry leaned toward him. "You're here because of the Belgian— through no fault of your own. And if you'd coughed up the goods on him the first time you were asked, maybe Jill Morone would still be alive."

Armedgian hung his eyelids at half-mast. "I don't know what you're talking about."

"Neither do I," Dugan said. "What are you talking about, James?"

"I'm talking about the feds wanting a little international feather in their cap. Van Zandt turns out to be a serial killer, they want the bust."

"The only thing we have on Van Zandt," Armedgian said, "is some speculation from an agency in Europe. That's all. He's had a couple of minor charges dismissed. You should have learned the same thing just by asking Interpol, Detective Landry."

Landry wanted to get in his face and point out that someone *had* asked, but this asshole would bring Estes' name into it, and then all hell would break loose. As it was, Weiss was giving him the eye.

"Didn't you contact them?" Dugan asked. "I thought you contacted them."

"Yeah, I contacted them." Landry kept his attention on the fed. "All right, I'll play. What are your people doing here? I don't want them underfoot, fucking up the drop."

Armedgian held his hands up. "It's your show. I'm here to consult and advise."

My ass, Landry thought.

"I've worked kidnappings," Armedgian said. "Have you checked out the drop site?"

Landry made his eyes wide. "Gee, should we do that?"

"Landry . . ."

"I understand it's very open," Armedgian said.

"I've got a man out there keeping an eye on the place," Dugan said. "It's a difficult location for surveillance. He's hiding in a horse trailer across the road from the show grounds."

"There's one road that circles through Equestrian Estates," Michaels said. "And a dirt side road that can be accessed through a gate near the drop site. "We can't have cars cruising through there."

He gave the fed the hard stare too.

"My people can tail Van Zandt, Lieutenant," Armedgian offered. "That way your people are clear of any harassment charges."

"Fucking magnanimous," Landry muttered.

Dugan scowled at him. "That's enough out of you or I'll feed you to Bert Shapiro myself."

Landry kept his eyes on Armedgian. "Lawyers or feds. We get fucked over either way."

He just hoped Erin Seabright didn't end up paying the ultimate price.

33

Bring the money to the place. *Sunday. Six P.M.*

Since there had been no further instructions, I had to assume the location of the drop was the place the kidnappers had originally chosen.

The Horse Park at Equestrian Estates show grounds had been in existence only since the 2000 show season, when it had been the site of the U.S. Equestrian Team Olympic team trials for dressage. Unlike the show grounds in Wellington, it was a compact and simple place, with four sand competition arenas used specifically for dressage, and three warm-up rings set in a U around the perimeter of a large grass field. Like most of the stabling at the equestrian center, the barns consisted of several huge tents with portable stalls, all situated at the front of the property. The stalls were occupied during shows only. The rest of the time, the place was a big empty playground in the middle of nowhere.

At the back and center of the property stood the only permanent structure: a grand-looking two-story stuccoed building with huge white columns out front. The building housed the show secretary's office on the first level, and the announcer's electronic control center on the second floor.

From the second floor one could survey the entire grounds. It was the perfect surveillance and sniper's perch if it could be accessed undetected.

The building sat at the very back of the property. Behind it ran a canal, the bank on the far side thick with trees. On the other side of the trees ran a trail used by dirt bikes and all-terrain vehicles, much to the dismay of people showing high-strung horses. If a person were to take the trail and get across the canal, they could use a staircase that ran up the back side of the building.

Certainly the kidnappers knew all of these things. They had chosen the spot. A strange choice, I thought. There weren't a lot of ways in and out. They would see the enemy coming from a distance, but so too would the enemy see them. Trapping and catching them was only a matter of manpower. Why not choose a busy place with lots of commotion, lots of people, lots of escape routes?

No police. No detective. You broke the rules. The girl will pay the price.

No way this was going to go well.

The kidnappers knew the Sheriff's Office was involved now. They couldn't risk showing up with Erin at such an open place. I couldn't see why they would risk showing up themselves. My conclusion was that they wouldn't.

Six P.M. Sunday. A week from the day Erin Seabright had been taken. I wondered if the timing was significant. I wondered if all the cops would be at Equestrian Estates in rural Loxahatchee while the kidnapper dumped Erin's body at the back gate of the equestrian center in Wellington—the spot where she had been grabbed.

I played the videotape of the kidnapping, wanting to see something I hadn't seen before, wishing for some sudden epiphany.

Erin standing outside the gate. Waiting. For who? A friend? A lover? A drug connection? Don Jade? Tomas Van Zandt? She doesn't seem nervous as the white van approaches. Does she recognize the van? Does she think this is the person she's supposed to meet? *Is it* the person she's supposed to meet?

Landry had told me he had contacted Narcotics to see about Erin Seabright's drug connections, if the bust for possession of Ecstasy wasn't just a one-time thing. I wondered what they had come up with. I would have known exactly who to look at for information two years before, when I'd been a part of the narcotics team. But two years is a long time in the drug business. Things change fast. Dealers go to prison, they go to Miami, they get killed. The turnover of personnel is especially swift regarding dealing drugs to high school kids. The dealers need to be at or around the age of their customers or they won't be trusted.

It was difficult for me to give very much credence to the drug angle anyway. If she was into a coke dealer or a heroin dealer for a lot of money, maybe. But it would take a hell of a lot of Ecstasy to run up a three-hundred-thousand-dollar tab that would hatch a desperate kidnap for ransom scheme. Erin's crime had warranted nothing more than a slap on the wrist by the juvenile court. She hadn't been charged with dealing, just possession.

I wondered what Chad Seabright, honor student, knew about Erin's drug use. I wondered how complete Erin's corruption of him might have been. He had no believable alibi for the night of the kidnapping.

But Landry hadn't asked me about Chad.

Do you think Don Jade could be Van Zandt's partner in this? In the kidnapping?

Landry hadn't asked that question for no reason. Had Erin been there to meet Jade? Was Jade the older man in her life? A good bet the answer was yes. But if that was true, then Jade would have had control over Erin, and she wouldn't have been a threat, even if she had known what had really happened to Stellar.

I thought again about the horse and the way he had died, and the fact there had been a sedative in his system. Paris hadn't pinpointed the drug. She had listed several possibilities: Rompun, acepromazine, Banamine.

The consensus was that Jade had killed horses before and gotten away with it. But if that was true, he would have known better than to sedate the horse first. He wouldn't have taken the chance of anything showing up in the necropsy.

What if the jab I had thrown at Michael Berne to rattle him was true? I wondered. What if Berne hated Jade enough to ruin him, hated him so much he would sacrifice an animal he himself had loved in order to frame Jade?

Berne would know as well as anyone a sedative in the horse's system would be a big red flag to the insurance company. The death would be ruled the result of foul play. The company wouldn't pay out. Trey Hughes would lose a quarter of a million dollars. Jade would lose his career, and possibly go to jail.

If what Erin had known about Stellar's demise was that Berne had orchestrated it, then Berne had a motive to get rid of the girl. But why risk the kidnapping plot? Was he that desperate for money? The chances of getting caught seemed far too great—unless he had a way to hang the kidnapping on Jade as well, but I couldn't see how he would pull that off. And if Van Zandt was a part of the kidnapping, I had seen no connection between him and Berne.

I got up from my chair and walked around the house, trying to separate the tangled strands of truth and speculation.

I knew in the marrow of my bones Tomas Van Zandt was a sociopath, a criminal, a murderer. It stood to reason: if he was responsible for one girl dying, he was responsible for another disappearing. He had the arrogance to think he could pull off a kidnapping for ransom. But who would he trust for a partner? And who would trust him?

All of it seemed too risky for Jade. He may well have been a sociopath too, but there was a world of difference between Van Zandt and Don Jade. Van Zandt was unpredictable. Jade was controlled and methodical. Why would he concoct a scheme that made him look like a crook and a killer? Why would he kill Stellar in a way that would make everyone jump to the conclusion he was guilty of the crime? Why would he risk kidnapping Erin for ransom?

If he had needed to be rid of her, why wouldn't he just make her disappear? If he was going to claim she had moved out of town, why wouldn't he ditch her car? Why leave it parked at the show grounds on the off chance that no one would ever look for it?

It didn't make sense to me. But Landry thought Jade was connected. Why?

Erin's connection to Stellar.

Erin had allegedly told Jade she was quitting. Told him and no one else.

Jade was the last person to see her.

He said she'd gone to Ocala. She hadn't.

Why would Jade make up a story like that—a story that could be easily checked out and discounted as untrue.

It didn't make sense to me. But somehow it made sense to Landry. What other information did he have that I didn't? What small thread that could tie Don Jade to the crime?

The phone numbers of the calls to the Seabright house.

I hated the idea that Landry had details I wasn't privy to. I was the one who had given him those numbers, but he was the one who could check them out. And I was the one who had given him the videotape of the kidnapping, but he had access to the technicians who could enhance the tape. I was the one who had tried to reach out to Interpol, to check out Van Zandt. But I knew that if Landry had made first contact with Interpol, no one would have held back from him the information about Van Zandt's past history as a possible sexual predator.

The frustration built inside me like a thunderhead. I was on the outside. It was my case. I was the one who had cared enough to try to help this girl. I was the one who had done all the dog work. Yet I was the one being shut out, information kept from me. Information available on a need-to-know basis, and it had been decided I had no need to know.

And whose fault was that?

Mine.

It was my fault I wasn't a cop anymore. It was my fault I'd brought Landry into the picture. I'd done the right thing and pushed myself out of the picture in the process.

My case. My case. The words pounded in my head like a drumbeat as I paced. *My case. My case.* The case I hadn't wanted. *My case. My case.* The thing that had reconnected my life to the real world. The world I had retreated from. The life I had given up on.

The conflicting emotions sparked off each other like stone and flint, igniting my temper. Unable to contain the pressure, I grabbed up one of the decorator's objets d'art and threw it as hard as I could against the wall.

The motion felt good. The crash was satisfying. I picked up another piece—some kind of heavy wooden ball from a collection in a bowl—and threw it like a baseball. A wild, animal sound ripped up my throat and exploded from my mouth. A deafening shout that lasted so long, my head was pounding from the sheer effort of it. And when it ended, I felt spent, as if a demon had been exorcized from my soul.

I leaned against the back of the sofa, breathing hard, and looked at the wall. The wallboard had two large dents about head-high. Looked like a good place to hang a picture.

I sank into a chair and held my head in my hands, and I didn't think at all for a good ten minutes. Then I got up, grabbed my keys and my gun, and left the house.

The hell if I would let James Landry cut me out. This was my case. I was in it to the end.

The end of the case or the end of me—whichever came first.

34

There is no surer way to tell which direction the wind is blowing than to spit into it.

Sunday is the marquee day at a horse show in Wellington. During the Winter Equestrian Festival, the big grand prix jumping competitions are held on Sunday afternoon. Big money, big crowds.

Just down the road from the polo stadium, where an international match would be going on at the same time, the stands and banks around the Internationale arena fill with hundreds of fans, owners, riders, grooms—all come to watch the best of the best jump a massive course of fences for prize money upward of a hundred grand.

Camera crews from Fox Sports dot the landscape. Vendor stands line the walkway on the high bank between the Internationale arena and the hunter rings below, teeming with people eager to part with their money for everything from ice cream to diamond jewelry to a Jack Russell puppy. At the same time the grand prix is going on, there are lesser events taking place in half a dozen smaller arenas around it.

I drove in the exhibitors' gate and down the row of tents, backing my car into a spot about three tents before Jade's. I had no way of knowing whether Van Zandt had ratted me out to the Jade camp. Fine if he had, I thought. My patience was too thin to play any more games.

I had not come dressed as the dilettante. Jeans and sneakers. Black T-shirt and baseball cap. Belt holster and Glock nestled in the small of my back under the loose shirt.

Circling around the back of Jade's tent, I entered as I had the first night I'd come there. Down the aisle of some other trainer's stalls where people I didn't know were talking, laughing, shouting at each other as they prepared for their classes. Horses were being groomed and braided, tack cleaned, boots polished.

Farther down the row, directly behind Jade's stalls, another trainer's horses stood bored in their stalls. Two had already gone that day, their short manes were still curly from having their braids let down after their rides. The others hadn't seen a brush that day. There was no sign of a groom in the vicinity.

Cap pulled low, I picked up a pitchfork and dragged a muck cart to one of the stalls, let myself in. The occupant of the stall barely spared me a glance. Head down, I picked through the bedding with the fork, working my way to the back of the stall, and peered between the iron frame of the stall and the canvas that made the wall.

In the stall behind, a girl with spiky red hair stood on a step stool, braiding Park Lane. Her fingers worked quickly, expertly. She sewed the braids in place with heavy black thread, every braid perfect and flat against the horse's neck. Her head bobbed as she worked, keeping time to a tune only she could hear on her headphones.

One of the many cottage industries of the winter show season is braiding manes and tails. With four thousand horses on the grounds, most of them needing full braids for the showring, and not enough grooms to go around, a tidy sum can be made every day of a show by a good braider. There are girls who do nothing but go from stable to stable, starting before dawn, braiding manes and tails until their fingers give out. A good braider can clear several hundred dollars a day—cash if the clients are willing to do business that way.

The girl braiding for Jade kept her eyes on her work and her fingers flying. She didn't notice me.

Paris paced in the aisle in front of the grooming stall, talking on her cell phone. She was dressed to show in buff breeches and a tailored sage green blouse. There was no sign of Jade or Van Zandt in the immediate area.

I doubted Landry had hauled either of them in. He wouldn't make a move before the ransom drop. If there was still a chance of them getting the money, the kidnappers had an incentive to keep Erin alive—provided they hadn't killed her already. Unless what Landry had on Jade was ironclad, taking him into custody was too risky. He still had nothing solid on Van Zandt. If he pulled in one suspect, the other kidnapper would still be free to do as he pleased to Erin. If he knew his partner was in custody, he might panic, kill the girl, and bolt.

Landry had to play the odds on the drop, hoping against hope the kidnappers would show up with Erin in tow, even if he knew the odds were against him.

I couldn't quite make out the conversation Paris was having. She didn't seem upset. The tone of her voice rose and fell like music. She laughed a couple of times, flashing the big smile.

I tossed a couple of forkfuls of manure into the muck cart, moved to the next stall, and repeated the process. Looking between the canvas and the post, I watched Javier emerge from the Jade tack stall with Park Lane's tack in his arms.

"Excuse me? Excuse me?"

I started at the sound of the voice behind me, and turned to find an older woman peering in at me. She wore a helmet of starched-stiff apricot hair, too much makeup, too much gold jewelry, and the severe expression of a society matron.

I tried to look confused.

"Can you tell me where to find the Jade stables?" she asked.

"Jade stables?" I repeated with a heavy French accent.

"Don Jade's stables," she repeated loudly and with very precise diction.

I pointed at the wall behind me and went back to digging through the shit.

The woman thanked me and went out the end of the tent. A moment later, Paris Montgomery's voice rang out: "Jane! It's wonderful to see you!"

Jane Lennox. Park Lane's owner. The owner who had called after Stellar's death, talking about moving the horse to another trainer.

Through my spy hole, I watched the two women embrace—Paris bending down to put her arms around the older woman, unable to get too near because of the size of Jane Lennox's bosom.

"I'm so sorry, Don's not here, Jane. He's tied up with something related to that poor girl's murder. He called to say he won't be back in time to show Park Lane. I'll be filling in for him. I hope that's not too disappointing for you. I know you flew all the way down here from New Jersey to watch Don ride her—"

"Paris, don't apologize. You ride her beautifully. I won't be disappointed watching you take her in the showring."

They went into the tack stall, and their voices became muffled. I moved to the stall directly behind them to listen through the wall. Their voices went from whisper to murmur and back, the volume increasing with emotion.

"... You know I love how you handle Parkie, but I have to tell you, Paris, I'm very uncomfortable with what's going on. I thought he'd put his past behind him when he went to France..."

"I understand what you're saying, but I hope you'll reconsider, Jane. She's such a good horse. She's got such a bright future."

"So do you, dear. You have to consider your own future in this. I know you're loyal to Don, but—"

"Excuse me?" A voice behind me asked sharply. "Who are you? What are you doing in there?"

I turned to face a woman with thick gray hair and a face like a wizened golden raisin.

"What do you think you're doing?" she demanded, opening the stall door. "I'm calling security."

I went with confusion again, shrugged, and asked in French if these were not the stalls of Michael Berne. I was asked to clean the stalls of Michael Berne. Was I not in the right place?

Berne's name was the only part the woman understood. "Michael Berne?" she said, her face pinched tight. "What about him?"

"I am to work for Michael Berne," I said haltingly.

"These aren't his horses!" she snapped. "What's the matter with you? Can't you read? You're in the wrong barn."

"Wrong?" I asked.

"The wrong barn," the woman said loudly. "Michael Berne. That way!" she shouted, waving her arm in the general direction.

"I am so sorry," I said, slipping out of the stall and closing the door. "I am so sorry."

I set the pitchfork aside, shrugged, spread my hands, tried to look sheepish.

"Michael Berne," the woman said again, waving like a demented contestant in charades.

I nodded and backed away. *"Merci, merci."*

Head ducked, shoulders hunched, hat pulled low, I stepped out the end of the tent. Paris was walking away on Park Lane, looking like a cover girl for *Town and Country.* The Jade golf cart trailed behind, Jane Lennox and her cotton-candy balloon of apricot hair perched behind the wheel.

I slipped back into the tent on Jade's row. Javier, who had apparently been promoted, was leading Trey Hughes' gray into the grooming stall. I waited for him to start working on the horse, then slipped unnoticed into the tack stall.

The crime scene unit had been through everything the day before. The sooty residue of fingerprint dust clung to the surfaces of the cabinets. The remains of yellow crime scene tape hung on the door frame.

I didn't like that Jade was absent, with the ransom drop only a couple of hours away. What detail of Jill Morone's death would he see to personally? He hadn't wanted to take time out of his life to answer questions about her when the cops had dug her corpse out of the manure pile. He wouldn't want to be bothered with details when he should have been on a horse. Details were Paris Montgomery's job as his assistant. The details, the scut work, the PR, the day-to-day. All of the nitty-gritty and none of the glory. The lot of the assistant trainer.

Not today. Today Paris would ride the star of the stables in the showring while the wealthy owner looked on. Lucky break.

I wondered how loyal to Jade Paris Montgomery really was. She was quick to pay lip service, but her compliments to and defenses of Don Jade always seemed to have a backside to them. She had spent three years working in Don Jade's shadow, running his operation, dealing with his clients, schooling his horses. If Jade left the picture,

Paris Montgomery might have a hell of an opportunity. On the other hand, she had no reputation in the international show-jumping ring. Her talent in the arena had yet to be realized. It would take the support of a couple of wealthy patrons to make that happen.

And in a little while she would ride Park Lane into the ring in front of Jane Lennox, who was on the verge of jumping the Jade ship.

I looked around the stall, one eye on the door, waiting to be found out. Paris had left the armoire open. Clean shirts and jackets hung neatly on the rod. Jeans and a T-shirt had been tossed on the floor. A leather tote bag was carelessly half-hidden by a discarded blouse on the floor of the cabinet.

Checking the door again, I squatted down and dug through the bag, finding nothing of interest or value. A hairbrush, a show schedule, a makeup case. No wallet, no cell phone.

On the right-hand side of the cabinet, at the bottom of a bank of drawers, was a small plastic lockbox bolted to the floor of the cabinet. I tried the door. The simple keyed lock was in place, but the box was cheap with flimsy plastic hinges that wobbled as I pulled on the door. A casual thief would leave it alone and move on to one of the many open stalls where purses were carelessly left in plain sight.

I was not a casual thief.

I glanced at the stall door again, then worked the door of the lockbox, jiggling and pulling at the hinged side. It moved and gave, tantalizing me with the possibility of coming open. Then a cell phone rang, playing the William Tell overture. Paris Montgomery's cell phone. And the sound was coming not from the lockbox in front of me, but from a drawer above my head.

With the tail of my T-shirt, I wiped my prints off the lockbox door, then rose and started opening the drawers above it. The caller ID window in the phone displayed the name: Dr. Ritter. I turned the phone off, clipped it to the waistband of my jeans, and let my T-shirt fall to cover it. I closed the drawer and slipped out of the stall.

Javier was in the grooming stall with the gray, his attention on his work as he plied a rubber currycomb over the horse's hide. The horse dozed, enjoying the process the way one might enjoy a good massage.

I stepped into the doorway of the stall, properly introduced myself in Spanish, and asked politely if Javier knew where I might find Mr. Jade.

He looked at me out of the corner of his eye and said he didn't know.

A lot of very bad things going on lately, I said.

Yes, very bad.

Terrible about what happened to Jill.

Terrible.

Had the detectives asked him questions about what he might know?

He wanted no business with the police. He had nothing to say. He was with his cousin's family that night. He didn't know anything.

It was too bad Señor Jade had not come by for night check that night and stopped the murder from happening.

Or Señora Montgomery, Javier said as he kept working the brush.

Of course, some people thought Señor Jade was the guilty one.

People always like to think the worst.

I also knew the detectives had spoken with Van Zandt. What did he think of that?

Javier thought only of his work, of which he had too much with both girls gone.

Yes, the other girl was gone too. Had he known Erin Seabright very well?

No, he didn't. He was nothing to those girls because he could not speak English very well.

That makes things hard, I said. People don't respect you. It never occurs to those people that you could feel the same way about them because they don't speak Spanish.

Young girls think only of themselves and the men they want.

Erin had her eye on Señor Jade, yes?

Yes.

Did Señor Jade have his eye on her?

No answer.

Or maybe Van Zandt was the one?

Javier only did his job. He didn't mind the business of other people.

That was the best way to be, I agreed. Why borrow trouble from others? Look at Jill. She said she knew something about Stellar's death, and look what happened to her.

The dead tell no tales.

His gaze flicked past me. I turned to find Trey Hughes coming up behind me.

"By golly, Ellie, you're a woman of many talents," he said. He seemed subdued, not his usual drunken, jovial self. "Speaking in tongues."

I lifted a shoulder. "A language here, a language there. It's nothing every girl in boarding school doesn't get."

"I've got all I can do with English."

"You're not riding?" I asked, taking in his casual attire. Chinos, polo shirt, deck shoes.

"Paris is taking him today," he said, reaching past me to touch the gray's nose. "She can undo all the confusion I wreaked on him in the last go-round Friday."

He looked at my outfit and lifted a brow. "You don't exactly look yourself today either."

I spread my hands. "My disguise as one of the common folk."

He smiled a sleepy kind of smile. I wondered if he had taken the mood elevator down with a little chemical assistance.

"I heard a little rumor about you, young lady," he said, watching me out of the corner of his eye as he fed a stalk of hay to his horse.

"Really? I hope it was juicy. Am I having a flaming affair with someone? With you?"

"Are you? That's the hell of getting old," he said. "I'm still having fun, but I can't remember any of it."

"Then it's always new and fresh."

"Always look on the bright side."

"So what did you hear about me?" I asked, more interested in whom he had heard it from. Van Zandt? Bruce Seabright? Van Zandt would spread the news to turn people against me for his own sake. Seabright would have told Hughes because he valued his client more than he valued his stepdaughter.

"That you're not who you seem to be," Hughes said.

"Is anyone?"

"Good point, my dear."

He came out of the stall and we walked to the end of the aisle to stand looking out. The sky had gone gray with the threat of rain.

Across the road the water of the lagoon rippled silver under the skimming breeze.

"So, who am I supposed to be—if I'm not who I seem?" I asked.

"A spy," he said. He didn't seem upset, but strangely calm. Perhaps he was tired of playing the game too. I wondered just how key a player in all this he was, or if he had simply allowed himself to be swept along by someone else's current.

"A spy? That's exciting," I said. "For a foreign country? For a terrorist cell?"

Hughes gave an elaborate shrug, tipping his head to one side.

"I knew that I knew you," he said quietly. "I just couldn't quite place the face. The old brain doesn't fire like it used to."

"A mind is a terrible thing to waste."

"I'd get a transplant, but I keep forgetting to call."

It was a terrible thing, I thought as we stood there side by side. Trey Hughes had had it all going for him: good looks, quick wit, money to do or be anything. And this was what he had chosen to become: an aging alcoholic wastrel.

Funny, I thought, people who had known me along the way might say a similar thing: *She had every advantage, came from such a good family, and she threw it all back in their faces. For what? Look at her now. What a shame.*

We can never know another person's heart, what gives them strength, what breaks them down, how they define courage or rebellion or success.

"How do you think you know me?" I asked.

"I know your father. I've had occasion to call on his services over the years. The name made it click. Estes. Elle. Elena Estes. You had the most glorious mane of hair," he reminisced. He had a faraway look as he stared through the haze of his memory. "A friend tells me you're a private eye now. Imagine that."

"It's not true. Call the licensing board and ask. They don't know me by any name."

"Good business to be in," he said, ignoring my denial. "Christ knows there's never any shortage of secrets around here. People will do anything for a dime."

"Kill a horse?" I asked.

"Kill a horse. Kill a career. Kill a marriage."

"Kill a person?"

He didn't seem shocked by the suggestion. "The oldest story in the world: greed."

"Yes. And it always ends the same way: badly."

"For someone," he said. "The trick is not to be that someone."

"What character do you play in this story, Trey?"

He tried a weary smile. "The sad clown. All the world loves a sad clown."

"I'm only interested in the villain," I said. "Can you point me in a direction?"

He tried to laugh, but didn't have the energy for it. "Sure. Go into the hall of mirrors and take a left."

"A girl is dead, Trey. Erin Seabright's been kidnapped. It's not a game."

"No. It's more like a movie."

"If you know something, now's the time to tell it."

"Honey," he said, staring out at the water. "If I knew anything, I wouldn't be where I am today."

He walked away from me then, got in his convertible, and drove slowly away. I watched him go, thinking I had been wrong at the start of this, when I had said everything led back to Jade. Everything led back to Trey Hughes—the land deal with Seabright, Erin getting the job with Jade, Stellar. All of it came back to Trey.

And so, the big money question was: was he at the center of the storm because he was the storm, or had the storm blown up around him?

Trey had an eye for the girls. That was no secret. And scandal was his middle name. God knew how many affairs he'd had in his lifetime. He'd had an affair with Stella Berne while Michael was his trainer. He'd been with her the night his mother died. It wasn't hard to imagine him having his eye on Erin. But kidnapping? And what about Jill Morone?

I couldn't imagine any of it. I didn't want to. Monte Hughes III, my first big crush.

I know your father. I've had occasion to call on his services over the years.

What the hell had he meant by that? Why would he have needed the services of a defense attorney the caliber of my father? And how would I find out? Call my father after all these years of bitter silence and ask him?

So, Dad, never mind that I defied you at every turn and dumped my education to become a cop. And never mind that you were always a lousy, distant, uninvolved parent, disappointed in me for the simple fact that I was not a child of your own making. Water under the bridge. Tell me why Trey Hughes has needed your esteemed expertise.

My father and I hadn't spoken in a decade. It wasn't going to happen now.

I wondered if Landry had interviewed Trey. I wondered if he'd run his name through the system as a matter of routine. But Landry hadn't asked me any questions about Trey Hughes, only about Jade.

I went to my car and climbed in to sit and wait. Paris would be getting on Hughes' gray soon. Trey would come back to the barn after for the postmortem of the ride. And when he left the show grounds afterward, I would be behind him.

Trey Hughes had just become the center of the universe. It all revolved around him. I was going to find out why.

ACT TWO

SCENE TWO

FADE IN:

EXTERIOR: THE HORSE PARK AT EQUESTRIAN ESTATES—SUNSET

Wide open spaces on three sides. Trees and a canal at the back of the property. A paved road curves past the front. No one in sight, but the cops are there, hidden.

A black car approaches and parks at the gate. Bruce Seabright gets out of the car and looks around. He looks pissed off and nervous. He thinks it's a trap.

He's right.

He opens the trunk and takes out two large blue duffel bags. He heaves the bags over the gate, then climbs over, picks the bags up, and looks around again. He's looking for a sign, for a person. Maybe he's even looking for Erin, though he would be just as happy if he never saw her again.

He starts walking up the drive toward the building, reluctantly. He has the expression of a man who will wet his pants at the first sudden loud noise.

Halfway to the building he stops and stands and waits. Slowly he turns around in a circle. He wonders what will happen next. He sets the bags down and checks his watch.

6:05 P.M.

Darkness is closing in. The security light comes on with a loud humming sound. The voice, the same mechanically altered voice from the phone calls, comes over the loudspeakers.

THE VOICE
Leave the bags on the ground.

BRUCE
Where's the girl?

THE VOICE
Leave the bags on the ground.

BRUCE
I want to see Erin!

THE VOICE
In the box. Ring one. In the box. Ring one.

BRUCE
What box? Which ring?

He is agitated, doesn't know which way to turn. He doesn't like not having control. He doesn't want to leave the money. He looks at the two rings nearest the building and chooses the one to his right. He takes the bags with him and goes to stand at the corner of the ring.

BRUCE
What box? I don't see any box!

He stands there, impatient. It's getting darker by the second. He stares for a moment at the judge's booth—a small wooden shelter—at the end of the ring, then goes toward it.

BRUCE
Erin? Erin!

He circles the booth cautiously. Someone might jump out and shoot him or stab him. Erin's body might fall out onto the ground.

Nothing happens.

He inches toward the door, pulls it open, jumps back.

Nothing happens.

BRUCE
Erin? Are you in there?

No answer.

Slowly, he sets the bags on the ground and inches toward the booth again, eventually stepping inside. There is no one in the booth. A videotape cassette has been left on the floor. Written in black block letters on a white label on the tape: PUNISHMENT.

THE VOICE
You broke the rules. The girl has paid the price.

Cops come out of the woodwork. Several charge up the stairs of the building. They pry the lock off the door, kick the door in, burst into the room shouting with guns drawn. The beams of their flashlights bob and sweep around the room. There is no one there.

As they approach the console of audio equipment situated under the bank of windows that allow full view of the grounds, they spot the simple timer that turned the machines on at precisely 6:05 P.M.

The tape is still playing.

THE VOICE
You broke the rules. The girl has paid the price.
You broke the rules. The girl has paid the price.

The voice echoes across the emptiness of the night.

FADE OUT

35

Trey Hughes never came back to Don Jade's barn.

I waited in my car, checking my watch it seemed every three min-utes as the time ticked on toward six. Javier led the gray, draped in a Lucky Dog cooler, away from the barn and came back leading Park Lane. Paris and Jane Lennox returned in the golf cart, then Lennox climbed into a gold Cadillac and drove away.

I checked my watch again: 5:43.

At another show grounds some few miles away, Landry and his team from Robbery/Homicide would be in place, waiting for the kidnappers to show.

I wanted to be there to see how the drop played out, but knew I wouldn't be allowed anywhere near the place. I wanted to know where Jade and Van Zandt were, what they were doing, who was watching them. I wanted to know where Trey Hughes had gone. I wanted people reporting these facts to me. I wanted to be running the case.

The old rush of adrenaline was there, speeding up my metabolism, making me feel a hum of electricity running just under my skin. Making me feel alive.

Paris emerged from the barn in street clothes, climbed into a money-green Infiniti, and drove toward the truck exit. I started my car and followed, leaving a pickup truck between us. She took a left on Pierson and we began winding through the outskirts of Wellington, passing through Binks Forest.

Molly would be in the Seabright house, tucked away in a corner like a mouse, eyes wide, ears open, breath held, waiting desperately for any word of Erin and what had happened at the ransom drop.

I wish I could have been there for her, as much as for myself.

I hung back as Paris brought her car to a stop at Southern—a busy east-west drag that led to Palm Beach one way or the rural county the other. She crossed to the Loxahatchee side of the road and continued down B Road, into the wooded darkness.

I kept my eyes on the Infiniti's taillights, very aware that we were traveling in the direction of Equestrian Estates.

A creepy sense of déjà vu crawled down my back. The last time I'd driven these side roads at night, I'd been a narcotics detective. The Golam brothers' trailer wasn't far away.

The Infiniti's brake lights came on. No blinker.

I slowed and checked my rearview as headlights glared through my back window. My heart rate picked up a beat.

I didn't like having someone behind me. This was not a heavily traveled road. No one came out here unless they had to, unless they lived here or worked at a nursery or a mulch-grinding place.

I was revisited by the sick feeling I'd gotten in the pit of my stomach that morning when Van Zandt had shown up at the farm and I had thought I was alone with him.

Until later, he had said when he kissed my cheek.

Ahead of me, Paris had turned in at a driveway. I went past, catching a quick glimpse. Like most of the places out this way, the house was a seventies vintage ranch style with a jungle for a yard. The garage door went up and the Infiniti rolled inside.

Why would she live out here? I wondered. Jade had a good business. Paris should have been making decent money. Enough that she could have lived in Wellington near the show grounds, enough to afford an apartment in one of the many complexes that catered to riders.

It was one thing to stick the grooms out here in the sticks. Rent was cheap—relatively speaking. But Paris Montgomery with her money-green Infiniti and her emerald and diamond heirloom ring?

The lights in the rearview brightened as the car behind me closed the distance between us.

Abruptly, I hit the brakes and turned hard right onto another side road. But it wasn't a road at all. It was a cul-de-sac ringed by several freshly cleared lots. My lights caught on the frame skeleton of a new home.

The headlights turned into the cul-de-sac behind me.

I gunned the engine around the curve of the drive, beating it back toward the main road, then hit the brakes and skidded sideways, blocking the exit.

The hell if I would let that son of a bitch stalk me like a rabbit.

I pulled the Glock out of its box in the door.

Kicked the door open as the other car pulled alongside and the passenger's window went down.

I brought the gun up into position, dead aim on the face of the driver: eyes wide, mouth open.

Not Van Zandt.

"Who are you?" I shouted.

"Oh, my God! Oh, my God! Don't kill me!"

"Shut the fuck up!" I yelled. "I want ID. Now!"

"I just—I just—" he stuttered. He looked maybe forty, thin, too much hair.

"Out of the car! Hands where I can see them!"

"Oh, my God," he whimpered. "Please don't kill me. I'll give you my money—"

"Shut up. I'm a cop."

"Oh, Jesus."

Apparently, that was worse than if I had been ready to rob and kill him.

He climbed out of the car with his hands held out in front of him.

"Are you right-handed or left-handed?"

"What?"

"Are you right-handed or left-handed?"

"Left."

"With your *right hand,* take out your wallet and put it on the hood of the car."

He did as he was told, put the wallet on the car and slid it across to me.

"What's your name?"

"Jimmy Manetti."

I flipped the wallet open and pretended I could see in the faint backwash of the headlights.

"Why are you following me?"

He tried to shrug. "I thought you were looking too."

"Looking for what?"

"The party. Kay and Lisa."

"Kay and Lisa who?"

"I dunno. Kay and Lisa. Waitresses? From Steamer's?"

"Jesus Christ," I muttered, tossing the wallet back on the hood. "Are you an idiot?"

"Yeah. I guess."

I shook my head and lowered the gun. I was trembling. The after-glow of an adrenaline rush and the realization that I had nearly shot an innocent moron in the face.

"Keep your distance, for God's sake," I said, backing toward my car. "The next person whose ass you run up might not be as nice as I am."

I left Jimmy Manetti standing with his hands still up in the air, pulled out of the cul-de-sac, and went back in the direction I had come. Slowly. Trying to regulate my heartbeat. Trying to get my head back where it belonged.

The lights were on in the house Paris Montgomery had gone to. Her dog was chasing its tail in the front yard. There was a car parked in the drive.

A classic Porsche convertible with the top down and personalized plates: LKY DOG

Lucky Dog.

Trey Hughes.

36

Obviously, they went in there** and set up the tape and the timer before they even made the last ransom call," Landry said.

They had gathered in a conference room: himself and Weiss; Dugan and Armedgian. Major Owen Cathcart, head of the Investigations Division, had joined the gathering and would act as liaison to Sheriff Sacks. Completing the group were Bruce and Krystal Seabright, and a woman from Victim Services whose name Landry hadn't caught.

The Vic Services woman and Krystal Seabright sat off to the side of the group, Krystal shivering like a Chihuahua, her eyes sunken, her hair a bleached fright wig. Bruce had been none too happy to see her there, insisting she go home and let him handle things. Krystal pretended not to hear him.

"There hasn't been an event at that facility in the last three weeks," Weiss said. "The place is kept locked up, but we're talking padlocks. Security has never been an issue because of the location. But it wouldn't be hard to break in."

"Any fingerprints?" Cathcart asked.

"A few hundred," Landry said. "But none on the audiotape, none on the videotape, none on the timer, none on the tape deck . . ."

"And is someone trying to get that tape to sound like a real human being?"

"They're working on it," Dugan said.

"And what's on the videotape? Let's see it."

Landry hesitated, glancing at Krystal and the Vic Services woman. "It's pretty rough, sir. I don't know that the family—"

"I want to see it," Krystal said, speaking up for the first time.

"Krystal, for God's sake," Bruce snapped as he paced behind her. "Why would you want to see it? The detective just told you—"

"I want to see it," she said with more force. "She's my daughter."

"And you want to see some animal attack her? Rape her? That's what you're saying, aren't you, Landry?" Bruce said.

Landry moved his jaw. Seabright set his teeth on edge. If he got through this case without popping the guy in the face, it was going to be a miracle.

"I said it's pretty rough to watch. There's no rape, but Erin takes a beating. I wouldn't recommend you watch it, Mrs. Seabright."

"There's no reason, Krystal—" Bruce started. His wife interrupted him.

"She's my daughter."

Krystal Seabright stood up, her trembling hands clasped in front of her. "I want to see it, Detective Landry. I want to see what my husband has done to my daughter."

"Me?" Bruce turned red in the face and made a choking sound in his throat like maybe he was having a heart attack. He looked at the cops in the room. "I am nothing but a victim in this!"

Krystal turned on him. "You're as guilty as the people who took her!"

"I'm not the one who brought the cops into this! They said no cops."

"You wouldn't have done anything," Krystal said bitterly. "You wouldn't even have told me she was gone!"

Seabright looked embarrassed. His mouth quivered with bad temper. He stepped closer to his wife and lowered his voice. "Krystal, this is neither the time nor the place to have this discussion."

She ignored him, looking instead at Landry. "I want to see the tape. She's my daughter."

"As if you ever cared," Bruce muttered. "A cat is a better mother than you."

"I think it's important for Mrs. Seabright to see at least part of the tape." The Vic Services woman put her two cents in. "You can always ask them to stop it at any point, Krystal."

"I want to see it."

Krystal walked forward, teetering unsteadily on leopard print stiletto heels. She looked as fragile as a glass ornament, as if one tap would shatter her into a million gaudy-colored slivers. Landry moved to take her by the arm. The Vic Services woman then finally got up off her wide ass to help, to come and stand beside Krystal Seabright and offer support.

"This is against my better judgment, Mrs. Seabright," Dugan said.

Krystal looked at him, eyes bugging out. "I want to see it!" she shouted. "How many times do I have to say it? Do I have to scream? Do I have to get a court order? I want to see it!"

Dugan held up a hand in surrender. "We'll play the tape. Just tell us when to stop it, Mrs. Seabright."

He nodded to Weiss, and Weiss fed the tape into the VCR that sat with a twenty-one-inch TV on a cart at the front of the room.

Everyone was silent as the video image faded in to a scene inside a bedroom in what looked to be a trailer house. The window gave it away: a cheap aluminum frame around filthy glass. Someone had taken a finger and written on the dirty pane: HELP, the letters backward so the word could be read from outside the trailer.

It was night. One lamp with a bare lightbulb lit the scene.

Erin Seabright sat naked on a filthy, stained mattress with no sheets, chained to the rusty iron frame of the bed by one wrist. She was hardly recognizable from the girl Landry had seen only in a photograph. Her lower lip was split and crusted with dried blood. Mascara ringed her eyes. There were red welts and bruises on her arms and legs. She sat with her knees pulled up, trying to cover as much of her nakedness as she could. She looked directly at the camera, tears streaming down her face, her eyes glassy with terror.

"Why won't you help me? I asked you to help me! Why can't you just do what they say?" she asked, a thread of hysteria quivering through her voice. "Do you hate me that much? Don't you know what he's going to do to me? Why won't you help me?!"

"Oh, my God," Krystal murmured. She brought a hand up to cover her mouth. Tears welled up in her eyes and spilled down her cheeks. "Oh, my God, Erin!"

"We warned you," the metallic voice said, the words drawn out, low and slow and slightly garbled. "You broke the rules. The girl will be punished."

A figure dressed in black from head to toe stepped into the frame from behind the camera—black mask, black clothes, black gloves— and moved toward the bed. Erin began to whimper. She shrank back on the bed, huddling against the wall, trying to hide, trying to cover her head with her free arm.

"No! No!" she screamed. "It's not my fault!"

The figure struck her with a riding whip. Landry felt himself flinch at the sound of the whip connecting with bare flesh. The whip came down again and again with vicious force on her arms, her back, her legs, her buttocks. The girl screamed again and again, a horrible piercing shriek that went through Landry like an ice pick.

Dugan stopped the tape without being asked.

"My God," Bruce Seabright muttered. Turning away, he rubbed a hand over his face.

Krystal Seabright fell against the Victim Services woman, trying to cry, but no sound coming out of her open mouth. Landry caught hold of one of her arms, Weiss caught the other, and they moved her toward a chair.

Bruce Seabright stood where he was, the asshole, staring at this woman he had married, looking like he was wondering if he could call it quits on that deal right there and then.

"I told you it would only upset you," he said.

Krystal sat on the chair, doubled over, her face in her hands, her pink skirt halfway up her thighs.

Landry turned his back to her, stepped up to Bruce, and said in a low voice, "If you could crawl out of your own asshole for three seconds, a little faked compassion would be a good thing right now."

Seabright had the gall to be offended.

"I'm not the villain here! I'm not the one who called you people in when the kidnappers said not to."

"No," Krystal said, lifting her head. "You didn't call anyone! You didn't do anything!"

"Erin would be home by now if not for that detective sticking her nose into it," Bruce said angrily. "I was handling it. They would have let her go. They would have known I wouldn't give in to their terrorism, and they would have let her go."

"You hate her!" Krystal shrieked. "You want her dead! You never want to see her again!"

"Oh, for Christ's sake, Krystal. Neither do you!" Seabright shouted. "She's nothing but a nasty little piece of white trash, just like you were before I found you! That doesn't mean I want her dead!"

"That's it!" Landry declared, moving toward Seabright. "You're out of here."

"I've given you a life you never would have gotten any other way," Seabright said to his wife. "You didn't want Erin messing it up. You threw her out of the house yourself."

"I was afraid!" Krystal cried. "I was afraid!"

Sobbing again, she fell off the chair onto the floor, and curled into a ball.

"Out!" Landry said, shoving Seabright to the door.

Seabright shrugged him off and went out into the hall. Landry followed, with Dugan coming behind him.

"I'm pressing charges!" Seabright shouted.

Landry looked at him like he'd lost his mind. "What?"

"I want that woman brought up on charges!"

"Your wife?"

"Estes! None of this would be happening if not for her."

Dugan looked at Landry. "What's he talking about?"

Landry ignored him and advanced on Seabright. "Your stepdaughter was kidnapped. That wasn't Estes' doing."

Seabright stuck a finger in his face. "I want her license. And I'm calling my attorney. I never wanted you people involved, and now look what's happened. I'm suing. I'm suing this department and I'm suing Elena Estes!"

Landry batted his hand to the side and backed him up against the wall. "Think twice before you start throwing threats around, you fat prick!"

"Landry!" Dugan shouted.

"I find one thing that ties you into the kidnapping, you can bend over and kiss your ass good-bye!"

"Landry!"

Dugan grabbed him roughly by one shoulder. Landry shrugged him off and stepped aside, his glare still on Seabright.

"Take a walk, Detective Landry," Dugan said.

"Ask him what she meant," Landry said. "Ask him what Erin meant when she said she had asked him to help her. When did she ask? Why didn't we hear about it? I want a warrant for that house and for that bastard's office too. If he's withholding evidence, he can rot in jail."

"Go," Dugan said. "Now."

Landry went down the hall, into the squad room to his desk, and dug through the pencil drawer for a pack of Marlboro Lights he kept there. He had quit smoking as a rule, but certain moments were exceptions, and this was one of those moments. He shook out one cigarette, took the lighter, and went out of the building to pace on the sidewalk and smoke.

He was shaking. He wanted to go back into the building and beat Bruce Seabright unconscious. The son of a bitch. His wife's daughter kidnapped and his solution was to do nothing. Let her rot. Let them rape her, kill her, throw her in a canal. Jesus H.

I asked you to help me! Why won't you help me? Do you hate me that much?

Seabright hadn't said anything about having spoken with Erin directly. Landry was willing to bet his pension Seabright had another tape stashed somewhere. A tape where Erin begged for help. And Bruce Seabright hadn't done a goddam thing.

But that wasn't why Erin was being punished, was it? She was in that filthy place, chained naked to a bed, being beaten with a whip because the rules had been broken and the Sheriff's Office had been called in.

It could have been that Estes had poked at the wrong hornet's nest. She'd spoken with everyone involved with Erin Seabright. Maybe Van Zandt had figured out she wasn't what she seemed to be.

All of Jade's crowd had been interviewed Saturday regarding Jill Morone's death. Erin's name had been raised. Jade might have been tipped off that way.

Someone in the neighborhood might have been watching, but Landry didn't believe it. He'd looked over the reports on the neighbors: their families, their professions, their connections to the Seabrights. Nothing.

Maybe the kidnappers had had the house bugged, but that seemed a long stretch. This wasn't some multibillionaire they were trying to shake down.

Or the kidnappers had inside information. That kid of Seabright's. Or Seabright himself.

What better way to distance himself from suspicion than to cooperate with the cops, then blame it on them when things went south. He would never have done a thing to help Erin if Estes hadn't stuck her nose in it.

He would have done exactly what Landry had said in the beginning: kept all the info to himself until the girl turned up dead—if she turned up at all. And he would have told his wife he'd done everything he could, everything he'd thought best. Too bad it hadn't worked out, but what the hell, Erin was just a white trash liability anyway.

The cigarette was gone. Landry dropped it on the sidewalk, ground the butt out, picked it up and threw it in the trash.

And how did Don Jade fit into the picture?

Estes had told him: Seabright sold land to Trey Hughes, Don Jade worked for Trey Hughes. Bruce got Erin the job with Jade through Hughes. The girl would have been better off running away from home to live on the street in Miami.

Everything goes back to Jade, Estes had said in the beginning. But that wasn't quite true. Everything went back to Trey Hughes.

Landry dug his cell phone out of his pocket and dialed Dwyer, who had the tail on Jade.

"Where is he?"

"Having dinner at Michael's Pasta. Specials of the night: penne putanesca and seafood risotto."

"Who's he with?"

"Some tiny old broad with big fake tits and orange hair. Can we pick him up?"

"No."

"What happened at the drop?"

"It was a setup. They knew we'd be there."

"How?"

"I've got a hunch."

"They've got medication for that now."

"Yeah, it's called an arrest. Do you know where the feds are?"

"Sitting with their thumbs up their asses. They say Van Zandt hasn't left the town house. The Mercedes is sitting in the driveway."

"And where's the Carlton woman's car?"

"Don't ask me. I'm doing *my* job."

"Great."

Landry wished for a second cigarette as he watched Dugan come out the door behind Bruce Seabright. Seabright went across the parking lot to his Jaguar, got in, and drove away. His wife was noticeably absent from the passenger's seat. Dugan turned and came down the sidewalk.

"I've gotta go," Landry said to Dwyer, and snapped the phone shut.

"What do you know about Elena Estes?" Dugan asked.

"She used to be a narc."

"What do you know about her being a private investigator?"

"I know she's not."

"Why does Seabright think otherwise?"

Landry shrugged. "Why does he think anything? He's a fucking asshole. He thinks it's a good idea to let perverts have an eighteen-year-old girl so they can beat her with a whip."

"What do you know about Estes in relation to this case?" Dugan asked. His face was tight with temper.

"I know there wouldn't be a case if she hadn't come into this office and told me what was going on," Landry said.

"She's involved in this."

"It's a free country."

"It's not that free," Dugan snapped. "Get her in here."

37

Suddenly living in rural Loxahatchee made sense. Secluded, away from the throng of horse people, it was the perfect place to conduct a clandestine affair.

Apparently, Don Jade wasn't the only one in his barn willing to play bedroom games to further his cause. If Trey Hughes was in that house for something other than a discussion of how his horse had gone in the ring that day, then Paris Montgomery had snagged Jade's most affluent patron. With malice aforethought.

Or maybe Jade knew. Perhaps she had his blessing. Perhaps she was Jade's insurance policy for keeping Trey's attention.

My gut said no. I had witnessed no overt displays of affection between Paris and Trey. Their interaction at the barn had appeared to be nothing more than client and trainer.

Paris was a smart, ambitious girl. If Paris made Trey happy, Trey could certainly make Paris happy.

As I drove back to Wellington, I wondered if Paris knew Hughes had been involved with Michael Berne's wife before her. That certainly hadn't insured Michael a place in the posh new stables—or Stella Berne either, for that matter.

I wondered how long the affair had been going on. Hughes had taken his horses to Jade about nine months previous, meaning they had gone up to Jade's barn in the Hamptons for the summer. Trey had likely spent the summer there, soaking up the social swirl. A relationship might have sparked.

Turning these things over in my mind, I drove back to Wellington and swung by Sag Harbor Court.

The Mercedes Trey Hughes had loaned to Van Zandt was parked in the driveway. In the visitor parking spots down the street, two men in shirts and ties sat in a dark Ford Taurus.

Feds.

I parked a couple of slots down from the sedan and approached the vehicle from the front. The guy in the driver's seat rolled his window down.

"FYI guys," I said, "I saw him this morning driving a dark blue Chevy Malibu."

The driver stared at me with cop eyes. "I'm sorry?"

"Tomas Van Zandt. That's who you're supposed to be sitting on, right?"

They looked at each other, then back at me.

"Ma'am? Who are you?" the driver asked.

"I used to be a friend of that prick Armedgian. Tell him I said that."

I left them sitting there like a couple of assholes, watching a car that probably hadn't left the driveway all day.

Tomas Van Zandt was a free man.

Until later . . .

I put my gun on the passenger seat of my car and drove home to wait.

There was no obvious sign of an intruder in the area of Sean's farm. I knew Sean would not have given Van Zandt the gate code. But my senses were humming just the same.

I parked my car at the barn and checked on the horses, walking down the aisle with gun in hand. I stopped to pet each horse, feeling my tension lessen a fraction at each stall. Oliver wanted to eat the gun. Feliki pinned her ears at me, to remind me who the alpha mare was, then expected a treat. D'Artagnon wanted only to have his neck scratched.

I thought of Erin Seabright as I performed the task, of the way she had laughed at Stellar in the video I'd found in Van Zandt's bedroom. I wondered if she let memories like that one comfort or torment her wherever she was, whatever was happening to her.

I wanted to call Landry and find out what had happened at the drop, but I wouldn't. He wasn't my friend or my confidant. He wouldn't appreciate my need to know. I hoped Molly would have called, but knew she wouldn't be the first to hear whatever news there was. Bruce would have been sent to the drop. Regardless of what transpired, there would be a postmortem of the operation at the Sheriff's Office. And during that time, no one would think or have the courtesy to let Molly know what was going on.

Nothing to do but wait, I thought, then remembered I had Paris Montgomery's cell phone in my car. I retrieved it on the way to the house and sat down with it at the writing desk.

The phone was a Nokia 3390. The voice mail icon indicated she had messages, but I had no way to retrieve them because I didn't know her password. I did know from experience, however, this model of phone automatically stored the last ten numbers dialed.

I scrolled to the last number dialed. "Voice mailbox" appeared in the screen. I scrolled to the next call: Jane L—Cell. The next: Don—Cell.

Headlights flashed in the drive.

It wasn't Sean. I never saw Sean's lights when he drove in because he always went directly into the garage, which was on the far side of the main house.

Irina, perhaps.

Perhaps not.

I set the phone aside, picked up the Glock, turned off the only light I had on in the house, then went to look out the window.

The security light on the end of the stable didn't quite reach the car. But as the driver got out and came toward my house, I could tell by the way he carried himself it was Landry.

My heart beat faster. He would have news. Good or bad, he would have news. I opened the door before he made it to the patio. He stopped and put his hands up, his eyes on the gun still in my hand.

"Don't kill the messenger," he said.

"Is it bad news?"

"Yes."

"Is she dead?"

"Not that we know."

I leaned against the door frame and let go a sigh, feeling relieved and sick at once. "What happened?"

He told me about the drop, the taped message rigged with a timer, the videotape of Erin being beaten.

"My God," I mumbled, rubbing my hands over my face, feeling it on only one side. In that moment, I wished all of me could have been numb. "Oh, my God. That poor kid."

You broke the rules. The girl will pay the price.

Breaking the rules had been my idea. I'd spent my entire life breaking rules and never thinking twice until it was too late. I never seemed to learn that lesson. Now Erin Seabright was paying the price.

I should have done something differently. If I hadn't been such a bully with Bruce Seabright, if I hadn't insisted on bringing the SO into the picture . . .

If I hadn't been me. If Molly had gone to someone else.

"Don't beat yourself up, Estes," Landry said quietly.

I laughed. "But that's one of the few things I do really well."

"No," he murmured.

He was standing very close to me. Our shadows overlapped on the flagstone as the front door light washed down over us. If I'd been a different woman, I might have turned to him in that moment. But I couldn't remember the last time I had offered my vulnerability to anyone. I didn't know how. And I didn't trust Landry not to hand it back.

"It's not all about you," he said. "Sometimes things just play out the way they play out."

I had used those same words with him just twenty-four hours before. "Anything I say can and will be used against me."

"Whatever works."

"Did it work when I fed it to you?"

He shook his head. "No. But I liked the sound of it."

"Thanks."

"You're welcome."

We looked at each other for a little too long, then Landry rubbed the back of his neck and looked past me into the house.

"Can I help myself to your scotch? It's been a hell of a day."

"Sure."

He went to the cabinet and poured himself a couple of fingers of whiskey as old as I was, and sipped at it.

I sat on the arm of a chair and watched him. "Where was Jade during the drop?"

"In West Palm, meeting with Jill Morone's parents. They flew down from Buttcrack, Virginia, this afternoon and demanded he meet with them personally."

"And Van Zandt?"

He shook his head, the line of his jaw tightening. "Good call this morning about your FBI friend."

"Armedgian? He's no friend of mine—or yours, I imagine."

"He's suddenly here to 'consult and advise.' His people are sitting on Van Zandt."

"His people are watching a car in a driveway. Van Zandt was out here this morning driving a Chevy."

Landry gave me the eagle eye. "What was he doing out here?"

"Serving me notice, I think."

"He knows it was you in his place last night?"

"Yes. I think so."

"I don't like that."

"Imagine how I feel."

He sipped his scotch and thought. "Well . . . he wasn't at the drop. We know that."

"That doesn't mean he's not connected to the kidnapping. Or Jade either, for that matter. I'm sure that was half the point of rigging the tape with a timer: so the bad guys could make airtight alibis for the time of the drop."

"That and to punish Seabright."

"They had to know you'd be there. They never had any intention of showing up with or without Erin."

"We still had to go through with it."

"Of course," I said. "But I don't like what it means for Erin. They know now they're not going to get the money. What do they have to gain by keeping her alive? Nothing."

"Fun and games with the riding whip," Landry said. He stared at the floor and shook his head. "Jesus. You should have seen him go at her. If he beat his horses like that, the SPCA would have him locked up."

"Jade?" I said. "I'm sure you know something about him I don't, but I'm having some serious doubts he's our guy."

"You're the one who told me everything came back to him."

"In a way, it does. But in a way that doesn't add up for me. He's sitting pretty professionally with Trey Hughes putting him into that new facility, buying expensive horses for him. Why would he risk that by doing something so outrageous as kidnap Erin?"

"Erin knew something about that horse he killed."

"So why not just get rid of her?" I asked. "This is south Florida. It's the easiest thing in the world to get rid of a body. Why get embroiled in a messy kidnapping plot?"

Landry shrugged. "So he's a psycho. He thinks he's omnipotent."

"I could go for that explanation regarding Van Zandt. But I don't see Jade risking everything on some scheme, and I don't see him partnering with a loose cannon like Van Zandt."

Landry took another sip of the scotch. Trying to decide whether or not to share with me, I thought.

"One of the phone numbers you gave me from Seabright's incoming calls belonged to a prepaid cell phone we traced to the Radio Shack in Royal Palm Beach. We couldn't get an ID from the clerks off Jade's photo, but one of them thinks he took a phone call from a man named Jade, asking him questions about the phones, and asking him to set a phone aside for him."

"Why would Jade do something so stupid?" I said. "He wouldn't."

Landry shrugged. "Maybe he figured a disposable phone would be untraceable, so it wouldn't matter who he talked to."

I got up to pace, shaking my head. "Don Jade hasn't gotten where he is by being an idiot. If he wanted a phone held for him, why not give a phony name? Why not give them just his first name? No. This doesn't make any sense at all."

"It's the lead we have," Landry said defensively. "I'm not going to ignore it. You know as well as I do, criminals fuck up. They get careless. They make mistakes."

"Yeah, well maybe someone made this mistake for him."

"What? You think someone's trying to frame him?"

"It looks that way to me. Jade has more to lose than to gain by any of this."

"But he's done it before—the insurance scam with the dead horses."

"Yes, but things were different then."

"Tigers don't change their stripes."

"Look," I said, "I'm not trying to defend him. I just think there are more rotten apples in this barrel than Don Jade. What did Michael Berne have to say for himself about the night Jill was murdered?"

"He was at Players for drinks with a client, the client was a no-show. Berne went out into the hall to call the client, and witnessed the scene between Jade and the girl."

"And after that?"

"Went home and spent the evening with his wife."

I rolled my eyes. "Ah, yes, the accommodating Ms. Alibi."

"What?" Landry said, looking irritated. "You think Berne masterminded the whole thing? Why?"

"I'm not saying that. I still don't see why anyone would risk getting caught at the kidnapping scheme. But Michael Berne hates Don Jade with a vengeance—and I mean that literally. Berne lost a lot when he lost Trey Hughes as a client. He's the definition of bitter. He might have killed the horse. Maybe he thinks if Jade was out of the way, he would get back in with Hughes. Even if that didn't happen, he would have the satisfaction of ruining Jade's life."

"And where does Van Zandt fit in with Berne? You still believe he killed Jill, don't you?"

"Yes, but maybe he doesn't fit in. Maybe he killed Jill and it didn't have anything to do with anything but sex," I said. "Or maybe he's partners with Berne, or he's partners with Paris Montgomery—who's screwing Trey Hughes, by the way—but I don't believe he's partners with Don Jade. And then there's Trey Hughes. This whole nightmare is revolving around him."

"Jesus, what a fucking mess," Landry mumbled. He finished his scotch and set the glass on the coffee table. "I wouldn't mention any of this to Lieutenant Dugan, if I were you."

"Why would I?"

Landry's pager went off. He checked the display, then glanced up at me. "Because he wants you in his office ASAP."

Landry held the door for me as we entered the building. I didn't have the manners to thank him. My mind was on the meeting ahead. I needed a strategy going in or Dugan and Armedgian would run me off the case on a rail.

They were waiting in the lieutenant's office: Dugan, Armedgian, and Weiss. Weiss gave me the glare as I entered the room, the flat cop eyes with a mountain of pent-up anger behind them. I dismissed him and went straight to Dugan, looking him in the eye, offering my hand.

"Lieutenant. Elena Estes. I'd say it's a pleasure, but I'm sure it won't be." I turned to Armedgian. "Wayne. Thanks for the info on Van Zandt. The whole truth would have been more helpful, but what the hell? Nobody liked Jill Morone anyway."

Armedgian's round face colored. "I can't give sensitive information to a civilian."

"Sure. I understand. And that's why you called Lieutenant Dugan here straightaway, right? To warn him, so he could have someone keep an eye on the guy, right?"

"We had no reason to believe Van Zandt was an immediate danger to anyone," Armedgian defended himself. "I hadn't been made aware of the Seabright girl's kidnapping."

"I'm sure that will be a comfort to Jill Morone's family."

"Your concern for the family is touching, Ms. Estes," Dugan said. "And surprising, considering the way you've treated the Seabrights."

"I've given due courtesy to the Seabrights."

"Not according to Bruce Seabright."

"He wasn't due any, as you've probably found out for yourself by now. Frankly, I'm not convinced he isn't involved in the kidnapping."

"I'm not interested in your theories, Ms. Estes," Dugan said.

"Then why am I here?"

"The Seabrights want to lodge a complaint against you. Seems you've misrepresented yourself to them."

"Not so."

"You are not a private investigator," Dugan said.

"I never told anyone that I was. The Seabrights have made an erroneous assumption."

"Don't try to bullshit me with semantics. If you want to play word games, become a lawyer."

"Thanks for the career advice."

"Too bad she couldn't have taken it before she got one of ours killed," Weiss muttered behind my back.

I kept my focus on Dugan. "I got into this to try to help a little girl who believed her sister was in trouble when no one—including this office—believed her. That's my only purpose in this, Lieutenant. If Bruce Seabright somehow feels threatened by that, you might want to have a hard look at why."

"We've got it under control," Dugan said. "I want you out of it. Now."

I looked around the room. "Gee, did I miss something? Have I been rehired by this agency? Because, if I haven't been, then I'm pretty certain you can't tell me what to do or where to go or with whom I might have a conversation. I'm a private citizen."

"You're impeding an official investigation."

"There wouldn't be an investigation if not for me."

"I can't have a citizen running loose, breaking and entering homes, tampering with evidence—"

"Breaking and entering is a crime," I said. "If you have some kind of proof I've committed a crime, then you should arrest me."

"Say the word, Lieutenant," Weiss offered. "I'll do the honors."

"Van Zandt is our business now, Elena," Armedgian said. "The sheriff's and the FBI's."

I looked at him, bored. "Uh-huh. Great job. He came to my house this morning and threatened me. Where were you then, Wayne? And you know what? I'll bet a hundred dollars you don't know where he is right now. Do you?"

The look on his face spoke for him.

"The Seabrights intend to file a restraining order against you, Ms. Estes," Dugan said. "If you go near them, their home, Mr. Seabright's place of business, we'll have to pick you up."

I shrugged. "You could have sent a deputy to tell me that. Unless you really want to talk about this case, Lieutenant, you're wasting my time."

Dugan arched an eyebrow. "You have pressing business somewhere?"

I pulled my cell phone out of my jacket pocket, scrolled through a few numbers, and hit the call button. I kept my gaze on the lieutenant as the phone rang on the other end.

"Van Zandt? Elle. Sorry I had to rush off this morning. Especially after you took all that time to scream at me and make me feel like I couldn't ride a bicycle, much less a horse."

There was a pause on the other end of the line. Only background noise. He was in a car. I figured to proceed with the conversation even if Van Zandt hung up on me. I wanted Dugan to know he didn't own me, and at the same time know that I could be an asset, whether he liked the idea or not.

"You think I was too tough on you?" Van Zandt asked.

"No. I like it rough," I said suggestively.

Another pause, and then he chuckled. "I don't know anyone like you, Elle."

"Is that a good thing or a bad thing?"

"I think that remains to be seen. I'm surprised you are calling me."

"The moth to the flame," I said. "You exercise my brain, Z. Sean and I are going to Players for a late dinner and a drink or three. Are you free?"

"Not at the moment."

"Later?" I suggested.

"I don't think I should trust you, Elle."

"Why not? I don't have any power. I'm the odd one out."

"You don't trust me," he said. "You think bad things about me which are not true."

"So convince me you're a good guy. It's never too late to make friends. Besides, it's only drinks, for God's sake. Bring your friend Lorinda. You can sell her Sean's horse over dessert. See you later. *Ciao.*"

I ended the call, put the phone back in my pocket.

"Yes," I said to Dugan. "I have pressing business. Seems I have a date with Tomas Van Zandt." I turned to Wayne Armedgian. "Do you think you can pick up the tail from a dead standstill in a parking lot?"

I didn't wait for an answer.

"It's been real, guys," I said, and with a wave of my hand, I left the room.

I felt dizzy. I felt like I had walked up to a giant and spit in his eye. I'd managed to alienate the head of Robbery/Homicide and a regional supervisory special agent of the FBI in one fell swoop.

What the hell. I'd been the alien going in. They had excluded me, not the other way around. I would have happily told them anything about the case I could, but they didn't want me. I had just put them on notice I couldn't be bullied. I knew my rights, I knew the law. And I knew I was right: They wouldn't have had a case if I hadn't badgered Landry into it, if I hadn't called Armedgian looking for information. I wouldn't let them pat-pat me on the head now and send me to the sidelines.

I walked up and down on the sidewalk outside the building, breathing in the thick, warm night air, wondering if I'd played it right, wondering if it would even matter or if it was already too late.

"That's some set you've got on you, Estes."

Landry came toward me with a cigarette in one hand and a lighter in the other.

"Yeah, it's a wonder my pants fit."

"Think Van Zandt will show at Players?" he asked, lighting up.

"I think he will. He likes the game too much. And it's not as if he's in imminent danger of arrest. He knows you don't have anything on him or he'd be in jail already. I think he'll show to rub your face in it—and mine."

On impulse I took the cigarette from his fingers and took a drag. Landry watched me, inscrutable.

"You smoke?" he asked.

"No," I said on a trail of smoke. "I quit years ago."

"Me too."

"Desk pack?" I asked.

He took the cigarette back. "It's this or a flask. I can't get suspended for this. Yet."

"Weiss has a real bug up his ass."

"He's short," Landry said by way of explanation.

"I know I'm not welcome in this," I said. "But it was my case first, and I can still serve a purpose."

"Yeah, I know. You just slapped my lieutenant in the face with it."

A hint of a smile pulled at his mouth. His approval meant too much to me.

"Subtlety is overrated and it takes too long," I said. "We don't have time to fuck around."

I took the cigarette for one last puff, my lips touching where his had been. I didn't want to let myself think there was anything erotic in that, but of course there was, and Landry knew it too. Our gazes locked and held, a current running between us.

"I've got to go," I said, backing down the sidewalk.

Landry stayed where he was. "What if Dugan wants you back inside?"

"He knows where I'm going. He can come and buy me a drink."

He shook his head in wonder. "You're something, Estes."

"Just trying to survive," I said as I turned and went to my car.

As I pulled around past the sidewalk on my way out of the lot, my headlights flashed on Weiss standing in the doorway to the building. Little prick. I figured he would make trouble for Landry sharing his smoke with me, but that was Landry's business. I had problems of my own. I had a date with a killer.

38

Women. Stupid, ungrateful bitches. Van Zandt spent most of his life courting them, flattering them—no matter what they looked like—carting them around to look at horses, giving his advice and counsel. They needed him to tell them what to do, what to think, what to buy. And were they grateful? No. Most of them were selfish and silly and didn't have a brain in their heads. They deserved to be cheated. They deserved whatever happened to them.

He thought of Elle. He still thought of her by that name, even though he knew it to be false. She was not "most women." She was clever and devious and bold. She thought with the hard logic of a man, but with a woman's slyness and sexuality. He found that exciting, challenging. A game worth playing.

And she was right: there was nothing she could do to hurt him. There was no evidence against him, therefore he was an innocent man.

He smiled at that, feeling happy and clever and superior.

He snatched up his cell phone, punched the speed-dial number for the town house, and listened to it ring unanswered on the other end. His mood spiraled back down. Another ring and he would get the machine. He didn't want to speak to a fucking machine. Where the hell was Lorinda? Off somewhere with that obnoxious dog of hers. Horrible, flea-ridden beast.

The machine picked up and he left a curt message for her to meet him at The Players later.

Angry now, he ended the call and threw the phone onto the passenger's seat of the cheap piece-of-shit car Lorinda had given him to drive. He hadn't wanted to tolerate the police following him around. Following him for no good reason, he had told her. He was the innocent victim of police harassment. She had believed him, of course, despite the fact that she had seen the bloody shirt. He had excused that away, and she had believed him in that too.

Stupid cow. Why she didn't rent a better car when she traveled was beyond him. Lorinda had money she had inherited from her family in Virginia. Tomas had taken it upon himself to do the research. But she wasted it on charities for abandoned dogs and broken-down horses, instead of using it for herself. She lived like a gypsy on the farm that had belonged to her grandmother, renting out the grand plantation house and living herself—with a pack of dogs and cats—in an old clapboard farmhouse that she never cleaned.

Tomas had told her she needed to get a face-lift and a boob job, and fix herself up or she would never get a rich husband. She laughed and asked him why she should get another husband when she had Tomas to look out for her best interests.

Stupid creature.

Women. The bane of his existence.

He drove east on Southern Boulevard, thinking about the woman he was to meet. She thought she could blackmail him. She told him she knew all about the dead girl, which, of course, she did not. But she had already become a problem before that, because of the lies she told the Americans about him. Bitter, vindictive cunt. That was the Russians. A more vicious race of people had never lived.

The death of this one would be, of course, the fault of Sasha Kulak. Tomas had taken her in, given her a roof over her head, a job, an opportunity to learn from him and take advantage of his vast knowledge—in the barn and in the bedroom.

She should have worshiped him. She should have wanted to please and service him. She should have thanked him. Instead, she had stolen from him and stabbed him in the back and spread stories about him.

He had, at great cost to himself, called any clients she might have known, might have contacted after she had left him, to warn them this girl was trouble, that she was a thief and probably on drugs; to tell them of course he hadn't done anything wrong.

And now he had to deal with her friend, Avadon's Russian girl. Avadon should have fired her on the spot Friday when the girl had tried to kill him in Avadon's own stable. Incredible what these Americans would tolerate.

He'd had his fill of Florida. He was ready to go back to Belgium. He had a flight already lined up. A cargo plane traveling to Brussels with a load of horses. Going as a groom, he never had to pay. One more day he would do business here, showing everyone he had nothing to hide, no reason to worry about the police. Then he would return to Europe for a time, and come back when people had better things to gossip about than him.

He slowed the car as he looked for the sign. He had suggested meeting at the back of the show grounds, but the girl had refused, insisting on a public place. This was the place she had chosen: Magda's—a shitty bar in an industrial part of West Palm Beach. A clapboard building that even in the dark looked as if it needed paint and had termites.

Van Zandt pulled in the drive alongside the bar and drove around back to find a parking place.

He would find the girl in the bar, buy her a drink. When she wasn't looking, he would slip her the drug. It was a simple thing. They would talk, he would try to assure her there had been a misunderstanding about Sasha. The drug would start to take effect. When the moment was right and she was incapable of protest, he would assist her outside.

She would appear to be drunk. He would put her in the car and drive away to a place where he could kill her and dispose of her body.

He found a spot to park, backing in along a chain-link fence that separated the bar's property from an auto salvage yard. The perfect place. Out of sight. This problem would be dealt with quickly and neatly, and then he would go to The Players to have a drink with Elena Estes.

I went into The Players alone. If Van Zandt showed with Lorinda Carlton, I would make Sean's excuses, but I wouldn't drag Sean any further into the drama than I already had.

The club was busy. Celebrants from the showring and losers drowning their sorrows. Most stables are closed on Mondays so everyone can recuperate from the weekend's competition. No reason to go to bed early on Sunday.

The place was a stage with a hundred players. Women showing off the latest in Palm Beach fashions and the newest plastic surgery. Swarthy polo players from South America hitting on every rich thing in a skirt. Minor celebs in town for a long weekend. Saudi Arabian royalty. Every pair of eyes in the place sliding to the next most promising conversation partner in the room.

I found a small table in the corner of the bar and settled in with my back to the wall and a view of the room. I ordered tonic and lime and fended off an ex-baseball star who wanted to know if he knew me.

"No," I said, amused he had singled me out. "And you don't want to."

"Why is that?"

"Because I'm nothing but trouble."

He slid into the other chair and leaned across the table. His smile had lit up many an ad for cheap long distance service and colorful underwear. "Wrong thing to say. Now I'm intrigued."

"And I'm waiting for someone."

"Lucky guy. What's he got that I haven't?"

"I don't know," I said with a half smile. "I haven't seen him in his underwear yet."

He spread his hands and grinned. "I have no secrets."

"You have no shame."

"No. But I always get the girl."

I shook my head. "Not this time, Ace."

"Is this character giving you a hard time, Elle?"

I looked up to find Don Jade standing beside me with a martini in hand.

"No, I'm afraid I'm giving him a hard time," I said.

"Or something," Mr. Baseball said, bobbing his eyebrows. "You're not waiting for this guy, are you?"

"As a matter of fact, yes."

"Even after you've seen me in my underwear?"

"I like surprises. What can I say?"

"Say you'll ditch him later," he said, rising. "I'll be at the end of the bar."

I watched him walk away, surprised at myself for enjoying the flirtation.

"Don't look so impressed," Jade said, taking the empty seat. "He's all hat and no cattle, as they say in Texas."

"And how would you know that?"

He gave me a steady look that belied the drink in his hand. He was sober as a judge. "You'd be surprised at the things I know, Elle."

I sipped my tonic, wondering if he knew about me; wondering if Van Zandt had told him, or Trey, or if he had been left out of that loop on purpose.

"No, I don't think I would," I said. "I'm sure there isn't much that gets past you."

"Not much."

"Is that why you were with the detectives so long yesterday?" I asked. "Because you had so much to tell them?"

"No, I'm afraid Jill's murder is a subject I don't know anything about at all. Do you?"

"Me? Not a thing. Should we ask someone else? Van Zandt is coming later. Shall we ask him? I have a feeling he could tell us some stories to make our hair stand on end."

"It's not difficult to get someone to tell you a story, Elle," Jade said.

"No. The hard part is getting them to tell the truth."

"And that's what you're looking for? The truth?"

"You know what they say: the truth shall set you free."

He sipped his martini and looked away at nothing. "That all depends on who you are, doesn't it?"

The girl was waiting under the back-door light. Her hair stood out around her head like a lion's mane. She wore black tights that clung to her long legs, and a denim jacket, and her mouth was painted dark. She was smoking a cigarette.

At least Van Zandt thought it was Avadon's girl. They never looked the same, these girls, away from the stables.

Van Zandt opened the car door and got out, wondering if he should simply lure her away from the building, shove her in the car, and go. But the threat of a possible witness coming out the back door of the bar was too big a risk. Even as he thought of it, the door opened and a large man stepped out under the light. He took a position there, feet apart, hands clasped in front of him. The girl glanced up at him, smiled bewitchingly, and said something in Russian.

Halfway between the car and the building, a sense of apprehension crawled over Van Zandt's skin. His step slowed. The big Russian had something in his hand. A gun perhaps.

Behind him, car doors opened and shoe soles scuffed the cracked concrete.

He'd made a terrible mistake, he thought. The girl was near enough that he could see she was looking at him and smiling wickedly. He turned to try to go back to the car. Three men stood in front of him, two built like plow horses standing on either side of a smaller man in a fine dark suit.

"Are you thinking you should not have come, Mr. Van Zandt?" the small man said.

Van Zandt looked down his nose. "Do I know you?"

"No," he said as his associates moved to take hold of Van Zandt, one on each arm. "But perhaps you know my name. Kulak. Alexi Kulak."

Do you believe in karma, Elle?" Jade asked.

"God, no."

Jade was still nursing his martini. I was on my second tonic and lime. A couple of cheap dates. We'd been sitting there fifteen minutes with no sign of Van Zandt.

"Why would I want to believe in that?" I asked.

"What goes around comes around."

"For everyone? For me? No, thank you."

"And what have you ever done that you'd have to pay for?"

"I killed a man once," I confessed calmly, just to see the look on his face. It was probably the first time in a decade he'd been surprised. "I'd rather not have that come back around on me."

"You killed a man?" he asked, trying not to look astonished. "Did he have it coming?"

"No. It was an accident—if you believe in accidents. How about you? Are you waiting for your past deeds to ambush you? Or are you hoping someone else will have their markers called in?"

He finished the martini as Susannah Atwood came in the room. "Here's what I believe in, Elle," he said. "I believe in me, I believe in now, I believe in careful planning."

I wanted to ask him if it had been in his plan for someone to murder Jill Morone and kidnap Erin Seabright. I wanted to ask him if it had been in his plan for Paris Montgomery to have an affair with Trey Hughes, but I had already lost his attention.

"My dinner companion has arrived," he said, rising. He looked at me and smiled with a cross between amusement and bemusement. "Thanks for the conversation, Elle. You're a fascinating person."

"Good luck with your karma," I said.

"And you with yours."

As I watched him walk across the room, I wondered what had prompted his sudden philosophical turn. If he was an innocent man, was he thinking this sudden turn of twisted bad luck was payback for the things he'd gotten away with in his past? Or was he thinking what I was thinking? That there was no such thing as bad luck, that there are no accidents, no coincidences. If he was thinking someone was hanging a noose around his neck, who did he like for a candidate?

From the corner of my eye I could see the baseball player homing in on the seat Jade had vacated. I got up and left the room, my patience for flirtation worn thin. I wanted Van Zandt to show up for no other reason than to rub Dugan's and Armedgian's noses in my obvious usefulness.

I believed he would show. I believed he wouldn't be able to resist the opportunity to sit in a public place, relaxed and pleased with himself, conversing with someone who believed he was a murderer and couldn't do anything about it. The sense of power that would give him would be too intoxicating to pass up.

I wondered what his business of the evening entailed, if it had anything to do with the kidnapping. I wondered if he was the man in black Landry had described viciously beating Erin Seabright with a riding whip. Sick bastard. It wasn't hard to imagine him getting off on that kind of thing. Control was his game.

As I stood outside the front doors of The Players, I pictured him in prison, suffering the ultimate lack of control, every minute of his life dictated to him.

Karma. Maybe I wanted to believe in it after all.

The beating wasn't the worst of it. The worst thing was knowing that when the beating was over, so too would be his life. Or perhaps the worst thing was knowing he had no control in the situation. All the power was held by Alexi Kulak, cousin of that Russian cunt who had now ruined his life.

While the Russian stationed at the back door kept anyone from coming out to witness the act, Kulak had personally slapped a wide swatch of duct tape over Van Zandt's mouth and taped his hands together behind his back. They shoved him into the backseat of Lorinda's rental car, which they drove through an open gate onto the grounds of the auto salvage yard behind the bar. They then parked the car inside a cavernous, filthy garage and dragged him from it.

He tried to run, of course. Awkward with his arms behind him and panic running like water down his legs, it seemed the door grew no closer as he ran. The thugs caught him with rough hands and dragged him back onto a large black tarp laid out on the concrete floor. Tools had been lined up on the edge of the tarp like surgical instruments: a hammer, a crowbar, pliers. Tears flooded his eyes and his bladder let go in a warm, wet rush.

"Break his legs," Kulak instructed calmly. "So he cannot run like the coward he is."

The largest of the henchmen held him down while another picked up a sledgehammer. Van Zandt kicked and writhed. The Russian swung and missed, cursing loudly as the hammerhead connected with the floor. The second swing was on target, hitting the inside edge of his kneecap and shattering the bone like an eggshell.

Van Zandt's screams were trapped by the duct tape. The pain exploded in his brain like a white-hot nova. It ripped through his body like a tornado. His bowels released and the fetid stench made him gag. The third blow hit squarely on the shin below his other knee, the force splintering the bone, the head of the hammer driving through the soft tissue beneath.

Someone ripped the tape from his mouth and he flopped onto his side and vomited convulsively, again and again.

"Defiler of young girls," Kulak said. "Murderer. Rapist. American justice is too good for you. This is great country, but too kind. Americans say please and thank you and let killers run free because of technicalities. Sasha is dead because of you. Now you murder a girl and the police cannot even put you in jail."

Van Zandt shook his head, wiping his face through the mess on the tarp. He was sobbing and panting. "No. No. No. I didn't . . . accident . . . not my fault." The words came out in gasps and bursts. Pain pulsed through him in searing, white-hot shocks.

"You lying piece of shit," Kulak snapped. "I know about the bloody shirt. I know you tried to rape this girl, like you raped Sasha."

Kulak cursed him in Russian and nodded to the thugs. He stood back and watched calmly while they beat Van Zandt with thin iron rods. One would strike him, then another, each picking his target methodically. Occasionally, Kulak gave instructions in English so Van Zandt could understand.

They were not to hit him in the head. Kulak wanted him conscious, able to hear, able to feel the pain. They were not to kill him—he did not deserve a quick death.

The blows were strategically placed.

Van Zandt tried to speak, tried to beg, tried to explain, tried to lay the blame away from himself. It was not his fault Sasha had killed herself. It was not his fault Jill Morone had suffocated. He had never forced himself on a woman.

Kulak came onto the tarp and kicked him in the mouth. Van Zandt choked on blood and teeth, coughed and wretched.

"I'm sick of your excuses," Kulak said. "In your world, you are not responsible for anything you do. In my world, a man pays for his sins."

Kulak smoked a cigarette and waited until Van Zandt's mouth stopped bleeding, then wrapped the lower part of his head with the duct tape, covering his mouth with several layers. They taped his broken legs together and threw him in the trunk of Lorinda's rented Chevy.

The last thing he saw was Alexi Kulak leaning over to spit on him, then the trunk was closed. Tomas Van Zandt's world went dark, and the awful waiting began.

39

I watched the world come and go from The Players that night, but Tomas Van Zandt never showed. I heard a woman ask for him at the bar, and thought she might be Lorinda Carlton: the hard down-side of forty with a low-rent Cher look about her. If it was her, then Van Zandt must have called her about meeting for drinks. But there was no sign of Van Zandt.

I saw Irina come in with some girlfriends around eleven. Cinderellas on the town, just in time to blow five bucks on a drink and flirt with some polo players before their coaches turned into pumpkins and they had to go back to their rented rooms and stable apartments.

Around midnight Mr. Baseball tried his luck again.

"Last call for romance." The winning smile, the eyebrows up.

"What?" I asked, pretending amazement. "You've been here all evening and no sweet young thing on your arm?"

"I was saving myself for you."

"You have all the lines."

"Do I need another one?" he asked.

"You need to take a hike, spitball." Landry stepped in close on him and flashed his shield.

Mr. Baseball looked at me.

I shrugged. "I told you I'm trouble."

"She'd eat you alive, pal," Landry said, smiling like a shark. "And not in a good way."

Baseball gave a little salute of resignation and backed away.

"What was *that* about?" Landry asked, looking perturbed as he settled into the other chair at the table.

"A girl has to pass the time."

"Giving up on Van Zandt?"

"I'd say I'm officially stood up. And I officially look like a fool. Did Dugan call off the dogs?"

"Five minutes ago. He was betting on you. That's something."

"Never bet on a dark horse," I told him. "You'll tear up the ticket nine times out of ten."

"But you can make it all back when one comes in," he pointed out.

"Dugan doesn't strike me as a gambling man."

"What do you care what Dugan thinks? You don't have to answer to him."

I didn't want to admit that it mattered to me to gain back some of the respect I'd destroyed when my career ended. I didn't want to say that I had wanted to show up Armedgian. I had the uncomfortable feeling I didn't need to say it. Landry was watching me more closely than I cared for.

"It was a gutsy move, calling Van Zandt the way you did," he reminded me. "And it might have paid off. What'd he say when you asked him if he was free?"

"He said he had some business to take care of. Probably dumping Erin's body somewhere."

"I saw Lorinda Carlton," Landry said. "I stopped her on her way out."

"Long braid with a feather in it?" I asked. "Stalled on the shoulder of the fashion highway?"

He looked amused at the description. "Meow."

"Hey, any woman stupid enough to fall for Van Zandt's act gets no respect from me."

"I'm with you there," he said. "That one got an extra helping of stupid. A hundred bucks says she saw that bloody shirt, even helped Van Zandt get rid of it, and she still thinks he's a prince."

"What did she have to say tonight?"

He huffed. "She wouldn't call nine-one-one if I was on fire. She thinks *I'm* evil. She had nothing to say. But I don't think she came here trolling for men. Strikes me her idea of a good time would be burning incense and reading bad poetry aloud."

"She asked the bartender if he'd seen Van Zandt," I said.

"Then she came here expecting him to be here. See? You weren't such a long shot after all."

The bar was closing down, wait staff putting chairs up and carrying glasses back to the bar. I stood up slowly, body aching and stiff from my adventures of the last few days. I dropped a ten on the table for the waitress.

Landry arched a brow. "Generous."

I shrugged. "She's got a shit job and I've got a trust fund."

We walked out together. The valets had already gone for the night. I could see Landry's car sitting opposite mine in the lower parking lot.

"I don't know any cops with a trust fund," he said.

"Don't make a big thing out of it, Landry. Besides, as you are so fond of reminding me, I'm not a cop anymore."

"You don't have a badge," he qualified.

"Ah, do I flatter myself or was that a backhanded compliment?" I asked as we arrived at the cars.

"Don't make a big thing out of it, Estes," he said with a slight smile.

"Well, I'll be a lady and say thank you, anyway."

"Why'd you become a cop?" he asked. "You could have been anything, or done nothing."

I looked around as I thought about how to answer him. The night was almost sultry, the moonlight glowing white through the humidity. The scents of green plants and wet earth and exotic flowers perfumed the air.

"A Freudian would yawn and tell you my choice was an obvious rebellion against my father."

"Was it?"

"Yes, but there was more to it than that," I admitted. "Growing up, I watched my father bend lady justice like a Gumby doll and sell her to the highest bidder. I thought someone needed to tip the other side of the scale, make an effort to even things out."

"So why not become a prosecutor?"

"Too much structure. Too much politicking. You might not have guessed this, but diplomacy and ass-kissing are not on my list of talents. Besides, prosecutors don't get to do neat things like get shot at and beat up."

He didn't laugh. He watched me in that way he had that made me feel naked.

"You're something, Estes," he murmured.

"Yeah, I'm something."

I didn't mean it the way he did. In the span of a week I had lost hold on just what I was. I felt like some creature emerging from a cocoon, not quite knowing what the metamorphosis had changed me into.

Landry touched my face, the left side—where feeling was more a vague memory than it was real. That seemed fitting somehow, that he couldn't really touch me, that I couldn't allow myself to feel it in the acute, nerve-shattering way I might have once. It had been so long since I had let anyone touch me, I don't know that I could have taken it any other way.

I lifted my chin and looked in his eyes, wondering what he could see in mine. That I felt vulnerable and didn't like it? That I felt anticipation and it unnerved me? That I didn't quite trust him, but felt the pull of attraction just the same?

Landry leaned closer and settled his mouth on mine. I allowed the kiss, participated, though with a timidity that may have seemed out of character. But the truth of it was that the Elena standing there at that moment in time had never been kissed. The experiences of the pre-exile me were so distant as to seem like something I'd once read in a book.

He tasted like coffee and a hint of smoke. His mouth was warm and firm. Purposeful, I thought. Nice. Exciting.

I wondered what he felt, if he thought me unresponsive, if he wondered at the way my mouth worked—or didn't work. I felt self-conscious.

The flat of my hand rested on his chest. I could feel his heart beating and wondered if he could feel mine racing.

He raised his head and looked at me. Waiting. Waiting. Waiting...

I didn't fill the silence with an invitation, though a part of me certainly wanted to. For once, I thought before acting. I thought I might live to regret it, but while I was bold enough to toy with a murderer and defy the authority of the FBI, I wasn't brave enough for this.

The corners of Landry's mouth turned upward as he seemed to read all of these things I couldn't sort out in my own mind. "I'm going to follow you home," he said. "Make sure Van Zandt isn't waiting for you."

I glanced away and nodded. "Thanks."

I was afraid to look at him, afraid I would open my mouth and ask him to spend the night.

I turned away from him and got in my car, feeling more scared now than I had that morning when I had thought I might have to stab a man to save my own life.

The drive to Sean's farm was uneventful. The main house was dark. A single light burned in the window of Irina's apartment above the barn. Van Zandt was not there lying in wait for me.

Landry came into the house and looked around. Then he went to the door like a gentleman and waited again for me to say something.

I fidgeted, chewed my thumbnail, crossed my arms. "I'd—ah—I'd ask you to stay, but I'm kind of in the middle of this kidnapping thing..."

"I understand," he said, watching me, his gaze very dark and intense. "Some other time."

If I had an answer for that, it stuck in my throat. And then he was gone.

I locked the door and turned out the lights, went into the bedroom and undressed. I took a shower, washing the scent of cigarette smoke out of my hair. After I'd toweled off, I stood for a long time in front of the mirror, looking at my body, looking at my face; trying to decide who I was seeing, who I had become.

For the first time in two years, I felt aware of myself as a woman. I looked at myself and saw a woman, instead of an apparition, instead of a mask, instead of the shell of my self-loathing.

I looked at the scars on my body where asphalt had stripped away skin and new skin had filled the gaps. I wondered what Landry's reaction would be if I were to allow him to see the full extent of the damage up close in good light. I disliked feeling vulnerable with him. I wanted to believe that he would look at my body and not be shocked, not say a word.

The fact that I was even contemplating these thoughts was amazing to me. Refreshing. Encouraging. Hopeful.

Hope. The thing I hadn't wanted. But I needed it. I needed it for Erin, for Molly . . . for me.

Maybe, I thought, just maybe I had been punished enough, that perhaps to drag it on any further failed to serve a purpose and became simple self-destructive self-indulgence. I hadn't done everything right in this case, but I had tried my best for Erin Seabright, and I had to let that count for something.

I went into the bedroom, opened the drawer in the nightstand, and took out the bottle of painkillers. With a strange mix of giddiness and fear, I took the pills into the bathroom and spilled them out on the counter. I counted them one by one, as I had nearly every night for two years. And one by one, I dropped them into the toilet and flushed them all away.

ACT THREE

SCENE ONE

FADE IN:

EXTERIOR: LATE NIGHT—EDGE OF SHOPPING CENTER PARKING LOT

The parking lot is mostly empty. A few cars in the rows near the supermarket, which is open twenty-four hours. The rest of the businesses are dark.

The girl runs toward the store. Her legs are weak and tired. She's crying. Her hair is a tangled mess. Her face is bruised. Her arms are striped with red welts.

She spots a pair of Palm Beach County cruisers parked together and veers toward them. She tries to cry out for help, but her throat is dry and parched, and hardly any sound comes out.

A few feet from the car, she stumbles and falls on her hands and knees.

GIRL
Help. Help me. Please.

She knows the deputy can't hear her whispered pleas. She is only a few yards from the car, but she doesn't have the strength to get up. She lies sobbing on the concrete. The deputy spots her and gets out of his car.

DEPUTY
Miss? Miss? Are you all right?

The girl looks up at him, sobbing in relief.

The deputy kneels down beside her. He calls to the other deputy.

DEPUTY
Reeger! Call for an ambulance! (Then, to the girl)
Miss? Can you talk to me? Can you tell me
your name?

GIRL
Erin. Erin Seabright.

FADE OUT

40

What kind of shape is she in?" Landry asked as he walked into the Palms West Hospital ER. The deputy who had brought Erin Seabright in hustled alongside him.

"Someone beat the hell out of her, but she's conscious and talking."

"Sexual assault?"

"The doc's doing the rape kit now."

"And where did you find her?"

"Me and Reeger were in the Publix lot down the street. She came running out of nowhere." He motioned Landry toward an exam room.

"Did she say how she got there?"

"No. She was pretty hysterical, crying and all."

"Did you see anyone in the vicinity? Any vehicles?"

"No. We've got a couple of cars cruising the area now, looking for anything unusual."

Landry rapped on the door and showed his badge to the nurse who stuck her head out.

"We're almost done," she said.

"How's it look? Anything?"

"Inconclusive, I'd say."

He nodded and stepped away from the room, pulling his phone out of his pocket. Dugan himself had gone to notify the Seabrights. Weiss had yet to show up.

He punched Elena's number into the phone and listened to it ring on the other end. He tried not to picture her in bed. The taste of her mouth still lingered in his memory.

"Hello?" She sounded more wary than weary.

"Estes? Landry. Are you awake?"

"Yes." Still wary.

"Erin Seabright is in the Palms West ER. The kidnappers let her go or she escaped. I don't know which yet."

"Oh, my God. Have you seen her? Have you spoken with her?"

"No. They're doing the rape kit now."

"Thank God she's alive. Has the family been notified?"

"Lieutenant Dugan is with them. I expect they'll be here soon. Look," he said as he spotted Weiss looking lost at the reception desk. "I've gotta go."

"Okay. Landry?"

"Yeah?"

"Thanks for the heads-up."

"Yeah, well, it was your case first," he said. He ended the call and clipped the phone on his belt, his eyes on Weiss.

"Was that Dugan?" Weiss asked.

"He's with the family."

"You talk to the girl yet?"

Before Landry could answer, the doctor came out of the exam room, looking. Landry showed her his badge.

"Detectives Landry and Weiss," he said. "How's she doing?"

"She's quite shaken, as you might imagine," she said. She was a small Pakistani woman with glasses that magnified her eyes about three times. "She has a great many minor cuts, abrasions, and contusions, though no evidence of broken bones. It looks to me as if she has been struck with something like a wire or a whip of some kind."

"Signs of rape?"

"Some vaginal bruising. Marks on her thighs. No semen."

Like Jill Morone, Landry thought. They would have to hope for some other source of DNA from the attacker, maybe a pubic hair.

"Has she said anything?"

"That she was beaten. That she was frightened. She keeps saying she can't believe he could do such a thing."

"Did she give a name?" Weiss asked.

The doctor shook her head.

"Can we talk to her?"

"She is mildly sedated, but she should be able to answer your questions."

"Thank you, Doctor."

Erin Seabright looked like an escapee from the set of a horror movie. Her hair was a tangled blond mass around her head. Her face was bruised, her lip split. She looked at them with wide, haunted eyes as Landry and Weiss entered the room.

Landry recognized the expression. He'd done a couple of years working Sex Crimes. He had discovered quickly he didn't have the temperament for it. He couldn't keep a lid on his anger dealing with suspects.

"Erin? I'm Detective Landry. This is Detective Weiss," Landry said quietly, pulling up a stool beside the bed. "You're a sight for sore eyes. A lot of people have been working hard to find you."

"Why didn't he just pay them?" she asked, bewildered. She held a plastic bottle of water in her hands, and kept turning it around and around, trying to find some comfort in the repetitive motion. "That was all he had to do. They kept calling and calling him, and they sent him those tapes. Why couldn't he just do what they said?"

"Your stepdad?"

Tears spilled down her cheeks. "He hates me so much!"

"Erin? We need to ask you some questions about what happened to you," Landry said. "Do you think you can do that now? We want to be able to get the people who did this to you. The sooner you tell us about it, the sooner we can do that. Do you understand?"

She didn't answer. She didn't make eye contact. That wasn't unusual. Landry knew she didn't want to be a victim. She didn't want any of this to be real. She didn't want to have to answer questions that would require her to relive what had happened. She felt angry and embarrassed and ashamed. And it was Landry's job to drag it all out of her anyway.

"Can you tell us who did this to you, Erin?" he asked.

She stared straight ahead, her lip quivering. The door to the examination room opened and she started to cry harder.

"He did," she said, glaring at Bruce Seabright. "You did this to me! You son of a bitch!"

She sat up in the bed and flung the bottle at him, water spraying everywhere as Bruce Seabright brought his arms up to deflect the object from his head.

Krystal screamed and rushed toward the bed. "Erin! Oh, God! Baby!"

Landry stood up as the woman tried to fling herself on the bed. Erin pulled herself into a ball at the head of the bed, cringing away from her mother, looking at her with hurt and anger and something like disgust.

"Get away from me!" she shouted. "All you've ever done is side with him. You never cared about me!"

"Baby, that's not true!" Krystal cried.

"It *is* true! Why didn't you make him help me? Did you even do *anything*?"

Krystal was sobbing, reaching out to her daughter, but not touching her, as if one or both of them were contained inside a force field. "I'm sorry! I'm so sorry!"

"Get out!" Erin screamed. "Get out of here! Both of you!"

A hospital security guard came in from the hall. Landry took hold of Krystal by the arms and moved her toward the door.

Weiss rolled his eyes and muttered, "Nothing like a family reunion."

41

Molly's call came on the heels of Landry's. I was already pulling on clothes. I told her I would go to the hospital, though I knew I wouldn't get anywhere near Erin's room. If Bruce Seabright caught sight of me, I would end up being escorted from the building. If he had the right kind of pull with the right people, and had gotten a restraining order from a judge on a Sunday night, I could end up taking a ride to the county accommodations. I had been warned, after all.

All that said, I didn't think twice about going.

When I walked into the waiting room, Molly came running to me. She was pale with fear, eyes bright with excitement. The contradiction was the difference between relief that her sister was safe and apprehension about what might have happened to her that she had to be in a hospital.

"I can't believe Bruce let you come along," I said.

"He didn't. I rode with Mom. They're having a fight."

"Good for Mom," I muttered, steering her to the couches in the waiting area. "What are they fighting about?"

"Mom blames Bruce for Erin being hurt. Bruce keeps saying he did what he thought was best."

Best for Bruce, I thought.

"Will you get to talk to her?" Molly asked.

"Not anytime soon."

"Will I get to?"

Poor kid. She looked so hopeful, yet so afraid of disappointment. She didn't have anyone in this mess but me. In her mind, the big sister she loved so much was her only real family. And who knew what resemblance there would be in Erin now compared to the Erin whom Molly had idolized just a week ago. Knowing what I had learned about Erin over the last few days, I had to think Molly's perception had been a dream even before Erin had been taken.

I remembered thinking, the day Molly had first come to me, that Molly Seabright was going to learn that life is full of disappointments. I remembered thinking she would have to learn that lesson the way everyone did: by being let down by someone she loved and trusted.

I wished I could have had the power to shield her from that. The only thing I could do was not be another someone who let her down. She had come to me when no one should have, and bet on that dark horse I had tried to lecture Landry about.

"I don't know, Molly," I said, touching her head. "You probably won't get to see her tonight. It might be a day or so."

"Do you think she's been raped?" she asked.

"It's a possibility. The doctor will have examined her and taken certain kinds of samples—"

"A rape kit," she said. "I know what it is. I watch *New Detectives*. If she was raped, they'll have DNA samples to match to a suspect. Unless he was particularly meticulous and used a condom, and made her take a shower afterward. Then they won't have anything."

"We have Erin," I said. "That's all that matters right now. Maybe she can identify the kidnappers. Even if she can't, we're going to get these guys, Molly. You hired me to do a job. I won't quit until it's over. And it's not over until I say so."

It was a good line at the time. In the end, I would come to wish that I hadn't meant it.

"Elena?" Molly said, looking up at me with her earnest face. "I'm still scared. Even with Erin back, I still feel scared."

"I know you do."

I put my arm around her shoulders and she leaned her head

against me. It was one of those small moments that I knew would remain stamped in my memory forever. Someone turning to me for comfort, and me being able to give it.

From somewhere in the ER came a crash and a scream and a lot of shouting. I looked down the hall that ran behind where Molly and I were sitting, and saw Bruce Seabright backing away from a door, looking stunned. Then Landry came out of the same room pushing a sobbing, hysterical Krystal along ahead of him.

"I'll find out what I can," I told Molly, knowing it was time to make myself disappear. "Call me in the morning."

She nodded.

I went past the reception desk to the ladies' room and ducked inside, betting Krystal wouldn't be far behind me. She came in half a minute later, crying, mascara striping her face, her lipstick smudged.

I felt sorry for her. In some ways Krystal was more a child than Molly. All her life she'd dreamed of having a respectable husband and a nice home and all the trappings. She had never imagined living the Barbie Doll life would have the same pitfalls as living poor. I'm sure it had never occurred to her that making bad choices in men crossed all socioeconomic borders.

She leaned against the counter, hanging her head over the sink, her face distorted with emotional anguish.

"Krystal? Can I help?" I asked, knowing I couldn't.

She looked up at me, swiping tears and snot from her face with her hands. "What are you doing here?"

"Molly called me. I know Erin is back."

"She hates me. She hates me, and I don't blame her," she confessed. She looked at herself in the mirror and spoke to her reflection. "Everything's ruined. Everything's ruined!"

"You've got your daughter back."

Krystal shook her head. "No. Everything is ruined. What am I going to do?"

I would have started by taking Bruce Seabright to the cleaners in divorce court, but then I'm the bitter, vindictive type. I chose not to offer that advice. Whatever decisions this woman would come to, she would have to come to them herself.

"She blames Bruce," she said.

"Don't you?"

"Yes," she whispered. "But it's my fault really. It's all my fault."

"Krystal, your life is none of my business," I said. "And God knows you probably won't listen to me, but I'm going to say this anyway. Maybe it is all your fault. Maybe you've made nothing but bad choices your whole life. But your life is not over, and Erin's life is not over, and Molly's life is not over. You still have time to do something right.

"You don't know me," I went on, "so you don't know that I'm an expert on the subject of fucking up one's own life. But I've recently discovered that every day I get another shot at it. So do you."

Ladies' room psychology. I felt like I should have offered her a linen hand towel and hoped she would leave a tip for me in a basket on the counter.

A large woman in a purple Hawaiian mumu came in the door and gave Krystal and me the glare, like she thought we were hogging the room to have lesbian sex. I glared back at her and she turned sideways and waddled into a stall.

I went out in the hall. Bruce Seabright was in the waiting area near the exit, having an argument with Detective Weiss and Lieutenant Dugan. Landry was nowhere in sight. I wondered if anyone had let Armedgian know about Erin's escape. He would want in on the interview in the hopes that Erin would finger Van Zandt as one of her kidnappers.

There seemed to be nothing for me to do but wait until the hostile forces left. I would hold out in the parking lot, stake out Landry's car. If I could get a moment alone with him, I would.

I turned and went down the hall in search of a cup of bad coffee.

The doctor offered Erin Seabright a stronger sedative. Erin snapped at the woman to leave her alone. The fragile flower flashing her thorns, Landry thought. He hung back in the corner, saying nothing as he watched the girl order the doctor from the room. She turned then and looked at him.

"I just want it to be over," she said. "I just want to go to sleep and wake up and have it be over."

"It won't be that easy, Erin," he said, coming forward to take his seat again. "I'll be straight with you. You're only halfway through the ordeal. I know you want it to be over. Hell, you wish it had never happened. So do I. But you've got a job now to help us catch the people who did this to you so they can't do it to someone else.

"I know you've got a little sister. Molly. I know you wouldn't want to imagine what happened to you happening to her."

"Molly." She said her sister's name, and closed her eyes for a moment.

"Molly's a pretty cool kid," Landry said. "All she's wanted from the beginning of this is to have you back, Erin."

The girl dabbed at her swollen eyes with a tissue and breathed a shaky sigh, preparing herself, settling herself to tell him her story.

"Do you know who did this to you, Erin?" Landry asked.

"They wore masks," she said. "They never let me see their faces."

"But they spoke to you? You heard their voices. And maybe you recognized a voice or a mannerism or something."

She didn't answer yes, but she didn't answer no either. She sat very quietly, her eyes on her hands neatly folded in her lap.

Landry waited.

"I think I know who one of them was," she said softly. Fresh tears filled her eyes as the emotions welled up inside her. Disappointment, sadness, hurt.

She touched a hand to her forehead, partly shielding her eyes. Trying to hide from the truth.

"Don," she whispered at last. "Don Jade."

42

Weiss came out of the hospital first, running for his car. As he drove past me, I could see he was on his cell phone. Something was going down.

Ten minutes later, Armedgian finally arrived and went into the hospital, then came back out a minute later with Dugan. They stood on the sidewalk, Armedgian angry and animated. Their voices rose and fell, the gist of the conversation drifting my way as I sat in my car with the windows down. Armedgian felt he'd been left out, should have been notified immediately, blah, blah, blah. Dugan was short with him. Not the FBI's secretary, get over it, all on the same page now, et cetera, et cetera, et cetera.

They went to their individual vehicles and drove away, dash lights flashing.

I got out of my car and went back into the ER, going down the hall toward the examination room Erin had been in. Landry came out of the room with a large brown paper evidence bag in hand: Erin's clothes, which would go to the lab to be examined for DNA evidence.

"What's going on?" I asked, changing direction and hustling to keep up with him.

"Erin says Jade was one of the kidnappers."

"Positive ID?" I asked, not believing it. "She saw him?"

"She says they wore masks, but she thinks it was him."

"How? Why does she think it was him? His voice? A tattoo? What?"

"I don't have time for this, Elena," he said impatiently. "Weiss and some uniforms are on their way to pick him up. I've got to get back to the station."

"Did she say anything about Van Zandt?"

"No."

"Who else then?"

"She didn't say. We don't have the whole story yet. But we're grabbing Jade before he can split. If he knows she's gotten away, he knows he's gotta get out of Dodge. If we can snag him now, we'll get him to roll on his partner."

The doors swooshed open and we went outside, headed for Landry's car. I wanted everything to stop, for time to stop right then so I could think before anything more happened. The plot had taken a hard left turn, and I was having a difficult time making the corner. Landry, however, had no intention of slowing down.

"Where did they have her?" I asked. "How did she get away?"

"Later," Landry said, getting into his car.

"But—"

He fired the engine and I had to jump back as he pulled out of the parking space and drove away.

I stood there like an idiot, watching him go, trying to digest what had just happened. It just didn't make sense to me that Jade would take the risk of kidnapping someone—or that he had the temperament for it. I couldn't see Jade as a team player in a thing like this.

Landry had developed Jade as a suspect, had circumstantial evidence against Jade. He had a vested interest in Jade being the perpetrator.

I wanted to know what Erin had said. I wanted to hear her story from her lips. I wanted to ask the questions and interpret her answers from my own perspective, with my own knowledge of the case and the people involved.

An ambulance came screaming toward the hospital, screeching to a halt in the bay as hospital staff ran out to meet it. A huge woman screaming blue murder came out of the vehicle on the gurney, calling for Jesus as arterial blood sprayed in a geyser from what looked like a compound fracture of her left leg. Someone shouted something about a victim from the second car coming in.

I slipped back into the hospital behind the mob as they rushed the woman toward a trauma room. Staff were running everywhere in the chaos of the moment. I went directly to the room where Erin had been and slipped inside.

The bed was empty. Erin had already been taken to a regular room. The exam room had not yet otherwise been cleared. A steel tray sat with suture equipment and bloody cotton balls. A speculum lay in the small sink, discarded after the rape exam.

I felt like the party was over and no one had invited me in the first place. Landry had Erin's clothes and the rape kit. There was nothing here for me to find.

I sighed and stepped back from the table, my absent gaze dropping to the floor. A small silver bracelet lay half-hidden under the table. I bent to pick it up. Made of silver, the links were fashioned in the shape of stirrups, one interlocking with the next. A couple of tiny charms hung from it—one a horse's head, one the letter E for Erin.

Just the thing for a horse-crazy teenager. I wondered if it had been a gift. I wondered if the gift-giver was a man, and if that man had betrayed her in the most terrible way.

The door swung open and I turned around to face a deputy.

"Where did they take my niece?" I asked. "Erin Seabright?"

"Fourth floor, ma'am."

"Will she have a guard?" I asked. "I mean, what if one of the men who took her comes here—"

"We've posted someone outside her room. You won't have to worry, ma'am. She's safe now."

"What a relief," I said without enthusiasm. "Thank you."

He held the door for me as I left the room. I walked away, disappointed. I couldn't get to Erin. I couldn't get to Jade. I didn't know where Van Zandt was lurking. It was three in the morning and I was locked out of the case again.

I slipped the bracelet in my pocket and headed home to sleep.

The calm before the storm.

43

What do you have to say about this, Mr. Jade?"

Landry placed the photographs on the table in front of Don Jade, side by side by side. Jade astride a horse, smiling at the camera. Jade standing beside a colorful fence in a showring, in breeches and boots, profile to the camera as he pointed to something. Jade on another horse, going over a fence. Jade with his arm around Erin, her face scribbled over in ink by a jealous Jill Morone.

"I don't have anything to say about them."

Landry reached out and turned the last picture over like a blackjack dealer flipping an ace.

"Until someone drew a line through it, the inscription on this was: To Erin. Love, Don. Do you have something to say now?"

"I didn't write it."

"We can have an expert compare handwriting samples."

"Don't even start the battle of the experts with me, Detective," Bert Shapiro said, sounding like he might die of boredom. Landry wished he would. "I've got bigger clubs in my bag than you do."

Bert Shapiro: walking, talking, designer-dressed prick.

Landry looked at the attorney with hooded eyes. "What's your connection to these people, Counselor?"

"This should be self-evident, but we are dealing with the Sheriff's Office, after all," Shapiro said to the room at large, amused with himself. Stubby little cocksucker. "I'm Mr. Jade's attorney."

"Yeah, I caught on to that. And Van Zandt's attorney."

"Yes."

"And who else in that little rat's nest? Trey Hughes?"

"My client list is confidential."

"Just trying to save you some time," Landry said. "Hughes will be in here next, talking to us about Mr. Jade. So, if he's one of yours too, you can just hang out with us morons at the Sheriff's Office all day. Enjoy our hospitality and bad coffee."

Shapiro frowned. "Do you have some legitimate reason for wasting Mr. Jade's time here, Detective?"

Landry looked around the room, the same way Shapiro had. "That should have been self-evident when Mr. Jade was Mirandized. He's charged with the kidnapping of Erin Seabright."

Jade pushed his chair back from the table and got up to pace. "That's absurd. I haven't kidnapped anyone."

"What evidence do you have to support the charge, Detective?" Shapiro asked. "And before you answer, let me point out to you that it's not illegal to have one's photograph taken by an ardent fan or employee."

Landry looked at Jade, letting the anticipation gain some weight. "No, but it is against the law to hold a young woman against her will, chain her to a bed, and beat her with a riding whip."

Jade exploded. "That's ridiculous!"

Landry loved it. The cool cat was in a corner now. Now the temper came out. "Erin didn't seem to find it amusing at all. She says you were the mastermind."

"Why would she say such a thing?" Jade demanded. "I've never been anything but kind to that girl."

Landry shrugged just to be annoying. "Maybe because you terrorized her, abused her, raped her—"

"I did no such thing!"

Shapiro put a hand on his client's arm. "Have a seat, Don. Clearly, the girl is mistaken," he said to Landry. "If she's been tortured, as you say, who knows what kinds of things the kidnappers put into her head. They might have convinced her of anything. They might have had her on drugs—"

"Why would you say that?" Landry asked.

"Because clearly the girl isn't in her right mind if she thinks Don had anything to do with this."

"Well, somebody's misunderstood something," Landry said. "When last we spoke, Mr. Jade denied having had anything other than a working relationship with Erin Seabright. Maybe he misunderstood the meaning of 'working relationship.' That doesn't generally involve sex between employer and employee."

Jade blew out a breath. "I told you before: I have never had sex with Erin."

Landry pretended not to be listening. He fingered the photographs on the table. "You know, we found these photographs this morning—Sunday morning—in the apartment shared by Jill Morone—victim of murder and sexual assault—and Erin Seabright—victim of kidnapping and sexual assault. Jill Morone was last seen alive having an argument with you, and you yourself admit you were the last person to see Erin before she disappeared."

"She came to tell me she was quitting," Jade said. "I had no idea she'd gone missing until you brought it up."

"Employee relations are not your strong suit, are they, Don?" Landry said. "Erin wants to leave you, so you chain her to a bed. Jill disappoints you, so you shove her face in a pile of shit and suffocate her—"

"My God," Jade said, still pacing. "Who could believe I would do any of that?"

"The same people who believe you electrocuted a horse for the insurance money."

"I did nothing of the kind."

"Erin knew, Jill knew. One's dead, one's lucky not to be."

"This is all speculation," Shapiro said. "You don't have a shred of evidence against him."

Landry ignored him. "Where were you a week ago Sunday, Don? Sunday late in the day, say around six o'clock."

Shapiro gave his client a look of warning. "Don't answer that, Don."

"Let me speculate," Landry said. "With your friend Ms. Atwood, who has the amazing ability to be in two places at once?"

Jade glanced down. "I don't know what you mean."

"You told me Ms. Atwood was with you Thursday night when Michael Berne's horses were being set loose and a woman was being assaulted not fifty yards from your barn."

Shapiro held a finger up. "Don't say anything, Don."

Landry went on. "The night Ms. Atwood was also seen in attendance at a charity ball in Palm Beach. Did you think we'd just take your word for it, Don? Or the lady's, for that matter?"

"We got together after her event."

"Don, don't—"

"Oh." Landry nodded. "You mean the same time she was also partying with friends at Au Bar?"

Jade sank back into his chair and rubbed his temples. "I don't remember the time exactly—"

"You would have been smarter picking Jill for your alibi for Thursday night, after all," Landry said. "She was willing to lie for you, and she was probably home alone at the time."

Shapiro was up now, hovering behind his client. He leaned forward and said, "Mr. Jade has nothing to say to you on this subject or any other. We're through here."

Landry gave the lawyer a look. "Your client can still help himself out here, Mr. Shapiro. Don't get me wrong. He's in deep shit, but maybe he can still climb out of it and take a shower. His partner is still out there, running around loose. Maybe Don here wasn't the one with the whip. Maybe the whole scheme was the partner's idea. Maybe Don can help himself out giving us a name."

Jade closed his eyes for a moment, inhaled and exhaled, composing himself. "I'm trying to be cooperative, Detective Landry," he said, still struggling to be calm. "I don't know anything about a kidnapping. Why would I risk doing something so insane?"

"For money."

"I have a very good career. I have a very good situation with Trey Hughes at his new facility. I'm hardly desperate for money."

Landry shrugged. "So maybe you're just a psycho. I once knew a guy killed a woman and cut her tongue out just to see how far back it went in her throat."

"That's disgusting."

"Yes, it is, but I see that kind of thing all the time," Landry said reasonably. "Now I see this deal: one girl dead, one girl missing, and a horse killed for the insurance money; and it all revolves around you, Mr. Jade."

"But it doesn't make sense," Jade insisted. "I would have made good money on Stellar as a sales horse—"

"Provided you could get him sold. I understand he had some problems."

"He would have sold eventually. In the meantime, I collected my training fee every month."

"And you'll collect your training fee for his replacement, too. Right?"

"Trey Hughes doesn't have to wait to sell one horse to buy another."

"That's true. But I've learned over the years there are few people greedier and less patient than the rich. And you stand to make a big commission on the replacement horse. Isn't that right?"

Jade sighed and closed his eyes for a moment, trying to gather himself. "I intend to have a long and happy working relationship with Trey Hughes. He's going to buy and sell a lot of horses in that time. I'll profit on all of them. That's how the business works. So, why would I risk that by kidnapping someone? The risk would far outweigh any possible gain.

"If, on the other hand, I live a law-abiding life," he went on. "I'm set to move into a beautiful new facility to train horses for people who will pay me a great deal of money. So you see, Detective Landry, you simply don't have a case against me."

"That's not quite true, Don," Landry said, pretending sadness.

Jade looked at Shapiro.

"What do you think you have, Landry?" Shapiro asked.

"I have ransom calls placed to the Seabright home on a prepaid cell phone purchased by Don Jade two weeks ago."

Jade stared at him. "I don't know what you're talking about."

"And do you have a witness who can positively identify Mr. Jade purchasing this phone?" Shapiro asked.

"I never purchased any phone," Jade said, peeved with his attorney for making it sound like he had.

Landry kept his gaze on Jade. "I've got Erin Seabright, beaten and bloody and scared to death, telling me you're responsible. It doesn't get any more real than that, Don."

Jade turned away and shook his head. "I had nothing to do with it."

"You got greedy," Landry said. "If you wanted her out of the way because she knew something about Stellar, you should have just killed her and dumped her body in a canal. You hold a hostage, things go wrong. People are unpredictable. You maybe wrote the script, but not everybody takes direction as well as a girl chained to a bed."

Jade said nothing.

"Do you own property in the Wellington area, Mr. Jade?"

"That would be a matter of public record," Shapiro said.

"Unless he put it in a partnership or a blind trust," Landry pointed out. "Will you share that information with us or make us dig for it? Or should I ask Ms. Montgomery, who keeps track of all your little details?"

"I fail to see what this has to do with anything," Shapiro said.

Again, Landry ignored him, his focus on Jade, watching every nuance of his expression. "Have you ever had any dealings with Bruce Seabright or Gryphon Development?"

"I know Gryphon Development is in charge of Fairfields, where Trey Hughes' barn is going up."

"Have you personally had any dealings with them?"

"I may have spoken with someone from their office once or twice."

"Bruce Seabright?"

"I don't recall."

"How did Erin Seabright come to work for you?" Landry asked.

"Trey knew I was in need of a groom and told me about Erin."

"How long have you been associated with Mr. Hughes?"

"I've known Trey for years. He brought his horses to me last year."

"Shortly after the death of his mother?"

"That's it," Shapiro announced. "If you want to go on a fishing expedition, Detective Landry, I suggest you hire a boat. Come on, Don."

Landry let them move for the door to the interview room, speaking only as Shapiro reached for the doorknob.

"I own a boat, Counselor," he said. "And once I get a trophy on the line, I reel him in, fillet him, and fry him. I don't care who he is or who his friends are or how long it takes."

"Good for you," Shapiro said, pulling open the door.

Dugan was standing on the other side with Armedgian and an assistant district attorney.

"You're free to go, Mr. Shapiro," Dugan said. "Your client, however, will be enjoying the county's hospitality for what's left of the night. Bail hearing tomorrow."

44

He told me to meet him at the back gate," she said quietly, her eyes downcast.

Landry had slept on a bunk at the station and come back to the hospital at the crack of dawn to wait impatiently for Erin Seabright to wake up. Jade would be arraigned later that morning. Landry wanted the state's attorney to have every scrap of ammunition possible to keep Jade in the tank.

"People gossip—especially about Don," Erin said. "He said he didn't want them talking about us. I totally understood that. I thought it was kind of exciting, really. Our secret affair. Pathetic."

"Had you had sex with him prior to that?" Landry asked. He kept his voice matter-of-fact. No accusation, no excitement.

She shook her head. "We flirted. We were friends, I thought. I mean, he was my boss, but . . . But I wanted it to be more, and he did too. At least, that's what he told me."

"So he asked you to meet him at the back gate. You knew no one would see you there?"

"There weren't any horses in those last two barns that weekend. That's where the dressage horses are stabled when they come to

Wellington for a show, but there wasn't a show for them. Plus it was Sunday night. No one hangs around."

"You hadn't told Mr. Jade you were quitting your job, moving to Ocala?"

"No. Why would I? I wanted to work for him. I was in love with him."

"What happened then, Erin? You went to the back gate to meet him..."

"He was late. I was afraid he had changed his mind. Then this van pulled up and a guy in a mask jumped out and—and—he grabbed me."

Her voice died out as another bout of tears came. Landry handed her a box of tissues and waited.

"Did you recognize him, Erin?"

She shook her head.

"Did you recognize his voice?"

"I was so scared!"

"I know you were. It's hard to remember details when you're afraid and something awful like that is happening. But you need to try to slow it all down in your mind. Instead of seeing it all happen so fast, you need to try to see individual moments, like snapshots."

"I'm trying."

"I know you are," he said quietly. "Take your time, Erin. If you need a break, just let me know and we'll take a break. Okay?"

She looked at him and tried to smile. "Okay."

"If you never saw their faces, why do you think Jade was one of the kidnappers?"

"He's the one who told me to be there at the back gate."

"I know, but did you recognize anything in particular about one of the kidnappers that made you think it was him?"

"I know him," she said, frustration showing. "I know his build. I know how he moves. I'm sure I heard his voice different times."

"What about the other guy's voice? Did he sound familiar? Did he have an accent?"

The girl shook her head and rubbed a hand across her eyes, exhausted. "He didn't talk much. And when he did, he whispered and mumbled. He never talked to me."

"Do you know where they were holding you?" Landry asked. "Could you take us there?"

Erin shook her head. "It was a trailer house. That's all I know. It was horrible. It was filthy and old."

"Could you tell if you were near a busy road? Were there any particular sounds you heard regularly?"

"I don't know. Cars, I guess, in the distance. I don't know. They kept me drugged most of the time. Special K."

"How do you know that was the drug?"

She glanced away, embarrassed. "I've had it before. At a party."

"What happened last night? How did you get away?"

"One of them—the other one—he dragged me out of the trailer and put me in the van. I thought he was going to kill me and dump my body somewhere, and no one would ever find me!"

She paused to catch a ragged breath and try to compose herself. Landry waited.

"He just drove around. I don't know how long. He had given me a shot of K. I was pretty out of it. I just kept waiting for the van to stop, knowing that when it did, he would kill me."

"You couldn't see out the windows?"

She shook her head. "I was on the floor. And then we stopped, and I was so scared! He opened the door and dragged me out. I was dizzy. I couldn't stand up. I fell on the ground, a— a—dirt road. And he just got back in the van and drove away."

Thrown on the side of the road like a sack of garbage. Something they had used and didn't need anymore. Still, she was damn lucky, Landry thought.

"I don't know how long I was laying there," Erin said. "Then finally I got up and started walking. I could see lights. Town. I just started walking."

Landry said nothing for a moment. He let Erin's story sink in. He turned it over a few times in his mind, more questions shaking loose.

So, Jade and company figured out they weren't going to get the ransom. They dumped the girl rather than face a murder rap. Only, the way Landry saw it, Van Zandt was Jade's accomplice, and he was already under the lights for one murder. Why risk Erin Seabright identifying them? Because they knew she couldn't do so positively? Because they had taken pains to make certain there was no physical evidence to tie them to her?

That remained to be seen, of course. The clothes Erin had been wearing were at the lab being scrutinized under microscopes and fluorescent lights, swabbed and stained and picked over with tweezers.

Maybe letting Erin go was just part of the game for them. Let the victim live, and let her live with the knowledge that she can't put them away. Let the vic live, and let the cops live with the knowledge of their guilt, but no evidence to prove it. Power trip.

The problem with that theory was that Landry had no intention of letting anyone get away with anything.

"Erin, did they ever talk about why they singled you out?"

She shook her head, her eyes on Landry's microcassette recorder sitting on the bed tray, tape rolling. "I was so drugged up most of the time. I know they wanted money. They knew Bruce has money."

"Did they call him Bruce?"

"They called him I don't know how many times—"

"When they talked about him," Landry clarified, "did they use his first name? Did they call him Bruce?"

Erin nodded, though he thought she didn't get the significance of her answer.

"Did you tell them his name?"

"No. They just knew it."

It struck Landry odd the perps would call Seabright by his first name. Familiar. Like a friend.

"I could have died because of him," Erin said bitterly. "I can't believe my mother stays with him. She's so weak."

"People are complicated," Landry offered, out of his element.

Erin just looked at her lap and shook her head.

"Erin, how many videotapes did they make of you while you were in the trailer?"

"I don't know. Three or four. It was so humiliating. They made me beg. They did things to me. They hit me." She started to cry again. "It was horrible."

That son of a bitch, Landry thought. Three or four tapes. Seabright had handed over one besides the tape he had picked up at the ransom drop.

"Erin, did either of the men have sex with you?"

The tears came harder. "They k-kept drugging me. I couldn't do anything about it. I c-couldn't stop them. I c-couldn't d-do anything."

"We're going to try really hard to do something about it now, Erin. We'll work together—you and me—to build the case against them. Deal?"

She looked up at him with tear-filled eyes and nodded.

"Get some rest," Landry said as he started for the door.

"Detective Landry?"

"Yes?"

"Thank you."

Landry walked out hoping he would be able to really give her something to thank him for sooner rather than later.

I was waiting down the hall when Landry came out of Erin's hospital room. He didn't look surprised to see me. He stopped outside her door, took out his cell phone, and made a call that lasted about three minutes. When he ended the call, he glanced in the opposite direction down the hall, toward the nurses' station, then came toward me.

"What's she saying?" I asked as we walked toward the emergency exit.

"She says it was Jade, but that the kidnappers wore masks the whole time and they kept her doped up on ketamine. She never actually saw Jade. She can't identify the other guy at all. She says he rarely spoke."

"That doesn't sound like Van Zandt," I said. "I've never met anyone who liked the sound of his own voice better than Tomas Van Zandt."

"But she'd know his voice, because of the accent," Landry said. "Maybe he's smarter than he looks." He sighed and shook his head. "She won't make a good witness."

He was frowning, and I could tell I had only a fraction of his attention. He was mentally replaying what Erin had told him, trying to find a way to work it into a lead or lead him to a piece of evidence.

"She doesn't need to be a good witness, yet," I reminded him. "You've got enough for Jade to be arraigned. Maybe you'll come up with some forensic evidence."

"Yeah. Don't strain yourself in your enthusiasm," he said sarcastically.

362

I shrugged. "What do you have on him I don't know about? Have you come up with anything from his condo?"

He said nothing.

"Anything from the girls' apartment?"

"Some snapshots of Jade. One of him and Erin together. Someone wrote on the back: 'To Erin. Love, Don.' Jill had the pictures stashed. She had scratched out Erin's face and name with a ballpoint pen."

"All the girls love Donnie."

"I don't see it, myself," Landry muttered.

"Have you found whether or not he owns or rents property other than the condo?"

"He wouldn't be stupid enough to hold Erin on property that could be traced back to him. And I couldn't get that lucky."

"How did she get away?"

"She says they let her go. They figured they weren't getting the money, so they tossed her in the back of the van, drove her around, and dumped her like an old rug."

"So, she can't say where they held her."

"No. A trailer house. That's all she knows."

"Could you tell anything from the last videotape? Any background sounds?"

"There was some noise in the background. The techno-geeks are trying to figure it out. Sounded like heavy machinery to me."

"What did Erin say about it?"

He looked out the window. "That she wasn't sure. That they kept her drugged. Special K, she says. It's easy to come by," Landry said. "Especially for people who work around veterinarians."

"But it's not a sedative we use on horses," I told him. "It's commonly used on small animals."

"Still, the access is there."

"What about Chad?"

"He never left the Seabright house last night," Landry said, opening his phone again. "Besides, Erin and Chad had an intimate relationship. You think she wouldn't recognize him while he was raping her?"

"Maybe he was the silent one. Maybe he just watched the partner do her. Maybe they had her so drugged up, she wouldn't have recognized Santa Claus if he was bending over her."

Landry scowled at me while he checked his messages. "You know what? You're a pain in the ass, Estes."

"Yeah, like *that's* news." I slipped down from the ledge. "Well, what the hey, Landry. Just kill them all and let God sort 'em out."

"Don't tempt me. Half the people involved in this girl's life belong in prison, if you ask me," he muttered as he listened to the phone. "We'll be executing a search warrant at the Seabright house in a couple of hours. I'll be sure Dugan includes drugs as part of the warrant inventory."

"What else are you looking for?"

"Erin keeps saying the kidnappers called Bruce Seabright multiple times, and that they made more than one video in the trailer. Three or four, she says."

"Jesus God, what's he doing with them?" I asked. "Selling them on eBay?"

"Yeah, and he'll claim he was just trying to defray the cost of the ransom," Landry muttered. "Asshole."

I sat down on the deep window ledge, the early morning sun hot on my back, and thought about Bruce Seabright's possible involvement. "So, let's say Seabright wanted Erin gone. He sets up the kidnapping scheme with no intention of ever bringing the cops in, or ever bringing Erin home. Why wasn't she killed right away? They could have made the tapes in an hour, killed her, and dumped her.

"Then I get involved and bring you in," I went on. "Now Bruce has to play along. Again, why not just have the accomplice get rid of her?"

"Because now we're watching him, asking questions. The accomplices see cops nosing around and they get scared."

"So they let Erin go so she can help you build a case against them?" I shook my head. "That doesn't make any sense."

"I'm playing with the cards I've got, Estes," Landry said impatiently. "Erin says it was Jade. I'm going with that. It'd be stupid not to. If the thing tracks back to Bruce Seabright, I'll go with that too. Felony makes strange bedfellows."

I didn't say anything. Occasionally, I do realize the value of discretion. Landry had his suspect and his circumstantial evidence. He had a half-sure victim and doubts of his own.

"I've got to go," he said, closing his phone. "The state's attorney wants a meeting before Jade's arraignment."

I thought I might be able to slip into Erin's room after he'd gone, but I could see the deputy assigned to the post had already come back from his coffee break.

"Landry?" I asked as he started down the hall. He glanced back at me. "Any sign of Van Zandt yet?"

"No. He never came back to the town house." He started to turn away and I called him back a second time.

I took Erin's bracelet from my pocket and held it out to him. "I found this on the floor of the examination room Erin was in last night. Ask her about it. Maybe it was a gift from Jade."

He took it from me, his fingers brushing mine. He nodded.

"Thank you," I said. "For filling me in."

Landry tipped his head. "Your case first."

"I thought you didn't share."

"First time for everything."

He looked at the bracelet in his hand, then walked away.

I left the hospital and took a drive around the parking lot with an eye peeled for a navy blue Chevy, but Van Zandt wasn't there. Nor was Krystal Seabright's white Lexus or Bruce's Jaguar. Ever the loving parents. Erin had told them to go, so they'd gone. Off the hook.

I have never understood people who have children but don't raise them, don't nurture them, don't help them become human beings. What other reason is there? To carry on the family name? To get a welfare check? To preserve proof of a relationship? Because that was what one was supposed to do at a particular time in one's life: get married, have kids. No one ever explained why.

I didn't know much about Erin Seabright's upbringing, but I knew she hadn't gotten where she was by being loved. She was, by her own sister's account, an angry, bitter girl.

I didn't like her sketchy tale. I knew from personal experience that angry, bitter girls want the people who hurt them most to pay for their sins. I wondered if she might blame whom she wanted to blame. Perhaps Jade hadn't loved her. Perhaps he'd broken her heart. And, in pain, in terror, under the influence of drugs, she might have projected his identity onto her tormentor.

365

Or perhaps the tormentor had put the idea there for her to believe.

I thought of Michael Berne again. It would have been simple for him to call Radio Shack and ask for that cell phone to be set aside. He could have sent a minion in to get the thing. If he had known about Erin's attraction to Jade, he could have played on that during Erin's captivity.

But who would Michael's partner be? He had no connection to the Seabrights I was aware of. He was on the wrong side of the relationship with Trey Hughes.

Trey Hughes, who kept my father's phone number in his wallet. Trey with his eye for the girls and his connection to every aspect of this sordid tale.

I didn't want to believe he could be a part of something so vicious as what had been done to Erin Seabright. I was still putting money on Van Zandt.

But it seemed to me I had pieces from three different puzzles. The trick would be coming up with a final picture that wasn't an abstract.

45

The assistant state's attorney seemed unperturbed by the fact
that Erin Seabright had not seen the faces of her captors. As Elena had
said, they had enough evidence to hold him on the charges, to arraign
him and make a strong argument for high bail or no bail. They would
then, by Florida law, have 175 days to bring Jade before a jury. Ample
time to put the case together, provided the additional evidence was
there to find.

The blood that had been found in the stall where Jill Morone had
died had been typed. If they could match it to Jade, they were on
their way to a murder indictment to add to the kidnapping charge.
They had put Jade's alibi for the night of Jill's death in doubt. He had
no alibi for the night the horse had been killed, the event Estes believed had kicked everything into motion.

Landry thought of Elena as he left the prosecutor's office. He
didn't like that she had doubts about Jade's involvement, and he didn't
like that it mattered to him what she thought. She had dragged him
into this mess, and he wanted it to lay out as simply as her original
theory had. Most crimes were like that: straightforward. The average
murder was about money or sex, and didn't require Sherlock Holmes

to solve. Kidnapping for ransom—the same. Good basic police work led to arrests and convictions. He didn't want this case to be any different.

And maybe the reason Estes' doubts bothered him so much was that some of those same doubts were chewing at the back of his mind. He tried to shake them off as he walked down the hall. Weiss came out of the squad room to meet him.

"Paris Montgomery is here. Asking for you," he added with an eye roll.

"Did you find anything at the Seabright house?"

"Jackpot," Weiss said. "We found a videotape stashed on a shelf in Seabright's home office. You won't believe it. It actually shows the girl being raped. We've got Seabright in the conference room. I'm on my way now."

"Wait for me," Landry said, fury burning in his gut. "I want a crack at that son of a bitch."

"There'll be a line," Weiss assured him.

Paris Montgomery was pacing behind the table as Landry walked into the interview room. She looked upset and nervous, though her emotional state had not prevented her from putting on makeup or styling her hair.

"Ms. Montgomery. Thank you for coming in," Landry said. "Have a seat. Can I get you anything? Coffee?"

"God, no," she said, sitting down. "If I have any more caffeine I'm going to start spinning around the room like a top. I can't believe any of this is happening. Don in jail. Erin *kidnapped*. My God. Is she all right? I just tried calling the hospital, but they wouldn't tell me anything."

"She's been roughed up," Landry said. "But she'll recover."

"Will they let me see her?"

"Immediate family only, for the time being. Maybe later today."

"I feel terrible about what happened. I mean, she worked for me. I should have looked out for her." Tears filled the big brown eyes. "I should have done something. When Don said she'd quit and gone— I should have tried harder to contact her. I should have known something was wrong."

"Why is that? Did you have reason to be suspicious?"

She glanced away; her expression seemed to have the kind of glazed look people get when they are watching memories run through their minds.

"Erin had seemed happy with the job. I mean, I knew she was having boyfriend trouble, but what girl her age doesn't? I just— I should have questioned her leaving so suddenly. But you have to understand, grooms come and go during the season. There's too much opportunity. Someone offers more money or health insurance or an extra day off and they're gone."

Landry offered no platitudes, no absolution. Someone sure as hell should have been paying closer attention to what was going on with Erin Seabright. He wasn't inclined to let anyone off the hook.

"Were you aware of any relationship between Erin and Don?" he asked.

"Erin had a crush on him."

"To your knowledge, did he act on it?"

"I—well—Don is very charismatic."

"Is that a yes or a no?"

"He's a magnetic kind of person. Women are drawn to him. He enjoys that. He likes to flirt."

"With Erin?"

"Well . . . sure . . . but I didn't think he would take advantage of her. I don't want to believe that he did."

"But he might have."

She looked uncertain, which was answer enough.

"Did Erin say anything to you about the death of the horse?"

"She was upset. We all were."

"Did she hint that she knew something about what happened?"

She looked away again and pressed two fingers against the small crease digging in between her eyebrows. "She didn't believe it was an accident."

"She took care of the horse, right?"

"Yes. She was very good with him—with all the horses. She put in extra time with them. She would come and check on them after hours sometimes."

"Had she checked on them that night?"

"Around eleven. Everything was fine."

369

"Why did she think it wasn't an accident?"

Paris Montgomery began to cry. She looked around the room as if looking for a crevice to disappear into.

"Ms. Montgomery, if Don Jade did what we believe he did, you don't owe him any loyalty."

"I didn't believe he'd done anything bad," she said in a small voice, making the excuse for herself, not for Jade.

"What happened?"

"Erin told me Don was at the barn already when she got there that morning. Early. Really early. We had horses showing that day, and Erin had to get there early to braid manes and get the horses ready. She told me she saw Don in Stellar's stall, doing something with the cord of the electric fan. She went over to the stall to ask him why he was there so early."

She stopped and tried to compose herself, her breath catching. Landry waited.

"She saw Stellar was down. Don told her the horse had bitten through the cord of the fan, and he held the cord up. But Erin said he had something in his other hand. Some kind of a tool."

"You think he cut the cord to make it look like an accident."

"I don't know!" she sobbed, covering her face with her hands. "I don't want to believe he could have killed that poor animal!"

"And now that might be the least of what he's done," Landry said.

He sipped his coffee impassively while Paris Montgomery cried for her sin of omission. He turned the new facts over in his mind. Erin could have fingered Jade for staging the accident. That might logically have led to her death, he thought, as it may have led to Jill Morone's death. But the evidence regarding the cell phone purchase indicated the kidnapping had been planned in advance of the horse murder. Therefore, the one thing had nothing to do with the other.

"What did you do when Erin came to you with this information?" he asked.

Paris dabbed at her eyes with a tissue. "I got angry. I told her of course it was an accident. Don wouldn't—"

"Despite the fact that Don *had* on several occasions previous."

"I never believed that was true," she said adamantly. "No one ever proved anything."

"Except that he's clever and adept at evading the consequences of his actions."

Even now, she rose to Jade's defense. "In three years I have *never* known Don to do one cruel thing to a horse in his care."

"What was Erin's reaction when you didn't believe her?"

"She was upset at first. We talked some more. I told her what I just told you about my experience working for Don. I asked her if she could believe him capable of hurting anyone. I made her feel ashamed for even thinking it."

"So, when Jade told you she had quit later that day—"

"I wasn't that surprised."

"But you didn't try to call her."

"I tried to call her, she didn't answer. I left a message on her voice mail. I went to her apartment a couple of days later, but it looked like she had moved out."

She sighed dramatically and looked at Landry with the big eyes, looking for forgiveness. "I would give anything if I could go back to that day and change what happened."

"Yeah," Landry said. "I'll bet Erin Seabright would too."

46

I went back to the day it all began. The day Stellar was found dead in his stall. The day Erin Seabright was snatched from the back gates of the Palm Beach Polo Equestrian Center. I laid it all out in black and ecru on sheets of expensive stationery I found in the writing desk. A timeline. When Jade had allegedly purchased the cell phone. When Erin and Chad had argued. When Stellar had been found dead. When Erin had been taken. Everything I knew about the case, I wrote down and I spread the sheets out in order on my bedroom floor.

I had become focused on the idea that everything had come out of the death of Stellar, but looking at the timeline, reflecting on what I knew, I realized that it wasn't so. The kidnapping plan was already in motion when Stellar died. Someone had purchased the disposable cell phone. Someone had lined up the trailer where Erin had been held, had gathered the video and audio equipment, had procured the ketamine to drug Erin and found the van used in the abduction. An elaborate plan with at least two people involved.

I wanted to know everything that had transpired that Sunday, the day of Stellar's death and Erin's abduction. I wanted to know what had gone on between Erin and Jade that day and prior to it. I wanted to know where Trey Hughes had been that day, and Van Zandt.

I looked at my timeline and all the things I did know. No matter how many times I went over it, the simplest explanation was not the best. But I knew plenty of people would have been happy to stop there. Landry among them.

I have never been able to do things the easy way.

I went back into the living room, pulled out the tape of the kidnapping, and shoved it into the VCR.

Erin standing at the back gate, waiting. She watched the van approach. She stood there as the masked man got out. She said, "No!" Then she ran. He grabbed her.

I rewound the tape and played it again.

I thought about the things she had told Landry, and the things she had not told him.

I thought about who had come under suspicion and who had not.

Don Jade was sitting in jail. Bruce Seabright was under a microscope. Tomas Van Zandt, known predator, suspected murderer, was nowhere to be found.

I went back to the writing desk and dug through the mess I'd made to find the piece of paper I had taken from Van Zandt's trash. The flight schedule of horses being shipped to Brussels. The plane was scheduled to leave that night at eleven. I would have to give that information to Landry. And Landry would have to pass it on to Armedgian.

Screw that. I wasn't giving Armedgian anything. If I could find a way to make him look like an idiot, I would. God knew, after the fiasco at The Players, neither Armedgian nor Dugan was going to have anything to do with me anyway.

I decided, when the time came, I would go to the airport and wait for Van Zandt myself, then call in Landry. If Tomas Van Zandt thought he could get away with murder in my country, he could think again.

47

He had no idea how long he had been in the trunk of the car. Night had become day. He knew that because of the heat. The fucking Florida sun was beating down on the car, the temperature in the trunk becoming unbearable.

He was going to die in this horrible place because of that Russian cunt. Two of them. Their faces blended together in his brain. He went in and out of delirium from the pain and the heat.

He would have tried to break out, but he couldn't move. He didn't know how many of his bones were broken. He would have tried to scream, but the lower half of his face was encased in tape. Many times in the hours past he had feared he would vomit and choke to death.

Like the fat groom. Stupid little whore. She had been ready to have sex with Jade. She should have been willing to have sex with him. Some of his beating was her fault. Kulak had known about her death.

An accident. Not murder. If he had gotten rid of her body the way he had wanted, no one would ever have known. No one would have asked questions about where was Jill. Who in the world could give a shit about that one?

If he hadn't been talked into dumping the body into that manure pit, plenty of what had happened wouldn't have. And maybe he would not now be waiting to die.

He could hear sounds outside the car. Machinery running, men's voices. Russians speaking Russian. Fucking Russians.

Something struck the car, rocking it, then it began to move forward. The noise of the machinery grew louder, like a beast from hell devouring everything in its path. The noise grew deafening—the roaring of the beast, the crunching of metal as the front end of the car collapsed.

He knew what was coming. He knew, and he started screaming, even though the sound could not escape his own head. He screamed the names of every woman who had turned against him.

Women. Stupid, ungrateful bitches. The bane of his existence. Many times he had said women would be the death of him. As always, he was right.

48

The scene was as nightmarish as anything Landry had ever watched. Erin Seabright, tied spread-eagle on the bed, screaming and crying as one of her captors violated her.

Dugan, Weiss, Dwyer, and he stood in a half circle, arms crossed, watching the tape play, their faces like stone. At the top of the half circle, Bruce Seabright sat on a chair, his complexion the color of putty.

Landry punched the power button off and slammed a fist against the side of the television. He wheeled on Seabright.

"You sick son of a bitch."

"I've never seen that before in my life!" Seabright shouted, coming to his feet.

"Landry..." Dugan warned.

Landry didn't hear him, he didn't hear Weiss' phone ring. He was hardly aware anyone else was in the room. He saw only Bruce Seabright, and he wanted to beat him to death with his bare hands.

"What? You were saving it for later?" Landry said. "Planning your own little film festival?"

Seabright shook his head vehemently. "I don't know how that thing got in my office."

"You put it there," Landry said.

"I didn't! I swear!"

"The kidnappers sent it to you, just like they sent the first one."

"No!"

"And if it had been left up to you, no one would have seen either of them."

"That— that's not true—"

"You lying sack of shit!" Landry shouted in his face.

Dugan tried to step between them, shoving at Landry's chest. "Detective Landry, step back!"

Landry stepped around him. "It wasn't bad enough you wanted rid of her? You wanted to see her tortured too?"

"No! I—"

"Shut up!" Landry shouted. "Shut the fuck up!"

Seabright stepped back, small eyes popping with fear. The backs of his legs hit the folding chair he'd been sitting on, and he stumbled and fell awkwardly back down onto it.

"Landry!" Dugan shouted.

Dwyer stepped in front of him, holding up a hand. "James—"

"I want a lawyer!" Seabright said. "He's out of control!"

Landry stilled himself, slowed his breathing, stared at Bruce Seabright.

"You'd better call God, Seabright," Landry said tightly. "It's going to take more than a lawyer to get your sorry ass out of this crack."

Jade's bail hearing took twenty minutes. Five minutes for business and fifteen minutes for Shapiro to hear himself talk. For what a guy like that charged by the hour, Landry supposed he ought to at least give the appearance of being worth more than the average suit.

Landry stood at the back of the courtroom, taking roll of the attendees. He was still trembling from the adrenaline and rage that had burned through him in the conference room. Like counting sheep, he counted heads. Shapiro's entourage of lawyers-in-waiting, the assistant state's attorney, a small pack of reporters, and Trey Hughes.

The prosecutor, Angela Roca, stated her intention to take the case before the grand jury and asked for bail in the amount of a million dollars.

"Your Honor," Shapiro whined. "A million dollars! Mr. Jade is not as wealthy as his clients are. For all intents and purposes, that would amount to denying bail altogether."

"Fine by us, Your Honor." Roca said. "Mr. Jade has been identified by his victim as a kidnapper and rapist. Additionally, the Sheriff's Office considers him a suspect in the brutal murder of one of his employees."

"With all due respect, Your Honor, Mr. Jade can't be penalized for a crime for which he has not been charged."

"Yeah, I caught that one in judge school," the Honorable Ida Green said sarcastically. Ida, a tiny redheaded New York transplant, was one of Landry's favorite judges. Nothing impressed Ida, including Bert Shapiro.

"Your Honor, the prosecution's case—"

"Is none of my business. This is a bail hearing, Mr. Shapiro. Need I enlighten you as to basic proceedings?"

"No, Your Honor. I remember vaguely from law school."

"Good. You didn't waste your parents' money. Bail is set at five hundred thousand, cash."

"Your Honor—" Shapiro began.

Ida waved him off. "Mr. Shapiro, your client's clients spend that much on a horse without batting an eye. I'm certain if they are as devoted to Mr. Jade as you are, they'll help him out."

Shapiro looked pissed.

Roca took the inch and went for the mile. "Your Honor, as Mr. Jade has lived in Europe and has many contacts there, we consider him to be a flight risk."

"Mr. Jade will surrender his passport. Anything else, Ms. Roca?"

"We request Mr. Jade be required to submit to a blood test and give a hair sample for the purposes of comparison to evidence in custody, Your Honor."

"Make it so, Mr. Shapiro."

"Your Honor," Shapiro argued. "This is a gross invasion of my client's person—"

"A colonoscopy is a gross invasion, Mr. Shapiro. Hair and blood samples are so ordered."

The proceedings ended with a bang of the gavel. Trey Hughes got up, went to the front of the courtroom, wrote a check for the clerk, and Don Jade was a free man.

49

I rewound the tape again.

I wondered if Landry's people had found any of the other video-tapes Erin had spoken of in Bruce Seabright's possession. If they had, I hoped he would be arrested and charged with something—hinder-ing, withholding evidence, conspiracy, something, anything. Regard-less of the outcome of Erin's ordeal, regardless of the origin or motive of what had happened, Bruce Seabright had exhibited a depraved in-difference to human life.

I thought about the tape of Erin's beating, which I had not seen, but which Landry had described to me as brutal. An eye for an eye, Bruce, I thought.

I hit the play button for the one tape I had.

How many times had I watched this? I didn't know. Enough that I should have seen every detail there was to see, yet I felt compelled to play it again and look for things I hadn't, couldn't, wouldn't see. Again and again, and still something bothered me, a feeling that nagged at the edge of my consciousness, and another I as yet could not put a finger on.

The van approaches. Erin stands there.

The van stops. Erin stands there.

A masked man jumps out. Erin says, "No!"

She tries to run.

I hit pause, freezing the image. A thick band of snow ran across the faces of Erin and her pursuer as they ran toward the gate. Without seeing her expression or his mask, the shot might have taken on any meaning. Out of context, the two people might have been lovers chasing each other out of joy. They might have been people running from a disaster or to the rescue of others. Without expression, they were two torsos in faded jeans.

The sluggishness of Erin's reactions bothered me. Was it disbelief? Was it fear? Or was it something else?

I let the tape run forward, watching the man catch her roughly from behind and spin her around. She kicked him hard. He back-handed her across the face with enough force to knock her almost off her feet.

Horrible. Absolutely horrible. Violence that was completely real. I couldn't deny it.

I watched him shove her down from behind and drive her face-first into the dirt. I watched him jab a needle into her arm. Ketamine. Special K. Drug of choice of rave-goers, date rapists, and small animal vets.

Erin had used party drugs in the past. She herself had told Landry it was the drug that had been used on her. How would she have known that unless her captors graciously filled her in, unless she had a working knowledge of the drug herself?

I thought about the things Erin had told Landry, the things she had not told Landry, the pieces of her story that didn't all fit the same puzzle.

She was sure Jade was one of the kidnappers, but she had never actually seen him. She was sure it was him—the man she'd had a thing for, the man she had supposedly dumped Chad for. Yet, without ever seeing his face, she could believe he would brutalize her. Why? Why would she think it? Why would he do it?

And while she was dead certain Jade was one of her captors, she didn't have a clue about his partner.

Then, after raping her, beating her, drugging her, and not getting the ransom for which they had gone to such elaborate lengths, her abductors simply drove her around and let her go. Just like that. And not only had they let her go, they had given her clothes back to her, even her bracelet.

I didn't believe her. I didn't believe her story, and I would have given anything to change that gut feeling. I wanted to doubt my own instincts as I had doubted them every day since Hector Ramirez had been killed. What irony that through this case I had gained back a belief in myself, and yet, I wanted nothing more than to be wrong.

I thought of Molly and wished I could have cried.

I would have prayed to be wrong, but I have never believed any higher power ever listened to me.

Feeling ill, I rewound the tape and forced myself to watch it again, this time in slow motion, so that I might even more closely scrutinize it, looking for something I was afraid I wouldn't find.

The quality of my equipment was average. Landry would have a much better look at the tape with all the high-tech equipment at the lab. Still, as I watched the tape second by second, I had a good view. Throughout the filming, the camera had remained focused fairly tightly on Erin, she appeared to be no more than eight or ten feet away. I could see that her hair was pulled back in a clip, she was wearing a tight red T-shirt that showed off her flat belly. Her jeans had a little white spot on one thigh.

As her assailant caught her by the arm, I could see she was wearing a watch. But I didn't see the one thing I wanted desperately to see.

Prowling the guest house like a caged cat, I thought of the people involved in Erin's life: Bruce, Van Zandt, Michael Berne, Jill Morone, Trey Hughes, Paris Montgomery. I wanted Bruce to be guilty. I knew Van Zandt was a murderer. Michael Berne had a motive to ruin Don Jade, but kidnapping made no sense. Jill Morone was dead. Trey Hughes was the center of all their universes. And then there was Paris Montgomery.

Paris and her backhanded loyalty to Don Jade. She had as much to gain by Jade's ruination as Michael Berne—even more. She had labored in Jade's shadow for three years with her cover-girl smile and her love of fine things and her hunger for the spotlight. She had run his life, run his barn, run interference.

I thought of the small, destructive "truths" Paris had confessed to me about the death of Stellar, even as she defended Don Jade. If she would say those things to me, what slivers of doubt was she putting into Trey Hughes' mind every time she slept with him?

On the morning Jill Morone's body had been found, Paris had been supervising Javier's cleanup of the crime scene. Even as she called their insurance adjuster about the damage to Jade's clothing and personal effects, she'd had Javier cleaning up the mess. I wondered now if news of Jill's murder had been a surprise to her at all.

I thought of the supposed rape and Landry's feeling that it might have been staged. I thought of Jill's body buried in the manure pit at barn forty, where it would surely be found. And when it was found, who would be the first suspect? Don Jade.

His clients might tolerate a few scandals, but the murder of a girl? No. Kidnapping? No. And with Jade out of the picture, and few wealthy patrons to believe in him, who would benefit most? Paris Montgomery.

I called Landry and left a message on his voice mail. Then I turned off the television and left the house.

At one end of the barn Irina was stretched out in a lounge chair in a bikini top and short shorts, dramatic black sunglasses shading her eyes.

"Irina," I called on my way to my car. "If Tomas Van Zandt comes by, call nine-one-one. He's wanted for murder."

She raised a hand lazily to acknowledge me, and rolled onto her stomach to tan her back.

I went to the show grounds, to Jade's barn, for a second shot at Javier. There was less chance on a Monday of his being caught speaking to me. The stables were closed. There was no reason for Trey Hughes to show up, or Paris. Perhaps he would feel more free to tell me what he knew.

But there was no one at Jade's stalls. The stalls had not been cleaned and the horses were clamoring for lunch. It appeared they had been abandoned. The aisle was an obstacle course of forks, rakes, brooms, and overturned muck buckets. As if someone had come through in a very big hurry.

I raided Jade's feed stall and tossed each horse a flake of hay.

"Don't tell me. Now you're pretending to be a groom?"

I looked out the back of the tent to find Michael Berne standing there in jeans and a polo shirt. He looked as happy as I had seen him since this mess had begun. Relaxed. His rival was in jail and all was right with the world.

"I'm a multitalented individual," I said. "What's your excuse for being here?"

He shrugged. I noticed for the first time he held a small box in his hand. Something from a vet's office.

"No rest for the weary," he said.

"Or the wicked."

Rompun. One of the sedatives used commonly on horses. Everybody has the stuff around, Paris had said as she spoke of the drug found in Stellar's bloodstream.

"Having a party?" I asked, looking pointedly at the box.

"I've got one that's hard to shoe," Berne said. "He needs a little something to take the edge off."

"Was Stellar hard to shoe?"

"No. Why do you ask?"

"No reason. You haven't seen Paris today, have you?"

"She was here earlier. Just in time to watch the INS cart her last groom away."

"What?"

"There was a raid this morning," he said. "Her Guatemalan guy was one of the first rounded up."

"Who tipped them off? You?" I asked bluntly.

"Not me," he said. "I lost a guy too."

The INS rolled in for a surprise raid, and a man in barn nineteen was one of the first to go. The one person left in Jade's camp who might have been persuaded to tell the truth—if he knew it—gone just as the case seemed to be breaking.

Trey had seen me speaking with Javier. He might have told Paris. Or perhaps Bert Shapiro had wanted the Guatemalan out of the country in the event he might know something about Jade.

"I hear he's in jail," Michael Berne said.

"Jade? Yes. Unless he's made bail. Kidnapping charges. Do you know anything about it?"

"Why would I?"

"Maybe you were here the night it happened. A week ago, Sunday, late in the day at the back gate."

Berne shook his head and started to walk away. "Not me. I was at home. With my wife."

"You're a very devoted and forgiving husband, Michael," I said.

"Yes, I am," he said smugly. "I'm not the criminal here, Ms. Estes."

"No."

"Don Jade is."

No, I thought as he walked away, *I don't believe that either.*

50

My phone rang as I walked back to my car.

"Meet me for lunch," Landry said.

"Your telephone etiquette is sorely lacking," I pointed out.

He named a fast-food place ten minutes away and hung up.

Erin Seabright caught Jade in the stall with the dead horse," Landry said. We sat in his car. A sack of food lay on the seat between us, filling the car with the aroma of charbroiled meat and french fries. Neither of us touched it. "She caught him doctoring the electrical cord on the fan."

"Erin told you that?"

"I'm on my way to ask her about it now. We didn't get into the whole dead horse saga this morning. I only asked her for details about her abduction. Paris Montgomery came in on her own and told me. There was a story on the morning news about Erin's escape from the kidnappers. Apparently, that put the fear of God in Ms. Montgomery."

"More like a vulture circling a dying animal," I said. "She smells opportunity.

"She says Erin caught Jade, and at the end of the day Jade kidnapped her? It doesn't track, Landry."

"I know. The kidnapping plot was already in motion."

"If that's what it was," I said. "Have the technical wizards enhanced that first videotape?"

"Yes, but I haven't had a chance to look at it. Why?"

"Look for the bracelet I handed you this morning."

"What about it?"

"Do you think the kidnappers gave it to her as a parting gift?" I asked. "I've watched that tape fifty times. I don't see a bracelet, but she was wearing one last night."

Landry looked incredulous. "Are you trying to say the girl is in on it? You're out of your mind. Estes, you haven't seen her. She's had the shit kicked out of her. You didn't see that tape of the perp going at her with the whip. And this morning Weiss and Dwyer found another tape in Seabright's office. It shows the girl being brutally raped."

That brought me up short. "He had it in the house? In his office?"

"Stuffed behind some things on a shelf."

I didn't know what to say to that. It was what I had been hoping for—for Seabright to be made to pay a price. But news of the taped rape was something else.

"It looked genuine?" I asked.

"Made the hair on the back of my neck stand on end," Landry said. "I wanted to take Seabright and choke him till his eyes popped out."

"Where is he now?"

"He's sitting in a holding cell. The state's attorney is trying to decide what to charge him with."

"What happened at Jade's arraignment?"

"Trey Hughes posted bail."

"I wonder if Paris knows about that."

"I'd bet he's paying for Bert Shapiro too."

"Have you interviewed him yet? Trey?"

"He's been asked to come in. Shapiro won't allow it."

"Run his name through the system," I said. "Trey has a checkered past. He told me yesterday he has a past professional acquaintance with my father. People don't hire Edward Estes for traffic mishaps."

Landry shook his head in disgust. "It's like a goddam bag of snakes, this bunch."

"Yes," I said. "Now we get to find out how many of them are poisonous."

Nothing breeds contempt more virulent than unrequited devotion. I drove toward Loxahatchee, thinking of Paris Montgomery walking into the Sheriff's Office to give up her boss on the horse murder and insurance fraud. Paris was a first-chair kind of girl who had been playing second fiddle to Don Jade for three years. She had helped him build his clientele.

She had defended him with one hand and dug the foundation out from under him with the other.

I wondered if it had been Paris who dropped the dime to the INS regarding Javier. She had been with Trey the night before. He might have told her he believed me to be a private investigator, and that he had found me conversing in fluent Spanish with the one Jade employee left who might have known something valuable.

Or perhaps Trey had called them himself. For reasons of his own. I tried to picture him as one of the kidnappers. Had the years of debauchery so warped him that he might consider kidnapping a girl to be a game?

The afternoon was already half-gone as I turned down the road to Paris Montgomery's house. In the dense woods of rural Loxahatchee, much of the light had already fallen victim to the long shadows of tall thin pine trees.

I drove past the house Paris lived in to the cul-de-sac where I had nearly shot Jimmy Manetti the night before. The half-built houses had been abandoned by their work crews for the day. I parked my car, took the Glock out of its hiding place, and made my way back down the road, ducking into the cover of trees as quickly as I could.

The house was much like Eva Rosen's: a pseudo-Spanish seventies rambler with mildewed white stucco and a cedar shake roof crusted with moss. I let myself in a side door to the garage, which was stacked with the property owner's lawn equipment and Christmas decorations. The money-green Infiniti was not there.

The door into the house was locked, and the lights on the security system panel showed that the system was armed. I walked around the exterior of the house, looking for an unlocked door, a partially open window. No luck.

Through the living room windows I could see a nasty once-white shag carpet and a lot of cheesy "Mediterranean" furniture no one from the Mediterranean would ever have laid claim to. The TV looked almost as tall as I was and had every kind of symbiotic machine hooked up to it—VCR, DVD, Dolby sound system with a bank of stereo equipment that looked like something from NASA.

I went around the side yard to the back, where a big redwood hot tub sat inside the requisite caged patio, along with an assortment of tacky patio furniture and sun-starved plants. The screen door was not locked, but the sliding glass door into the dining room was secure. I could see mail on the dining room table: magazines, bills.

A second sliding glass door at the far end of the patio led into a bedroom with orange shag carpeting. The drapes were pulled back, revealing a king-sized bed with a red velvet spread. A painting of a naked woman with three breasts and two faces hung above the or-nate, fake wood headboard. A TV sat on an open-sided stand at the end of the room. I checked the titles on the stack of videos on the bottom shelf and wondered if I was the only person in south Florida without a collection of porn.

Somewhere beyond the yard, the engine of a piece of heavy ma-chinery had fired up with a throaty growl. My luck someone had come back to the construction site down the road and was about to bulldoze my car.

The backyard was dim with shadows, but the sky above the tree-tops was still an intense blue. The racket was not coming from the di-rection of the new houses down the road, but from beyond those trees, beyond Paris Montgomery's backyard, to the west.

A large motor grumbled constantly, the intermittent crunching and chewing of materials being fed through some big machine. A mulch grinder, I guessed, and I almost turned away. Then I paused.

Landry had said there was a sound of heavy machinery in the background of the video showing Erin being beaten by her captors. A sound Erin hadn't been able to remember when he'd asked her about the place where she was held.

I walked toward the back of the property. Dense with young trees and wild bamboo, vines knitting all of it together, the back border of the yard was a jungle that would have eventually swallowed up the yard and the house if allowed.

The thump and grind of the machine grew louder. A truck engine revved and the beep-beep-beep of warning sounded as it backed up.

Trying to see through the curtain of greenery to the property on the other side, I almost missed it. The thing sat in the tangled growth like an ancient ruin. Gray and rusted, once an alien thing that had become almost an organic part of the landscape over the course of time. A trailer. What might have been a construction boss's office once, with a window on the end of it that was coated with dirt on the inside. Someone had scratched through the filth with their fingertip, writing a single word: HELP.

51

Life can change in a heartbeat.

I had nearly missed it. I had been a heartbeat from turning and walking away. Then, there it was: the real reason Paris Montgomery had taken this shitty house too far from the show grounds. I had thought she had come here to be away from prying eyes, and I was right. But her affair with Trey Hughes was not the only thing she had wanted to hide.

The trailer squatted in the overgrowth like something from a bad dream. The sight of it evoked memories I wished I didn't have.

Adrenaline runs through my bloodstream like rocket fuel. My heart pounds like a piston. I'm ready to launch.

I pulled my gun and moved in close along the side of the trailer. Only when I was right on top of it could I see the path where someone had walked around the end to get to the twisted, rusted metal stairs that hung off the back side of the trailer.

Despite the fact that the sun hadn't touched this yard in an hour or more, and the temperature was in fact cool, I was perspiring. I thought I could hear myself breathing.

I've been told to stay put, to wait, but I know that's not the right deci-
sion . . . wasting precious time . . . It's my case. I know what I'm doing . . .

I felt the same push now. My case. My discovery. But a hesitation,
also. Apprehension. Fear. The last time I had made that decision, I had
been wrong. Dead wrong.

I leaned back against the side of the trailer, willing my pulse to
slow, trying to slow my thought process, trying to shut out the emotions that had more to do with post-traumatic stress than with the
present.

Paris would have rented this property months ago, I reasoned. If
this place had been chosen because of the privacy, because of the
trailer, that extended the period of premeditation to before the season
had begun. I wondered if Erin had been chosen for her job because of
her potential as a groom or as a victim.

My hand was shaking as I pulled out my phone with my left hand.
I dialed Landry's pager number, left my number and 911. I called his
voice mail, left Paris Montgomery's address, and told him to get here
ASAP.

And now what? I thought as I closed the phone and stuck it in my
pocket. Wait? Wait for Paris to come home and find me in her backyard? Let opportunity and daylight pass, waiting for Landry to call me
back?

It's my case. I know what I'm doing . . .

I knew what Landry would say. He would tell me to wait for him.
Go sit in my car like a good girl.

I've never been a good girl.

It's my case. I know what I'm doing . . .

The last time I had thought that, I had been very wrong.

I wanted to be right.

Slowly, I went up the metal stairs that over time had sunken into
the sandy earth and settled away from the trailer, leaving a gap of several inches between the two. Standing to the side of the door, I
knocked twice, and called out "Police."

Nothing happened. I couldn't hear any movement within the
trailer. No shotgun blasts came through the door. It occurred to me
Van Zandt might be inside, hiding out until he could catch his plane
to Brussels. He might have been Paris Montgomery's partner in it all,

helping her to oust Jade and secure her place in Trey Hughes' life, while Van Zandt indulged himself in his hobby of dominating young girls. Perhaps the ransom was to have been his fee for helping to ruin Don Jade.

And Erin's role in the game? I wasn't sure now, in light of what Landry had told me about the videotapes of her being raped and beaten. The tape of her abduction, which I had watched a dozen times, made me question whether Erin was truly a victim. Perhaps Paris had lured her into the plot with the opportunity to punish her parents, and once the plan was in motion had given her over to Van Zandt. The idea sickened me.

Standing to one side, I held my breath as I opened the door a crack with my left hand.

Billy Golam jerks open the door, wild-eyed, high on his own home cooking—crystal meth. He's breathing hard. He's got a gun in his hand.

A bead of sweat ran down between my eyebrows and skittered off my nose.

Leading with the Glock, I ducked into the trailer and swept the barrel of the gun from left to right. There was no one in the first room. I took in only the swiftest impression of the furnishings: an old steel desk, a pole lamp, a chair. All of it covered in dust and cobwebs. Piles of old newspapers. Discarded paint cans. The stale, musty smells of dust and cigarettes and mildew growing beneath the old linoleum floor assaulted my nose. The sounds of the machinery outside seemed to resonate and amplify inside the tin can trailer.

Cautiously, I moved toward the second room, still leading with the gun.

I hadn't seen the video of Erin's beating, but I knew from Landry's description this was where it had taken place. A bed with a metal-framed headboard sat against the back wall. A filthy, stained mattress with no sheets. Bloodstains.

I pictured Erin there as Landry had described her: naked, bruised, chained by one arm to the headboard, screaming as her assailant beat her with a whip. I pictured her as a victim.

A few feet from the foot of the bed stood a tripod with a video camera perched atop it. Behind the tripod a table littered with empty soda cans, half-empty water bottles, opened bags of chips, and an ashtray full of butts. There were a couple of lawn chairs, one with a copy of *In Style* magazine left on the seat, the other with clothes tossed carelessly over the arm and back and dropped on the floor beside it.

A movie set. The stage for a twisted drama with a final act yet to be played out.

The roar of the machines outside had ceased. I felt the silence like a presence that had just come through the door. The skin on my arms and the back of my neck prickled with awareness.

I moved to stand beside the wall next to the doorway into the first room, the Glock raised and ready.

I could hear, but not see the exterior door open. I waited.

Movement in the front room. The sound of shoes scuffing and thumping on the old linoleum. The rattle of the old paint cans knocking together. The smell of paint thinner.

I wondered, if I stepped through the doorway, who I would confront. Paris? Van Zandt? Trey Hughes?

I moved into the doorway and leveled my gun on Chad Seabright.

"You're going to lose your seat on the student council for this."

He stared at me as paint thinner puddled on the floor around his shoes.

"I'd ask what you're doing here, Chad, but that seems obvious."

"No," he said, shaking his head, eyes wide. "You don't understand. It's not what you think."

"Really? I'm not watching you prepare to destroy evidence of a crime?"

"I didn't have anything to do with it!" he said. "Erin called me from the hospital. She begged me to help her."

"And you—a complete innocent—just dropped everything to commit a felony for her?"

"I love her," he said earnestly. "She screwed up. I don't want her to go to prison."

"And what would she go to prison for, Chad?" I asked. "She's supposed to be the victim in all this."

"She is," he insisted.

"But she told you to come here and burn the place? She told the detectives she didn't know where she'd been held. How is it you knew to come here?"

I could see the wheels spinning in his mind as he scrambled for an explanation.

"Why would Erin be in trouble, Chad?" I asked again. "Detective Landry has the videotapes of her being beaten and raped."

"That was her idea."

"To get beaten? To be raped? That was Erin's idea?"

"No. Paris. It wasn't supposed to be real. That's what Erin said. It was supposed to be like a hoax. That's what Paris told her. To ruin Jade so she could take over his business. But everything got way out of hand. Paris turned on her. They almost killed her."

"Who are 'they'?"

He looked away and heaved a sigh, agitated. Sweat greased his forehead. "I don't know. She only talked about Paris. And now she's scared Paris will try to take her down with her."

"So you'll burn the crime scene and everyone calls it even. Is that it?"

His Adam's apple bobbed as he swallowed. "I know how it looks."

"It looks like you're in it up to your eyeballs, Junior," I said. "Up against the wall and spread 'em."

"Please don't do this," he said, blinking back tears. "I don't want any trouble with the cops. I'm supposed to go to Brown next fall."

"You should have thought of that before you agreed to commit arson."

"I was only helping Erin," he said again. "She's not a bad person. Really, she isn't. She just— It's just that— She always gets a raw deal. And she wanted to get back at my father."

"And you didn't?"

"I'll graduate soon. It won't matter what he thinks. Erin and I can be together then."

"Up against the wall," I said again.

"Can't you have a little sympathy?" he asked, crying now, taking a step toward the wall.

"I'm not the sympathetic sort."

I moved farther into the room as Chad moved toward the wall that divided the spaces. A slow dance of unwilling partners trading places. I kept the gun on him. My gaze darted to the side as I stepped past the open door.

Paris Montgomery was coming up the steps.

As I turned my head, Chad turned and charged me, his face twisted with rage.

My gun went off as he hit my forearms and deflected my aim. I stumbled backward, his weight coming against me, paint cans and stacks of old newspapers tripping me. My breath went out of me as we hit the floor, the back of my head banging so hard I saw stars.

The Glock was still in my right hand, my finger jammed through the trigger guard. The gun was out of position, my trigger finger bent at an unnatural angle. I couldn't shoot, but brought the gun up and slapped the body of it as hard as I could against Chad Seabright's head. He grunted, and blood ran from a gash in his cheek as he tried to get a hand around my throat.

I swung and hit him again, the barrel of the Glock tearing across his right eye. The eyeball exploded, fluid and blood raining out of the collapsing tissue. Chad screamed and threw himself off me, hands over his face.

I rolled away from him, trying to get my legs under me, slipping through paint thinner, clawing at anything that might give me purchase.

"You bitch! You fucking bitch!" Chad screamed behind me.

Grabbing the leg of the metal desk, I pulled myself up. I glanced back to see Chad, one hand pressed against his ruined eye, the other swinging a paint can. The can caught me on the left jaw and snapped my head sideways.

I fell across the desktop, grabbed the edge with one hand, and dragged myself over as Chad struck at me with the empty can again and again.

Hitting the floor on the other side, I fumbled to pull my gun free of my broken finger. Adrenaline blocked the pain. I would feel it later—if I was lucky.

I expected Chad to come over the desk, but instead as I looked up I saw the translucent flash of orange and blue across the room as the paint thinner was ignited and the gases exploded upward.

Gripping the Glock, my left forefinger on the trigger, I pushed myself to my feet and fired as Chad went out the door and slammed it shut behind him.

The far side of the room was in flames, the fire licking hungrily up the cheap paneled wall to the ceiling, catching on the piles of paper on the floor. It burned toward me. It burned toward the second room. The trailer would be fully engulfed in a matter of minutes. And as far as I could see, there was no way out.

Landry could see the glow of the fire a mile away, though he hoped against hope—even as he stepped on the gas and went with lights and sirens—that the source of the blaze would be something else, somewhere else. But as he neared the address Elena had given him, he knew it wasn't. The county dispatcher was calling the code over the radio.

Landry pulled in the yard, jumped out of the car, and ran to the back of the property.

The walls and windows of a small house trailer were silhouetted against the backdrop of orange.

"Elena!" He screamed her name to be heard above the roar. "Elena!"

Jesus God, if she was inside . . .

"Elena!"

He ran toward the trailer, but the heat pushed him back.

If she was inside, she was dead.

Coughing, I ran for the second room, flames chasing me, flames already shooting up the wall around the doorway. I could smell the paint thinner that soaked my shirt. One lick of a flame and I would be swallowed whole.

Another exit door was located in the far back corner of the second room. The smoke was so thick, I could barely see it. Stumbling over chairs, I ran for it, hit it running, turned the doorknob and shoved. Locked. I twisted the deadbolt and tried again. Locked from the outside. The door wouldn't give.

The fire rolled into the room like a tide on the flimsy ceiling.

Jamming the gun in the back of my jeans, I grabbed the video camera off the tripod, tossed the camera on the bed and swung the tripod like a baseball bat at the window where Erin Seabright had written the word HELP in the dust. Once. Twice. The glass fractured but stayed in the frame.

I slammed the end of the tripod against the glass, trying to knock the glass out, afraid that when I did the flames would rush to the fresh oxygen. It would char my skin and melt my lungs, and if I didn't die instantly, I would wish that I had.

I saw the flames coming and thought of hell.

Just when I'd thought I might redeem myself...

One last time I rammed the tripod against the glass.

Elena!" Landry screamed.

Once more he tried to approach the trailer and was knocked flat as something inside the place exploded. Flame rolled out the broken windows in billowing clouds of orange. In the distance he could hear sirens coming. Too late.

Shaken, sick, he pushed himself to his feet and stood there, unable to do anything or think anything.

My first thought was that it was Chad standing in the yard, watching his handiwork, thrilled with the idea that he had killed me. Then he started toward me and called my name, and I knew it was Landry.

Clutching the video camera against me, I tried to run toward him, my legs like rubber, weak from effort and relief.

"Elena!"

He grabbed me by the shoulders and pulled me along with him, dragging me away from the burning trailer toward Paris Montgomery's patio.

"Jesus Christ," he breathed, sitting me in a chair, going over me with his eyes, with his hands. His hands were trembling. "I thought you were in there."

"I was," I said, coughing. "Chad Seabright set the fire. He's in this with Paris and Erin. Did you get him? Did you get them?"

He shook his head. "No one in the house but her dog." The Jack Russell was at the patio doors bouncing up and down like a ball as it barked incessantly.

Sirens screamed at the front of the house. A deputy came running around the side of the garage. Landry went to meet him, holding up his shield. As I sat coughing the smoke out of my lungs, I watched him motion toward the house. The deputy nodded and drew his weapon.

"Are you hurt?" he asked me as he came back and crouched down in front of me again. He touched my cheek where the paint can had struck me. I couldn't feel it, didn't know if any damage had been done. I guessed not as Landry moved on, inspecting me.

"I broke my finger," I said, holding up my right hand. He took the hand gently and looked at the finger. "I've had worse."

"You goddam knothead," he muttered. "Why didn't you wait for me?"

"If I had waited for you, Chad would have burned the place—"

"Without you in it!" he said, standing. He paced a little circle in front of me. "You never should have gone in there, Elena! You could have compromised evidence—"

"We would have ended up with nothing!" I shouted back, pushing to my feet.

"We?" he said, stepping into my space, trying to intimidate me.

I stood fast. "It's my case. I brought you into it. That makes *we*. Don't even think of trying to shove me out again, Landry. I'm in this for Molly, and if it turns out her sister was a willing participant in this thing, I'm going to strangle Erin Seabright with my own two hands. Then you can put me in prison and I'll be out of your way for the next twenty-five years."

"You were almost out of my way permanently!" he yelled, swinging an arm in the direction of the fire. "You think that's what I want?"

"It's what everybody in the SO wants!"

"No!" he shouted. "No! Me. Look at me. That's not what I want."

We were toe to toe. I glared up into his face. He stared at me, his expression slowly, slowly softening.

"No," he whispered. "No, Elena. I don't want you out of my life."

For one rare moment, I didn't know what to say.

"You scared the hell out of me," he said softly.

Likewise, I thought, only I meant in the present tense. Instead, I went back to the other topic. "You said you'd share. My case first."

Landry nodded. "Yes. . . . Yes, I did."

Trucks from the Loxahatchee fire department arrived, the lead truck barreling into the backyard. I watched the firemen leap to action as impassively as if they were on a movie screen, then looked down at my hands. I still held the video camera. I held it out to Landry.

"I saved this. You'll get fingerprints."

"This was where they held her?" he asked, looking back at the trailer.

"Chad said Erin was in on it at first, but that Paris turned against her. But if Paris turned against her, why isn't she dead?"

"I guess we'll have to ask Paris that question," he said. "And Erin. Do you know what Paris is driving?"

"A dark green Infiniti. Chad has a black Toyota pickup. And he's missing an eye. He might turn up at a hospital."

Landry arched a brow. "Missing an eye? You gouged out his eye?"

I shrugged and looked away, the horrible image still so strong in my mind it turned my stomach. "A girl's gotta do what a girl's gotta do."

He rubbed a hand over his mouth and shook his head. "You're some kind of tough, Estes."

I'm sure I didn't look tough in that moment. The weight of the emerging truth of the case was weighing down on me. The adrenaline rush of the near-death experience had passed.

"Come here," Landry said.

I looked up at him and he touched my face with his hand—the right side, the side that I could feel. I felt it all the way to the heart of me.

"I'm glad you didn't die," he murmured. I had the feeling he wasn't talking about now, about the trailer.

"Me, too," I said, leaning my head against his shoulder. "Me, too."

52

Landry put an APB out for Paris Montgomery and Chad Seabright. All county and state units on the road would be on the look-out for the money-green Infiniti and Chad's Toyota pickup. Additional alerts had gone to the Coast Guard, and to the West Palm Beach and Fort Lauderdale airports, as well as to all small airports in the vicinity.

One of the reasons south Florida has always been a conduit for drugs is the fact that there are many ways in and out, and a quick exit can take you to another country in short order. Paris Montgomery knew a lot of people in the horse business, a lot of very wealthy people, people who owned planes and boats.

And she knew one who was shipping horses to Europe that very night: Tomas Van Zandt.

"Has he been located?" I asked Landry. We sat in his car in the front yard of Paris Montgomery's rented house.

"No. Armedgian's guys scored the fuckup of the century there."

I told him about the horses flying to Europe. "My bet is they both try getting out of the country tonight."

"We've alerted the airlines," Landry said.

"You don't understand. Flying cargo is a whole different ball game. If you ever want a good scare thinking about terrorism, fly transatlantic with a bunch of horses sometime."

"Great. Weiss and the feds can go sit on the cargo terminal."

The Loxahatchee fire chief approached the car as Landry reached for his cell phone. He was a tall man with a heavy mustache. Out from under the gear, I imagined he would be slender as a post.

"Treat it as a crime scene, chief," Landry said out the window.

"Right. Arson."

"That too. Have you located the owner of the property?"

"No, sir. The owner is out of the country. I've contacted the property management company. They'll get in touch with the owner."

"Which property management company?" I asked.

The chief leaned down to look across at me. "Gryphon Property Management. Wellington."

I looked at Landry as his cell phone rang. "Time to have another chat with Bruce. Is he still in custody?"

"No. They cut him loose. Landry," he said into the phone. The muscles in his face tightened and his brows pulled low. "What the hell do you mean, gone? Where was the fucking guard?"

Erin, I thought.

"When?" he demanded. "Well, that's just fucking fantastic. Tell that deputy when he gets his head out of his ass, I'm gonna rip it off his shoulders and shout down the hole!"

He snapped the phone shut and looked at me. "Erin's gone. Someone set a fire in a trash can on the other side of the nurses' station and the deputy at her door left his post. When he came back, she was gone."

"She's with Chad."

"And they're running." Landry started the car. "I'll drop you at the emergency room. I've got to roll."

"Leave me at my car," I said. "I'll drive myself."

"Elena . . ."

"It's a finger, Landry. I'm not going to die of it."

He heaved a sigh and closed his mouth.

It was a slow night in the ER. My finger was x-rayed and found to be dislocated rather than broken. The doctor shot my hand full of lidocaine and manipulated the finger back into a straight line. I refused the cumbersome splint in favor of taping the finger to its neighbor. He handed me a prescription for painkillers. I gave it back.

On my way out I stopped at the desk and asked if anyone had come in with a severe eye injury. The clerk told me no.

I checked my watch as I walked out of the hospital. Five hours until Van Zandt's plane left for Kennedy Airport, then on to Brussels.

Every uniform in Palm Beach County was looking for him, looking for Paris, looking for Chad and Erin. Meanwhile, Don Jade was out on bail, and Trey Hughes had written the check.

It all revolved around Trey Hughes—the land deal, Stellar, Erin—and to my knowledge, no one was looking for him. I went in search. If he was at the center of it all, maybe he held the key.

Last I'd known, Trey had a house in the Polo Club, a gated community near the show grounds that caters to horse people with money. I headed in that direction, taking the back streets that would swing me past Fairfields on the way.

The gate stood open at Lucky Dog Farm. I could make out the shape of a car near the construction boss's trailer. I turned in and my headlights washed over the back of Trey's classic Porsche. I killed the engine and got out, the Glock in my left hand.

The only light I could see was the big security light on the pole, but somewhere nearby Jimmy Buffett was singing a song about the joys of irresponsibility.

I followed the sound, walking the length of the huge, dark stables, and around the end. A second-story balcony ran the length of the building, overlooking the jumping field. Candles and lanterns illuminated the scene. I could see Trey dancing, the end of his omnipresent cigarette a glowing orange dot in the dark.

"Come on up, honey!" he called. "I thought you'd never get here! I started the party without you."

I climbed the stairs, keeping my eyes on him. He was high. On what, I couldn't know. Cocaine had been his thing in the eighties. It was making a comeback when I'd checked out of the Narcotics division. Nostalgia among the tragically hip.

"What are we celebrating, Trey?" I asked as I stepped onto the balcony.

"My illustrious and stellar life," he said, still dancing. He held a bottle of tequila in one hand. His aloha shirt hung open over a pair of khaki pants. He was barefoot.

"Stellar," he said, and started to laugh. "What a bad joke! Shocking!"

The song ended and he fell back against the railing and took a long pull on the bottle.

"Were you expecting me?" I asked.

"No, actually I was expecting someone else. But you know, it doesn't really matter, does it?"

"I don't know, Trey. I think it might—depending on your reasons. You were expecting Paris?"

He rubbed his face, tiny embers of cigarette ash floating around his head like fireflies. "That's right. You're the private eye, now. The gumshoe. The private dick—or is that politically incorrect? It really should be private pussy, shouldn't it?"

"I don't think Paris will be here tonight, Trey. She's been unavoidably detained."

"Yeah? What's she up to?"

"Running from the law," I said. "She and Chad Seabright tried to kill me today."

He squinted at me, waiting for the punch line. "Honey, what have you been smoking?"

"Come on, Trey. You've been to her place a hundred times. I know about your affair. Don't try to tell me you don't know anything about the trailer, about Erin."

"Erin? Somebody kidnapped her. The whole fucking world's going to hell on a sled."

I shook my head. "It was all a play. Didn't you know? A play for you."

I could see his face in the candlelight. He was trying to find his way through the fog in his brain. Either he didn't know what I was talking about, or he wanted to convince himself he didn't know.

"A three-act play," I said. "Deceit, double-crosses, sex, murder. Shakespeare would have been proud. I don't know the whole script yet, but it begins with a quest for the holy land—Lucky Dog Farm— and its king—you."

The last of his puzzled smile faded away.

"Here's what I know so far: The story opens with a girl named

Paris who wants very much to be queen. So much so that she plots to ruin the one person standing between her and the fulfillment of her dreams: Don Jade.

"It shouldn't be that hard to do, she thinks, because he's already got a bad reputation. People are ready to believe the worst about him. They'll believe he would kill a jumper who wouldn't bring top dollar. Insurance fraud? He's done it before and gotten away with it.

"His groom disappears. He's the last person to see her. Turns out she's been kidnapped. And when she gets away, who does she name as one of her abductors? Don Jade.

"Surely, Paris thinks, now Trey will dump him. Jade will be in prison soon, at any rate. And she'll become queen of Lucky Dog Farm."

"That's not a very funny story," Trey said. He put his cigarette out on the cast stone railing and flicked the butt out into the night.

"No. It isn't. And it's not going to have a happy ending either," I said. "Did you think that it would?"

"You know me, Ellie. I try not to think. I'm just a Dixie cup on the sea of life."

He sniffed and rubbed his face again. A round patio table squatted like a mushroom in front of an open set of French doors that led into a dark room. A dozen candles burning on the table spilled their light over a glass tray of cocaine that had been cut into lines. Near the tray lay a .32 caliber Beretta pistol.

"What's the gun for, Trey?" I asked, reassured by the weight of my own weapon—even if it was in the wrong hand.

"Rats," he said, digging another cigarette out of his pocket. He flicked a lighter and took a drag, exhaling into the night sky. "Maybe a little Russian roulette later."

"That'll be a very short game," I said. "That's an automatic weapon."

He smiled and shrugged. "The story of my life: stuck in a rigged game."

"Yeah, you've got it hard. How much did you inherit when Sallie died? Eighty million? A hundred?"

"With a string attached to every one," he said.

"They don't seem to be holding you back from spending."

"No."

He turned and looked out at the property, nothing to see but a patchwork in varying shades of black.

"Why did you bail Jade out, Trey? Why did you get him Shapiro?" I asked, moving to stand down the railing from him.

He flashed a smile. "Because your father was unavailable."

"You've never been more loyal than a tomcat your whole life. Why stick by Don Jade?"

"He made me what I am today," he said with another crooked smile.

"He killed Sallie, didn't he?" I said. "You were with Michael Berne's wife, fucking your alibi, and Jade was at the house, hiding in the shadows. . . . And now you can't walk away."

"Why would I walk away from all this?" he asked, spreading his arms wide. The cigarette bounced on his lip. "I'm king of the world!"

"No, Trey," I said. "You were right the first time. You're the sad clown. You had it all. And you're going to end up with nothing."

"You know a little something about that, don't you, Ellie?" he said.

"I know all about it. But I'm climbing out of that hole, Trey, and you're going to end up buried in it."

I pulled my phone off the pocket of my jeans and tried to dial Landry's number, my right hand awkward, still half-numb and under the numbness a hot, throbbing pain waiting to come fully to life. Landry needed to know Trey had been expecting Paris. She had probably thought to come to him for a car the cops wouldn't be on the lookout for. Perhaps she thought to come to him for money to live on in Europe. Or perhaps she would try to convince Trey to go with her. Wealthy fugitives on the lam in Europe's glamour capitals.

I took a couple of steps back from Trey, switching hands with phone and gun, my eyes on him, the pathetic playboy, Peter Pan corrupted utterly by time and self-indulgence.

Landry's line was ringing as Paris Montgomery came out of the darkness beyond the open French doors. Without hesitation, she scooped the Beretta off the patio table and pointed it right at my face.

53

We manage a lot of properties, Detective," Bruce Seabright said. "I have nothing to do with most of them."

"I only care about what you have to do with this one," Landry said.

They stood in Seabright's home office. Seabright turned around in a circle and heaved a sigh up at the ceiling. "I don't have anything to do with it!"

"We both know that's not true."

"I don't know where that videotape came from," he said. "Someone planted it."

"Yeah, right. You stick with that story. I'm asking you about the property in Loxahatchee."

"I have an attorney," Seabright said. "Talk to him."

"This is an unrelated line of questioning."

"And I told you, I don't have anything to do with the rental property."

"You expect me to believe that someone involved in Erin's kidnapping just happened to rent that property from your company?

The same way these people you sent Erin to for a job just happened to turn out to be killers and rapists and Christ knows what all."

"I don't care what you believe," Seabright said, reaching for his phone. "I had nothing to do with any of this, nor did my son. Now get out of my office or I'm filing harassment charges."

"File it up your ass, Seabright," Landry said. "You and your rotten kid are both going to jail. I'll see to it personally."

Landry left the office, thinking he just wanted to drive the lot of these people out to Lion Country Safari and dump them inside the pen with the big cats.

Krystal Seabright was standing in the hall a few feet from the office door. For once, she didn't look stoned, but stricken. She held a hand out to stop him from passing her, her mouth opening to form words that didn't come out.

"Can I help you, Mrs. Seabright?"

"I did it," she said.

"I'm sorry?"

"That woman came to me, to my office. I rented her that property. I remember her name. Paris. I've always wanted to visit Paris."

She didn't know quite how she should be reacting to the news, Landry thought. With guilt? With shock? With outrage?

"How did she happen to come to you?" he asked.

"She told me a friend sent her." Tears shone in her eyes. She shook her head and looked toward her husband's office. "Was it him? Do you think it was him?"

"I don't know, Mrs. Seabright," Landry confessed. "I guess you have to ask him."

"I guess I do," she murmured, staring at the office door. "I have to do something."

Landry left her there in the hall, glad he was just a cop. He could walk away from this mess when it was over. Krystal Seabright wouldn't be so lucky.

54

I stared at the barrel of the gun in Paris Montgomery's hands. Jimmy Buffett was still singing in the background.

"Put down the phone and the gun," Paris said to me.

I now held the Glock in my weak and damaged right hand. I could have tried to raise it up and call her bluff, but I couldn't have done it convincingly. I couldn't have pulled the trigger if I needed to. I weighed my options as Landry's voicemail message came on the line.

Paris came toward me. She was angry and she was afraid. Her neat little scheme was fraying at the edges like a cheap rag.

"It seemed a simple plan, didn't it, Paris?" I said. "You got Erin to help you frame Jade. She and Chad got to ruin Bruce Seabright in the process. It would have worked like a charm if Molly Seabright hadn't come to me for help."

"Put down the phone and the gun," she ordered again.

I clipped the phone onto my jeans and glanced at Trey, who stood flat-footed and expressionless.

"Why did you let Van Zandt in on it?" I asked. "Or did he force his way in?"

"I don't know what you're talking about."

"Then why are you pointing a gun in my face, Paris?"

She glanced at Trey. "This is all Don's doing," she said. "He killed Stellar. He kidnapped Erin. He killed Jill. It's all Don, Trey. You have to believe me."

"Why?" he asked. "Because it's part of your plan?"

"Because I love you!" she said emphatically, though her eyes were on me, sighting down the barrel of a gun. "Erin saw Don kill Stellar. Don did horrible things to her, to punish her. And he killed Jill."

"No, he didn't, honey," Trey said wearily. "I know he didn't."

"What are you saying?"

"You had night check the night Jill was killed. You left my bed to go do it. Just like you did the night before, when Berne's horses were turned loose."

"You're confused, Trey," Paris said, an edge in her voice.

"Generally, yes. Life's easier that way. But not about this."

She took another step toward me, her patience wearing thin. "Put the fucking gun down!"

I heaved a sigh and slowly crouched down as if to set the gun on the floor, then ducked and rolled sideways.

Paris fired twice, one of the bullets hitting the floor near me and spitting up shards of travertine marble.

I switched my gun to my left hand, trying to steady it with my right, came to my feet, and rushed her before she could adjust her position to fire at me a third time.

"Drop it, Paris! Drop it! Drop it!"

She turned and bolted for the stairs at the far end of the balcony. I ran after her, pulling up short as she turned the corner and fired off a shot behind her.

Cautiously, I peered around the corner, looking down on an empty stairwell faintly illuminated by the glow of the security light. She could have been waiting beyond the landing, tucked against the wall, waiting for me to charge after her. I could see myself turning the corner on the landing and the bullet hitting me square in the chest, my blood the only color in a black-and-white scene.

I went instead to the end of the balcony and looked down. She was gone. I ran down the stairs. The engine of Trey's Porsche roared to life as I hit the ground. The headlights blinded me as the car leapt toward me.

I brought my gun up and put a round through the windshield, then dove to the side.

Paris tried to swing the Porsche around, tires spinning, dirt and gravel spraying out behind it. The car skidded sideways and slammed violently against the side of the concrete building, setting off the horn and alarm system.

Paris shoved the door open, fell out of the vehicle, got up and started to run down the driveway, a hand pressed to her left shoulder. She stumbled and fell, got up and ran another few steps, then stumbled and fell again. She lay sobbing on the ground within sight of the sign proudly announcing construction of Lucky Dog Farm.

"No, no, no, no, no!" she whimpered over and over as I reached her. Blood ran between her fingers from the bullet wound in her shoulder.

"The game is over, Paris," I said, looking down at her. "You're out of luck, bitch."

55

Molly sat curled up in a little knot on her bed, knees pulled up beneath her chin. She was trembling and trying hard not to cry.

She listened to the fight going on below her, their voices coming up through her floor. Bruce shouting. Things crashing. Hateful and angry, her mother shrieking like something from a nightmare, like nothing Molly had ever heard. An eerie, high-pitched tone that rose and fell like a siren. She sounded insane. Bruce called her insane more than once.

Molly feared he might be right. That maybe the tight band that had held Krystal together all this time had just broken, and everything she had held repressed inside her had come bursting out.

As the shrieking rose again, Molly jumped off the bed, locked her door, and struggled to shove her nightstand in front of it. She grabbed the phone Elena had given her, scrambled back to her spot against the headboard, and dialed Elena's cell phone.

She listened to the phone ring unanswered. Tears spilled down her cheeks.

Below her the noise abruptly stopped and a strange, horrible silence took its place. Molly strained her ears for any kind of sound, but the silence pressed in on her until she wondered if she'd gone deaf.

Then came a small, soft voice drifting up through the vent as if from another dimension. "I only ever wanted a nice life. . . . I only ever wanted a nice life. . . ."

56

Landry arrived on the heels of the ambulance that had been called for Paris. My shot through the windshield had clipped her shoulder. She had lost some blood, but she would live to see another day, and another and another—all of them from a prison cell, I hoped.

Landry got out of his car and came directly to me, holding a finger up at the deputy who had secured the scene, warding him off for the moment. Deputy Saunders, my escort from the night Michael Berne's horses had been turned loose, stood watching me, not willing to accept my word for my innocence.

Landry dismissed him, his focus on me.

"Are you all right?"

I gave him the half smile. "You must be tired of asking me that. I'm fine."

"You've got more lives than a cat," he muttered.

I filled him in on what had happened, what had been said, my take on it all.

"What made you come here in the first place?" he asked.

"I don't know. I thought Paris might try to get to Trey. It all revolved around him—around Trey, around his money, around this place."

I looked back at the barn, the massive walls washed in the colored lights from the ambulance and county radio cars. Trey was being escorted in handcuffs to one of the cruisers.

"I believe Trey and Jade cooked up a scheme to kill Sallie Hughes so Trey could inherit and build this place. I confronted Trey about it. He didn't even bother to deny it. That's why he's stayed loyal to Jade. He didn't have a choice. Paris wanted Jade out of the way so she could have it all. And in the end, none of them will end up with anything," I said. "All the deceit, all the scheming, all the pain they caused—it's all for nothing. Everybody loses."

"Yeah," Landry said as the ambulance rolled out with a cruiser behind it. "Cases like this one make me wish I'd listened to my old man. He wanted me to be a civil engineer."

"What did he do for a living?" I asked.

His mouth quirked. "He was a cop. What else? Thirty years on the Baton Rouge PD."

"No sign of Van Zandt yet?" I asked as we walked back toward our cars.

"Not yet. The guy at the cargo hangar told us Van Zandt's horses arrived by commercial shipper a while ago, but they haven't heard from Van Zandt all day. You think he was in it with Paris?"

"I still believe he killed Jill. But Trey said Paris got out of his bed to go check the horses that night. Jill's body was left to be found, and whoever put it there knew everyone would connect it to Jade. That furthers Paris' plan."

"We know Van Zandt was at The Players that night," Landry said. "He was all over the girl. Say he followed her out, thinking to pick up the pieces after Jade had broken her heart. Maybe she said no and he didn't want to hear it. She ends up dead."

"Paris comes on the scene and convinces Van Zandt to dump the body in the manure pit," I speculated. "Was he involved in the rest of it? I don't know. Chad tried to tell me someone had actually raped Erin, that Paris had let things get out of hand. Maybe Van Zandt came into it and took over."

"If that's what happened, I'm sure she'll spill it," Landry said.

"She's in custody, he's not. Nothing ruins a partnership faster than threat of jail time. Good work, Estes."

"Just doing my civic duty."

"You should still have a badge."

I looked away. "Oh, well, don't you say the sweetest things? I wouldn't express that opinion around the SO, if I were you."

"Fuck 'em. It's true."

I felt embarrassed that his compliment meant so much to me.

"Any news of Chad and Erin?" I asked as my phone rang.

Landry shook his head.

"Estes," I said into the phone.

"Elena?"

The tremulous sound of her voice sent fear through me like shards of glass. "Molly? Molly, what's wrong?"

I was already hustling toward Landry's car. I could see the concern on his face as he kept pace with me.

"Elena, you have to come. Please come!"

"I'm on my way! What's happening?"

In the background I could hear pounding, like someone banging on a door.

"Molly?"

And then a strange and terrible keening sound that ended with her name.

"Hurry!" Molly said.

The last thing I heard before the line went dead was an eerie voice: "I only ever wanted a nice life. . . . I only ever wanted a nice life. . . ."

57

Okay," Landry said. "Here's how we're playing it. I'm going in first with the uniforms."

I let him talk, not caring what he said, not caring what his plan was. All I could think of was Molly.

If someone had harmed that child . . .

I thought of Chad and Erin running at large. If they had come back to the house—

"Elena, did you hear me?"

I didn't answer him.

He turned in at the driveway and ran the car onto the lawn. A radio car turned in behind us. I was out of the car before it was stopped.

"Dammit, Estes!"

The front door was open. I went through it without a care to what danger might be on the other side.

"Molly!"

Landry was right behind me. "Seabright? It's Landry."

"Molly!"

I took the stairs two at a time.

If someone has harmed that child . . .

Landry went toward Seabright's home office. The house was eerily silent, except for a small, faint sound coming from beyond the office doors.

"Seabright?"

Landry moved along the wall, gun drawn. In his peripheral vision, he saw Elena bolt up the steps.

"Seabright?" he called out again.

The sound was growing more distinct. Singing, he thought. He sidled along the door, stretching his arm as long as he could to reach the doorknob.

Singing. No, more like chanting. "All I ever wanted was a nice life."

Molly!"

I had no idea which of the closed doors belonged to her. I stood to the side and opened the first one I came to. Chad's room.

If someone has harmed that child . . .

I shoved open another door. Another unoccupied bedroom.

"Molly!"

If someone has harmed that child . . .

The third door opened an inch and hit something. I shoved at it.

"Molly!"

If someone has harmed that child . . .

The doors to the study fell open, revealing a gruesome tableau. Krystal Seabright stood behind her husband's desk, covered in blood. Blood streaked her bleached hair, her face, the pretty pink dress she had been wearing when Landry had seen her earlier. Bruce Seabright was slumped over his otherwise immaculate desk, a butcher's knife sticking out of one of perhaps fifty stab wounds in his back, neck, and head.

"Jesus God," Landry murmured.

Krystal looked at him, her eyes glassy and wide.

"I only ever wanted a nice life. He ruined it. He ruined everything."

If someone has harmed that child...

I pulled back, took a deep breath, and rammed the door with my shoulder as hard as I could.

"Molly!"

The block on the other side of the door gave a few inches, enough for me to wedge into the opening and shove it a few inches more. Someone had piled half the furniture in the room as a blockade.

"Elena!"

Molly ran into me full force. I fell to my knees and caught her in my arms and held her as tightly as I had ever held anyone in all my life. I put my arms around Molly Seabright and held her while she cried, and held her for a long time after that.

For her . . . and for myself.

58

All I could say to Molly as I hugged her tight was that it was over. *It's over. It's over. It's over.* But that was a lie of such grand proportions, all lies that had come before it were dwarfed in comparison. Nothing was over for Molly, except having a family.

Krystal, fragile in the best of times, had shattered under the pressure. She blamed her husband for what she believed had happened to Erin. The kidnapping, the rape. Landry told me she had suspected Bruce of sending Paris Montgomery to her to rent the Loxahatchee house where the whole drama had been staged.

She had reached her limit. In the end, one might have tried to put a nobler face on it and said Krystal had defended her daughter, had taken revenge for her. Sadly, I didn't believe that at all. I believed killing Bruce had been punishment not for ruining her daughter, but for ruining her fairy tale.

I only ever wanted a nice life.

I wondered whether Krystal would have stayed with Bruce if she had found out that what they had all been put through had been orchestrated at least in part by her daughter. I suspected she would have put the blame squarely on Erin and no one else. She would have found a way to excuse Bruce's sins and keep her pretty life intact.

The human mind has an amazing capacity for rationalization.

Landry sent Krystal to the Sheriff's Office in a cruiser, then drove Molly and me to Sean's farm. Not a word was said about calling Child Protective Services, which was standard operating procedure in a case like Molly's.

We rode in silence most of the way, drained of our emotions and our energies, weighed down by the magnitude of what had gone on. The only sound in the car was the crackle of Landry's radio. An old familiar noise for me. For a moment I felt as nostalgic for it as I ever had for any song from my adolescence.

As we turned in at the Avadonis gate, Landry used his cell phone to call Weiss at the airport. There was still no sign of Van Zandt, and the plane was ready to taxi onto the runway.

Exhausted, Molly had fallen asleep leaning against me in the backseat. Landry scooped her out and carried her into the guest house. I led the way to the second small bedroom, thinking what an odd family unit we made.

"Poor kid," he said as he and I walked back outside onto the little patio. "She'll grow up in a hurry."

"She's already done that," I said, sitting down sideways on a delicate iron chaise with a thick cushion. "That one was a child for a minute and a half. Do you have kids?"

"Me? No." Landry sat beside me. "You?"

"Always seemed like a bad idea to me. I've watched too many people screw it up. I know how badly that hurts."

I knew he was watching me, trying to read into me, into my words. I looked up at the stars and marveled at the vulnerability I had just shown him.

"Molly's great, though," I said. "Figures. She raised herself watching the Discovery Channel and A and E."

"I was married once," Landry offered. "And I lived with a woman for a while. It didn't work out. You know: the job, the hours, I'm difficult. Blah, blah, blah."

"I never tried. Go straight to 'I'm difficult. Blah, blah, blah.'"

He smiled wearily and produced a cigarette and a lighter from his pocket.

"Car pack?" I asked.

"Gotta get that corpse taste out."

"I used to drink," I confessed. "To cleanse the palate."

"But you quit?"

"I gave up everything that could dull pain."

"Why?"

"Because I believed I deserved to hurt. Punishment. Penance. Purgatory. Call it what you like."

"Stupid," Landry proclaimed. "You're not God, Estes."

"A welcome relief to all true believers, I'm sure. Maybe I thought I should beat Him to the punch."

"You made a mistake," he said. "I don't believe the Pope is infallible either."

"Heretic."

"I'm just saying, you've got too much good in you to let one bad mistake shut it all down."

The half smile tugged at the corner of my mouth. "I know," I said. "I know that now. Thanks to Molly."

Landry glanced back over his shoulder at the house. "What are you going to tell her about Erin?"

"The truth," I said on a sigh. "She won't stand for anything less."

The prospect drove me to my feet. As exhausted as I was, still I was restless, frustrated at the injustices of Molly Seabright's life and the inadequacy of my people skills. Crossing my arms against the damp night air, I walked to the edge of the patio.

"On the first day of this, I remember thinking Molly was about to get a lesson in life. That she would learn the way everyone learns that she can't count on anyone but herself in this world: by being let down by someone she loved and trusted. I wish now I could change that for her."

Landry came to stand beside me. "You can," he said. "You have. She trusts you, Elena. You haven't let her down. You won't."

I wished I could have been that certain of myself.

His pager went off. He checked the number, pulled his phone off his belt, and returned the call.

"Landry."

I watched his face, sensed his tension.

When he ended the call he turned to me and said, "Erin and Chad were picked up on Alligator Alley, halfway to Venice. She's claiming Chad abducted her."

59

You're eighteen," Landry said. "In the eyes of the law, you're an adult. You made bad choices that have big consequences, and now you're going to pay. The question is, are you going to take the big fall, or are you going to try to make life easier for all of us?"

Chad Seabright stared at the wall. A heavy gauze patch covered the socket where his left eye had been. "I can't believe any of this is happening," he muttered.

A state trooper had spotted Chad's pickup speeding on the highway known as Alligator Alley, the road that connected Florida's east coast with the Gulf Coast. A chase had ensued. A roadblock had eventually stopped them. The pair had been returned to the gracious accommodations of the Palm Beach County justice system, where both of them had been seen and treated in the infirmary.

Now they sat in back-to-back interview rooms, each wondering what story the other was telling.

Had Bruce Seabright survived, Landry did not doubt that Chad would have had a lawyer the caliber of Bert Shapiro sitting at his elbow. But Bruce Seabright was dead, and Chad had taken the first public defender out of the pool.

Assistant State's Attorney Roca tapped her pen on the table impatiently. "You'd better start talking, Chad. Your girlfriend has been telling us quite a tale in the other room. How you kidnapped her to extort money from your father. We have the videotape of you beating her."

"I think I should see that tape," the public defender said.

Roca looked at him. "It's quite convincing. She'll be a very sympathetic witness."

"That's a lie," Chad said, sulking, petulant, scared. "Erin wouldn't do that to me."

"Wouldn't do what?" Landry asked. "Tell us how you grabbed her out of the hospital while the guard was trying to put out the fire you set?"

Chad shook his head emphatically.

"You don't think Erin would tell us how you raped her and kept her doped up on ketamine?" Roca said.

The public defender sat there like a toad, his mouth opening and closing, no words coming out.

Landry sighed and stood up. "You know, I've just about had it with this," he said to Roca. "This little shit wants to take the fall. Fine. Let him rot. His father was an asshole. He's an asshole. Get him out of the gene pool. Go make a deal with the girl. You know a jury will get out the hankies for her."

Roca pretended to consider, then looked to the PD. "Talk to your client. The charges are going to be a potpourri of felonies: kidnapping, rape, attempted murder, arson—"

"I never raped anybody," Chad said. "I only went to that trailer yesterday to help Erin."

"To destroy evidence for her because she was the mastermind of the whole plot?" Roca said.

Chad closed his eye and tipped his head back. "I *told* you: Erin told me she was in it to start, but Paris turned on her. I didn't have anything to do with it! None of this is my fault. I was just trying to help Erin. Why should I be punished for that?"

Landry leaned across the table, looming over him. "People are dead, Junior. You tried to kill a friend of mine. You're going away."

Chad put his head in his hands and started to cry. "It wasn't my fault!"

"And what about the tape we took out of your father's home office, Chad? The tape showing the alleged rape. The tape that was conveniently left on a bookshelf. How did it get there?"

"I don't know!"

"I do," Landry said. "You put it there."

"I didn't! I didn't have anything to do with it!"

Landry sighed in disgust. "Well, you know what, Chad? I know for a fact that you did. You can either take responsibility and do yourself a favor here, or you can dig that hole deeper with every lie that comes out of your mouth."

He went to the one-way mirror in the wall, raised the blinds, and flicked a switch on the intercom.

Roca stood up. "Think about it, gentlemen. The best deal goes first. He who hesitates loses."

Why would Chad take you from the hospital, Erin?" Landry asked.

"He must have been the other one," the girl said in a voice as weak as a kitten's. She kept her eyes downcast, as if she were afraid or ashamed. Tears fell like tiny crystal beads down her cheeks. "He must have been the other kidnapper. That must be why he never talked. He knew I would know it was him."

"And so he walked into your hospital room in broad daylight, and kidnapped you a second time so you couldn't tell anyone how you couldn't identify him in the first place?" Landry said.

She put a trembling hand over her mouth and cried. Her public defender, a plump motherly woman named Maria Onjo, patted her on the shoulder.

Landry watched impassively. "Chad tells us you and he are in love. That you went with him willingly."

Erin's jaw dropped. "No! That's not true! I— We—had a relationship for a while. Before I moved out of the house." She shook her head at her own stupidity. "We only did it to make Bruce crazy. He couldn't stand the idea of his perfect boy involved with me," she said bitterly. "Chad was furious when I broke it off with him. He told me. He told me he wouldn't let me go."

Maria Onjo offered her a box of tissues.

"Erin," Roca said. "Chad claims you were in on the kidnapping, not him. That the whole thing was a play to discredit Don Jade, and to embarrass and extort money from your stepfather, and that things got out of hand."

"Out of hand?" Erin said, incredulous and angry. "They raped me!"

"And you didn't notice that one of them was Chad?" Landry said. "The guy you'd been involved with, slept with."

"They kept me drugged! I told you that. Why won't you believe me?"

"It might have something to do with the fact that the doctor who examined you the night you came in couldn't conclusively say you'd been raped."

"What? But—but— You saw the tape."

"Oh, I saw it," Landry said. "It was horrible, brutal, vicious. And if it was real, you should have had massive bruising and tearing in your vagina. You didn't."

Her expression was that of someone trapped in a nightmare. "I can't believe this is happening to me," she murmured to herself. "They beat me. They raped me. Look at me!"

She shoved her sleeves up to show the red welts the whip had left.

"Yeah," Landry said. "That's very convincing. So, you're telling us Don Jade and Chad were partners in your kidnapping, along with Paris Montgomery. How does Chad know Don?"

"I don't know."

"And why would he be partners with the man who stole you away from him?" Landry asked. "I don't get that."

He could see her frustration level rising. Her breathing was becoming shallow and rapid.

The PD gave Landry a glare. "You can't expect Erin to make your entire case for you, Detective. She can't know the minds of the people involved in this."

"I don't know about that, Ms. Onjo. Erin was intimate with Chad, worked for Don Jade, claimed to be in love with him. Seems to me if anyone could know the answer to these questions, it would be Erin."

Onjo patted the girl on the back. "Erin, you don't have to do this at all—"

"I haven't done anything wrong!" Erin said to her. "I don't have anything to hide. It wasn't my fault!"

Landry looked at Roca and rolled his eyes. "So how did Chad hook up with Jade, Erin? As far as I can see, the only thing Don Jade and Chad Seabright have in common is knowing you. I can't picture them being friends."

"Ask them!" she snapped. "Maybe they fell for each other. I wouldn't know."

"And they were both in on it with Paris Montgomery, right? They held you in a trailer in her backyard."

Erin put her face in her hands. "I don't know!"

"Erin is the victim in this," Onjo said. "She's the last person who should be sitting in jail."

"That's not what Chad is saying," Roca said. "That's not what Paris is saying. They're both saying the kidnapping was Erin's idea. Paris came up with the plot to kill the horse and implicate Jade. Erin pushed her to fake the kidnapping to extort money from her stepfather and drive a wedge between Seabright and her mother, as well as to implicate Jade in a crime that would ruin his career."

"And you know what?" Landry said. "That story makes a lot more sense to me than Chad and Jade as sociopathic secret bisexual lovers."

"This is a nightmare!" Erin sobbed. "They *raped* me!"

Landry sighed, got up, stretched his shoulders, rubbed his face. "I'm just having a hard time with that, Erin."

Onjo pushed her chair back and stood up. She was no taller standing than sitting. "This is barbaric, and it's over." She called to the guard outside the door.

"You're not going to stay for the movie?" Landry asked, gesturing toward the television and VCR on a metal cart in a corner of the room.

Onjo scowled at him. "What are you talking about? What movie?"

"They made videos," Erin said. "They made me do things. It was horrible."

"I don't think they made this one for public consumption," Roca said. "You may want to reconsider your strategy, Erin. I tend to give the best deal to the person telling me the fewest lies."

Landry pushed the play button on the VCR.

"You're a very talented actress, Ms. Seabright," he said. "If you hadn't turned to a life of crime, you might have made it all the way to triple-X porn."

The tape was a copy of the one that had been in the video camera Elena had saved from the trailer. Behind the scenes of the alleged kidnapping. Outtakes. The actors rehearsing.

The image that filled the television screen was of Erin posing suggestively on the bed, smiling seductively at the camera. The same bed she had been chained to in the videos that had been sent to Bruce Seabright. The same bed she had huddled into in the video that showed her taking a beating so brutal, even hardened cops had been shocked to see it.

Maria Onjo watched the tape, the color in her face draining away with her defense.

Erin looked from her attorney to Landry. "They made me do that. I had to do exactly what they said or they beat me!" she cried. "You think I *wanted* to do that?"

Her own image stared out at her from the television screen as she touched herself between her legs, then licked her fingers.

"Yeah," Landry said. "I do."

A male voice in the background on the tape mumbled something, then he and Erin both laughed.

Erin shoved her chair back from the table and got up to pace. A caged, cornered, angry little animal. "I had to play along," she said. "I was afraid they would kill me! What is wrong with you people? Why won't you believe me? It was Chad. I know that now. He was punishing me."

Something struck the one-way mirror from the back side. Erin and Onjo jumped. Landry looked at Roca.

On the screen, Chad Seabright walked around in front of the video camera and joined Erin on the bed. They kneeled face-to-face on the stained mattress.

"How do you like it, baby?" he asked.

Erin looked up at him and smiled like a vixen. "You know how I like it. I like it rough."

They both started to laugh. Two kids having fun. Actors rehearsing.

Landry glanced over at the one-way mirror, nodding to someone on the other side, then went to the door and opened it on the excuse of telling something to the guard outside.

"You fucking bitch!" Chad Seabright screamed into the room as a deputy pulled him past in handcuffs. Seabright tried to jerk away, lunging toward the interview room. "I loved you! I loved you!"

He tried to spit at her from ten feet away. Landry stepped to the side, frowning in distaste.

"Some people just aren't well brought up," he commented as he closed the door.

Onjo puffed up. "This is outrageous! Terrorizing my client with her attacker—"

"Give it up, Counselor," Roca said wearily. "A jury takes one look at this tape, and your client can kiss her movie future good-bye."

"I want a deal!" Chad shouted. "I want a deal!"

Erin jumped up from her chair. "Shut up! Shut up!"

"I did it for you! I loved you!"

Erin glared at him with venomous disdain. "You stupid fucking idiot."

Landry went out onto the sidewalk to stand in the hot afternoon sun and smoke a cigarette. He had to get the taste of other people's lies out of his mouth, burn out the stink of what they had done.

Chad Seabright had copped to everything, giving up his claims of innocence in order to hurt Erin. He claimed Erin had come to him with the plan. They would fake her kidnapping, and collect the ransom from Bruce Seabright. If he didn't pay one way, he would pay another: with his reputation, with his marriage. At the same time, Don Jade would be implicated and ruined, and Paris Montgomery would get what she wanted—Jade's business and Trey Hughes' stables.

A simple plan.

The three of them had sat down together and come up with the scripts for the videotapes as if they were shooting a movie for a film class. According to Chad, the beating had been Erin's idea. She had insisted he actually strike her with the whip for the sake of realism.

It was Erin's idea. It was Paris Montgomery's idea. It wasn't Chad's fault.

Nothing was ever anybody's fault.

Chad had been deceived and used by Erin. He was an innocent. Erin's mother hadn't raised her right. Bruce Seabright didn't love her. Paris Montgomery had brainwashed her.

Paris Montgomery had yet to be questioned, but Landry would eventually have to listen to her while she cried and told him how her father made her play the skin flute when she was three, and how she lost out on being the homecoming queen in high school, and how that all warped her.

Chad claimed not to know anything about Tomas Van Zandt or about the death of Jill Morone. Landry figured that would turn out not to be anyone's fault either.

What Landry wanted to know was: If nothing was ever anybody's fault, then how was it people ended up murdered, orphaned, lives destroyed? Paris Montgomery and Erin Seabright and Chad Seabright had made decisions that had ruined people's lives, ended people's lives. How was all that nobody's fault?

60

In the uncertain hour before the morning
Near the ending of the interminable night...

I recalled those lines again as I sat tucked up against the back of
the chaise on my patio, watching the sunrise the day after Chad
Seabright had cut a deal with the state's attorney.

Chad had turned on Erin. Erin had turned on Paris Montgomery.
Paris had fingered Van Zandt as Jill Morone's killer, trying to win
herself points with the state's attorney. They all deserved to rot in hell.

I thought of Molly, and tried to apply T. S. Eliot's words as a caption to what she was going through, and to the journey of her life. I
tried not to dwell on the irony that it had been Molly who had fought
to bring her family back together by hiring me to find her sister, and
at the end of it, Molly was the only one left.

Bruce Seabright was dead. Krystal's mind had shattered. If she had
ever been of any real support in Molly's life before, it was doubtful she
ever would be again. And Erin, the sister Molly had loved so much,
was lost to her forever. If not by a prison term, by Erin's betrayal.

Life can change in a heartbeat, in an instant, in the time it takes to make a wrong decision . . . or a right one.

I had given Molly the news about Erin's involvement in the plot the night before and held her in my arms while she cried herself to sleep.

She came out onto the patio then, wrapped in an enormous green blanket, climbed onto the chaise, and curled up beside me without saying a word. I stroked a hand over her hair, and wished I had the power to make that moment last a long, long time.

After a while I finally asked, "So what do you know about this Aunt Maxine person?"

The Sheriff's Office had located Krystal Seabright's only living relative in the area, a sixty-something widow in West Palm Beach. I was to drive Molly to her in the afternoon.

"She's okay," Molly said without enthusiasm. "She's . . . normal."

"Well, that's highly overrated."

We were silent for a time, just looking off across the fields at the sunrise. I searched awkwardly for words.

"You know I'm terribly sorry for everything that happened in the end, Molly. But I'm not sorry you came to me that day and asked me to help you. I'm a better person for knowing you.

"And if I don't like this Maxine broad," I added in my crankiest tone. "You're coming straight home with me."

Molly looked up at me through her owlish little glasses and smiled for the first time since I'd known her.

Great-aunt Maxine lived in a nice complex of apartments, and seemed as advertised: normal. I helped Molly in with her things and stayed for a cup of coffee and a fresh oatmeal cookie. Normal.

Molly walked me out, and we suffered through good-bye.

"You know, you can call me anytime for anything, Molly," I told her. "Or even for nothing at all."

She smiled a soft, wise smile and nodded. Behind the lenses of her glasses, her earnest blue eyes were shimmering with tears. She handed me a small card cut out of a piece of stationery. She had printed her name and new address and phone number beside a tiny sticker of a purple pansy.

"You have to send me your final bill," she said. "I'm sure I owe you quite a lot of money. I'll have to pay you in installments. We can work something out."

"No," I murmured. "You don't owe me anything at all."

I hugged her tight for a long while. If I could have, I would have cried.

By the time I returned to the farm, the day was slipping away, the sun pouring molten orange along the flat western horizon. I parked my car and wandered down to the barn.

Irina had Feliki in the cross-ties, dressing her legs with witch hazel and alcohol, and wrapping them for the night.

"How's tricks?" I asked.

"Is fine," she said, her concentration on making the right front bandage match perfectly with the left.

"I'm sorry, I haven't been much help lately," I said.

She looked up at me and smiled softly. "Is fine, Elena. It doesn't matter. I know the things that matter."

I was tempted to ask her the meaning of life.

She moved to the mare's hind legs and sprayed on the alcohol concoction.

"Have the police yet found the Belgian?" she asked.

"No. It seems he simply vanished with Lorinda Carlton's rental car. They'll get him eventually."

"He pays for his crimes, I think," Irina said. "I believe in karma. Don't you?"

"I don't know. Maybe."

"I think yes."

She was singing when I left the barn.

Landry had parked himself in a lounge chair by the pool. He was watching the sun set through his shades. I sat down beside his legs and blocked his view.

"What do you know, Landry?"

"People are scum."

"Not all of them."

"No. I like you, Estes," he said. "You're a good and decent human being."

"I'm glad you think so. I'm glad I think so too," I confessed, though I didn't think he probably understood the depth of what that really meant to me.

Or perhaps he did.

"Trey Hughes rolled on Jade today," he said. "He says it was Jade's idea to off the old lady so Trey could inherit. Not his fault the guy followed through with it."

"Of course not. And what does Jade have to say?"

He just shook his head. "Did you get Molly settled in?"

"Yes. She'll be all right. I miss her," I confessed.

Landry reached out and touched my hand. "You'll be all right too."

"I know. Yes. I will be. I will be. I am."

"You are," he agreed, his hand squeezing mine. "What do you say we get to know each other?"

I smiled the half smile and nodded, and we walked toward the guest house hand in hand.

Life can change in a heartbeat.